The Power of Unity

Vincent Havelund

iUniverse, Inc.
New York   Bloomington

iUniverse books may be ordered through booksellers or by contacting:

iUniverse
1663 Liberty Drive
Bloomington, IN 47403
www.iuniverse.com
1-800-Authors (1-800-288-4677)

Because of the dynamic nature of the Internet, any Web addresses or links contained in this book may have changed since publication and may no longer be valid. The views expressed in this work are solely those of the author and do not necessarily reflect the views of the publisher, and the publisher hereby disclaims any responsibility for them.

ISBN: 978-1-4401-9605-8 (sc)
ISBN: 978-1-4401-9604-1 (ebook)

Printed in the United States of America

iUniverse rev. date: 12 / 09 / 09

Contents

All Bible quotations are from the King James Bible.

Introduction

This book is meant to be a simple assessment of the world as it was in the past, where it will be in the future, and where it has been from 1929 to 2010. It's not possible that there could ever be a comprehensive writing on world lifestyles in such a simple book. What has been done is to give a bird's eye view of events, past and present and how the world will be in the future, only the major players in future development have been looked at.

The changes that we can see and that have evolved over the millennia irregardless, of wars famines and pestilence is what we have now. What we want to know; is what will happen in the future as the changes occur and we emerge into a new world. That new world has got to bring a new order, even if the reader is an atheist or even an agnostic we all know there are tremendous changes coming. The intent is not to write a history lesson quite the opposite, what we have done is write a novel type book with a simple glimpse of our world in camera.

Medicine is moving ahead very fast and life expectancy will explode, this will be worldwide, and the advances in medical science is too big for a comprehensive story here. The problems associated with a world that will soon grow to a population of over eight billion; will include the need for a full global infrastructure to match, and is a book on its own.

Information that is very fast now, cannot get faster, but it will get easier and more efficient, the new creative systems that are involved, are mostly under development already. The problem here is the control of information; as people begin to feel the stress that comes with so much new knowledge, and knowledge without understanding has little value!

Transport of all types is in the process of evolving and will in the near future have to compete, fast trains, big airplanes, safe cars free of fumes, flying solo without wings, green clean factories and renewable energy will further clear the atmosphere!

In the future the development of Space travel and the hoped for ability to colonize a distant planet, will become a small possibility not a crazy dream. Science will challenge the veracity of Spiritual Faith; and attempt to replace that with Self Faith. This will create a lot of confusion and further exacerbate world tensions, as the religions deny the findings of the scientific reality, but we believe science and religion is compatible.

The harvesting of renewable energy will be the most important industry in the world, as the major economies must learn to develop nuclear and renewable energy. The possibility of cleaning up the present dirty energy, we use such as coal and oil is another source for the future that the big companies are working with. The need to balance the energy supply to avoid future cost explosions created by skyrocketing oil prices is vital to keep the world's financial stability more secure.

Author's Profile

The writer was born in NZ on Oct 25th 1935 and lived there until August 1970. He came to Australia before there was the need for a passport between the two countries.

He has worked in many industries as a Professional Public Officer for small companies for many years in both Australia and NZ? In his early days that position entitled him to represent his client companies, at the Australian Tax Office and in the Equity Court of NSW? The Laws are now changed as the Legal Profession objected to that area of Law allowing none accredited practitioners to do legal work, which seems quite fair in retrospect? The writer did take accounting as a young man, but did not sit the final exams.

The areas of work that was undertaken has been numerous and created quite an interesting background, he has worked for many different industries over the last almost fifty five years? In NZ he owned and developed a very big wholesale meat company which failed for personal reasons after initial great success. It was at the time the biggest privately owned meat company in NZ; the loss when the companies as a group failed was large, financially and personally?

The industries he has had interests in were: Mixed dairy farming, Meat, Timber Soft and Hardwood, Fat Lamb Export, Heavy Interstate Transport, Mushroom Farming, Truck Stops and Restaurants, Professional Public Officer, (Australia only) International Finance in USA, London, Sao Paulo Brazil, Vienna etc; Shearing (NZ Only) Union Rep (NZ only) Canning of Tuna Fish, (Fiji only) Property Development, etc. The above interests are the source of the many short stories Vincent has written, from Humorous & Timid to Serious the vein is always, quick snatches of a very diverse life all in camera?

Chapter 1

World from 2010-2100:
Step one towards world unity.

Big reductions to the World's Global gas emissions will be well started in all developed and developing nations by 2020 and well underway towards control by 2050. The use of renewable energy will be well developed and taking up over 50% of energy used worldwide. Fossil (Dirty) fuels will have been cleansed so that the emissions are very low and no longer spewing gas into the stratosphere. The start towards healing the huge hole in the stratosphere (If really there) will have started by 2080, and the world's scientists are becoming hopeful they can do what is needed. The dramatic reduction in the use of fossil fuels; and the worldwide agreement on the cleansing of these fuels, has reduced the Financial and Political power of all oil producing countries worldwide. Having said all of that it seems the truth is that the monitoring of the barometric reading shows an increase worldwide of 0.06%, but this is the average spread. In some places the increase is up to 0.3% in others nothing. The point is that over the last one million years there has been variations at least 10 times, in other words once in every 100,000 years there is a variation; that can throw planet earth into chaos. We wait the truth is the great hole really there or are we just experiencing another chaotic change! Maybe the problems we have had are real, but not affecting the climate as much as claimed by most of the world's scientists!

The world will divide into four common market groups, serious and genuine discussions will have started by the year 2060, as the world politicians come to realize there is no alternatives, and serious changes are vital to the worlds overall systems? The world division into common market groups will be completed by 2078! There will be four major groups and membership will be optional, but will be taken seriously as the world starts to unite into and around the differing groups. Every country big or small will have to join one or the other of the groups, as we have suggested in the following writing. All energy costs will be controlled and firm budgets will be possible by 2020, but to get full advantage of the price controls there must be a genuine proposed intent by a country; to join in membership to one of the major groups. The cost control we refer to here is energy costs! The rise and fall of energy costs during the 20th century has created a fear worldwide of being at the whim of the fossil fuel producing countries, and alternative sources of clean energy fuel has been cultivated. Countries that are not members of one of the groups will not be part of the fixed cost agreements for all fuels, these countries must still buy on the various spot markets. The politicians in control of many of the Fossil fuel producing countries had become extremely arrogant, because of the large amount of money they were receiving from fossil fuel. In some cases instead of developing their internal infrastructure; these countries were wasting their prosperity on political maneuvers, just to gain prestige. The need for belonging to a group is beginning to be understood even by these political adolescents, they must change or their peoples will in the end rebel.

Travel will be very cheap by the year 2050, and the world will have become just one big village, flying will be just an everyday occurrence. State to state flights will just be like getting on a bus, as it has been between various states in the U.S for many years, and this mode of travel will grow in all countries. The competition to the airlines will come from high speed rail this will keep prices very keen, and the young people especially will take full advantage.

The Internet cannot become any faster, but it will become very convenient; as a result the flow of information will be enormous, as instant knowledge becomes available to all at the touch of a few buttons. There will be no way anyone can escape from the everyday bustle of life; the methods of communication will have become all pervasive. The pressure from so much information will create more and more stress, and this will become a major mental health problem. Many of the advances muted for the future of the internet, and the population as a whole has come true, but there will be many disadvantages, and the internet will become just too intrusive to be acceptable to many people.

Medicine will have developed hugely, all people from birth to death will be labeled and their health records will be on line immediately, anywhere in the world at a glance. Medical progress will be so great it is too big to set out here in detail, but Cancer and Heart Disease will be controlled. The Brain however still retains a lot of its mystique as scientist try to bridge that deep unknown. This will automatically increase the average age in most areas of the world, medical magazines predict an average age of 120 years in the advanced world, but we are not in a position to comment professionally.

Religion is as ever having differences and problems, mainly through religious disagreements between the major groups. Catholicism East and West, Judeo Christians, Muslims, Hindu's Jews and all of the cults will be under pressure from the effects, of the impressive achievements of so many areas of scientific progress. The scientific community will be challenging the truth of creation and gradually they will be reaching the young generation, so that Atheism is growing very quickly. The Roman Catholics will be under great pressure from followers to soften the approach on several issues, but the most serious will be appointment of woman Priests, easing birth control, and the issue of Pedophilia among the Priests. Advances in Medical, Travel, Media Internet, PC Computers etc; Space, Astrology which further aggravates the religious problems, as confusion develops strongly amongst the flocks. The use of fear as an instrument to control the various flocks will no longer be so very all embracing, even the none Christian flocks will begin to question their leaders.

The cashless society will be being tested by the year 2020 in several small countries, in readiness for complete implementation by 2030 and beyond. When the trials are completed the American led group will lead the way, followed by Europeans, Russia/China, and finally the Muslim countries. This will be one of the biggest changes to be implemented for several centuries; the effects of this change will even be greater than the Industrial and the Information revolutions.

The world's population will be stabilized at eight billion by 2100, but has been settled fairly well by birth control agreements. All countries have legislated for birth control! All religions have been forced to reach a formula to bring deaths to births into balance; any excess children born have to be handed over to the State to raise? There will be no knowledge of the whereabouts of child or parents to each other, from the time of birth. This control is the most important after the Global warming challenge, and again must be successful.

The Space program will be a little inhibited by the lack of funds for the American program, as the U.S needs to bring its external debts under control. There will be huge funds spent by the Chinese and the Russians, but they will be duplicating what America already has. The hope is that America can keep its secrets secure; if they don't then the others will soon catch up and overtake. The hope is that India and America can develop together, and by so doing keep well ahead of all others. We believe that the Space program will not be as dynamic in the U.S in the future as it has been, but there will still be sound development, and the Americans are far ahead anyhow. Hopes of finding other life in outer space won't be realized as quickly as hoped, but the dreams will persist. Once the American Group again earns financial ascendancy the Space program will again push ahead, with NASA finally getting the funds it needs. This won't happen until the years 2035, by this time the financial balances will again be cleared; it will take this long to bring world debt into proper balance. This includes dealing with the world's poor, and the need to provide them with food clothing and homes.

Financial prosperity will have returned to the U.S. and Barack Obama will have done a good, but not sensational job of reducing foreign debt that will be after his second term, which he will win easily. The American People will have lifted themselves up, in the belief that their first Afro American President will lead them in the right direction, and he has succeeded in doing a good job. Obama will have during his first term bought the internal accounts back to break even, but has had terrific pressure from the international demands on his Presidency. He will win a second term and the second term will be the start of improved trade relations, and the external accounts will improve, but only marginally. The democrats will then win another term with a new President, who knows even Michel Obama may have a try, in the primaries anyhow.

China and Russia will both become financial giants, as will Germany and France! During this period England will decide to link with the U.S. rather than the European market! The wealthy countries will already be accepting the need to, and be well on the way towards; setting up their groups of common markets. The poor countries will understand the need by now of population control! The help of the wealthy countries will be linked to the abolition of starvation etc worldwide!

Apparently the greatest challenge the world faces today is climate change which is dangerous for every nation on earth rich or poor, so say the scientists. The Population explosion has a top priority for world control. Next is the surge of terrorism that has been spawned from the ranks of the Muslim believers i.e. Muslim Extremists. The fourth challenge is the control of the internet security, the danger to the secrets accumulated by America, and other advanced countries have got to be protected, but that's easier said than done. As the big countries are prepared to pay huge sums of money to traitors, who have access to and would be prepared to sell those valuable secrets.

After that is the challenge to the economies posed by overvalued assets both in the inflated housing sector and the industrial sector, that condition is current with the new world countries in particular. There may be a period of inflation, which may mask the desperate situation the world economy is in. America is no longer in the position to expose herself to more huge trade deficits, and this must be stopped, but the creation of jobs on a very big scale may not be the answer. If that job creation can be linked to reduced energy costs, there will be the needed trade off set, but the competitive position of the American car industry is also vital to the recovery in the economy it must happen urgently. The competition from all over the world to the motor vehicle industry must be stopped, and the American icon producers supported with Govt; funds.

Then for America while looking at balancing the budget as promised by their new President, there is the enormous trade deficit which must top USD10.5 trillion dollars by the end of y/e 2009. The American system of world policeman needs to be changed and others must be forced to help financially. NATO funded by the world wealthy economies must take up the world policeman job; this cannot be allowed to continue to drain the American economy. The financial problems that put the Western economies in danger are very real, because of the deterioration that Capitalistic system that has developed, over the past one hundred years. An alternative to Democratic Capitalism must be found it is no longer viable it just does not work anymore! The understanding that China has the new financial muscle to be at the top of the world in financial strength belies the truth. America in terms of real financial muscle is still at the top, her asset spread is huge! It needs be noted that no other country has the real infrastructure to take over as the world's financial engine, if the USA fails the world fails, and then there would be none on top!

World Free Trade Groups

Group one: Chinese/ Russian Free trade group. China, Russia & Manchuria.

Group two: European Free trade group. North, East, & West Europe, African Continent.

Group three: American Free trade group. America, South & Central America and Mexico, Canada, India, South East Asia, Australia & NZ, England, Israel, Japan, Korea, Philippines, Malaysia, Singapore, Burma, Bangladesh, Thailand, Cambodia, Greenland.

Group four: Muslims Countries group. Indonesia, Pakistan, Afghanistan, Iran, Iraqi, Jordan, Syria, Lebanon, Saudi Arabia, Turkey.

Notes:

Only the main countries are listed in each group.

Tariffs to none group members will vary by group, not country.

Group Currency will be introduced similar to the Euro. The near future will see the introduction of the cashless society.

Muslim Groups may have problems between Shia and Sunni, but others should not interfere.

This will be stage one towards a World Government.

Free trade groups will still apply even after a world parliament is introduced.

The future of our world

Global warming is, the start of mankind having a common goal, the salvation of planet earth. The prime objective of the grouping of world economies; is to give the people of the world a path by which we can all work together, for the common good. Unless the global warming issue is dealt with as a priority, there may be no extended future for all of us anyhow. It is this prime issue that will drive us together, and it's by attacking the problems in unity, that we will find answers to the world's problems.

Man has proved how creative he is; therefore science must solve the main problem! First, there is little use of the so many wonderful advances envisaged if we, the human race no longer exist, because we didn't get our priorities right. In close second place are the world group economies, because unless we get our cost balances right in this area, we cannot pay for the global warming battle anyhow.

The days of loose tax controls, black economies so prevalent in the wealthy countries, criminal waste not only of keeping criminals in jail, but loss of their contribution to societies income must be properly harnessed. All of this is now within the scientific capabilities of the wealthy countries, but must be expanded at little cost to the various groups. Criminals must be sentenced to working for the state to repay their wrongdoings, it is not sensible to have criminals living comfortably, as they do in some countries while the citizens pay to keep them. The criminals must be made to work their sentences out, only those that are truly dangerous must be jailed, and the death sentence must be more liberally applied, in the attempt to reduce violence. The Old Testament must apply to violence in applying the death sentence, thou shall not kill.

Since the Bible refers to a cashless society we believe this is also inevitable, therefore we should plan for the near future, when the plastic card is supreme and is the only class of legal tender to pay accounts etc. If all payments are to be made by either plastic cards for the retail industry and automatic transfer for all commercial work, it will be difficult for criminals to operate. The only way there can be a deviation is by the old agrarian method of farm gate trading, but it will be difficult to set up to any great scale. All business set up from illegal funds needs to be confiscated and sold off by the Govt; with the funds going to treasury.

The use of fossil fuels must have a cleaning process, there must be no more carbon gasses being created, the technology to fix fossil fuels we have, but we have to reduce the costs. The huge profits from fossil fuels must be more adequately taxed; this will be done by the enforcement of cleansing these fuels as they are burnt. Natural fuels such as Wind, Solar, Hydro, and Methane gathering from waste are the apparent major sources there may be others, science must find them if there are ie compressed air? Electricity must only be created from the above sources once they are cleansed. A method of harvesting Methane from animals in high production low cost countries such as New Zealand, where the total none pet domestic animal population is probably at least twenty animals to one human, should be applied.

When the fossil fuels are well depleted, and this refers not only to oil, but also coal, the alternative nuclear fuel must have been established, to gradually take over the short fall from renewable fuels. The need is for the Govt; to control outputs, and balance them so the phase out is relative to the nuclear takeover of final needs. The dramatic panics of global overheating must be contained and sensibly dealt with; the effects are so severe and so important, that an individual national piece meal approach will not work. The Kyoto international proto cols approach, without all of the big polluters is just a joke, which is now being rectified.

Within the total goal we will see the steady solution to, or of is the first priority, so that having found the first common goal; we can realize the good in man and expand onto a series of common goals. This will happen because as the people are educated and begin to understand, they will expect more from world leaders. Education even in the poor countries will become possible, as the internet becomes more streamlined, and able to reach the poor? This is similar to religion, an uneducated class was able to be controlled even by a modestly educated lay class, but education has changed that. This is why the Inquisition was possible the poor peasants were like sheep to the slaughter literally, and even the aristocrats often could not read or write.

In order of importance we have global warming, almost simultaneously improved economic control in the cashless society, tax and crime reform, religion, health, education, poverty, etc; all of these needs need to be addressed on the basis of group interaction, and all are vital to the successful continuation of mankind.

The world will successfully divide into trade groups, this grouping will be well and truly completed by the end of the 21st century. The next step will be the formation of a world Govt; this will be completed by the middle of the 22nd century that is the important step of the 22nd century? The Groups and then World Parliaments when formed will have a quorum of Minister's selected from the four groups, but first we will discuss how the first groups will start and be interacting together.

The idea will be to have each group as independent entities working together, and all fully self contained within their own groupings, for everything as far as possible. Territorial integrity will still apply to each country at all times. There will be no bar to intergroup trade except for the different tariffs that will apply, such tariffs will depend on the grading of each group; any subsidies for their individual countries must be paid internally by the group financial conciliation depts.

For example Group three may have a tariff allowance to group one, of 8% on all sales to a group one member. The group one member that is the buyer may have an internal tariff of 12%. Group three will discount the sale direct to the buyer by 8% then the treasury of group one will credit another 4% in the monthly reconciliation of the accounts. If a country is tariff free then they will get reverse credits as listed above.

Each group will pay to the group leader the monthly fee charged by agreement at the time of the Free Trade Agreement first being set up. The group parliament will meet on an agreed timetable at which time all fees and costs will be set, and they will be changed as needed.

There is no need to change the basic International Trade and Tariff rates for the different countries these will all remain the same, the idea is to put in place the Bible Prophecies that tells us that World Govt; is inevitable. To achieve that aim the groups will create the structure, whereby World Govt; is practical.

The Christian community may be tempted to move back to a trading system, the problem will be in trying to do that, as there will be so few who have the knowledge. Sadly in the Western world in particular, the art of barter has been lost, people are just too used to buying packaged food from supermarkets. The idea of wearing animal skins for clothing is anathema, and homes built out of straw with no central heating are unthinkable. There are trade cards that work on trading only, and they may gain some credence in a cashless society, but the fees being charged at present are too high for any great acceptance. And to make this barter system work it will have to be trade for trade, there doesn't seem to be a set off for paying a net debit account.

This would be because the system could be undermined if exceptions are allowed, so in other words to trade something one must have an equal value to cross trade with.

From the time of birth until death ones health and lifestyle will be kept on a computer system which we presume, will be incorporated into one card. Obviously our birth certificate will also be on the health card! Our other cards such as driver's license etc; will be incorporated into the Passports, and life insurance and Superannuation will also be incorporated into that one; card just for convenience.

The internet will be all pervasive as the information trend continues; information and knowledge will be available instantly to all, but knowledge without understanding will be of little use. The understanding of knowledge; will be a constant barrage of T/V shows explaining the meaning of everything. It will be those who care to watch and learn that will benefit from the strengthening and changing society. It is this very changing that will create unity, because the teaching will be universally the same. The explanation of the common knowledge will be the same in Germany as in Australia, on the other side of the world. What we are saying is, young Germans will get the same information as young Australians, thus there will be unity gradually developed between the nations.

There is no way would be criminals will be able to defeat the system to any great extent, there will still be the small amounts of graft etc; but the big time swindlers will be having a hard time to exist. What will be the use of a great wad of criminally obtained credit one cannot spend, it's probable there will still be options to spending etc; but only to the extent of what the gangsters can consume, not much more. Prostitution will have to be paid by credit card, as will any other activity that operates in private; this will ensure tax controls are tightened naturally.

The black economy will no longer be able to exist because there will be no cash, again only trade credits can be used for payments, and these trade activities will be easy for the Govt; to trace. The same applies to tax, there will be no loopholes of any great amount, and tax havens will go out of business. This will not stop the setting up of legitimate tax set offs, but the trading in assets will be honest and efficient; as all Govts; will be able to easily trace what the wealthy are doing. We stress here there will be no hindrance to cooperate activities, because these are legitimate business activities, but the ability for Govt; surveillance is obvious. The effect when all assets hidden in safe tax havens, must be bought to book or lost, there will be a windfall to many Govts when this happens.

The Foreign Debt:

The American foreign debt is much the result of the years of living beyond their income by the Americans. But the negative cash flow that results from high purchases of foreign produce, fewer sales to foreign markets keeps growing ever bigger, it has to be stopped. A good example is China; this country has had such a big positive cash flow, creating a very strong credit account worldwide. China is now the biggest debtor country in the world, and the U.S. is the biggest Creditor hows that for a real problem? The problem is that China by keeping its currency undervalued is creating a difficult position to compete with. China also has a large business Diaspora population that is well established in many countries; take the Philippines for example a third world country where the business community is strongly Chinese. This is a common situation in many of the poor countries of the world, and will grow ever stronger as the Chinese Diaspora grows and flourishes.

Nationalism:

Society will change quite naturally, as the level of national commitment to the international group grows. This does not mean any appreciable change in love of one's own nation; it means a greater sharing and caring as the people become aware of boundaries beyond their own, but within the group to which ones country belongs.

Personal ambition for the future will gradually transcend beyond the boundary of one's own country, and will become one that embraces the future of the group as a whole. The worlds young will grow up knowing they belong to a society, with boundaries that extends beyond their own, and nationalism will decrease. As nationalism decreases the ambition for military conquest will decrease, and the era of negotiated settlements will really be upon us. We stress we are referring here to the internal groupings not the external ones, and we acknowledge some groups will be more aggressive than others. War after all is a major industry, without which some countries would be in major trouble financially ie the USA.

Historically Nationalism has been the scourge of mankind, because it has allowed the evil in individuals to grow. A tremendous list of names can be written starting from the evil of Cain killing Able! The sad truth is that these individuals have been eulogized by their peers and victims, (subjects) as being great ie; Napoleon was a great administrator and tireless worker, but is venerated as a War Lord. What a contribution he could have been for the benefit of mankind, as it was he was a curse. He was able to light the flame of Nationalism, that's exactly what Hitler did he lit the flame, in the breasts of an extremely nationalistic nation, and by the end of his atrocious career up to sixty million people had lost their lives.

History has a way of twisting facts to suit a purpose, the great German Conrad Adenauer is the father of Western Germany, but he isn't as interesting as Hitler he never murdered anybody. Another way of expressing nationalism is mad ambition! When we examine the truth of Hitler and Stalin, two madmen who went to war and between them had murdered, close to one hundred million people we see the reality of mad ambition. The sad truth is many still admire these two men; and see them as great; this is the reality of the inability to see truth. Books by the hundreds and movies by the score, about those two are still best sellers as morbid curiosities to citizens of a blood lusted world.

The hope that Nationalism can be rationalized; by a renewed society, or at least controlled is a goal for which we should all strive. The first and greatest human triumph will be if war can become a past madness that can be replaced by a common sense; that is always negotiable. When we don't need nuclear deterrents to find peace through fear, but rather can negotiate answers to our problems, through common sense, we will be on the path to universal love and goodwill, to all mankind of all creeds and color.

CULTURE:

There is no attempt to mix culture with Nationalism, the two are very different! Culture is a pride in ones past and present, and the way one's own culture has developed over in some cases millennia, in others such as the New World, the first millennia has not yet been reached.

Culture includes many things, Language, Dance, National Dress, Food, and so many other activities that are exclusive and inclusive, to our own home country and background. There is no harm in being proud of one's ancestors, and having them constantly in one's memory, we need to be proud of where we have come from. But more we need to be proud of where we are going, because to help ones brother in need and at the same time help one's own self is only smart, and is in accordance with God's will for us all.

As we look into the past we see a continuous history of violence and ignorance to the plight of others, but now we are on the brink of world annihilation because of our own lack of care for others, we need to become aware of danger ahead? Some of the worlds cultures have been an abomination, ie sacrifice's to an idol God, but this is not culture this is nationalism, the sacrifice of others for the benefit of one's own country is a strong example of nationalism.

If we look at the starving millions in say Ethiopia and do nothing this is self it is neither culture nor nationalism it is the worship of self, a good culture would say what can we do? Now let's do it all together let's go let's do it! Such a culture is united, we have so many starving millions because we say leave it to the church, that's our old cultural excuse, we hide behind the church because our culture tells us we are believers, and that what the church has to do is to protect our culture. We are casual believers, Easter, Xmas, Weddings, Christening and Deaths that's when we believe. But you see our culture tells us to do something so we say, let the church do the job, that's what they are there for! My Mum and Dad told me that and they were always right! Sure that's our culture but sadly our culture is dying, it's like anything that's left without nourishment it dies and with that death; some of our culture dies too. So let's unite as one and let's look to the good things we know how to do, let our selfish self die; and let our instincts for our love of our culture spring to life again.

Sport:

Sport and the ambition to represent ones nation is not the same as nationalism, or culture. The ambition to excel at a personal level and to represent other's, (Ones own nation) is a hugely different truth! One is motivated initially by the challenge of self to achieve personal goals, and the ambition to lift ones performance to national then International level is healthy. If one is able to achieve and set healthy examples to others then one is doing a good thing for mankind! To be an example to others one's life must be on a parallel, with ones achievements in any chosen public activity! The problem is that many of our sports people are very young and while excelling at their sport are only starting to learn about life and its many strictures. The young are only learning to live, alcohol, fame, excessive money, immaturity all of these strictures are at the learning point for many athletes they may be at the apex of their sport, an achievement most of us will never reach, but they are also at the peak of exposure to the public, and the pitfalls are many and varied.

Sport is becoming an over paid job, it is no longer individual effort for the good of all. At what stage does sport lose its real value and become just another human abomination? It's when the goal is not to do well for the good of all, but becomes the vehicle for the good of the few. Unfortunately this is where the professionalism of sport is taking us! Sport starts off at the University's and other places! But then peaks out when an athlete's outstanding achievement becomes a saleable commodity! The reality of good for all becomes the good for self, and thus becomes a negative on society not a positive, and this is a sad truth. The business of profits through propaganda becomes a spoiling advertisement, and thus a drag on the entire population.

We are not saying the rewards for sporting achievement should not be won, but we are saying that society has to grow up and mature. The truth is that most sports people are there for the sport, the expressed appreciation of the people is nice too, but money is the ruination of the original decent ideals. The enormous amounts of money that goes to the promoters etc; just adds on to the total cost and kills sporting ideals as they were once expressed. The only way this inequality can be redressed is through special tax rates over and above certain approved levels. Excessive promoters' business profits should also come under special tax rates, not to kill motivation, but to get sporting incomes back to realistic levels. The suggestion here applies to all activities that are performed by people who love what they are doing, but are paid excessive amounts simply because the public will pay and they do pay gladly?_

IT or Computer security and controls:

The Internet has become a great boon to modern life; in deeper context is a bigger advance than the industrial revolution two hundred years ago. There are major problems in the area of security; even hackers getting into small operators computers are just playing games and they are a headache. But what about the real world! In the commercial world the theft of money and commercial secrets are severe, by value in the billions of dollars annually. We shudder to think what happens in the public arena, and we worry more when we think of what secret's America must have, are they safe after all many of us live under their umbrella?

What happens if one of the terrorist countries learns a way to block the computers worldwide, hell if our home computer is down we are stuck cos we have got too used to that damned thing, but that really is nothing. If the bank computers breaks down it's another nuisance, but again not earthshaking. But oh what if the Pentagon or the White house systems were to be down, where the hell would we all be? We would be exposed to attack from terrorists etc; we should not delude ourselves, we in the West need to know the Americans are there, and we can shelter under their cover but for course we let them pay the bill they have lots of money?

Let's imagine a situation where some rogue state wanted to attack the USA with Nuclear Missiles, assume they first blacked out the World Wide Web then launched their missiles. The blackout would stop American retaliation, if the entire time they were out was only 15 minutes; that would be too long. In another scenario assume the stock market was falling, and the internet was suddenly locked out, what sort of panic would there be?

Apparently China has been proved to have been active in hacking into supposedly secure sites in America, how does the U.S. protect itself from them because protect themselves they must, the free world depends on them? One thing would be certain it will not only be the Chinese that would like to steal American secrets, and they have done it before. The secrets of the atom bomb was stolen by the Russians, and speeded up their nuclear advance by many years. That is the last thing we would want to see happen at present, the security of American secrets are vital to world peace.

We have read a prominent American writer's book and he writes the Chinese traders need America! To us that is just bulldust! The Chinese have been insular for at least 5,000 years, they need nobody, and we should not kid ourselves that they do. China needs the USA for at most ten years to have the money and time to fund the building of its infrastructure. Then once that is complete there will be no more need, then they can concentrate on building their own economy. When we include Hong Kong, Taiwan and the Diaspora Chinese there will be over 1, 5 billion of them, so how the hell are they to be controlled if they manage to steal the U.S. Secrets. We have Europe with populations falling, and China that has to control their population if they can. This is why Europe should be linking with Africa, because of population growth. However it is vital that population control is made effective, if only for the sake of our over loaded planet. It is also why the USA led group needs to be linked to India and the SEA nations.

What we must realize is those American secrets protects us all, not just Americans, sadly for them they have to pay all of the bills, but the world is safer if they can secure their secrets, long may they do just that.

RELIGIONS OF THE FUTURE:

All real religions are good, it gives man something outside of himself to put first, and to have fear in certain situations, but the problem is man has always been evil until now, but the future needs to see change. India is a good example in this modern age, the recent problems between the Muslims and the Hindu's are really sad. Why does this have to be so and has it been always this way? The short answer is yes!

If we go back to biblical times we know that Abraham the original Jewish Patriarch had two sons Isaac and Ishmael. The Jews descend from Isaac and the Christians were just a Jewish sect at the beginning, since Jesus and his followers were all Jews. Muslims descend from Ishmael and they have two main sects the Shias and the Sunnis. The Jews disdain the Christians and the Christians disdain the Muslim's. The Muslims hate each other, but is this how the founders meant what they left behind to be. The persecution of the Jews isn't a phenomenon of the now it's the reality of being HIS chosen people. The Jews have always been persecuted when they stray from Gods' word! We Christians know Jesus said he came not to bring peace, but problems and family upset, this he did and it has always been so, but why?

Surely it's because we Christians have never lived as he taught us too. We westerners cannot understand why the two Muslim sects hate each other, and are quite happy to kill each other indiscriminately or so it seems to us. But is it not so, that throughout history at differing times, the various Christian denominations have done the same? And the Christians should know and remember the Muslims have a great and honorable past, it is the evil intent of the few, (Satan's Servants) who are propagating hate. The Christians need to point to their own evil past and remember! It would be a good lesson for real Christians to remember Spain and Grenada, when the Moors were driven out, the Christians supplanted them. They were Spanish Catholics and they bought with them the inquisition, has there ever been a greater evil inflicted on the ordinary people than that evil. We are not referring to wars here; we are referring to the Catholic Church!

Throughout mans biblical times existence, there has been more killing in the name of some type of God than for any other reason. The blood lust that permeates the nature of man is greatest when Religion is the subject, and becomes the argument. Hitler perceived himself as some sort of a religious figure, Stalin reverted for a short time during the war back to the Saints he had prayed to when he was in the ministry, as a very young man. So many men with vast amounts of human blood on their hands, have tried to justify themselves through the excuse of religious zeal. But once again we get back to nationalism and ambition!

King Richard the Lion Heart of England, Sheikh Saladin and their armies fought each other to a standstill for religion ostensibly, but because of a Roman Catholic pope in reality. Both sides were afraid they were going to lose followers to the others religion, and so we had the many years of the Christian Crusades, for the Popes ambition. The horrors inflicted on the Roman Catholic believers by the Spanish Inquisition were surely madness? So much so that is hard to believe could have happened, even in medieval times!

But let's get back to modern times and consider where we are now. All religions have their extremists and all extremists are narrow minded and inflexible, this is what makes them extremists. In those far of days of the Crusades the Roman Catholics were the extremists, attacking the Muslims.

Of course the Muslims as could be expected were just as determined to retain the status quo and repel the Christians, which they did.

Now we have Muslim extremists who are determined to destroy the Christians and Secular world, and any others such as Hindu's etc; but in reality all we have is more murder in the name of a God. Surely in modern society this is just silly! Western society is now one hemmed in by fear; there is nothing we do in our everyday life that isn't in some way infected by the change in our society, because of fear. But the big problem now is man has the ability for total annihilation which is why these extremists are to be feared, after all is it such a great leap of the imagination to believe, that if they will blow themselves up given the chance they will just as easily blow up the whole of mankind?

This is the present barometer of problems with the Muslims, as for their Faith we know that not, all we know is how our lives are now permeated by fear, and that fear is created by the Muslim extremists. We don't even know what the problem is, apparently it's because in some way we have insulted their homelands, because as infidels we are not welcome. Well as one simple man to another we don't want their homeland, we have our own thanks? The ambition of the Politicians and others for money and political gains are a detriment to the many, and the many must pay for the greed of others. What we can say is please don't create problems for us, because the result of that is problems for all. We don't believe that the average Muslim is any different than us in many ways, but there are differences let us quote an example.

There are two families living side by side one Muslim and one Secular. The Secular one is a typical secular family that belongs to a society with a decreasing population, they have two children. The Muslim family is also average but they have five children! The two Families have the same income, and both have only one member of the family working, both families manages their finances well. As the families grow up the Secular children get more attention than do the Muslim children, because their parents have the cost of only two children to provide for. The youths in the big family see themselves being treated differently they object, and are soon seen as being in rebellion because they feel they are being treated unequally, they believe this because they see the Secular children as getting more. They probably are but whose fault is that? Do we blame the family with two children, or does the family with five off spring create its own problems? Surely the real answer is the parents of the big family have to work harder and earn more, after all they created the larger family?

We are not saying either is wrong, but the children of the large family are disadvantaged! How is society supposed to balance out the two families so both sets of children are treated equally, this is a big problem, that should not exist. This is a social and cultural problem not religious, the two families have different aims, the Secular family profess no or have little religion, the other strictly adheres to and keeps all of the religious rules that they are being taught. What becomes obvious is that the society those two families are living in; is incompatible to one or the others needs, but need that be so, is it possible to balance those needs? Sure it is if the big family works together they as a group when they get a little older can do better than the small family, it's all in the education, and understanding? We came from a big family of six siblings, we grew up and each one helped the other to get a nice home, nice car etc; just because we all worked together, mind we are all well educated?

We can promote failure when we separate out the families and put them in enclaves of their own, and this compounds the problem! In enclaves of their own in a material sense the one will prosper in the broader society. The other large family will be in a common apparently disadvantaged group, and with the other large families around see themselves as completely discriminated against. This is untrue but it appears as if they are right, in Australia with the many Govt; incentives for all families to have more children there is a comparative peace, but there are still problems. There needs to be an education available that teaches the big families the advantages they have, and how to use them.

But even there the feelings of being discriminated against are untrue and unfair; it is part of a supposed social injustice that breeds unhappy Youths. We say Youths because these are the volatile sections of any and all communities that is where the extremists come from. Even in the Secular community we see young men who join up with extremists, they see it as an adventure, or even a way to see the world and fight for a just cause. The question of course must be do they really know what they are fighting for, if they do then no one can object, but if it's just an ill conceived passion of the moment, then they are not informed and are being voluntarily led astray.

When we consider the Muslim countries they are what we in the west would see as communities that are just so far behind the developed world, but we must ask why that is so and what can be done? The same thing applies to Africa where the religious background is different again largely Pagan and Animist, the one thing all of these countries has in common is heat, sand and lots of children.

The importation of these problems to advanced countries that are ill equipped to deal with such social problems, must for now be avoided. The families must be educated before they are transplanted to new social conditions, the immigrants of the past have had no problems, but we are seeing problems now and they will grow. But the world must look forward to equality of all in the future, that's why we advocate the groups of nations so that all are treated well, even if not fully equally.

There is no use planting families into enclaves and leaving them to fester into nests of young radicals, who will flock to any organization that will offer the sustenance above and beyond what they think they are getting. This is an educational problem and must be dealt with before these families are resettled. There must be a point at which the world knows what it is doing, and tries to create harmony worldwide; by harmony we mean that all peoples have food and clean water, the basic human need. Beyond that we need to look to the wants, a home and clothing and work of some sort, so that all men can support their families with dignity. In saying that we know that some lazy people care little for dignity!

The west needs more children but we need them to socially integrate, and to do this only the families can do the job, and if they are to be accepted into our societies then they must recognize what is needed. The last thing that is needed is radical Sheikhs preaching a mixture of Islam and separation from the mainstream. The greatest damage that is being done to the Muslim Youths is the teachings of the Sheikhs, who are separatist and destructive!

Main stream Muslims don't want them either, but they are there in the Mosques they are teaching they are destructive, and they must be stopped. The teaching of hate is the last thing we need in the entire free world! This is something that has to be stopped and we hope with the integration into Free Trade Common Market Groups, we will see the beginning of enlightenment.

SCIENCE AND RELIGION:

The future is going to see the collision of science and religion as science develops, and attempts are made to teach Faith in self and the error of Spiritual Faith, which has for millennia been a chief source of inner strength to untold millions of people.

The head on collision of Evolutionism and Creationism is very close and there needs to be a better approach from the Religious folk who by definition must walk in Faith, this is what the Evolutionists decry. Creation is a belief that has been a belief since man first walked on earth; evolution has been a philosophy since the time of Darwin some two hundred years. The theory of a single sell amoeba being the ancestor of all life on earth; is very hard to believe in, and will be rejected by the great majority of mankind. The evolutionary solution assumes there can be no spirit that the spirit is just a figment of the imagination, this is inflammatory to many people and must be answered sensibly, not by vague hypothesis that have no meaning in fact.

The symbolism of the Bible must not be used as a anchor by which creation can be ridiculed by the evolutionists, the truth is that creation and evolution can be given a compatible profile, but this is too big a subject for this book, it requires books devoted to the subject not just a few lines.

When we examine the theory of creating the world in seven days we see that as merely symbolic, Moses is interpreting thoughts put in his head by God, it is not unreasonable to think of a day in Gods mind as totally different than ours. In Gods mind a day could be a thousand years even a million years, this seven day symbol should not be a great barrier to creation. Being created in God's image we suggest is referring to the Spirit! The Bible tells us God is a Spirit, so to be created in his image is to be a spirit surely, thus we believe only man has a spirit? It is simply silly to be saying that man has nothing to face the future for, we are spirit and our spirit cannot die, that is not symbolic that is a fact and what those who have faith believe in. So in the end the bones and artifacts the archeologists are working with, does not create a big difference between the two beliefs.

The compatibility of the two disciplines are seen as impossible, but we question why this is so and who is to prove those claims? Certainly the evolutionists will point to what they see in their scientific successes as a proof of their claims and they may be right, but equally they could be wrong. The creationists will claim they are right no matter what evidence is claimed, and they have every right to believe what they are saying, and they can be just as right or wrong. We wonder if there could be a third way, can the bible be interpreted a little differently.

If we assume that Moses when he interpreted the first five books of the bible never knew how long a day is in Gods world. God is infinite therefore surely one day to him could be way beyond our comprehension. We read the Bible verses that refer to creation and assume one day is 24 hours, who says that is so, certainly not Moses in our Bible which is a standard King James Version. Who knows what is meant by the big light and the small light in the heavens, this is surely symbolic.

When God says man is created in his image, what is meant? God is a Spirit so he has no form unless he chooses to take one, and he could take any form he chooses, who are we to try and restrict him to the shape of a man. How many of our neighbors can we look at and say they look like us individually, and how do we account for the so many differences? The scientists will say that's just our level of evolving from apes, is that why the white races were supposed to be superior? Because they have evolved further than other races? Well we don't feel comfortable with either assessment, nor do we want to dispute Darwin's theories he may be right?

Many people find comfort in their Spiritual Faith and consider it as what keeps them going, there needs to be a search to find a path towards compatibility that's what we prefer to search for. Before we start we want to stress this isn't a philosophy, we are trying to expound it is a search for compatibility with Science and Religious belief, or a belief in both.

The belief is growing that there are many Planets/Worlds out there that have conditions, which could host some form of life as we know it? Why could it not be that such life is evolving and they are many millions of years behind us in the process? Maybe it's the other way around and there are worlds far more advanced than ours, and they are sending out probes to find people compatible with them. Perhaps there is a Pantheon of Gods each with worlds that they are creating. Are such thoughts really so silly and are they harder to understand than a big black hole that exploded and is ever expanding so that the Universe, or Universes are in the millions and we are just part of the many?

Why couldn't our own God having completed creating us, now be in the process of creating other worlds in a different Universe? The thought to us is fascinating maybe we are just part of a huge family of worlds, and we are just evolving from world to world. This is just as likely as the old and not so old science fiction movies that portray different forms of life that are just so ugly to look at? We aren't fiction writers we are merely hypothecating on what could be, certainly our thoughts aren't any more farfetched than science?

The previous paragraphs may be a lot of silly rubbish but it's better than taking away all hope of an afterlife. Personally I need something tangible to believe in, and not somebody telling me that they have theories that go back fourteen billion years. The theory of everything is great for the smart people who sit around and dream of what everything really is, and their wonderful string theories. We are not trying to debunk anyone or thing we just want someone to come up with theories that give us hope, and we aren't referring to Theologians who can only create more mystery.

Jesus told us he had many mansions to visit, the Theologians interpret that as meaning he went to visit the Aztecs or some other ancient tribes. He then spent some forty days out visiting. Is that any sillier than what we are saying? We wander if it is much more difficult for ordinary people like us to believe in, than some piece of string and the philosophy of everything. We admire the Scientists so much and long may their theories exist, but you see people, to me what I believe in is no more just a theory than theirs? To close this chapter let us say we believe in the Trinity, the Father, Son and the Holy Ghost and that's that. If somebody wants to call their God Allah and if their

Prophet's name is Mohammed, or if you belong to other beliefs, all we have to say is God Bless You All and long may we all live. We pray we can all find Love and Peace together, each for the other!

THE FREE TRADE GROUPS:

GROUP ONE: CHINESE-RUSSIAN GROUP.

Global warming is really paramount to China many of her cities are already lost in the industrial smog, they managed a little control for the 2008 Olympics but only with a lot of luck. China will have to work in unity with all of the other groups, to help halt the coming disaster if they don't, them more than most will suffer. Russia needs clean air too maybe not as much as China, but still unity is needed from within their peoples as well. It's a world effort not just one country the world for once in unity, let's pretend we are all preparing for the Olympics.

The sheer size of this group both in Land Mass and Population sizes outstrips all others easily! Both lead Nations are strongly nationalistic, and both from ancient times have been the target of foreign ambition. Russia especially in recent times were targets of invasion by the French and Germans! The nationalistic fervor with which the Russian people fought off the invaders were intense and none can deny their total love and commitment to their homeland! China has been the target of trade colonialist nations for many years, the recent return of Hong Kong has fixed that problem for the present.

The separation of Taiwan will be a problem that will need to be settled, this will be a pre requisite of Chinese assimilation in the final structure. However since national integrity has to be maintained none of these type problems should be insurmountable. China and Russia both have problems from the past, but the advantages will over ride all such concerns in the moves for national advantages; with integrity.

As we look into the future we see this will be the hardest block of all, from the point of view of development and group financial assimilation. Both lead countries have an undeveloped approach to the personal freedom for its peoples. Any other countries that become part of this Group will need to be ones with a similar type peoples that are already well developed to this stricture. Economically this group will have a balanced internal economy, and both will enjoy a period of fast growth in the area of infrastructure building. It is in this area the continuing need of foreign income will continue to be important for a period of time, until the infrastructures are built up. However when the infrastructures are completed, they will be very self contained and with a huge internal market, they will never need any outside markets?

This need for foreign trade will be of a short duration maybe ten-twenty years, during which the money will be needed to build their respective infrastructures. Because of the enormous and corresponding high density populations in the adjacent Indo Asian nations, whatever the final structure of the group it will be easily self contained, but starting from a low average income base. This will mean a dynamic period of internal growth in the near future, as industry and agriculture switches from international, to group internal trade. The average growth of incomes will be above world norms, until gradually as income increases; so the standard of living will catch up to the countries, that are already fully developed.

The peoples of these countries are more malleable than most others; this is because of their history! It is for this reason the advantages of a Common Market will more easily accrue to them, than in some of the other groups. The nationalistic zeal may however create difficulties initially until the actual benefits start to show in a practical sense. Because of the low level of education in a very big percentage of the peasant type peoples; it is natural there will be strong initial disapproval to what is needed, but in the end agreements will be achieved, and fears from the masses will be lessened.

As the education and advantages start to accrue the control of the tax systems that will begin to work, will bring stronger budgets. This money will come from the control of criminals and the black money market, all worldwide problems. These stronger budgets will allow for money to be spent on education and social welfare, hitherto unheard of in these countries. Even starting from a low base the effects will be quick because of the natural intelligence, and work ethic of the Chinese and Russian peoples, and they will take full advantage of any chances they get.

The uneven benefits from the new wealth in both main countries, will also even out as the state gains the benefit; of greater administrative controls. The Beauracracy will be huge, but the trickledown effect often ineffective in the USA, will actually work in this group because the business community will also even out. The economies of these two countries will also benefit, out of being able to see the mistakes made in the Western World. The taxes avoided by the crafty Entrepreneurs in the past, will be a handy added income to the treasury coffers of both countries.

There will be a more even monetary spread into small business; and that is the key to an effective cash flow regime, that will naturally spread the wealth more evenly, than has ever been the case in the past. This is a capitalistic approach and will need to be controlled, but the change into a cashless society will help to monitor everything; that is happening in business, and thus improve the Govt share of net income. In other words the taxes due and payable will be properly assessed and collected, this will strengthen the treasuries of all countries.

All countries in the South East Asia area that are the ones most likely to join this group, have great but very hard recent pasts; this has created populations that will be highly appreciative of all future benefits. As in all things and people; it will be easy to spoil them in ways that would not be seen as spoiled, in the developed world.

Because the Nationalistic fervor is high in these countries and suspicion of the developed world so high, in the upper levels of their political agendas, there will be allowances that will have to be made in all moves; towards this Common Group formation. However we need to remember there is no loss of national identity, even though the necessary changes will be many, but all is value to increased world harmony. The common currency may be difficult; if one country wants to pursue a policy of cheap money on the world stage, but once greater economic strength is achieved true values will be necessary; with a currency that floats on market.

GROUP TWO: EUROPE, AFRICA:

This group potentially includes the most and the least developed, this is the correct mix in the need to create a balance in the group and in the eventual worldwide prosperity. Global warming and the green house effect will be the dominant or first priority of this group as it will for all of the others, and this will be very expensive, but so it will be for the whole world. The effect on all mammals including mankind will be catastrophic if a united effort is not achieved; doing nothing is not an option.

Led by Germany and France, these two countries are among the most successful in the developed world. Germany is a highly efficient industrialized country and France is a high cost highly subsidized; agricultural country that is very independent; and looks set to continue the practice of being different, and often controversial. France, Spain, Portugal and Italy all have common links back to the Roman Empire that was why the nick name the Romance Countries. The French tend towards a left leaning political preference, this has led to an expensive system of subsidies to its agricultural output, demonstrations by French Farmers in the glow of the international media is not uncommon.

Germany is a highly organized country that revels in many areas of success, a highly skilled workforce, scientific achievement, an unmatched labor output, sound government, and a creative ability to recover from economic adversity that is a repeating phenomenon of the German nation. The destruction of the Berlin wall and then reunification of East and West, once condemned by poorly informed journalists as impossible has been successful. This isn't unexpected everything the Germans do they do well, and so it has always been; right back to their Barbarian roots.

The Common Market is already established with their common currency, the national bonding is far more difficult, but is progressing quite well. The large national component of this group includes of the old Roman Empire, which can be a help or a hindrance; time will tell which is the most effective. This total international bonding isn't one that is natural, but is a must for future world stability; this probably applies more to groups two and three than one and four.

The Europeans have a large job among themselves as we look to East, West and North; this is the area that could correspond with a little overlapping, to the one in the bible (Daniel) referred to as steel and clay. This area will be highly successful once the bonding is better understood up in the North, since this includes so many areas that are largely inhabited by the Balts. These are a very hard working people if less imaginative than their neighbors in the East and the West. They tend to react more as defenders, not aggressors as the French and Germans have been in their past. The Low Lands and the East are extremely advanced cultures; that have developed a very high level of Social Welfare, this will need to be brought under control, the cost to their budgets are hard to balance. The past of the lowlands have been very dynamic as business and God fearing peoples, but their recent development has tended towards sexual tolerance; far greater than the rest of the developed world. The Dutch preservation of much of their land with a system of dykes to keep out the North Sea, has been over many years very impressive. The high water table can be seen in the drainage on the farms quite clearly as one travels through the country!

There tends to be a balance between the Low Lands and France in the protective tariff shields over their revenues or net sales, this is needed when having to compete against low cost countries such as Australia, NZ and the Argentine. The ability to control or hold these costs while others catch up is of great importance, the East also have high costs. In fact the European Market as it is now is insulated and costs are held high because they have to be, attempts to bring them down wouldn't work there has to be a method, and this is available through Africa's membership of this group.

Africa with its starving millions are less than attractive to the developed world, but if looked at in context a balance can be seen. Group one that has got to lift their huge populations gradually, in so doing they have to lift their capacities, they have a huge poor population but they are on the move already. If we now look at Europe and Africa we see the wealthy and the poor, with the need to develop the poor. But develop in this sense also means to help them to integrate into a producing largely wealthy (But not entirely) community, and in so doing become producers themselves. The creation of wealth here is synonymous with group one, but they are creating wealth internally, we know this is easier. But the balance is there, group three has the South, Central America's and Mexico as the poor they must lift and integrate, all up there is a fair mix.

Africa will yield a lot of minerals that the group two will have a priority to get, because as a matter of diplomacy the Europeans will be helping their development; on an agreed formula. They will not be taking an advantage of as in the old Colonial Era, or through unbalanced investment yields as is happening now with the Chinese who have mineral contracts. Africa will get the advantage of the European know how, Europe will get access to minerals that they badly need. This doesn't stop the sale of the mined minerals to other groups, what it does is give Europe a priority and a vested interest to see their group as a whole prosper.

All up group two will be in balance with the rest of the world, and the difficulties will be no harder than the others, but it is a more obvious case of lifting an extremely poor continent from the depths of poverty. Europe east and west will face a challenge such as never before and they must succeed. But in obtaining help from the other groups there will be a more genuine approach, because of the Group parliament having a far stronger incentive to succeed.

As with the Muslim Group there will be severe religious difficulties, Africa is largely Animist and Pagan, with small helpings of other religions. These are Roman Catholics, Muslim and Protestants, all of these churches will probably want to send as many missionaries as they can, but the pressure needs to be controlled and no beliefs discriminated against. What is very obvious is that the four groups have a prime purpose, of first lifting the worlds disadvantaged to improved conditions, as efficiently as possible. By working in groups the worlds poverty will be reduced, there is no goal for religious balance at this stage that can only come with world cooperation in the future. There will be religious freedom to all as the need for cooperation is spread; historically mankind has suffered from discrimination that gets out of hand very easily. It will be in Africa that this problem may be worst, but will eventually be dealt with in the later world unification. This isn't meant as a distrust of any religion or cult, it is simply a fact that can only be dealt with by world govt.

The use of resources that break down continually often between Russia and Europe has to be redressed, until that is done there will be continuing problems which are quite natural. It is far easier for Russia to send their energy surpluses to China and the other side of the world into Indo China than dally with Europe, and its recalcitrant former allies on the black sea. The future income off Russia's resources will be immense, but they won't be of benefit to Europe. These products will go to their common market comrades be they China or South East Asia, what matters is they can be paid full market value, without all of the intrigue they are having at present. Both Russia and China will have wealthy economies, and they will bring their political and religious differences into proper and long lasting focus. The change in the energy sources worldwide will change the focus on fossil fuels, and the need to cleanse all fuels will be of paramount importance. With the change to clean renewable fuels, there will be a shift in focus, and the importance of fossil fuels to many economies will lessen to a very large degree.

The aim of the individual groups should be the initial synchronization of production of products based on the areas competitive costs and thus through to resale, at post tariff prices. The cost of labor and material allowing business to compete and to maximize yields on capital employed; must be within an environment that is controlled by Govt. The acquisition of funding and there are many other needs to make business function, in an environment that creates motivation is vital, but cannot be left to business to create. Just as Govt; cannot utilize resources of all types to maximize yield in the world of business, business cannot be left to manipulate resources if continued success is to be enjoyed.

Big business that requires large resources and labor, thus require the same level of Govt; control, and can be extremely wasteful. This is because there is often a poor use of labor with horizontal integration, and then poor utilization of the said resources. Small to medium business can be difficult to control and hard to administrate, which is why the acquisition through takeover is popular. This takeover regime is an easy way for the few to gain large unearned profits! The once accurate claim of efficiency through size is a myth, from the public point of view? These activities have a persona created by Hollywood that is unbalanced!

The mythological image of big business efficiency is wrong, there is a point where this myth breaks down, because of the historical greed of mankind, and it's at this point that the cost to the public gets out of whack. This happens through the lack of competition created by the making of a big business artificially, the example can be seen using Microsoft? This huge business was not created artificially through takeovers therefore should be left to go its own monopolistic way; they have earned that right from their birth out of nothing. This reality also applies to the likes of Ford G.M. etc! The day may come when the monopoly of Microsoft is broken, and they have to compete meantime they have earned their rights. The ancestry of big companies need to be looked at closely, natural growth is one thing, acquisitive growth quite another?

At present it is usual to transport work from an expensive production area to one that is cheap, but this creates antagonism as jobs are lost and resources are shifted, it is important the public can see an equalizing set off. By that we mean, if cars are to be produced in France and sold in the Australia & New Zealand there is a need to be able to show the workers who have lost jobs where there has been an advantage. To say to those redundant workers, well there is a trade balance within the external trade accounts with the country that has now got your jobs; there must be a demonstration of that truth.

For example assume cars that have been produced in France and sold to A&NZ yet there is an account deficit with France! This is a disaster and creates not only job loss but National disorder! Rightly the workers in the G.M plants in Australia feel their Govt; has let them down and the dislike of France grows, the infestation of aggravated nationalism will be destructive and must be balanced.

In the past because the French gained the market for Lamb meats at the expense of Australia and New Zealand; in spite of the high French prices. This is as has happened in the past so the growing animosity to the French is insidious, and the French earn a reputation of unfair competition in its trade links. The high cost of Lamb meat that had to be subsidized in the Common European market was/is deeply resented by the A& NZ farmers they have been kicked out, not traded out. This is what we mean by uneven business flow that needs to be properly communicated to the Farmers in A&NZ, they need to know why they lost markets. New Zealand went into recession for many years and the areas once growing lamb is now growing pine trees. Many meat producing factories now lay idle in NZ and the pine trees take many years to reach cash flow and capital yields, which of course is why that period of severe hardship in NZ. Our People look at that and ask why our men went to war to support those, who later undermined us and created years of hardship to us through aggravated recession for several years in NZ.

It is necessary for France to trade out the difference on the basis of buying from the losers in A&NZ to understand the displacement or shifting of work. But more properly if A&NZ has French cars because they are just for the wealthy, then the cost imbalance needs to be rectified. France needs to through its Govt; to buy products from A&NZ that they must sell on the same basis, the French cars are being sold. If the French were to buy wine from A&NZ to compete on their French market with their own product, then we have balance that can be understood.

More properly what really needs to happen is for France to reduce the price of its cars, or sell them to a tariff free country in their own trade block. The Govt; down under must tax the French cars out of the market place; and look to produce and sell more luxury cars internally. The trade balance then finds its own level within its own trading block, and gradually the dislike of the French accumulated from the past in A&NZ will dissipate. As the local groups find trade efficiencies the trade potential grows within the European Market! As there develops reciprocating but subsidized trade, in the various groups so trade will balance and the rich will be really subsidizing the poor.

Let's forget cars and talk basic food! France should sell subsidized food to Africa and does so by way of trade debits, not unproductive free welfare credits. Africa takes those trade credits and converts them to promote its own if necessary new business! This is done on the basis of pre agreed sales again within the group, the welfare credits should then be given on the basis of the group buying African products. In this way the wealthy are really helping through trade, they are issuing real credit in two ways, and Africa can in this way start seriously developing. We only refer to France because we are from NZ and we know the pain our people went through when our products lost out to the French subsidized product. It was painful, it lasted for several years and the people were not properly told why, it was typical poor communication and detrimental unfairly to both France and New Zealand.

GROUP THREE: AMERICA AND OTHERS:

This group appears to be the wealthiest, but that may not be correct at present, the cost of America's military and space programs has been very high, and in the financial arena there are severe problems ahead for this group. This group is the one that has the most problems hidden in the closet as the investment problems sheet home, affecting all areas of the economies. America's future is in the South Pacific the Indian Sub Continent and in the South of North America.

This will change the perception of world affairs in relation to America, as India and America's family of countries to the south link up with her, to create a very effective grouping that will prosper, but has the same number of problems probably several more than other groups. America has a rapidly aging infrastructure, huge foreign debt, and a military that is at war with a mystery moving enemy, and they are the terrorists of the present day. What America does have is a huge military and scientific knowledge earned from its space program, but its security program is struggling to meet its countries real needs. This is gleaned from one of its chief security people from the past who has written of his own experience in advising five Presidents. HIs fear is of the sheer size and complexity of the problems, there was no criticism here, merely concern for the future of the writers own much loved country.

The primacy of big financial services business has proved very accurately, the weakness in the Capitalist system that is America at present. The fact that huge American based and capitalized listed financial services groups, could still falter in spite of their supposed huge capital base, needs in depth discussion. First we find the huge financial base is a myth, because there was inadequate cash available to withstand depositor fears. The cycle of investments are really a mirage and why did that happen! That's easy to understand the answer is human greed on a huge scale, not only in company boardrooms, but spread throughout the investing public; this we explain under the chapter headed money that is in the following comments.

Greed is evil in whatever guise it comes, money, influence, political, power, etc; there is many guises to greed, but naked greed usually refers to money. The growth of investment geared to what is really unearned income is like a disease and infected 74% of the American public. The so called Baby Boomers came of age and this utterly spoiled generation really believed the propaganda, they were the chosen ones, what bull dust. All that happened was their generation that took up the slack when the men returned from war, and the lost breeding time was underway especially in the Allied Countries. The Axis countries were a little slower to start, but they also started breeding with a vengeance, thus the Baby Boomers, really just a new generation of spoilt kids.

That generation has always been closeted because of the times, unparalleled growth, and high home ownership created by their parents. The fact of buying a home that created a capital base for many who had no financial understanding has now shown up as a disaster, suddenly there was a generation with an asset base they did not understand. They are the financially inept people who had assets but lacked knowledge to look after their assets, and who were ripe for the picking by unscrupulous business men, in many areas of their society. In short it was a generation of lazy greed, they thought they were suddenly really financial gurus, but their success was really because their parents had done everything for them. In truth they are just a totally spoilt generation, many who don't have a clue of real life!

It's in the home owners industry that the hidden rot is, and will take time to mature. The new world countries, America, Australia, Canada and New Zealand have hidden problems that will take time to work through the system if ever. While it is true that the problems were in houses being sold with contracts that gave false mortgage ratings, to poor new home buyers, so that equity was little or nothing, but that is just the start of the problems.

There is also the high ratio of no interest loans that means homes are only being loaned to buyers, this is because they have no equity and are only paying interest if that? The ratio of no interest loans in America was up to 64% of the total loan book, but these are not necessarily the loans to the poor who have been the first to lose out and to have their homes repossessed. This money went mostly to Mum and Dad investors who now have to service debts on none performing investments, therefore the repayments are being made out of income. The tax deductibility of these payments will vary according to the various State and country tax profiles.

The rot will gradually work the way through the markets, but it will be hard to create confidence; when investors know they have to mature losses if they want to change their port folios. This only means the big percentage of their investments are into poor performing investments, so to roll over they have to mature their losses and bring them to book. The money they will have for reinvestment will be less, and their cash after rolling over will not pay out the debts because they leveraged too high. Thus they are caught most will have no choice, but to hold and hope their investments come right, if they are to be rescued only the Govt; can create their life line. Let's hope for their sake the answers can be found without more dishonestly in the corporate boardroom, but this will need to be carefully monitored.

The drop in market has created an investment for buyers of investment homes at bargain prices; this will mature the yield on the bank loans and show the equity loss immediately. These sales will not show a return on Govt; loans, in fact it is problematic whether the capital to the banks are paid in full, because of the over leverage in the first place. The stock market and other investment loss in values will require a changing in the movement of money; that will be more severe in many ways. The banks will have matured their own books, but the buying spree will affect the value of homes on which loans have been acquired only for investment, these are the ones that won't be matured and is the rot in the system. Only Govt; action can possibly help, but since the investment to the banks by Govt; should be paid back by the banks, this money may be able to be used to clean up the rot in the Capitalistic system. This will depend on the values they yield when sold, but one thing is for sure those who have cash or access to cash should make a financial bonanza?

Like the other two systems there are the very poor people of the group that will require help to get themselves actually progressing out of their poverty. The main area we are referring to here is the South Central America and Mexico. In the Sth Pacific there are countries that are very poor, but are in the first stages of developing alone ie the Philippines is a good example. Most of the poor countries in the South East Asia and Indo China are countries that are moving quite well alone, as is India. The deep South Pacific Countries Australia and New Zealand are developed countries, and attached to them there are the tiny Islands that will have to be permanently sheltered.

The countries of South East Asia have proved their, (tiger economies) ability to deal with problems when their economies were under threat, they showed their viability. The adjustment they need is no different than all of the others in this evolving financial climate, but to rely on the discredited supremacy of America in the financial arena would be foolish, and the Asians are certainly not foolish. The financial future (markets) is going through dramatic changes, and there will be advantages to the group as it moves itself into taking full advantage, SEA and India will be at the fore front of the changes. The capital markets in America at this stage are weak, and there is medicine that has to be applied to rectify the problems, whether or not the changes will be accepted; is conjecture at this point.

Pure democratic capitalism is under threat, and the external debts owed by America are not going to vanish quickly. The direction the new President is taking his country needs to be allowed to mature before accurate comment can be made. One thing is certain and that is America needs help, in its investment banking arena, the wise guys are discredited, but as usual are still close to the action.

The shifting of energy exposures, new employment, Housing the poor, and a myriad other problems, not least war and global warming gives an agenda that has so many problems, that the whole structure needs revamping. The American superiority in technical knowledge for war and space creates a security industry that is a huge drag on the internal accounts. This is fine but our fear is how secure is this industry, the cheapest way for others to advance in the military and space surely is to steal the American's secrets, this is what is most to be feared, apart from global warming of course. All members of this potential group needs to understand the very serious security problems!

India is a country that has huge potential within the group concept, but she has a lot of new shaping to do as she tries to teach and rouse up her untouchables. This area alone will create a big infrastructure need, but the rewards will be substantial, not only monetarily but to the people, it is well time the untouchables are lifted out of their negative stupor. India is booming in the IT industry, but India must become a major manufacturer, she has such an advantage provided she can harness what she has. The IT industry has proved the point but that has limits, all of the group members need trade set offs, and this is what India has got to do to move forward. The development of their untouchables into an efficient work force, and the tapping of their business Diaspora are the key for the development opportunity that is available. The widening of the business base using their highly skilled business community must be used effectively as soon as possible. The capital that must be raised within the Common Market Group is vital, the contents are all there to help bring this group into full viability, it's just a matter of whether they can work together to do what is needed?

Even though Geographically England should be with the European Countries, it will find it more expedient to move over to group three, because of the ethnic and historical unity with those peoples especially with the new world. These are countries that are all highly developed and apparently self sustaining; and they have natural affinity with the UK, but appearances are deceptive. Australia has close ties with America, NZ has similar ties but far less so, and of course Canada has a close relationship with America in the NAFT agreement. Most of the islands are connected in some way to either Australia or New Zealand and there are ties with big, but poor neighbor New Guinea. Israel is an integral part of this group her association through religious links with the U.S.A. plus their strong Diaspora links there creates the very strong link. Even though there are no links to the Asian countries such as India, religion won't stop the first stage, religion must wait until the one world system is finally and fully realized but it is coming.

Australia and New Zealand are exporters and cheap producers of their surplus products, but their labor and some material costs are expensive. Add to this the tyranny of distance, and what we can see is that the people are the key in both of these countries. Both countries by comparison with their Asian neighbors have high total costs, but they have proved what can be done because they are among the world's developed nations in spite of their difficulties. This is because of the ethnic background and level of education, but like all others they cannot stand alone, nor can they stand still, they are capitalists and in that philosophy none can stand still, that's a fatal mistake they will not make.

The Australian Federal Govt; has made noises about Petro Dollars, that will be a serious mistake since those dollars will have to be guaranteed. Even though the Govt; has AAA rating and will get the money cheap it will in the end be expensive!

The Canadians are ethnically the same and just as creative, to survive next door to America as an independent and flourishing economy, with such difficult climatic conditions is proof of their ingenuity. Their industry like all others needs investment money and the American money is not now so available so what do the Canadians do now? Their NAFTA with the U.S. and Mexico isn't enough now, they need a deeper security, and they will find that, but they cannot find it through Petro Dollars this is the way to disaster. We repeat again the bible says, and the borrower is the slave to the lender.

The Green house problems will finally come to be the top world priority and leading the charge will be this group, because of the U.S high responsibility in this area as the most capable with her vast technical knowledge she will be in the forefront, and the group will join with her to search for answers. Answers will be found as the world changes gear the change will be slow but sure, and by the end of the 21st century the readiness to the discover the one world economy, will be well on the way?

Green house control will be a common goal for the entire world, this is one area that has priority, but needs international collaboration to have real affect. There is going to be an explosion in so many issues, Information, medical, etc and this American led group will be in the forefront because of the enormous information the U.S has, this presupposes they can keep the information secure as the big wealthy nations, try to steal all of the secrets they have.

Democratic Capitalism within group three will be the philosophy that is for sure, there is India the biggest democracy in the world, and America the most powerful nation in the world, the world leader in this system of Govt; occasionally she swings a little to the left, but it will never be much, the people are at heart avid capitalists so they won't swing very far left.

GROUP FOUR: THE MUSLIM COUNTRIES:

Again above all things the first priority must be unity in fighting Global warming through excessive green house gasses emitted in every country in the world. The countries of Islam are just as exposed as the entire secular world.

The Muslim countries will have to cooperate so that world peace can be found, but first they have to find peace among their own groups The Shia and the Sunni. The development of the Muslim countries also have the wealthy that must work together to help their poverty stricken neighbors. Only the Muslims can control Muslim countries it is just a vain dream for western countries to try to democratize Muslim countries. These are natural societies that are best left to their own theocracies, why must the west continue to reap hatred. It really is none of the business of the Secular and Christian world's; they must stop interfering in Muslim countries, but conversely the Muslims must stop exploiting the world they don't have common aims with. The Muslims in the past have been leaders in technological development; it is a mystery to us why they seem to have lost their way. Their society left so much behind when they were ousted from Spain and there was so much of beauty they left, why have they now sunk into such a morass of religious self destruction that seems foolish. It seems to us that Muslim Terrorists are doing more damage to their own peoples, than they are doing to others.

The Muslims world has a big advantage on the Secular world, because the Secular find their people with insufficient annual births, there are not enough to replace deaths in their languishing populations. The Muslim birth rate far outstrips deaths so their populations are growing quickly, and in the process creating poverty. They are emigrating to escape from their poverty by shifting to Secular or Christian countries. A continuation along this path will perpetuate hatred all around, as the Muslim Youths drift into extremist organizations and increase the tension; this is the main source of manpower for these extreme organizations that are so difficult for the developed world to deal with. Terrorism is a phenomenon that is costing the whole world dearly, but more especially the Secular world as it tries to create sound security, in several areas at the same time.

The desire to democratize the Muslim world is wrong, that path has led to failure and hatred, it is none of the business of the Secular world if the Muslim world allows religious interference in their Govt. Comments in the press about the terrible conditions for women in the Muslim Theocracies is best left to their Mullahs to deal with, these countries don't want our democracies they want their own Theocracies, and that what they should have!

The conditions in Iran, Saudi Arabia etc; are American influenced! The wealth of Saudi Arabia accrues to their Royal Family, but we ask so what? The wealth which accrues from oils sales to the world will continue, where else are they going to sell their oil. Iran makes a hell of a lot of noise and threatens to block of the Persian Gulf; let them that's the sort of face off that is needed, not nuclear threats yet, let them do what they want to do, their economies are tied to oil prices and revenues just as much as the rest of the world. They have no alternatives they would have to turn to China with no floor on the prices paid, China would love that, but they too need stability.

Yes indeed it's easy to write this stuff, but what else must be done, the capitalists want the oil and want to control through the spread of democracy it cannot work. Democratic Capitalism in a group of countries that want to introduce their own brands of Dictatorial Theocracy it is their own wish, and must be allowed to happen. Their own people must truly decide if they really want the Theocracies, and if they do well so let it be, what is the point of the U.S Billions to Pakistan and Iraqi just to name two that have failed. The plentiful supply of U.S funds must dry up; and their aid to States that don't really qualify must cease there will be enough need for money within the American led Group.

There is no way we in the free world can interfere or give aid or advice to these Muslim Dictatorial Theocracies, they definitely don't want our help; they see anything the Americans or anyone else does to help as interference. The point is if the women of their world feel discriminated against, they will have their own suffragettes just as we did in the West, and they will get what they want. If there are voting rights to be won, then again let it all happen like it did in the West, it isn't going to happen because we say that is what is right. There is way too much interference and it must stop, there is now no fear of communism it's a completely new world and all must decide for themselves?

Speaking as a practicing Christian our God is a Dictator, he dictates we shall live in love for one and all, he that lives by the sword shall die by the sword. It is glaringly obvious we don't live by our own Bible, it is all just one big sham and it has always been so. The self righteousness of the Christian world is just a joke; whatever the Muslim's believe they stick to it far more effectively than do our Christian counter parts.

Muslim controlled Petro Dollars are available and the interest rates are reasonable, but the strings of business attachments need to be understood. It is true though there is going to be a swing away from traditional funding sources, is the future with the Arabs we wonder! The Petro Dollars should be loaned to their Muslim businesses, not to the west because the circle is dangerous. The dollars are loaned to the west to sustain and grow their economies for the benefit of their own peoples; Petro Dollars will be unbalanced if used for the benefit of the already wealthy nations? What needs to happen is for the money to be used to develop Muslim countries such as Indonesia, Pakistan, etc they need multi Billions, maybe Trillions and if they need business expertise there will be those in Secular countries who will sell their labor and thus their knowledge. It is silly to move the money to the west, although it would be satisfying, there is no place for human avarice here we are referring to common sense, not self satisfaction.

There are many advertisements for Petro Dollars to be loaned at low rates of interest, but this isn't going to help the Muslim countries and that is very wrong. Whichever way we look at it that money needs to go for the development of Muslim countries, why do the Petro Dollar countries want to lend to the wealthy countries, it can only be short sighted at best. The only advantage to the lenders is by lending to the west they can charge full interest rates and get sound security, whereas lending to Muslims they should lend interest free and that's the big problem.

We see the pictures of wealthy oil tycoons using their wealth to invest in the west, this is fine but it won't solve the problems with the west. Those problems are too deep and it needs the money to go to Muslim business, so they can supply work to fix their own mixed up youths. The philosophy of lending to western style business and trying to get them to fix Muslim problems is a very wrong approach. Muslim business must borrow off Muslim lenders so they can create economies; that will keep their people at home! The reality is that there is too little business in their own countries, to employ their own people so they want to export the problems abroad. The silly part is they then send money to the extremists to destroy what they have financed, in this way they think they can win all around, but it won't work because that approach isn't viable. They must either support business in their own Diaspora, and help set up new business, but whatever they do they must take their own responsibility to lift their own people, out of despair to optimism. Why should the Muslim community be any different than the Secular community, that they dislike; when with the help of Petro Dollars they can show the west what they can do, the dislike and misunderstandings would stop really quickly?

EXTREMISTS:

It is pointless saying the followers of Muslim Faith are peaceful; the point is that it is from these peaceful people, we have the phenomenon of serious lawlessness that challenges world peace. The apparent cause for the economic conditions that prevail in many countries that adhere to the Muslim Faith is blamed on the Countries that claim to be Judeo/Christian dominated. The truth is these Muslim countries need to use the oil riches to develop their own industries; they should not sit back and allow the west to borrow the money, while they do little or nothing. They have to look back at the great Muslim achievements of the past, and step forward to repeat that past greatness; because greatness it was they had, and a very high level of social accomplishments.

The truth is it is the high birth rates that is one of the reasons in fact one of the biggest problem they have, then because their large families have difficulty finding work they blame all others but not themselves. It's the inflexible adherents to the Muslim Faith that produce the extremists, and then support the trouble makers in their quest. All religions that have a militant minority have internal problems; the truth is that at present the problems are within the Muslim community.

Many Muslim Youths use the false excuse that they are treated badly, even if it is true, they bring the problems on themselves, thus they become fodder for the Extremists. The extremists are even among the Sheiks who agitate for more freedom, but it is these Sheiks who speak out so harshly against the countries they have chosen to live in. These Youths are the agitators the Western world has got to get tough about and stop playing footsie with them. The truth is they are the ones the extremists look for, and need to perpetuate and support the extremists in their war with the west! During the WW11 the Japanese immigrants were incarcerated until the peace had been won, it's time now to do the same to trouble making young Muslim males?

There is no way the Muslims can be placated because the basis of their Faith is negative to cohabitation with the none Muslim world. The Muslim's believe that they should be free to do what they like in free world countries, yet preserve Monotheism, in their own Islam countries. If the boot was on the other foot and the Muslims had the controls that the Secular world has, there is no way they would be as sensitive to the problems that we would be having, rather they would exploit their advantage. There have been several examples of Christians being accused of trying to convert Muslims to their faith, and this has landed the Christians in jail, this alone has created hatred on the part of the secular peoples, we don't even ask if there is any reaction among Christians, but we hope not.

The Crusades of the Middle Ages which were religiously motivated between Christians and Muslims; are examples of the hatred motivated then, but conditions are worse now than they were then? This is because we have the infiltration of our advanced economies, by Muslims living on various hand outs to sustain them.

We also have the Birthrate in most developed societies becoming lower than ever, the opposite to Muslims who find ideal conditions for their high birthrate. They are able to exploit the countries that have taken them in, and then grow their numbers so rapidly problems must come. This is natural but a serious problem for their host countries, who find their own people complaining about the Muslims who they feel don't want to mix. On top of that the locals believe the Muslims want to treat them locals as strangers in their own countries. What we get is Youths against Youths, and the leaders egging both sides to ever greater heights of delinquency.

It is foolish to concentrate on whether or not there is adequate security against terrorists in the entire developed world; the first thing to be accepted is our world has had to change so much to accommodate the problems that the developed world now faces. The added costs to try and secure all of the Western world, as it is now, is a major victory to the Terrorist organization's no matter who they are or where. These people have thrust such an extra cost on the western world, that there is confusion everywhere.

The taxpayers and consumers must pay but the results are poor; we are perpetually on the defense and it matters not what anyone says we can all see the effects. One only has to take a flight from say America to Australia and the difference from pre 9/11 to now is incredible. We don't mind the disruptions, what we mind is the extra cost involved all thanks to the extremists, and they are nearly all Muslim. The terrorist organizations are well financed, but where does that money flow come from? We presume it's from the Mosques etc and donations from the flock who attend those Mosques, which means they are financed by the Muslim flocks. To us then it's not just the Youths it's also the flocks that finance the terrorists, and then claim they are not involved.

The costs to the Americans must be tremendous as they try to find answers to the new world war, huge new security divisions that struggle to be cohesive and effective. The enormous number of new employees that have had to be trained at such a great cost, and yet the Home security is still not effective relative to costs. This is only America what about Europe and even the smaller countries like Australia and Canada, in fact all those that have had to upgrade their security systems at so much extra cost.

Various American writers advocate different strategies, but it seems to us all are playing to the Muslim Empire because Empire it is. From a practical point of view the Muslims are the aggressors, but it is all watered down so as not to give religious insult. That is fine, but it seems to us the Western world endures an enormous amount of insult from the Muslims, no matter at what level we care to look at. We don't deny the great majority of the Muslim followers are peaceful, but there is no denying where the extremists are spawned from, they are Muslim Youths, and it is in such Youths they find new followers!

In Australia we have had a Muslim Cleric describing Australian Women as just meat, and that's only for starters. The "drive by" shootings and Lebanese gangs are Muslim not Secular, and we ordinary folk are supposed to say yes but that's ok they are just young Muslims, that are unable to integrate. But these Youths are loudly proud that they are different, they don't hesitate to parade their antagonism to their host countries!

These Muslim Extremists are all encouraged by the Sheiks who are loud and clear in their denunciation of our way of life, why should we keep accepting such abuse? The old axiom applies one rotten apple ruins the box, there are rotten apples in the Muslim case, since we can't toss the rotten apples out then we will have got to get rid of the apples before they all go rotten. That's what the extremists know and work on; when the balance is in doubt be very sure the passive Muslims will support the Extremists, not the rest of us whatever our breed and religion.

The Muslim Countries need to be isolated into a group of their own, not pandered to, because we want to catch Osama bin Laden and his murderous cronies, which of course presumes we really do want to catch that mass Murderer. There will never be a safe agreement with the Muslim countries, they should be set adrift on their own if necessary, and if they are to be enemies so let it be, but let's cut out the pussyfoot approach. We have our silly rules of accommodation that means we must take in families of these Muslims to keep them together is it not better to send them all back home then we are not importing more problems?

We want to stress we are not anti Muslim, but we are against letting them destroy the freedoms we in the west once had. If the Muslims that are already in the countries that have taken them in; let's be very sure they want to be American's, Britain's, Australian's, etc; because if they don't let's send them home. Families must sign allegiance to their adopted new homes, that's great, but if their children must continue to go astray then we should deport the troubled families.

The British have many Pakistani's that will never be faithful to Britain, the French, Dutch and Germans are having problems, how long are we going to accept this rubbish, if these young men want to go back to Pakistan let them stay there, at least we will know where the enemy is, not waiting for a stab in the back.

We have no trouble with peaceful Muslims, but they spawn problems and that's not acceptable. Any young men who want to train in terrorist camps should all have their passports cancelled and deported. This sort of threat may make them more appreciative of what their new countries give them and theirs, this may make them think twice before they stray.

The Western Countries including (America) are proving again just how weak they can be in answer to threats from outside influences, we cannot do this or that we have this or that rule, that's fine if we are dealing with those who will recognize the same level of integrity, but Muslim Extremist's wont. Let us finally say again let's hope there is no deportations, but if necessary let's not hesitate to act decisively.

SUMMARY: 2010-2100:

The Global warming problem will have been fixed and there is no warming caused by excess pollution, but there is the real knowledge that there are still dangers. The scientists know now it's up to them; to find the final solutions to keep the earth temperatures in line, with what is needed to continue on at a comfortable level. That means they have to control the earth's temperatures at a level that keeps the polar caps intact, and that we don't have a home that descends back to an ice age, or that we don't live in fear that this may happen at any time.

The period as set out above and as imagined it would be in this chapter has been extremely dynamic, and the unity of the four world groups has been very successful, but religion remains the stumbling block. The many changes have been prolific and have at the same time; there have been some impressive changes within the lives of much of mankind. There has been a big improvement in the conditions of people living, in what were the severely depressed countries. The peasants in Russia, China, India and South East Asia, have had greatly improved living conditions and look set to continue. South & Central America and Mexico is also now on solid ground and conditions are good. Africa has finally had a big turn around and there is no longer any poverty on that continent and the minerals are being extracted and valued properly. The African countries have benefitted from their link with the Europeans, and the Europeans have benefitted from Africa!

There has been a continuing uniformity of world conditions, as the countries that at the start of the period were developing countries, are now developed countries. The countries that were at the start poor countries are now developing countries and doing very well. The developed countries that originally were wealthy anyhow, have slowed back, but are still fully developed. All that has happened is that there is improvement worldwide for all, and living condition are now very good for all peoples, on all continents.

There are three super powers now, America, China, Russia, are all in that top class. Then Germany, France, England, Japan, Iraqi and Iran are in the top powers but they are not in the Super class. The Muslim nations have set up a powerful and successful group of their own! But having achieved success in the financial arenas they are now very successful, and they again have to thank the Jews for their financial success. Strange as that seems it is true, the Arabs and Muslims have never been overly strong on financial affairs, so just like the Moors back in 1431 AD they have wisely used Jewish knowledge to their own advantage. Just as the time after the Moors left Spain and they had help from Jews, so it has been the same again. The Muslims have looked for and found peace with the Jews, and have had the Jews to help them lay down sound financial foundations. The problems in the Middle East have dissipated as it was finally accepted the Jews could not be driven out, quite suddenly there was agreements reached and peace is now strongly entrenched.

The cashless society has been fully implemented worldwide and there is separate currencies for each group. Tax fraud and criminal activities have been controlled, and all business founded with dishonest money has been confiscated by the State and sold. All money received from the sale of those dishonestly funded assets, has been paid into the Govt treasury accounts.

Travel and information has reached a fabulous level of creativity and most cars run on compressed air, there will be compressed air stations all over the world. The world food production is sufficient for the population with self grow gardens in homes being very common. Super food markets are not as dominant as before, because people are buying a lot on the internet and get special deliveries. The food ordering is all done automatically and as the food is used the orders are placed and deliveries can be accepted and checked by Robots. Payments are made automatically from personal accounts, and clothes etc are also all approved and paid for by home Robots. It is now normal for both parents of the family to work, but the full home care as well as children control is now done by Robots. Cooking can be ordered up and prepared or pre timed to set the cookers going, and the food is ready to eat when the family gets home from work and school.

The medical profession has now got full control of Cancer and heart problems! Cancer can be cured and new hearts can be grown to replace defective hearts. There is no need any more for transplants because the body can be made to grow replacement parts as needed. Life expectancy has been increased to an average of 150 years for men and 170 years for women.

The internet is now an everyday tool available to all at a very cheap price, and education is available even to the very poor, and computers are a thing of the past. All systems are so micro now that there is no need for big bulky terminals, even the wristwatch or mobile phones are superior computer terminals. Monitors are now built into either the mobile phones or glasses; it is only a matter of choice.

Religion is still a very strong cause of dissension and the Muslims and the Christians still don't get on. The Muslims and Hindus are still at war with each other and the cults are still there in great numbers.

Chapter 2

The ancient world

We want herein to examine the changing world social systems which have evolved over the last up to 10,000 years. Since the time of Christ Agrarianism, Feudalism, Socialism, Communism, Slavery, Tribalism, Barbarians, Dictators, Capitalism, etc; of course there were/are many others such as Animists & Pagans etc but those are not what we are referring to in this writing.

Taxation naturally has been and is one of the continuing problems of the various forms of Govt; whether it was during the Roman Empire, and its long period of social pre eminence with the huge cost to its various Emperors, Socialism and Capitalism have been a natural element of society, from the time of the Emperors right up until the present. The attempts to avoid paying a fair tax share has always been part of the attempts by most strata's of society, but of course the wealthy are the most successful; since they have the ability to pay for skilled advisors.

The intent is to try and make available the understanding to the working classes, and provide them with a greater knowledge of world development past, present and the future. In many ways the modern world offers so much, including the supposed freedom of the peoples of the developed world. But there has been so many changes over the last two millennia, that most of us don't quite understand just how society has got to where it is at, nor how it will evolve during the worlds journey into the future.

None of us want to go back to having to harness the horse and buggy when wanting to take the family out for a Sunday afternoon drive, nor do we want to hang a meat safe outside to try and keep our food cool or from going rotten. Of course we could always salt our meat and take the washing down to the river to clean; those are the memories of ancient times. That's what was the bondage of the past, but the bondage of the now which drives our lives is money and the debt, to buy all of all those fine consumer goods! In truth we are still in bondage, the modern bondage of demand debt we see something we want it, we buy we borrow, that's the now. The future will have to find a new system, and as at now it seems we will have a cashless society, but that doesn't mean freedom from debt!

With debt the bondage is to money lenders ie banks etc; and is explained quite clearly in the Bible when it writes, the borrower is slave to the lender. So is that very much different now, than when we had Feudalism or several different types of bondage? All of the poor people were bonded to their Overlord or Bishop down to the peasants, all owed allegiance to one another in some way. The modern consumer society is all based on demand and/or productivity and the borrowed money to pay for what we buy. If we don't have the cash why we just borrow it and pay it back over an agreed term, thus we become in bondage to consumer debt. But we must remember that consumer debt is what fuels our economies, if the demand in a country's falters enough to effect the GDP then the problem becomes one that could go into recession which is what capitalist economies do.

Industry has become synonymous with the new consumer debt and interest system, our whole society depends on debt owed by the masses, therefore we are slaves to the lender, and each year the debts grow larger. The debt is insidious for the poor in that like ancient times when the poor were bonded to the wealthy, now we are bonded by loan contracts. Only home owners with a high equity have an asset that appreciates in line with a countries annual inflation rate. A country that doesn't have a Gross Domestic Product that is growing has a problem, after a period that country is in recession, therein lays the insidious debt trap, and if the people stop buying the demand is gone, so they have to be encouraged by what politicians like to call a stimulus package?

The other modern concept is information! If for example we want to research information for this book, all we need to do is go to one of several different internet search engines, and we will have so much information it becomes difficult to disseminate. We therein have so many who we presume to be experts giving opinions that it becomes confusing, and sadly often leads to misinformation. It seems as though everyone who has an opinion on a subject, and has the knowledge of how to download that information onto a search engine has done so. All seem to have various levels of expertise and many make sense, no longer do we have to go to libraries or University to learn or try to learn. The trick is of course to know how to turn information into serious knowledge and understanding, and not become befuddled by that huge volume of information.

Simple explanations are meant for those who would like to know what is happening, and what will happen in future. This book is not deep enough to be of interest to University Intellectual's! We want to write for those lower level of educated people who want to know more; and have so many legitimate queries about everything. Prophecy is an important part of the bible guidelines, and needs to be given at least some attention, by those who profess to be believers in whatever creed they follow. This book has prophetic outlines, especially for the period post 2008, and the bible has a strong influence on all thoughts or opinions expressed herein! Nor do we want to enter into discussion on the various religious denominations, all we are interested in is trying to understand what is, we don't have the background to try and give in depth opinions. That's mainly because we have none, blessed is he who has an open mind to all points of view, and yet can preserve their own opinions, if you feel threatened or antagonized by another's point of view, then your mind is closed.

Maybe if the Peoples of the Middle East were more open minded, they would be more integrated as the Lord originally intended. And had Joseph completed properly the job he had been expected to do, if he had cleaned out the promised land properly those many years ago, there would not have been the so many problems in the promised land as there has been ever since? But there is no point to equivocate, he did not and since then peace in the area we have had not.

From Roman times when many men and certain sections of the Aristocracy had to spend so much time in the military and they only came home on occasions of leave or holidays. It was not uncommon for men to spend their entire life in military service, followed by their Sons. In later Empire times of emergency even the Youths were liable to be pressed into temporary service. The Roman economy was based on tribute or taxes from what was called the Provinces, Egypt being the golden contributor, but with what Sicily and Spain also paid into the Emperor's treasury, there was a big income flow. This was money which was then used in his administration, or in some cases such as Nero and Caligula their misadministration.

THE ROMANS & GREEKS:

The Genesis of the Roman Empire was really around 800 BC but the huge growth really followed on from Alexander the great. The Empire Alexander annexed, was after his death split into three great areas, Asia, Egypt and Europe, with three independent rulers. (Former Generals) After many years of internal strife amongst Alexander's Generals, they finally settled on the various areas over which they would take control. The remains of Alexander were finally interred in a site in Alexandria. The Roman Empire was just starting to find its strength, and eventually all of Alexander's territories were absorbed. The best known of course is Egypt and Cleopatra who was a Ptolemy. The original Ptolemy was one of Alexander's Generals; the one who took over Egypt! Queen Cleopatra and her impact on Rome has of course become a Hollywood blockbuster, much to the loss of historical fact.

The structure of The Roman Empire; needed a boost such as the annexation of Egypt to be able to really do what was done on such a large scale. In modern terms the population of the Empire at its greatest (seventy million total) wasn't really that large, but the land mass is the same. In monetary terms to maintain such a military force, was unthinkable at any time in history. The role of being the world's police in retrospect seems fair, in that all of their subject countries were tributary to the Roman Treasury. At its biggest the Roman military was no more than 1.5% of the total male population! This could be compared with the other great Colonizing powers which were normally about 10% of the male populations.

'The Romans were brutal there is no doubt of that, but that was symptomatic of the times as well; looking at the records of the other regimes Babylonians, Persians etc they were compatible'. The fact is that Rome arose at a time of international change; Rome became a great trading entity and as such was able to field a permanent army. The method of military control however eventually destroyed Rome! The areas of income was, trading internally, tributes from subject countries, the sale of slaves caught in battle, the capture of the wealth off defeated countries etc. The trouble became that the military was paid by the Commanding Generals of the Eastern and Western Divisions of the military and eventually they couldn't pay. The lack of countries to defeat, the reduction in tributes, and the loss of vigor in the Roman Legionnaires, in simple terms they ran out of strength and money!

The Mighty Roman Empire lasted longer than any other throughout the ages; many of the monuments left over from those ancient times are still very obvious, and are favorite tourist attractions. Some are either still in use ie; some roads or museum pieces such as the remnants of the Coliseum, and even some parts of the old Capitol Hill. Tourists are still shown the outline of where Nero was reputed to have sat and fiddled while Rome burned. Of course we only have the guide's word we know not, just how accurate her comments were! In the Coliseum one can still see the area where the wild animals were held; and another for the human prisoners waiting to die, as entertainment for the people. The area where Gladiators, Criminals or Slaves were held, before being sent out to fight is still easy to see and can be walked through, while one thinks of the past?

The Emperor out of his income often paid for such entertainment for the masses, and this type of show was sometimes used to curry favor by an Emperor from the masses! The Emperor also out of his own income supplied an amount of bread daily to members of the City of Rome free, but this hand out was often abused in different ways. This quota of free bread was only for male Roman citizens, and at one point slaves were being freed so they would qualify for the free daily bread, which was all they had to avoid starvation. This ration was the equivalent of two medium sized loaves per day.

Grain was the main sustenance of the average Roman citizen, there was a vast array of imported goods from all over the Empire available. These products were only within the budget of the wealthy to buy and consume, but the wealthy were a very small portion of the total population. The slave laborers of Roman agricultural farming and grazing were not efficient, and did not produce a great variety of consumer goods. There was a limited range of grain crops grown, but very few, if any root crops were known about to be cultivated. In some isolated cases private family labor was used to compete with prices at market, against products grown by slaves, but such produce were not competitive in price, and the families soon gave up and reverted back to buying slaves to do the work.   _

The taxation of the different sections of the Roman population, and its tributary countries went through many different stages, as the various Emperors' have used different methods to sets rates and collect taxes. The income or tribute from Sicily, Spain and Egypt was totally owned by the Emperor and was used by him to pay for the military, constructions including roads, and water aqueducts etc.

The sale at auction of different areas of tax collection rights, gave the winning bidder, the right to collect taxes at the rate as set out by the Emperor from the general population of Rome. This system was also used throughout most parts of the Empire! The collector when placing a bid had to calculate the rate of tax payable, plus normal business expenses and profits within that bid. The winning bidder also had to pay the value of their winning bid immediately, and so were effectively, creditors to the Empire. Some tax agents made big profits from the rights won at auction, and became very wealthy from their business as tax collectors. There were very few contractors who didn't do well, but it was the most unpopular occupation of all, with all among the different classes of peoples, who were liable to pay taxes.

Apart from the military and agriculture there were only a few different major professions, actually worked at in Rome. Most work done by the

State was road building and water works, and there were a few trades such as building and mining etc; but relatively only small amounts were worked at by the citizens. Most Govt work was done by slave labor, and most contracts were managed by private management contractors for the State. Govt work was done much like the modern concept of Public Works, except for the use of slave labor!

Mark Antony a favorite of Julius Caesar and one of the influential Lover's of Cleopatra, Egypt's ambitious leader had rebelled in Egypt and had in place a type of Socialist, Capitalist State which it was expected they would have expanded, had they not been defeated by the adopted Son of Julius Caesar. Octavian (Augustus) their nemesis favored slavery, and returned Egypt to selective slavery answerable only to Rome, after he had defeated the rebels.

The Emperor Tiberius who was notoriously frugal in his approach to financial expenditure on Empire needs left enormous treasury assets at his death in the form of gold and silver. These credits were quickly dissipated by his nephews and successors, Caligula, Claudia and Nero who was all notorious spendthrifts, their parties and grand shows of licentious pleasure are still notorious as examples of expensive foolishness.

Nero tried to increase his tax revenues, by reducing the amount of silver minted into the coins used as legal tender throughout his Empire, thus deliberately inflating the value of his treasury artificially. This was an unsuccessful attempt to avoid increasing tax, on the general populace the system failed badly. The reduction of mineral value in his coins by 10% simply meant that merchants increased their prices to cover the lower value they received from the Nero currency issue, thus of course creating inflation. Nero earned immortality as the Emperor who supposedly played the fiddle while Rome burned (untrue); he then blamed the newly emerging Jewish Cult, Christianity, for the conflagration and ordered all Christians to be fed to the Lions. (True)

The most common method of working the land during Roman times was the use of slaves, these mainly men captured by the various Legions and sold, could be bought at the numerous auctions, held quite frequently throughout the Empire. Slaves were not cheap, and still had to be housed clothed and fed, no matter how poorly this was done, it was still a cost. In Roman times much of the land remained fallow, because the owners found it financially unviable to work. This was because the motivation within the slave labor system was poor yielding in terms of profit, and of course slaves paid no tax.

The Christian spread throughout the Empire, were later blamed for the passivity that allowed the German Barbarians to get control of Rome, by the continuous warfare they waged on that city and its western provinces. Another opinion was that the Christian influence prolonged the Empire, but one thing is certain was that the final collapse of the Western Empire was welcomed, even by the citizens of Rome. A thousand years later the same happened in Constantinople, the Roman Capital in the East. The constant poor Govt; performance in the Senate, and lack of municipal services was more demoralizing than the Barbarians at the end. Because there was no longer anyone for them to fight, and no spoil to take everything of value was gone, so the Barbarians settled in and gradually were civilized by Roman influences.

The final failings of the Empire were quite comprehensive! The failure of the Military to work with its own legionnaires; and the need to use 'German Barbarians to protect the Empire, high inflation as the currency was despoiled by the Emperors, in their efforts to balance their budgets. The lessening of tributes from foreign countries, and the consequent turn around in revenues that could not be rectified, and thus further eroded the Roman Treasury. Once the receipts started to get smaller from the tribute paying countries the end was inevitable, in simple terms Rome went broke'!

The first serious conflict between the Germanic Barbarians and the Romans, was when Julius Caesar crossed the Rhine, and defeated the Germanic hordes near what is now Austria in 53-55BC. The German Barbarians including its many tribal links were over hundreds of years, integrated into the Roman Legions, as the Roman fighting men began to lose their vigor, and the Empire had no choice but to hire mercenaries. The Roman male population in the military never exceeded one million under arms at any time; this was at most less than 1.5% of the total population. This refers to Roman citizens (not including mercenaries) the total population of the Roman Empire at its Peak, was less than seventy million including women, children and the aged population. The success of the Roman Legions was their discipline and weapons of war, these were in every way superior to their opponents, but when that superiority failed then so did Rome.

The Western Catholic Church which had not yet been formed, or at least had not yet gained any strong foothold in the West, imitated the structure of the Roman Senate including the naming of its leaders, such as Bishop's etc. The Eastern Orthodox Church, which dated from the time of St Paul's travels, planting Churches in Asia grew strong very quickly. Constantine The Great ordered that the Catholic Christian Church would be the official church of the Roman Empire from around 316 AD.

The demise of the Roman Empire in the end was helped by serious inflation, the value of the silver and bronze in the minted coins, were reduced steadily following Nero's example. At the end of the Empire the value of gold or silver minted into the coins, was no more than 2% to 5%, and so the money to pay the military was worthless, and inflation was totally out of control. Hyper inflation experienced in later years in some modern economies, was well known in the Roman World. As the Emperor's continually defaced their currency values, businessmen merely increased their prices, and thus any effort to stabilize the economy was breached by hyper inflation!

The Germanic Hordes (Tribes) East and West, within their many associated Barbarian tribes which were all related ethnically, and would be far too numerous and boring to portray herein. But it is useful to know that in the later years of the Roman Legions, many Legionnaires and Officers in the Roman military were Germans. The Germans were integrated into the Roman Legions, but never into the Civil Administration, their forfeit of any and all such honor's was of little interest to them, they much preferred the military commands which ultimately exercised real control.

At the end the Roman Empire had become largely symbolic, as without its mercenary armies, Rome could not have been defended. Julius Caesar had long ago set the precedent, which was then exercised by a few Commanders over the ages; the simple act of stationing one's Legions on the hills just outside Rome was an unspoken threat to the Senate. The simple decision by Julius Caesar to appoint himself as the first Emperor of Rome was the catalyst that created the rebellion that led to his murder on the steps of the Senate, but was a precedent for quite a few other Senate failings over the millennia.

Julius Caesar after his successful campaigns in the western area, described the Germans as long haired and dirty, totally undisciplined, and more akin to animals than human beings, but he credited them with being wonderful fighters, who if or when, they came under the command of efficient generals, would be hard to beat. Caesar's further comment was that in the cold weather they bred incessantly and the women fought just as strongly and brutally as their men.

They lived in small houses which were kept warm with small internal fires, but the stifling living conditions were unbearable to all but the German's. Under the dirt and hair, the Germanic Barbarians were a tall blue eyed blonde race, extremely handsome and strong. This was by comparison with The Huns who were squat and ugly, but equally strong and brutal. The Christianization of the German Barbarians and the Anglo Saxon's was accomplished by the Aryan Tribes, but it was their own type of worship, they did not accept the divinity of Christ.

The German social system was tribal, and the leader or chief would appoint another top man to take his place, when he felt no longer strong enough to command, this led to the fittest and strongest always being the leader of the various tribes. They were not good agriculturalists; they were mainly herders and grew only a few grain crops, which often failed because of the cold icy weather. The receipt of potatoes from France was a crop that could withstand the cold weather, but the consumption of a root crop to ease famine conditions was strongly resisted. 'The French King Louis 16th had tried to encourage his People to eat potatoes, by eating them himself. The potato originated in Peru and was bought to Europe by the Spanish, but there was a strong resistance to potatoes, because they are a root crop and the Europeans thought of them as inedible, for quite some years'.

'The Germans rubbed their bodies and long hair with rancid butter, and the smell in spite of the cold was ghastly to the Roman noses. The Germans in the West were far more vigorous and aggressive than their cousins in the East, including the Balt's, Verv's etc, up into today's Yugoslavia Russia etc; this lesser power in the East and North was why the Roman Empire in the East, governed through Constantinople, lasted almost one thousand years longer than in the West. But finally both East and West succumbed to the German hordes not in battle, but by simple uncontested integration! The civilizing effect of Roman culture changed the Germans from Barbaric, to what became more a civilized society as the Germans became romanized'.

The continuous attacks by the German Barbarians on the Western Empire was eventually victorious as the Roman Senate became unable to fund a properly organized Army, and therefore the defense of Western Empire sank into almost nothing. At the end the notoriously successful Roman Legions just sank into a miasma of nothingness, and the Citizens of Rome were better off with no legions to protect them. The Germanic Hordes having no longer any need to battle the Roman Legions themselves began to ease off their attacks, and Rome became peaceful once again. By this time the Roman Currency was worthless and all merchants were looking for alternative methods of buying and selling.

The Agrarian Society was a form of three tier delegation of authority that expanded and commercialized over hundreds of years, it was really already part of life in Roman agricultural life, except that the Romans depended on slaves captured by the Legions then sold by them for profit. There was a little agriculture in Rome the staples of Olives, Wine and Grains were badly managed, because of the vast amount of products coming through Rome from the subject countries. The local farmers produced enough to sustain the great majority of the population in Rome and its provinces, and there was a small amount of building etc; that created employment for some skilled artisans.

There were vast trading enterprises that bought all types of goods by boat, from all over and beyond the Roman civilized world. The fastest way to mobilize the legions was by boat, which meant that there was quite a large fleet of quite large boats, but all propelled with slave labor at the oars. 'The attempt by Rome to defeat the Phoenicians of Carthage was finally a disaster, when for good reasons the Roman fleet was lost at sea; before battle with the enemy was joined. Carthage was defeated later and the city of Carthage totally destroyed'!

The roads of Rome built for the fast movement of the Legions are still in use in some parts of the old Empire even today. The decay that set in was really beyond anything the Roman's could do, the Empire really just expired from old age just like anything that is man made, but it did survive for over two millennia in the East. The modern day Super Powers seem destined to be of a far shorter duration, 'British Empire was very short lived by comparison'.

'The only major cultures that have lasted longer than Rome has been the Chinese and the Indian Nations but they were totally internal and the expansion was within the close neighbor's not over vast distances as were the Romans'. Both of these countries have over 5,000 years of history! But just as the Roman's had grown by conquest of far flung subject countries, the two Asian countries had many internal conflicts in either coordinating their countries into one major unit. As in the case of China the first Emperor joined his nation into one kingdom in 221BC, or in India a country that constantly was under internal turmoil, a lot of which was both cultural and religious in character.

'There was no doubting the Roman superiority when they were at their peak, in spite of the constant attacks in the West from the various Barbarian tribes, and on one occasion a near disaster, Rome survived. There was a short lived threat from Hannibal when he attacked unexpectedly after taking his army with elephants over the Alps; he then struck cleverly and decisively. Hannibal a Carthaginian had been raised by his Father to hate all things Roman, and had he continued on his successful campaign right into the Empires' Capital Rome, there was a good chance he may have succeeded to vanquish Rome; he for some reason did not attack the city when he had the chance. It was not to be and after several defeats Hannibal was to die in rather ignominious circumstances his, former glory forgotten. His beloved Carthage was ravaged and burned to the ground, completely destroyed, the Romans' were determined that the city and its Phoenician sea faring people would never rise again to menace Rome at any time in the future, and it never did'?

The Augustine dynasty 5BC – 68AD started well with Augustus and Tiberius, both of these Emperors were good stewards and they started the period of the Roman Emperors, very strongly. Unfortunately their following Heirs, Gaius, (Caligula) Claudius and Nero were the worst Emperors ever; especially Nero who left a heritage that will never be forgotten. He murdered his Mother and his Wife, and he fed thousands of the new Jewish sect, Christians to the Lions, and killed many others by immersion in boiling tar when the lions could not eat them quickly enough. The accusation against the Christians was that they were instrumental in burning down Rome; in fact all knew the guilty party was Nero himself. Nero's place in history is as the Emperor who fiddled while Rome burned down. Then blaming the Christians for the fires which lasted for two weeks, and slaughtering them by the thousands. He was murdered himself by one of the Praetorian guards, reputedly he died screaming for mercy, while he was being stabbed another version is that he committed suicide? But there are several versions of his death recorded!

Just as Rome absorbed military advantage from the Greeks, she was also the recipient of many obvious Greek developments such as art, mathematics, philosophy etc. The modern world has had the advantage of all of the ancient Empires; the reality is though that the Western world has been advantaged most by the Greeks and the Romans.

The Greeks were a great society and developed a culture that is considered as classical even today. Alexander the Great was the Son of King Phillip and he and his Father were aggressive but sensitive leaders; well attuned to the needs of their commanders. Alexander's early death was a surprise, but may have been quite a fortunate event; he did not get old enough to become a brutal tyrant as so many Dictators throughout history have done. Alexander the Great built Alexandria, which in its day was one of the great cities of the world. Greece were the founders of democracy, and their development of human, but not female rights were far sighted at that time.

The Greek female would in modern times be termed a mere drudge to their husbands needs with little thought for themselves. The theory of male love is first theorized as a natural human relationship back in 400 BC approximately, but we are not referring to physical love. The Greeks saw Male love as a bonding process in the art of war, but that degenerated to physical love within the military, just before the Athenian conquest by Alexander the Macedonian, it was he that banished such foolish antics, as unbefitting the armies including his own.

The Roman females were in fact treated far better than their Greek counterpart, because in the home they were in charge, but of course away from the home the men took over and were in charge. By contrast the Greek female was at the same time, about 300 BC a mere chattel and was considered as there only for breeding and looking after the home, which her husband occasionally visited. She was there to breed Sons, daughters were of little consequence! Her sexual needs were also never considered whereas the Roman considered it manly only if his wife reached orgasm within sex!

ENGLISH:

Julius Caesar was the first Roman to go to England and it was him that decided to annex that country, this was in spite of his recognition that the English Tribes; were just as difficult to control as the German Barbarians. Caesar left and after his death there was a lot of turmoil in Rome after his assassination and England remained remote and quiet, the Roman occupation was in place, but not developed until the time of Emperor Claudius!

The later Roman Emperor Claudius was the one who promoted and supported the Roman occupation of England, and he did actually visit the territory in about 51 AD. There had been hesitation with continuing the occupation under Augustus, Tiberius and Gaius, (Caligula) because of the doubt that the country could be made financially viable. Had Gaius not been murdered the Romans would probably have pulled back, the Senate had voted against continuing the occupation. The tributes were too small, or conversely the costs too high, because the country was just too far away from Rome. Because of the Imperial insistence by Claudius the occupation continued, and after his visit Claudius even considered the occupation of Scotland, but he was persuaded of the foolishness of that action by his advisors.

Queen Boadicea, who rebelled against the Romans, was an outstanding leader of her people; she came very close to expelling the Romans completely from England! But just failed in that she lost the last battle her army had been going to fight against them, after having been so amazingly successful until then. Originally the Queen had been supportive of the Romans, but having been personally subjected to Roman brutality by members of one of the legions, and seeing her daughters raped, she came to hate them intensely. She was a gifted leader, but the Romans would not negotiate with her a mere woman.

English agrarianism was originally a separation of control between the Kings and the Catholic Church! The church was becoming ever more important as it became a major land owner, through the inheritance of estates left to the church by members of the Aristocracy when they died. Agrarianism is in the main similar to feudalism, but lacks the military commitments which came later via; Feudalism as society became more warlike, and was developed because Kings could not afford to keep a full time army. The attempts to bring safety to the people and the realm was via the social structure of Feudalism, which was first, introduced into England by William the Conqueror? After his Norman takeover of the Crown of England from Harold the reigning Saxon King. The defeat of King Harold at the battle of Hastings in 1066 AD; was the start of years of difficulty in England. As the victors the Normans were on the top of the social ladder, and the Saxons at the bottom. Under the Feudal system the King had the right to take, confiscate, and give land to the Barons and all of his Aristocratic followers. And he did so in the best way he knew how, that would help to consolidate his position as the undisputed King of the realm!

The Feudal system originated from the need to keep an army available at all times, against surprise attack from other regions looking to increase their armies, or to defend the land in times of war from others, such as those looking for internal expansion of their land holdings. The cost to keep an army perpetually under arms was prohibitive so the King would divide blocks of land and give them to his Barons Etc; of the realm, in return for them swearing fealty to himself and his family. Only the Romans had been able to keep a full time army, and only they had the organization of forced tribute to fund that army. But even the Romans found the English just too expensive, because they were too warlike, like their German Barbarian Cousins, the English were always fighting among themselves as well as fighting the Romans.

In time of war or battles of any type; the King needed to be able to field an army against any aggressors. The Barons would field the Knights from whom they had received oaths of fealty! The Knights would bring with them their tenant farmers who were committed to fight for their Lords. In this way an army could be raised but not a professional one, by comparison with the Romans they were a rat tag untrained noisy mob. Only the Knights had any training and this was only sporadic, mainly just at tournaments organized by the Barons or the King.

All of the surrounding villagers would be committed to the same Lords, at the various levels! In the time of danger the peasants would enter the great castles within its defenses and live there with their Lord until the danger passed, or the battle was lost and the castle taken. In such a circumstance it would be normal for the captured Knights and Leaders to be offered for ransom, but the peasants would simply have a new master at arms. The big castles with the hundreds of rooms look like big useless hunks of timber, bricks and mortar now. But in those feudal times were the last resort for safety and defense for the serfs and peasants, who had been guaranteed safety by their Lords. As far as was possible the castles were built in areas that would be difficult for those making an assault, but as easy as possible for the defenders. There was usually a moat around the entire perimeter of the main buildings, and there were various other defensive war machines that could, and were used to discourage all invaders.

The frequent tournaments that were held were in many ways training; for the Knights of the entire surrounding areas who had committed themselves to one cause generally the Kings. The pomp and ceremony was meant to encourage and motivate the Knights, to great heights of glory as they achieved hero status, much as the athletes of these modern times. If the King had sponsored the tournament and was in attendance, they were considered to be great social events, which would be followed by a Royal Ball afterwards. The English Court was always considered to be very poor compared to the French Court, which was said to be so colorful and gay. Many were the Ladies who had returned to England, spoke disparagingly of their new life of boredom in England

There were Barons with varying amounts of land under their control; a great Baron may have a hundred blocks of Land that he had passed out to one hundred Knights. The Knights would in turn divide up the blocks, and hand down the smaller blocks to Serfs or Peasants, who were under his protection. In return they would be committed to support their Knights in times of war. There was different methods of paying what we would call rent, but the main type of payment by the serfs was to share the produce with their landlord; be they knights of the realm, or if their land was owned by the church then the church representative would be the Bishops or Landlords, for the church.

Small amounts of money could be made by selling some of the produce, but that could only be after the proper distribution to their lord including tax. Only when enough for the full year for the family, and all commitments, only if there was a little left could that lot be sold. The crops that were to be planted and the amount of land committed to animal husbandry, was decided by the Lord of the manor. Animal grazing was not considered very important as the yield could not compare with intensive cropping of all types, only pigs with their rapid breeding and growth could be grown quickly, and was suitable for meat. A cow for milk and a horse for heavy labor were also important, on the small lots of land that were the usual allotments, dogs were not needed. A few sheep for wool were also kept for spinning, and then knitting into clothing.

The farmer's family usually produced butter, but separators were not yet invented, the cream was simply skimmed off the top of the milk. Therefore in ancient times the high protein producing breeds, like the modern day Jersey breed cattle were preferred. The cream so gathered would then be held until the next day and beaten into butter. The curds and whey that was left would be drunk by the family, or used for Yoghurt. Full cream milk was also used to make cheese, whatever was needed was made in the kitchen at home by the women and girls of the family. The grains grown would be sown and stored in the silos for the full year, but often such storage was at the castle, so there were supplies in event of a siege battle.

There was no refrigeration so supplies were sent up to the castle daily, there was normally a system whereby the provisioning would be rotated, so the work was balanced and fair to all. A lot of the meat and perishable foods were preserved by salting and smoking, jams and preserves were done for the full year. The advent of potatoes that could be preserved by sprinkling with lime, for the full year's supply added a root crop that the English had no trouble to accept. The English were good producers, but they had good and fertile land as well as a good climate. A big advancement was the first meat safe that was covered on two sides with a type of mesh wire that could be hung outside and kept cool; by the winds blowing through. Perishable food could then be kept two even three days extra, if the breezes were regular and cool?

The laborers would be enfranchised to their lords, and even in the case of marriage some agreements, gave the Lord the right to give or with hold permission. There was little hope of improving ones position in society, even if one had great skills, there was no place those skills could be demonstrated. It was below a Lords dignity to engage in any sort of fight with a commoner, even in training there was a class structure that had to be upheld.

These class taboos have remained in the European cultures right up to the 20th century, and is why starting afresh in a new country was so popular. A proud boast of the USA has been, anybody can do or be anything over here! The USA. Is in theory a classless society and anyone with the right drive and ability could rise to the top of their chosen vocation.

In times of danger there were the Castles to which the populace would retreat, these were what was considered to be their castle, and all would fight to defend that castle. In times of war the Barons would assemble the Knights who owed them fealty, and these would be the Knights of the realm, who would be fighting for King and Castles. The Serfs and Peasants would field an agreed number of fighting men, to support their Lord Knights; these would be the common foot soldiers. If a King was intending to go to war, he would normally first meet with the Knights and Barons of his realm, and battle strategies would be planned.

The intense hatred by the deposed Saxon Lord's against the Norman's prompted the need for a tighter control of all of the people! William when he gifted the Estates confiscated off the Saxon nobility to his own loyal followers, changed the social structure from an Agrarian Slave Command System that had developed after the Roman's left Britain, to a Agrarian then a Feudal one. The resulting acrimony after William lasted for many years, but there was little difference between the two systems other than the commitment to fight, for the Crown in the Feudal system. This commitment was built into the contract by the Aristocracy, or by their Overlords in the case of the serfs or peasants. Great Britain with its internal associated countries of Scotland, Ireland and Wales, and its highly productive climate and soils were ideal for Agriculture. The economic systems in those dark centuries and then the reconnaissance, was normally agrarian or feudal in the western countries.

In simple sequence from the time of the Roman's in England, was first the Roman Slave system mainly prisoners of war sold on behalf of the Roman Legions. Then came the Agrarian System followed by the Feudal and then the Industrial revolution. Henry the 8th controlled the Feudal system even more tightly, after he severed the English ties to the Catholic Pope in Rome. He set up his own religion and confiscated all Church property into his own control! This meant that the land became controlled by the Monarchy, (Himself) and was distributed amongst his own Aristocracy.

Henry as a complete Dictator was not what, one, in modern day England would be happy to have as the Land Lord. The capricious nature of Henry the despot especially in his old age was terrible; the wounds, caused by a javelin thrust in one of his legs in a Tournament, gave him severe pain at the end of his life. The rotting flesh must have been hard to put up with, especially by Henry himself, as he wasted unto death. The daughter of Henry the 8th Elizabeth born of Jane Boleyn, eventually ascended to the throne after the death of her half brother James first. James born of Jane Seymour died young, and the death of Elizabeth's half sister Mary, left the English throne to Elizabeth first. Mary born of Catherine of Aragon the original wife of Henry, and from whom he tried for years to get the marriage annulled, married a Spanish Prince, after she became Queen of England. She had desperately wanted the marriage, in the hope of bearing a male heir to the English Throne, and returning England back to Catholicism. Her half sister Elizabeth first never married, thus she was known as the virgin Queen, but for some critics the virgin label may not quite be right.

The first seeds of the British Empire were unknowingly sown by Elizabeth, and her estate by the time of Queen Victoria as prophesied, straddled the earth. The proud English proclamation that the sun never set on the British Empire came true, and Queen Victoria was the Monarch, when that proud boast was fulfilled. An intense pride in their Nations accomplishments in defying the Spanish, and the setting up of their own religion, created the basis for future success. Queen Elizabeth one was probably one of the most astute politicians of her time. It was her who knowingly or not, first initiated that independence that has kept the UK strong; and it was from her time the superiority of the English Navy first shone through and developed. The pride in her fleet, and the success of her captains at effectively humbling the mighty Spanish Armada, created that indomitable Spirit that propelled the English forward. The greatest success of Winston Churchill was that he symbolized that British Spirit, and self belief, which is why once in spite of being just a small island Britannia ruled the waves?

Elizabeth had sponsored such fine naval men as Captain Drake, who under different circumstances, would have been little more than a Pirate of the high seas, sailing under the queens colors. But that was the age of chivalry and none would suggest the Queen was associated with Pirates, they would not even think about their virgin Queen as being such a bad person, but she was a backer of pirates! The Spanish and the English were deadly enemies, the Spanish had tried to defeat England with its great Amada, but they failed and England from then ruled the waves.

The Spanish had only recently expelled the Moors from their country, and their treasury was in need of new funds, they had spent enormous sums of money on their international pre-eminence. This was why the Spanish Court, mainly Isabel was keen to find a way to get the fabulous wealth, that was supposed to be available from finding a new route to India. It was Isabel who had decided to back Christopher Columbus, on his quest to find a passage to the Indies, and the riches that was there to be picked up so easily. Over the lifetime of Elizabeth first, the taking of gold bullion from Spanish Galleons by her sea captains, was a favorite past time; and England became very rich in the process. It was this wealth that enabled England to dominate the high seas and build an Empire, which it was doing very successfully indeed.

The first real set back was the loss of the American colonies to rebels and aided by the old enemy France. Louis 16th in spite of his weak treasury reserves, felt it important that his country support the American rebels, and he did so. This was done in spite of his huge problems at home, and was probably his final major international commitment, before he was executed as was his Queen, Antoinette.

The next step of big dimensions, that propelled England quickly forward, was the Industrial revolution. Strangely the Chinese had done much of this industrial production; over a thousand years earlier, but had never developed their genius internationally or in fact at all. The use of machinery and an original type of time and motion labor controls, were initiated in Britain, but the use of child labor somewhat tarnishes the memories, of that period in English industry. The import of raw materials from her colonies, then the production in the mills in Bradford etc; to produce cloth and other goods, which was then exported to the world at great profit. This was just the start of the industrial revolution that propelled England forward, and into the position of being the greatest empire on earth at that time?

From the start of the industrial development by England which was rapid, the system spread first to Germany, Holland, then America, Japan, the

Korea's, Taiwan. Now the real giant China is starting to awaken to its true potential. England then lost her advantage in her financial lead, as the new world system was developed by America. We now have capitalism fueled by demand debt, but this is a system that seems to be out of control worldwide, and is what we say will fail within 70-80 years at the most.

England had no choice but to honor its peace agreement with Poland, so that when Hitler unilaterally invaded Poland she with France had no choice, but to declare war on Germany. The English Prime Minister Mr. Atlee came back from a meeting in Berlin with Hitler, declaring Peace in Our Time, only to be made a fool of a few days later with the attack on Poland. The Labor Party was then in a shambles, and Great Britain had no choice but to honor the peace agreement she held jointly with France and Poland. It was obvious that the Labor political regime was not one that could deal with war, out of the following political turmoil Winston Churchill emerged as the wartime leader of the English.

The rapid advance of the German war machine, in the occupation of all of Western Europe including the Lowlands and France; left only England standing in defiance of Hitler and his military machine. It was fortuitous for England that the need for oil and fuel, from the Caucasus persuaded Hitler to turn his attention to the East; in opening up this second front he weakened his forces in the West. Never the less without the entry of America into the war the English could not have succeeded. The Americans had to come into the war on two fronts, the Japanese in the South and the Germans in the West. The determined resurgence of the Russians in the East, and the industrial might of a newly awakened American Goliath, caused the war to finally swing against the Axis and towards the Allies.

Although the UK has become a mere shadow of the world dominant nation she once was, she still stands undefeated as a small island nation that stood alone, against the might of the Axis powers, while none stood with her. The Americans were the deciding power that defeated the Axis powers, but it was England that stood when all others had fallen, and it was the English lead in industrial development, from which the Americans were able to copy and unleash their unparalleled power; that in the end subdued the world.

We should not forget the forces sent by her Empire to fight on the side of the mother country! Almost five million troops were sent as soon as possible by her colonies, but this was not enough to stem the tide, it also needed the productive might of America, to fully equip those armies.

GERMANY & FRANCE:

The Germanic Barbarians of course were prominent on the ancient world stage, and are still prominent now. The Germans lived within a tribal economy with the tribe choosing the man most suitable to lead, there was never such a thing as hereditary rights, until the latter days. The tribes spread all the way up into Northern and Western Europe, and were interrelated within their many and varied tribes. The countries that trace back to the closest relationship are Holland, England and Germany, this is a direct ancestral

Link. Over the years it has often been said that if only the Germans and the English could have fought together, they would have easily subdued the world, but even the Dutch have no time for their cousins the German's. A war link between the three is not geographically feasible, and for some reason there is a deep dislike between the countries. Holland has always got on well with the English, two of the most successful international companies in the World are Anglo Dutch, Royal Dutch Shell for one and Unilever is another.

The Germans have always been an aggressive fighting people, and were for many years a scourge to the Romans with their constant attacks on Roman subject countries. Through the years they have been very successful, but only because of their own efforts, their own lands were wooded plains, and they were mainly hunter gatherers. They were not heavily into growing apart from their few planted grains crops, sometime successfully sometimes not. The weather patterns in the 15-1600 BC era the land was often frozen over, not good for grazing or gardening; so these were very lean times that drove the Germans out looking for better lands, and more of it. It was in the end the German Barbarians that defeated Rome, but it wasn't necessary for them to fight for control of Rome, they simply moved into the place vacated by the Senate and the military, and over a period became romanized themselves.

The two world wars were initiated by the Germans, but it is the historical hatreds that permeate that area West and North of Europe that has made it such a tinder box of war in the 20th century. The Poles and Balts were always considered to be inferior to themselves by the Germans, and peace had always been difficult to maintain. Yugoslavia was a melting box of Religious hatred anyhow, and the accidental assassination of a German Aristocrat Franz Ferdinand in Yugoslavia; started the First World War, that dragged on for four years. That war ended in the defeat of the Germans, and the victory of the allied forces led by the much hated English, left the huge repatriation costs payable by the German's.

This war and its humiliating loss was the object of hatred to Hitler, and his refusal to continue the repatriation of the debt to the English accrued from that war, was one of his early triumphs. The Labor Government in

England tried to preserve peace, with a policy of accommodation to Hitler's demands! This debt repudiation plus his war production policies pulled his country out of any effects, still being suffered from the Great Depression. Hitler was a Messiah in the eyes of the German masses, his many schemes of capital works were embraced with German fervor. This includes 5,000 miles of quality highways, the famous Autobahns of the Hitler era!

In modern warfare the outcome can depend on the access to fuel supplies, sufficient to fuel the machines of war. No longer was the outcome dependant on the cavalry (Horses), support of the infantry, (Foot soldiers) war was now heavily mechanized and had to be supplied with fuel. In the West Rommel couldn't get to the oil by a mere 40 miles short of the Suez. Montgomery and the 8th army held the Germans up and finally drove them back, from getting the Suez fuel, this was the beginning of the end at Tobruk for Rommel's army. Russia's weather defeated Hitler as it had beaten Napoleon before him, both of these Dictators armies bogged down and their soldiers died by the hundreds of thousands in the frozen wastes of Russia. But strategically the Germans were denied access to the badly needed fuel!

The Spanish through their Sth American possessions had bought back the potato from the mountains of Peru, but being a root plant the German Barbarians could not be persuaded to eat them. After several years and at last in desperation, they were persuaded to try; and they have been eating them ever since. The German cuisine as they have settled down over the years has developed into a unique quality that is high in pork fat contained in Sausage (Wurst) and Salami and they are a meat eating people. The sausages and salami in the production formulas' contain a lot of pork fat.

Pigs have been popular for years in many cultures because of their many advantages, the main one being the rate at which they breed and grow to maturity. There is a disease (Leptospirosis) that can pass from Pig to Humans, but in those days they would not have known if they were afflicted. This disease is propagated by feeding rubbish to pigs; from which the resulting germs pollutes the pigs flesh, and then that of the persons who eat the meat. The disease is painful and not deadly, but isn't seen much nowadays, because pigs now are fed on special grain only diets. In most developed countries it is illegal to feed pig's food scraps from restaurants; that could be contaminated. The internal organs of the pig are identical to human beings; this is probably why that disease is spread from pigs to humans easily?

There was an outbreak of Leptospirosis in New Zealand fifty years ago, that changed the pig industry there dramatically. The growing of Pigs in Germany, Holland and Denmark has become highly sophisticated, but perhaps it is a cruel industry. The pigs in those countries are grown very big with the breed now most common being the large white, with baconer's up to 100K/s and backfatters up to 200-250K/s. The Europeans want the hard fat that grows down the backbone; it is stripped off and used in Sausage and Salami production, which is fine in a very cold climate; but unhealthy in a hot climate. The problems for Europeans especially the Dutch and Germans, when migrating to warm climates is they still eat their foods from home that are saturated in pork fat, and not suitable for eating in warmer climates.

Growing animals in the very cold climate is far more difficult than in the warmer climate. In cold climate countries such as Holland and Germany, the growers are forced to keep their animals indoors during the winter; this means there are very few larger herds of any type. This may have changed with modern facilities; we refer here to early and pre 20th century.

The same potato problem applied to the French, even though Louis 16th tried to persuade his French people to eat potatoes, they would not. The King let it be known he ate potatoes for breakfast; still no reaction from his subjects they were starving, but they would not eat potatoes, because they came out of the ground. Had the king been able to get his subjects to eat potatoes, there might have been no French Revolution, and History in Europe would have been very different. Just imagine no Napoleon to allow England to show her military genius at Waterloo! There would have been none of the depravations and plunder throughout Europe by the French, and there would have been no slaughter of the aristocrats? Thus the demand agrarian economy in France would have been safe and all, if only; the French could have been persuaded to eat potatoes!

The French as in most things see themselves as the best at everything but especially in Cuisine and High Fashion. This may be quite true, but it was not always so, there is no denying the French have the flair for style etc. Historically the French and the English have had a mixed love, hate relationship starting in full strength from 1066 AD, with the invasion of the British Isles by William the Conqueror. The subjugation by the Normans from France, of the English Saxons, the hatred was to last for centuries, even though all of the different tribes trace back to the Barbarian tribes of Western Europe.

The French revolution created fear in the royal houses of Europe, because of so many of them being inter linked by many years of incestuous marriage, which meant most of the Royal families were/are linked. This included Russia and England, even the English Royals felt insecure, during and after the French slaughter of their aristocratic families. The advent of Napoleon and his self elevation, and the crowning of himself as Emperor of Europe, did not secure anything he was after all not of the Royal blood!

The French have had their periods of domination of Europe; the most recent was the occupation by the forces under Napoleon Bonaparte the

Sicilian. Napoleon wanted to annex Egypt as well as the British Isles, but over extended himself as he did when he tried to occupy Russia. The French losses in the attempt to occupy Russia, was a huge disaster and weakened Napoleon force's badly, The end of Napoleon and his dreams of European domination ended at Waterloo, crushed by the hated English. In spite of this example, Hitler tried to occupy Russia, but he suffered the same fate as Napoleon; huge losses in the frozen lands his armies had over run; and then couldn't get out of in an orderly manner.

If we look back over the centuries the French have been strong contributors to the dominant Western Society, but the 20th century has seen that pre eminence diminish. The attempt to create an eminent society, within the Current Market Community; has both the Germans and the French leading the way. Morocco and the Sahara was once a French Colony; that was after years founded by the French Foreign Legion. After many years of struggle to gain control of this vast area mainly consisting of sand, the French had what was considered to be a new Colony, but we have yet to see what advantage they got out of that sandy area of the world. Perhaps the reputation earned by their Foreign Legion, is enough to make their acquisition worthwhile, there must be some value there somewhere.

AFRICA & EGYPT:

Africa the cradle of the world has been a problem continent for a long time, and will be for quite a while to come. This continent has been peopled by blacks belonging to different tribal groups with the Zulu's being the most prominent; if only because of their magnificent bodies and their exceptional height. Shaka Zulu built up the greatest native tribe ever in Africa, but in the end was murdered by two of his half brothers, because his reign was sinking into a brutal Dictatorship, which they felt had to be terminated. Shaka was a brilliant man a front line warrior who led by example, an astute general who could command and plan down to the finest detail, battle strategies. He was well aware the white man must in the end take over his beloved country; he could see the English had superior numbers, but more importantly far superior weapons. He sophisticated the African attack procedures that had endured for centuries, and the changes were what led to the Zulu superiority which he used to the utmost advantage. The training for the use of his techniques was against another great African Tribe the Masai!

From the religious point of view; the many different tribes mostly practice different types of cults, with the Animists being the most numerous. The economy has always been one that mostly trades between the tribes, and was really a slave command economy. For many years within many mainline church's to be colored was to have the mark of Cain, because one was cursed with the mark of Cain as in the Bible when Cain killed his brother Able. This has led to a tremendous amount of self righteousness among the predominately white cultures, but has now largely been forgotten. The black churches of America have done a lot to dispel the myth of color preference in the Lords Kingdom. But there is no doubt that slavery was a result of this false teaching in several main line churches, and created a lot of hatred over the years. Only the enlightened religionists were able to see the error of those teachings and oppose black slavery. Strangely slavery is still thriving as a worldwide business, but now it's all colors, creeds and women for the sex trade, who are the main victims, such is the evil of man.

We must stress here that this is different than the early aversion to Asians by the rest of the community. In that instance the great numbers of the Asian populations were and are feared by many. The thought of the Asian numbers which includes India, as well as South East Asia and includes Indo China boggles the mind. There are not many people in this world, that don't become confused when they try to imagine why the Asians are so dominant racially, except themselves of course!

South Africa has been a country much fought over by two countries wanting to gain control, one was the eventual winner England, the other the Dutch or more correctly the Boers. Of course we should not overlook the main Black tribe the Zulu's who had also to be subdued before a discernable economy could be developed. The fighting between the English and the Boer's was interspersed with the English having to fight the Zulu's. The creation and promulgation of Apartheid was the result of the Boer Prime Minister Dr. Verwoerd, who was the complete hater of the colored peoples of the world, but he especially considered the Blacks as some type of animal; which had to be separated from white people. The acquisition of Native lands is synonymous with the English Colonial methods, perhaps the most difficult countries they have ever penetrated have been in Africa. South Africa with their aggressive Natives was always going to be difficult, but the secondary opposition from the Boers; made for very hard times for the English military.

The development of slavery on a big scale was at first condoned even by the English, and certainly by the French, Spaniard and Portuguese. These were the peoples that aspired to getting control of the new English colony, the emerging United States of America. The Civil war fought between the Southern States, (Rebels) and the Eastern States (Union) was largely about slavery, and most of those slaves were sourced from Africa. It was also because the Southerners wanted to secede from the Union, into a separate country, and that was never going to be acceptable in the North.

The point was that the slavers were assisted in their search for slaves by the African Chiefs; the boats would pull into a port in Africa and would choose and buy slaves at auction. The slaves that were being auctioned off were those captured in tribal wars, and gathered by the victor's to be sold at the auctions, that were arranged on behalf of the various original slave owning chiefs. Hence we have the current Afro Americans who are descended from those early slaves!

After the Civil war when the slaves were told they were now free many demurred as they had always been slaves, fed, clothed and housed by their masters. The fear was that they would not be able to look after themselves; once they had lost their owners. Many slaves just wanted to stay where they were, and many just wanted to stay on as slaves for their various masters. After the war slaving was illegal so the wishes of the slaves did not matter, they were now free and had to leave; the only master they had ever known.

All of the many African Countries have long histories dating back to Biblical times, ie Ethiopia and its queen of Sheba is an example. That country dates back to a flourishing economy before King Solomon's time. The Queen took a camel caravan of exotic presents with her to give to Solomon, she wanted to hear him speak; so she could listen herself to the King's wisdom. We are told she was very impressed and went home very satisfied with all she had seen and heard, about Solomon and his Kingdom. Another story about her relationship with Solomon says they produced a child together, but that is probably just another myth. There is also a black tribe found in Africa who are Jews, and are descended from one of the lost tribes. They have kept the Jewish Law more faithfully it is claimed, than the tribes that were not lost, they have now been absorbed into the Jewish Nation in Israel.

During the 20th century there have been a few disasters in Africa that have made the news, and caused hesitation when it has come to investment; this creates the situation whereby development is stunted. Opportunities now exist that have started to revert to the old style of investment; by mineral hungry countries, like China, but also to a lesser degree India. Examples of Uganda and the Congo stay in the memory of atrocities committed in these two countries. In the Congo Patrice Lumumba was killed because of his efforts to bring an improved life style for his people, after being separated from Belgium. Idi Amin was a monster responsible for mass killing in Uganda, reportedly over 800,000 of his citizens died as victims, of yet another mad man of the 20th Century.

The city of Tobruk was an important breakthrough area for the allies during WW11, it was here the English claim the fortunes of war changed. Seen in camera the truth is it was here the allies shut the Germans out from what they most needed, fuel supplies through the Suez Canal. This area was also vital to the Romans as well, even though in their years the aim wasn't to get fuel; for heavy war equipment.

Egypt was the bread basket of the Roman Empire, a vast assortment of Egyptian produce was collected by the Roman's as tribute and taxes, then shipped to Rome where it was ware housed. The products were then repackaged and distributed for sale throughout the Empire, branded as Roman products. The Egyptian's relied on the fertility gained from the annual flooding of the Nile River, which renewed the soil quality annually; this was the source of their superior output in a big range of products. The economy of Egypt was really one of command and demand agrarian, although those that tilled and worked the soils completed the same cycle every year. They were not told what crops they were to grow, but the values were based on demand, many of those working the land were slaves working for their Egyptian Masters, they did the same old thing year in and out.

Every year the flooding of the Nile River was vital for the revitalizing of the soil! The annual floods bought fresh silt down, and when the river flooded that soil settled on the land, and it was how the soil was fertilized every year. It also meant the soil was easy to work, the top soil that came down from the river made the soil soft pliable, and easily worked with the simple tools they then had. The growth was quick and two crops per year was the norm!

During the earlier years the land was owned by the Pharaohs' and his ministers were responsible for the land and the crops. Their jobs were to acquire a share of the crops based on total yield, but included in that was the tax surcharge. Compared to many other societies of the time the Egyptian family enjoyed quite a good life style, they were able to live quite comfortably. That was until the Roman's came and then the life styles got harder, as Tribute and Roman taxes had to be added to the Pharaohs' percentage. In later years just before the Romans came; life changed as the Priests began to own land in their own right. The end result was there were the Roman taxes, the Priests command production and what was left over went to the Pharaohs', by this time there was little left for those that did all of the work?

Eventually the Priests owned just over a third of all land, and that was the point at which the Egyptian economy started to get very hard for the common folk. When the Romans came and added in more taxes life became real hard, but there was a lessening commitment to the Pharaohs' military as a strong military was banned by their overlords the Roman Empire. The only military they had was enough to protect themselves an army of attack and occupation from the time of the Ptolemy's/Romans, a full military was banned.

There was the need to contribute by all members of the laboring classes to the construction of special Govt; works such as the Pyramids as one example.

The wonderful treasures that were part of those found in the tombs of Pharaohs' that had not been plundered by grave robbers, gave an indication of the wealth shared among the wealthy classes of Egypt. Embalming was only affordable by the wealthy, contrary to modern mythology that all were embalmed the service was only available to the very wealthy. The ordinary Egyptian could never aspire to being mummified, but they could lift themselves to a better social class, this was not a common reality in the ancient world. Of course the Roman's system provided for raising ones quality of life, all one had to do was earn the right in the coliseum as a successful Gladiator. If in this example one failed to improve one's station in life one did not care, because he would be dead.

Egypt was when at its peak quite successful at war and defending its lands! In the time of the Pharaohs they had a seriously effective war machine, and the early Pharaohs extended their domains quite extensively. Even Israel was subjected to defeat and plunder by the Egyptians in the Middle Ages; of the Egyptian Empire building period. By the time of Alexander the Ptolemy's and then Julius Caesar, they had passed their independent peak and had been under Grecian control for several hundred years, the Ptolemy's were Greeks.

Cleopatra first had an affair with Julius Caesar and then with Mark Antony, Egypt became a confusion of political intrigue as all tried to gain favor in Rome with the Senate. Augustus the first of the Claudian Emperors defeated Mark Antony and his fleet at Antioch. It was after that defeat that Cleopatra committed suicide and Mark Antony died, also by his own hand. Cleopatra was the last of the Ptolemy's after her Egypt was firmly controlled from Rome! Later it became the headquarters for the Commanding General of the Eastern Legions, until after Constantine had built Constantinople.

CHINA:

This is the country that is the coming giant of the future, but if examined in context has been the giant of the past. Many western people in all classes of life fear China if only because of the sheer size of its population, the thought of so many people in one country boggles the mind of many, and well they should be apprehensive. Over the last one hundred & fifty years China has grown from Three hundred million, until the census in 2001 the population excluding Hong Kong and Taiwan was just under One point three billion people.

China's economic past goes back over 5,000-10,000 years, and their achievements in many facets of their Society; have been on a greater and grander scale than most others. Many of their inventions have shaped the world, ie paper and ceramics, then later explosives for fireworks and that is just a few of the many inventions that could be credited to the Chinese. There have been many other industrial inventions; that had they been continued would have placed China 1000 years ahead of the western world. The point is however they did not continue, and in so not doing, lost the edge they could have held.

The real cause has been the amount of fighting among themselves; because the country was so split up by minor Kingdoms with many Kings; and the outside world was always considered inferior. China was in so many ways just like Europe in the third century BC; China was a part of a huge sub continent and had many Kingdoms. China became one huge Kingdom when all of the minor Kingdoms were finally subdued by its first Emperor; and it stayed that way for two thousand years. Conversely the German Barbarians contained the Romans at the Spanish borders, and the Roman Empire had many different races that were never able to be politically bought under one system, such as was achieved in China. The Chinese development was agrarian, the feudal structures as developed in Europe was not a part of the Chinese system of security. The managerial structure from the Emperor down was always brutal; with beheading on the spot practiced, this seemed to keep the peasants and the administration under a type of control, probably a method the western minds don't understand. And from the common people's point of view, such as we are; we don't really want to understand, the thought of their callous attitude to human life; even now boggles the mind for us.

The Chinese have always thought of themselves as superior to all other cultures, and they were always aggressive towards Japan and Korea their close, but much smaller neighbors. The Japanese have been taught by their Samurai cultural forbears that they are superior, especially to all other Asians, this has put them at odds with the Chinese who think of Japanese as being low class. When the Japanese invaded Nanking they considered they were killing animals less than human, much like the German attitude to the Jews? The slaughter of twenty million Chinese by the Japanese in the period just before WW11 in Europe, further estranged the two countries?

Strangely the Japanese war atrocities have never really been bough to account, and if taken in context would be every bit as brutal as the Germans. Obviously in the end China's population is over ten to one in favor of China, so the Chinese must in the end prevail against the Japanese. Their population ratios to the rest of the world except India are huge, and with India, Manchuria and Russia they are all part of the one Continent. Short of a few atomic bombs on selected targets that population advantage will always be constant. Neither Country has great mineral resources that have yet been found, but China has a far greater chance to develop than Japan through its huge labor force. Now that China has progressed from their old economy, towards the creation of the new type of economy; that is business friendly.

The old economy was through the Emperors and a type of agrarian demand economy existed, that would be the most beneficial to the State. Before 231BC China was split up into six different kingdoms; all with separate kings and economies as was typical in Western Europe. But then they had the coming of the first Emperor who over ten years through victories at war bought the country together under one Kingdom. The system then developed remained the same for over 2000 years!

The battles of which there were many were very bloody, but he eventually bought all the different states under his own banner, and centralized control? The Emperor then decided to promote himself and officially raised his position to the status of a God! This was surely a mistake because from that time on; his reign was beset by constant wars, as he struggled to hold his now united nation together. The first Emperor was a masterly War Lord, but having bought all of the Kingdoms together, he developed an intense paranoia in his quest for eternal life. It is thought he killed himself with the ingestion of too many medicines containing mercury; he eventually died of lead poisoning. Despite all of the difficulties the Emperor had in uniting the country, China remained under central control; but the self appointed Man-God paid a heavy penalty? He died as a result of his fear for his life; in short his own success killed him.

Chinas' history has been tumultuous over the thousands of years, the size of the united country and the constant need to try and keep the people at peace, has been difficult and getting harder as the population grows so quickly. Over the recent past this has been thwarted many times by outside human greed, from foreign countries. China has been so conspicuously grand and apparently wealthy; that all comers have wanted to share that prosperity. The usual Colonial European powers were clamoring for trade rights, France, Spain, USA, England etc; in the end the English gained sole trading rights, over all of the competitors. It has been sad to see China seemingly deteriorate from its former grandeur to a period of strife, as politics has split the country asunder?

The success of communism within the mainland, and the aggrandizement of Mao tse Tung, almost to the stature of a God, created a period of turmoil in China. Chiang ki Shek took his conservative party off shore to Taiwan, and has created a separate country; which is strongly disputed by the Chinese Communist party on the mainland. The aim of the Chinese has been to take back its territories, Hong Kong and Tibet they have got and Taiwan they are still aiming to get. Taiwan has created a successful economy of its own, and its support by the USA has so far stopped China forcing its will; and taking back Taiwan unilaterally!

The problem became one that England having won a trade agreement could not export to China enough, because the Chinese really had not much use for English products. Slowly as the trade imbalance grew in favor of China, illegal trading was attempted to create an artificial balance? Opium was introduced by nefarious English business people, seeking to find a product that the Chinese population wanted. The Chinese took very quickly to smoking Opium, and it became a scourge that was frowned on by the Chinese authorities. This eventually led to the opium wars, because of the Chinese Govt; decision to close down all illegal drug activities, of both Chinese and English traders? The destruction by Chinese Govt; agents of large stores of opium held by both English traders and Chinese resellers, caused the anger on both sides that culminated in war. The power of the western media created the illusion that the fault was with the Chinese, and that China was a country full of opium addicts. This was totally untrue, it was the English that tried to seduce that country by addicting the people to opium, and then blamed the Chinese Govt; for their own brand of English driven evil.

The huge land mass is cultivated by the Chinese peasants who keep working and demanding little except food, clothes and a home with a small plot of land; on which to feed and raise their families. The apparent docility of the population should not be under estimated, the abuse over the ages has meant a cynicism that if they are forever abused; could break through into violence. The explosion in the population has also created a change in the normal life styles. In the past the young could be expected to take over from parents the home etc; they would then care for their parents in their last years. This is changing as more of the young go searching for city jobs, the elderly are being left to fend for themselves, and the change is dramatic and traumatic?

Like in India the Europeans were dazzled by the exotic goods they found in China, and wanted more ever more, the silks and other wonderful goods on display were an attraction to all. China was one country that did not become interested in the Colonial British Empire, they probably believed they had more of everything than the English had anyhow, even if these Britishers were spread all over the world. There has been no time in their long history that the Chinese have wanted anything from anywhere else, this isolation has in some ways left them behind. The annexation of Hong Kong by the British was due to expire in 1957; and the return of that colony to the Chinese Mainland, was as far as the Chinese were concerned a major coup. The return of Taiwan to becoming part of China is still one of intense importance, as China claims its right to have returned all of its former lands. Tibet is one of those countries that China considers as Chinese territory. The forced takeover of Tibet and the exile of the Dalai Lama has been of worldwide interest, but China will not be dissuaded they claim Tibet is a colony of China and that is the final word, none else matters anymore!

The dramatic change in the way the Western world has developed, and the danger of the Internet information being spread so easily and widely, forces the Chinese Govt; to recognize those western values that are being portrayed on the Internet. That information spread means the Chinese and their Government have no choice, but to move into the main stream of the world. In doing that the rest of the world waits in wander to see what is going to happen. One thing is certain there is going to be changes in the world order, and America as top dog needs to be very careful of her future performance. The reality is that China is the Debtor Nation now; and all Creditor Nations need to remember the bible, that tells us, and the borrower will be the servant of the lender.

China has always been so large it was considered beneath them to even consider exploiting other Nations, they have had everything they needed. Their problem has been other Nations wanting to in some way colonize and exploit them. The wily Chinese have always managed to keep the foreign devil away and guessing what would happen next, in the Chinese political spectrum? For many years they played the Europeans and Americans off against each other; but eventually they were forced to award a mandate to the most aggressive nation of them all at that time, England in her prime?

Vietnam was an early victim of Chinese aggression, but that was a costly victory won by the first Emperor Quin Shi Huang at a huge cost. The marshes bush and rivers as well as the tenacious fighters, that are the Vietnamese created huge difficulties. The canal that runs into the centre of Vietnam was built by the first Chinese Emperor; this had to be done before he could defeat the Vietnamese. _____

THE ROMANCE COUNTRIES:

During the late 13th century France was occupied by the English and was doing badly in their attempts to drive the hated English out. A young girl who heard voices came forward and proclaimed she had a mission to save her beloved country and would drive out the hated armies of the occupiers. She managed to convince Charles 6[Th] of her Godly credentials and did just what she claimed the voices had told her to do, drive out the English.

This girl was betrayed by the French nobility who were supposed to be her main supporters and she was captured by the English using the simple expedient of paying her ransom. She was claimed to be a Witch and was burnt at the stake, that girls name was Joan of Ark. Joan of Arc was a Hero no matter what her source of bravery was, who cares were the voices came from she must have been blessed by an Angel because she was so very successful. Charles the 6th was a weak individual who instead of being grateful to Joan of Arc betrayed her shamelessly and he is remembered in French History for that cowardly act. She been captured at Bordeaux and a ransom had been raised, but never arrived so the ransom from the English was accepted!

The Spanish were the most powerful of the Western European Nations during the Dark and middle Ages. Christopher Columbus was a Portuguese who was financed into his expedition to find a passage to the East by Isabel and Ferdinand of Spain. Mexico and the Central and South America's became subject eventually to Spain, while Brazil was annexed by Portugal. North America was initially settled by the English and the French pretenders, but broke away from England with help from France, starting with the forever famous Boston Tea Party. Eventually the American Rebellion against England succeeded when George Washington won a strategic battle that eventually led to his being elected the first President of the USA.

The Islamic Moors ruled Spain for over 400 years, and their splendid palace in Granada remain a testimony to Islamic Glory. The Spanish had been under the rule of the easy going Moors but they were replaced by the hard driving Christians and their Inquisition. While driving out the Moors; the Christians also caused about 250,000 Jews to relocate to Turkey, to avoid the persecution and execution of Jews during the Inquisition. The other bad habit the Christians had was borrowing of the Jews and forgetting to ever repay their debts. The Spanish at this time in history was to become the pre eminent nation in Europe, and also including France totally committed to the Catholic Faith. Both countries were totally committed to the eradication of heresy via the inquisition. The Jews that relocated to Turkey were welcomed strongly by their new Islamic overlords; they quickly established a strong rapport with the Moorish Sheiks. The Moors were a dark skinned people, and were not well versed in the ways of finance; they therefore had a great use and respect for the Jews and their money expertise. It was Jewish influence that eventually persuaded the Turkish Moors to take over Cyprus.

The Spanish were extremely brutal in their subjugation of the native peoples of the South America's. After initially confiscating all of the gold they could find off the native people, the next step was to mine everything they could. The natives were conscripted into the mines with little or no pay, under severe slave conditions. The conditions were bad enough, but the natives were also exposed to foreign diseases; and died off in large numbers. They also succumbed to poor food and clothing, and being completely neglected in the mad drive for ever more gold from the mines. They were forced to work in atrocious conditions normally almost naked, with little food and no shelters or homes! The treatment of their slaves was every bit as cruel as any of the other Imperial Nations supposedly earning wealth for the Crown. The English had no rights in the newly discovered lands including Mexico, but they stole a lot of gold from the Spanish Galleons as they sailed heavily laden with gold to Spain. It was this period that escalated the hatred for the English; that was never far beneath the surface in all of the romance countries, these are Italy, Spain, Portugal, and France!

It was also this gold that built the financial foundation; that eventually led to Great Britain's domination of the high seas, and her Empire that was eventually spread worldwide. It was here that 'Elizabeth one' proved she was a 'Statesperson without Peer' in those days; it was her that set down the foundations for the coming Empire. The Royal encouragement of the English Navy, and the Spanish attempt at conquest by its massive naval Armada, forced the English to a big effort to build up their fleet to war readiness. The Spanish saw their mission as one blessed of God, theirs was a mission to bring the Godless rogue nation into proper control, for some reason the expedition failed. What they succeeded in doing was the opposite of their intentions, they motivated the English to increase their efforts to ensure their own safety, and this eventually led to their domination of the high seas. Over the years reconciliation through marriage etc has tried to be negotiated without much success. 'The attempts at finding a Spanish husband for Elizabeth were laughingly rejected by the English virgin Queen!

Support from the Portuguese had been denied, which was why Columbus sought and got the support he needed from Spain. The reason for the Columbus expedition was to find that much dreamed of seaway to the Indies, he initially thought he had found the path he was looking for. It didn't take long to realize the mistake, but truthfully what he did find was more valuable than what he had been looking for. 'The amount of golden ornaments for which it seemed, as if the natives had little value', was soon turned into a gold rush by the new colonists? 'The Spanish and the Portuguese had certainly found gold, but they proceeded to prostitute their own religious ideals', as they went crazy in the quest for gold.

In the years following there was a period during which great amounts of gold bullion was being mined, and sent by their Galleon's back to Spain. This provided a great opportunity for English plunder by Pirates, and increased Spanish frustration, as they saw their legitimate property being stolen! Many of these English Buccaneers had been or were being financed and encouraged by Elizabeth, or so it was claimed by the angry Spanish Royalty. The valuable pirated gold cargoes that were being stolen and bought back to England, created the basic funds for English mercantile expansion. England continued to defy the Spanish, but the real impetus and powerful growth came after the Industrial Revolution. The English were able to capitalize on their growing Empire to expand further, for example India and South Africa both became part of the Empire. England like Rome before it was taking in raw materials from its subject countries, processing that material and selling it again through its captive markets. The biggest difference between Spain Portugal and England was religion. 'The English were Protestants and the others Catholic, but unlike the Latin's the English never forced their Religious affiliations'; but they did encourage their missionary's. The Anglican missionaries left to their own devices proved good proselytes' and the conversion of the natives where ever the English went was quite good. The Catholics went to the same places and were never hindered, but they were never allowed to force their beliefs like they could in the other European colonized countries.

The natives were free to accept their own brand of beliefs usually they were cultists or some other religion of their own. It was the brutal methods used by the European countries, to force their beliefs on their newly acquired subjects, which forever condemned them in future world opinion. It is a notable truth that in most of the countries that were occupied by the Latin countries, and their Roman Catholic attachments to the Papacy, the people were left very poor. It is also notable that there was no effective government systems left in place, most went through periods of political instability created by Dictatorships. This has meant the people have been unable to find material advancement, and most are now not even among the developing nations, they are extremely poor, or as in the case of Venezuela have oil riches.

The Portuguese were as cruel as if not crueler than the Spaniards and the mines they worked were exceptionally cruel as the natives were forced to work unpaid, but as slave labor. Many books have been written documenting the activities Portuguese cruelty in their mines over years! The Portuguese was relentless, and if quotas were not met the punishments inflicted were beyond belief; to our modern societies. What made the cruelty more appalling was that the Spanish and the Portuguese were supposed to be bringing Gods love, to those poor unfortunates.

Catholicism was bought to the natives in the form of whips and curses, those who did not want to get baptized were basically tortured unto death. In some cases alleged against the Portuguese but unproven in law, women heavy in child had their stomachs ripped open and their unborn child murdered, that's if it had survived. Then the mothers if they couldn't immediately go back to work were thrashed unto death. The Portuguese were the worst, but the Spanish were a very close second, when it came to inhuman cruelty in the name of their God. We need to point out these are allegations not proven in Law, but seems to be in line with other atrocities committed in the name of God's inquisition in many European Countries.

The Spanish Armada was meant to punish the English and put them in their place again, subservient to Spain and the Catholic Faith. The much bigger Spanish boats with heavier guns were cumbersome compared to the smaller English ones, but even so the battle was fairly even. It was when the English sailed fire boats into the packed Spanish Armada that the two fleets came apart with the Spanish trying to find a route to clear their way out of the battle formations. This route was found and the renewal of the battle at a soon to be set time was never fought, because the Armada was heavily battered and lost a lot of ships, because of the rough weather in the English Channel. The result was that the Spanish Armada went home with heavy casualties, and the English gave thanks to their Anglican God for a resounding victory.

The Latin's in combination with the Catholic Church, kept their peoples pretty much under control using the agrarian command system that applied to the church and royalty. But they would just conscript men into their military whenever they felt the need to take up arms for a war such as against the much hated English.

Perhaps the worst accusations that can be leveled against those European Countries, was the cruelty propagated in God's name. The most heinous crimes committed in God's name was perhaps the so called Spanish inquisition, people in their thousands were executed for heresy and all manner of serious sin. Most of the confessions that were obtained from accused sinners were forced by torture; the victims once they confessed were executed, normally by burning at the stake.

INDIA:

'India is the fabled land the myth perpetuated over the centuries by stories of great wealth created by Gold, Silver, Spices, Exotic animals, and wonderful buildings' everything the western mind could conjure up as wonderful, came from India. What was no myth was the Indus Valley where great wealth did come from, and that was located on the Southern tip of India, but now with the separation was also part of Pakistan. 'The Indus Valley was incredibly fertile and wealthy in minerals and gemstones hence the fables of India', because much of this wealth travelled out to the west through India, and in its day resold through Rome.

It is wrong to think that India had a monopoly, which since the Indus Valley was in Indian Territory she would be expected to have certain privileges, but she did not; she merely had the best access and then the ability to send the riches out by boat to distant places, such as Rome. The Arab camel caravans travelled great distances over land; from western Arabia they also traded in products from the Indus Valley. Many of the fabled goods and spices from the Indus Valley were however from India, the trade between the Indus and India was very much a barter system, since India had a lot of the products the Arabs wanted. The Indian products were sold by the Indus Valley peoples as their own products, and conversely the Indians sold all of the products as their own. Both were really correct since the Indus Valley was in India, but it was just that the products from the Indus valley became fabled, and synonymous with India.

India is a mass of contradictions her colorful and varied population is extremely volatile because of several different factors. Religion has always been a problem if only in the sense that some have originated in India, and gone on to create huge divisions within the subcontinent. Buddha and his teaching very quickly gained a big following among the people, but just as quickly created opposition and even hatred, from other religions such as Muslims and Hindus. The Buddhist philosophy of life and its passive beliefs, gradually took hold in other countries more strongly than it has in India. Tibet is a good example!

The cast system that is peculiar to India, originated with the Brahmins, as the superior peoples, but at the same time a caste was established that gave recognition to the aged, but again only from the top social class. The lower classes then gradually came into being and a full class system, over the ages became established. The castes gradually developed so the Brahmins became the wealthy and professional classes, and all others totally subordinated. The problem was the lower classes (castes) became passive and never had ambitions to rise above their station in life. This is much the same as the Europeans, but the Indians mark the castes on the forehead; so one always lives with ones place in the system, and in the process with such a huge mass of people, motivation to move up is killed off.

There are four different levels of castes the bottom one being known as untouchables, these are the ones that will need to benefit from the new influences that will pervade their country in the future. The third and fourth castes are the ones that internally could propel India into a significant world economy, provided the problems of self debasement could be overcome, the opportunity is there. The Indians at the top are entrenched, and very aware of whom they, are they won't do any manual labor. The second class is the aged so they aren't the producers of the future either. The third class are well on the way as the developed economies begin to see India as an IT hub, this class has good English skills. It is the untouchable class that can create that labor force that could match China, the problem is the lack of drive as already noted. The Chinese don't have that lack of motivation, the peasants are leaving their homes looking for a better life; that may not happen with the Indians, but to really compete they must. The opportunity is there, but can they muster their peoples to rise to the challenge, only the future will tell?

The jewel in the English Crown was India which was before the partition off, of what was to be Pakistan a Muslim State. The separation had become necessary because of the incessant fighting between Muslim's and Hindu's. Mahatma Gandhi had tried unsuccessfully to unite and get the negotiators for the two religions to agree but he was unsuccessful. India was/is a fabulous country with an economic background that has bounced up and down for over 5,000-10,000 years. The English was the successful of the many Colonial predators that had been trying to get control of India. When they did get control the English plundered the natural wealth of the country, but economically gave little in return. There could be future advantages for India as she benefits from the Language, Political and Legal Heritage, those were the only things, and the British couldn't take with them when they had to leave. The Indian contribution of men for the defense of Empire was of the highest caliber, Indian soldiers have earned a fine reputation in the heat of battle.

The opposition of Jamir, who at that time was the leader of the Muslim's, to the continuation without separation of the country was inflexible. He was suffering from serious Diabetes and had been told he had a limited life left perhaps 12 months, but no more. Gandhi as well as the last Governor General, Earl Mountbatten, were both trying to avoid separation they all knew the cost in human lives for the Muslim proposals. Jamir was totally inflexible, but he hid his sickness being determined to leave Pakistan as his gift to the Muslim world.

The loss of human life in the huge changes that were necessary has been quoted at between 1-1.5 million people died in the transition. This was because of the Muslim's being shifted out of India and the Hindu's and Sikh's being shifted out of Pakistan, the cost to all was tremendous. There is continuing disruption to world peace as Pakistan has been accused of collusion with terrorists, and creating the sanctuary for Taliban fighters, from Afghanistan. The former General Sharif as President of Pakistan promised, so much in return for American money, but did very little. Sharif eventually resigned because of political pressure, but we have little doubt he left with a lot of ill gotten money as his reward for doing little.

The British East India Company at first facilitated the commercial control of India, but in the end she was assimilated into the British Empire, because of the need for political controls the company could not give. There was little advantage initially to the Indian people from its relationship with the British, but there will be good future advantages. Quite a large number of the upper casts learned to speak, read and write English. The democratic background was kept when the British left, as was the economic systems, for good or bad. The final English loss of control was a result of WW11; as there was no way she could defend her Empire. Winston Churchill could only watch sadly as his beloved British Empire in the Southern Sea areas, slipped away as the Japanese over ran Singapore in very little time, and the English reign in the Deep South was over.

England and its commonwealth had always believed that India and Singapore were supposed to be impregnable, and would be forever British. When the Japanese over ran Singapore very quickly, it was a major shock to the English who could do nothing? The superiority of the English was a myth; and is now but a memory of the White Sahib, who in the end was just another man. The English enjoyed a period of great affluence from what was plundered from India by her traders and others; the loss has been and is serious to the English economy.

The usual flock of missionaries that followed any new British Colonies, had little success in India, there was reputed to be over 300 different cults of a great diversity, well established before the coming of the white man. There are in the Indian sub continent about 50,000 Christian Groups of different denominations in different stages of development, another 40,000 mosques and some 35,000 Hindu houses of worship. Like China if India is to develop it must build the infrastructure, it is in the process of building thousands of k/s of good roads, but that is just a start.

The different economic systems that have controlled India for over 5,000 years is more akin to slavery, so effectively it was a more command demand agrarian system than any other, but her caste system may help them in the near future. The white man was supposed to be superior, and expected to be venerated by a people that had a far longer historical past. It is proper to say the common Indians live no better under the Raj, than they did under the English, perhaps the greatest charge against them was their foolish English pomposity. In India every Englishman became in his own mind a superior being, an illusion created by their self importance, much the same as the obnoxious Yank that came after the Poms.

Gandhi's passive resistance to the English was slow and tedious method of mutiny, only such a man could have succeeded where he did, but in the end the religious problems caused his assassination. 'Gandhi was much loved and his untimely death cut short the ideals that he had fought so long and hard to achieve. It seemed at the time of his death he was making real progress, with the religious divisions that was tearing his country, India apart'. His fasting had bought the major protagonists the Hindu's and the Muslim's together, but in the negotiations he failed, but even the separation of Pakistan, has not bought lasting peace.

India has always had a large Hindu population, and has a large religious variety of small worshiping cults, which keeps the country in danger of sudden surges of violence. One Indian advantage in the future of the world's compression into strategic alliances, is its large business community outside India, all who are proudly ethnic and very well aware of the way their country must move? They are also well aware of the opportunities that will accrue in the future! The Indians have proved their ability world wide as business men, not quite as spread out as the Chinese, but very successful never the less. The Indian low caste (untouchables) has not been able to spread out as easily; as the Chinese coolly types, probably because of the inhibitions bred into them by the caste system. In the future with more learning from the mixing with other peoples via the internet, these untouchables may be able to work and be low cost producers, again much the same as the Chinese peasants to China, they will be vital to India, but all must forget the untouchable tag that is a system from the past, and must die with that past.

There is an opportunity for an Indian alliance within the countries of South East Asia, then jointly an umbrella alliance with the American's. The American's cannot compete economically within production and consumer trade patterns, with the giant that will become China as they develop. The best alternative is for America to link up with India the world's second biggest country in terms of population. India seems to be heading more towards the IT industry, but that will expand as she develops laterally. India's has her casts and the lowest cast the untouchables, but the advantage is in the class separation. As India expands it will start to produce in specialized areas, this will be unlike China that is developing horizontally. China wants to spread and develop her production industries, very widely across the full international markets. The big problem in India will be the many religions; the Hindu's in particular seem to be in constant strife with their Muslim neighbors. Pakistan as well won't want to see India flourish as she would do. And if in some way assimilated into a Common Market Group with America, India would benefit exponentially.

SOUTH & CENTRAL AMERICA, MEXICO NORTH AMERICA:

Mexico is a nation with a turbulent past, exacerbated by its Spanish connections and the losses of its lands to the USA. The loss of Texas and Lower California to the United States was a very hard blow, which even now is hard for the Mexicans to accept. This loss was the cause of much bloodshed with immigrants from the USA, who wanted to settle in a country the Mexicans still thought of as their own. The Mexicans have the advantage with Canada in that they have the NAFTA that was signed into law by President Bill Clinton, and seems to have worked quite well. The number of illegal Mexican immigrants, known as wetbacks working and living in America is very large and growing, as the Mexicans continue to break through immigration on the American border, just south of San Diego.

All of the South and Central American countries have low cost labor, but they have to be united in a group to be efficient, those in the South are very unskilled workers, but more problematically the men are rather lazy. Mexico needs to be included in these low labor cost countries. South & Central America and Mexico should be set up in, and with other Pacific Rim countries into the proposed Free Trade Agreement with America. And all of this should happen within the American Common Market Group! The link of this group with India will encourage these countries to see this is the only way open to the future. The problems here is the lack of skilled workers, and the attitude of the men to work, many men think all work is for woman and sex should be available with multiple women at the whim of men, we quote Peru as a classic example of this attitude. Their woman are good workers, but this attitude is a dead end, and will change as the advantages start to flow through, or if we like trickle down to the poor. The subsequent improvement in the conditions of the peasant class people, of which there are a lot in this group, will identify the product spread and also the future improvements possible, this will eventually lead to international group harmony.

The NAFTA free trade agreement has worked quite well for Canada and Mexico it will need time to integrate the rest of the countries, but it will be workable quite quickly. The aversion by the Latin's to the American Gringo is very strong, but that will change because there will be no choice, and even less choice as the Free Market Groups start to work and integrate properly. Conversely the Americans would be wise to learn to be a little less arrogant, towards their Southern neighbors. There has been millennia of mistreatment of the Southern People's of the American Continent, this is a problem that will have to be redressed if there is to be a sound rapprochement between North and South. But integration will succeed because in the end all will want it to proceed, and 'the leftist regimes in the South, will reconcile with the two major regimes of the North'.

In general the South Americans have suffered from bad political leadership; Argentina in particular has been badly served. The Peron's husband then wife held up the countries development badly; as they used the country as a type of personal fiefdom, then the abuse by the military Generals made the country look quite foolish. The General's decision to unilaterally take over the Marianas islands from the British, gave Margaret Thatcher the chance to grandstand, and the English a chance to remember their great days. But that undermined the Generals and they were soon displaced from Govt! The economy is modern, but with a narrow base, it is historically a beef grazing country with millions of acres of plains for beef cattle and horses. There are minerals that can be mined when and if investment funds are found! Argentina is a country that has benefitted by a lot of European Immigrants before and after WW11; the problem has been one of widening the countries production base and attracting mining investment. Most of this business activity has been stunted by the poor political quality, which creates a lack of confidence in the ability to guarantee stability. The strong Spanish background creates a feeling of emotional instability this is the typical Latin temperament, and seen as a national failing.

Uruguay is a small country with conditions much similar to New Zealand in the South Pacific. Again this country has been disadvantaged by political instability and has suffered from the lack of foreign investment. Uruguay is considered to be the education capital of South and Central America, because of the success of its universities in turning out an abundance of genuine Professionals. Many of these local people have immigrated to other countries worldwide, and many have returned to successful careers in the Latin countries of their birth. Uruguay has also had a big influx of European immigrants, but the last of their native population have been gone many years ago.

Chile has been a political football, and suffered from the interference of the CIA when they helped to destabilize the democratically elected leftist Allende Govt, in favor of the Pinochet alternative. Allende never had a chance to create a stable Govt; right from the start he was undermined and his authority usurped. General Augustus Pinochet took over from Allende, and there followed one of the most brutal South American Dictatorship Regimes, the South has ever had. Many thousands were reputed to have been taken and just vanished! There are claims of military style execution, but there were no corpses to prove the claims! There were attempts to put Pinochet to trial in the World Court, but he died at a grand old age, in this way escaped justice.

Peru and Ecuador are both very poor countries with again unstable Govt; one of the Leaders was of full Japanese descent and created a lot of problems in his country of birth Peru. Bolivia was the birthplace of Simon Bolivar who died a martyr for the communist cause after building up a relationship with Castro. Columbia became a major drug exporting country to the U.S and created strong links with the drug cartels in the States, mainly Florida. The drug industry and its fabled ability to generate billion in cash money has been an interference to the Columbian development, but the Govt; is now gaining some political control that bodes well for that countries future.

Venezuela has gained oil riches and a leader who has grand ambitions of becoming a world statesman with Castro as his example, Paraguay has done very little and the same applies to the small Central American countries.

Brazil is the probable success story of the South! This is a huge country with massive resources as well as the major part of the Amazon River running through its states. There is a very big mixed population with a big percentage of Mulatoes (Mixed black and native bloods) living there. Brazil is developing at a rapid pace and will be the major economy of the South Americas, probably producing more than the rest of the countries combined. This growth will be very rapid and whatever happens Brazil will become a major economy. The future development will begin quite quickly, the rate of development in the region of the Amazon River, and its rain forests give concern to naturalists for the conservation of many plant, insect and animal species still undiscovered.

SOUTH EAST ASIA:

The need to specialize will be spread across various countries in South East Asia this will create spread and will nullify the fear of Chinese domination. The Indian cast system allows her peoples and its casts; to more easily to assimilate themselves with other nations, since they are already so divided themselves. It will be easier for India to reach cooperative production units within the countries of South East Asia, than it would for say the hated Japanese. Because of her record for brutality, the Japanese can only ever get full cooperation of the surrounding countries by conquest. All of the countries we have indicated have populations that are hard working, and highly malleable when given the chance. Strangely the white Anglo countries in the south Australia and New Zealand seem passive in their memories of Japans past, because they are enjoying an easy life selling their minerals and agriculture to the Jap's; it seems money over rides past memories.

The best way to combat the Chinese giant will be for the group including India and the SEA countries, to be consummated as suggested herein? If the group can agree to implement production and sales goals that balances the need of all countries in this Common Market Grouping, that would be led by America, trade could be internal and an advantage to them all. Countries may have a special product that no others could compete with, for example NZ is an Agricultural Country that may specialize in Milk and Meat, Australia would have Minerals and India as well as IT would have different consumer products she produces for their own group. If all of the nations settle in to produce products for which they are best suited, they could match and beat China if need be. The secret will be in lateral not horizontal growth, the split of countries requires that cautious approach. The consolidated flows internally could bring balance that would be competitive with China, the feared giant, but a lot depends on the Indians being able to motivate its untouchable caste people.

The South East Asian countries which are, Brunei, Burma, Cambodia, Timor, Indonesia, Laos, Philippines, Thailand and Vietnam are all low cost labor producers if given a chance. These countries linked with Australia, New Zealand, New Guinea and the Pacific Islands could be a highly effective united group, the ones that lack unity with this group can be negotiated with. The key to these countries becoming a superior economic force is India, but India has much to win with this grouping as do all of the other countries named. The old allies, America and the British Isles would also benefit from the link as will the many countries in South and Central America, Mexico and Canada. Israel is to many the Pariah of the group, but that criteria is wrong, but this is a Muslim opinion generally.

Indonesia has the biggest Muslim population in the world and its only real investors are companies who have been there since Dutch colonial days. They understand the country and are working along quite happily, since the Dutch were expelled and self Govt; was proclaimed. Indonesia is not considered a great investment by Western Bankers, that's why there has been a poor investment background,

Cambodia has had a bad recent past with hundreds of thousands killed for political reasons by the Khmer Rouge and their leader Pol Pot. The Philippines has suffered from bad politicians and is starting to go ahead now. Eastern Timor is recently separated of from Indonesia and is the world's youngest democracy. Thailand and Vietnam are both doing well and finding financial stability. Laos, Burma and Brunei will all fit in well with the proposed American Common Market Group, they are all Asian countries starting to find stability. The Vietnamese have developed a thriving economy, but as with most Asians they are very much into family units producing together. They are used to selling via village markets and some of the business types will buy and sell to other consumers, but it is what westerners call a cottage industry.

The terrible past with their years of war including the Chinese pre bible times about 200 BC and the French and the Americans has been overcome and the country is recovering to a strong family/tribal type economy. The fact that they are a communist country loses its negativity as they like China, seem to be embracing a more modest approach to communism.

One of the many industries that are growing fast is fish bred and grown in underground home fishery tanks. The whole process is quite amazing, the entire family is involved and the cycle of growing and harvesting is all well controlled, but it seems only Asians could run such an industry successfully. We dread to think just how bad the arthritis will be after some years of sleeping eating and living on top of their fish tanks. The process reminded us of Europe in cold snowy weather when the animals live inside during the winter, the houses smell dreadful, even though the floors are covered with straw and changed daily.

All of the South East Asian communities need to be more critically controlled by their Govt! This region nicknamed the Tiger economies because of their aggressive business approach; and ability to recover from a serious downturn, that could have been very serious throughout the South Pacific including Australia and New Zealand, had they not quickly recovered like they did. The need for more Govt; overview is not meant as in to interfere, what we mean is more help on an international level. The need to assist in the recovery from the past disadvantages is needed, so that the obstacles from the past are cleared. Then the way ahead will be clear and even further improved financing methods become relevant to the present. The recent past finance methods have quickly become irrelevant as the worlds wealth shifts; from the developed countries to China and the Oil rich states. The developed nations have got to stem the negative flow and as quickly as possible reverse the trend, if they don't they will be over taken by China and Russia. This refers to financial affairs; none can over take America in their military or Space knowledge.

Indonesia has suffered from the colonial regime of the Dutch, which was replaced by the corrupt Suharto regime that created a big vacuum in the treasury. The strong man Suharto and his nepotistic regime have created a big poor country with a huge population that suffers still from the Suharto's families criminal activities. This is the biggest Muslim country in the world, and is the type of country we have referred to when we suggest Muslim Petro Dollars, should be used to modify and create business opportunity for Muslim's. Indonesia is quite well endowed with minerals, but the World Bank's historically have refused to provide finance for business development. The reason that was given for the refusal to back those entrepreneur's; who wanted to invest in Indonesia, was the poor work ethics of the Muslim peoples, which created too much risk for the Australian banks.

This is why the Petro Dollars need to be directed towards business opportunities in this big undeveloped country, there are many great opportunities that cannot be taken up because of lack of money. The Indonesians have the expertise and can see the opportunities themselves, they lack the money to invest, but they would if they could. The problem is that as the world moves to clean coal for example, the amount of money needed to develop and sell coal increases greatly; none of the costs can be absorbed by cash flow because there is none. This is just a small example of how Petro Dollars should be used as risk capital, for their own religious brethren, and it is seriously wrong when that money is offered to the west. The west won't invest there, the only ones that are there are those that were there from Dutch Colonial times, and they are taking out as much as they can, just as they did when the Dutch were in charge.

Cambodia a great country of the past, is another country that could use Petro Dollars, but they are Buddhists and still outside western guidelines. The communist madman and his regime murdered these wonderful people in their millions, and was never bought to trial. We know this is not a Muslim country so Petro Dollars have no incentive to support them, but it is an area that is in dire need of help.

Laos, Burma, Malaysia, the Philippines, Thailand, Timor and Brunei, these are all countries that could do with Petro Dollars, they are a mixture of religions but they could benefit greatly from help from Petro Dollars. They have proved their viability in the past so are reliable investment propositions for the future even without the proposed group formation we herein propose.

JAPAN AND RUSSIA:

The fear of China's future influence in the South Pacific pervades all of the adjacent nations, including Japan and Korea. It would be a disaster for Japan; if China should get a very strong trade hold on the South Pacific, Japan has no minerals and is why that country needs free trade relations; minerals were after all what Japan was fighting for in WW11. Unfortunately the brutality and excessive killing by the Japanese has created bad memories; and now could put them in a tight position if China moves to ever greater heights of dominance. The countries of the New World led by America have tended to forget Japanese brutality, but one wonders if this may be partly because the Americans dropped two Atomic bombs on them to finish WW11 in the Pacific?

Because of the accrued hatred between the two countries, China would find it difficult not to exact revenge. The fact that the Japanese killed over twenty million in China and Manchuria before WW11; presumably eliminates Japan from any alliance which includes China in the near future. The Japanese perpetrators of the horrors they committed in China, Nanking and Manchuria, are eulogized as National Heroes in Japan; which gives an insight into the Japanese mindset. If we consider the War Trials at Nuremberg that finished with the top Nazi's being hung, then think of the Japanese praising up the murderers in their midst, we can only ask why this is? Apparently the Japanese have wiped the records of their atrocities from their school books, so their young are ignorant of their parent's misdeeds in the 1930-45 periods. They have not wiped out the American atom bombs from their records though! It is true many of us see the killing from the American Atom Bombs as some retribution, for what the Jap's did and for which they have never apologized too.

Similarly Japan has bad relations with Russia, these countries' fought a war, and they still argue over who owns the islands off the coast of Japan. The Russian problems are mere bagatelle though, it is just indicative of the poor relations Japan has in South East Asia, China and Russia. Korea is not well disposed towards Japan either, again from past military experience with the Japanese warrior system. Japanese think of the Koreans as less than human, and have demonstrated this repeatedly in their disrespect for the Koreans! The Samurai background of Japan, which teaches the Japanese they are superior to all others, is deeply imbedded in the Japanese self image. This possibly may have been correct up until Pearl Harbor it's not now, and the time has come when the Japanese will have to accept that reality, and be responsible for their brutal past. If the Americans had not supported the Japanese the way they did, financially after the war the Japanese and the Germans would not have reached the pre eminence they have done. The Americans had refused the Japanese the minerals and financial releases, they requested before Pearl Harbor, yet at the end of the war they gave them everything they needed, too rebuild. The Americans did what they did to help build bulwarks against the communists in the South and the West; they knew both countries were immune to communist intrigue.

The Japanese are always a force to be recognized, but are universally hated they are not even respected. We say this in spite of their achievements in lifting themselves up to such a high economic success; the future will not respect them just because of money. They need to share the wealth worldwide which doesn't appear to be the Japanese idea of a good thought which is hardly surprising. It is interesting to note that in 1990 or there about, the top five banks out of the world's top 100 were Japanese, the fact they were carrying a massive amount of over leveraged lending gives an indication of Japanese logic. All of their funding was internal and as at then severely over leveraged, this is part of the reason for the stagnation in their economy that has plagued that country for over a generation. There is no indication yet as to how well the Japanese will finally come out of the doldrums, but there is no sympathy for them worldwide; they are still a hated race of people. Sadly money hides all things even the horrific past of Japan!

There needs to be no mistakes or misunderstanding, China is still very much a Communist country, but the pragmatic Chinese have come to know they must be part of the real world. One of the big problems between the Asian and the Western worlds is the method of negotiation. The Asians want to deal on a very personalized basis, the first priority is to gain the confidence of their opposite number, this can be a slow process, but the Asian mind is very patient, The Westerner wants to negotiate and get it all down on paper, so that the notes can be transposed into a legal agreement. Westerners are impulsive, the Asian mind is not, they will feed their opposite numbers with scrumptious dinners, then sit and talk all day and night, but in the end get no where they are quite happy to do that day in and day out till they get what they want. If they have a strong hand they will sit forever, they are too polite to say no, they will just sit and tire their negotiators out.

The Chinese people are unique, there is not only a hell of a lot of them, but they are able to be controlled by their leaders. Chiang ki Shek and Mao tse Tung confirmed how malleable they are as a race! But more accurately their ancient past and servility to the Emperors, most of whom had little compunction to lop of heads, shows just how servile they are? Having said that we also know just how their sheer numbers can easily create domination if used properly! This seems to be the case now as the Chinese communist leaders show, how much they are prepared to cut through red tape to expedite; quick membership to the WTO. We believe they will be just as quick to accept other world organizations, what this does is shows their confidence to compete in all arenas, without a lot of contract red tape.

There are often surprises in store when the Westerner thinks they have a deal, and the Chinese think they are starting to make progress towards a possible future agreement. When it becomes obvious that there is a long way to go the Westerners tend to get off balance, this is so obvious that now the Chinese deliberately use this impatience to their own benefit. After many years of dealing with Diaspora Chinese we know how unflappable they are, but from a westerns point of view how utterly frustrating. The writer has spent many frustrating days and eaten many multi course dinners, before finally getting some progress to an agreement. The Chinese thrive on such an approach, as a westerner used to western style business we found their approach frustrating, but we learned and in the end got better. What we did was make it obvious how much we were enjoying ourselves eating so much free food, and we pretended we were happy to eat free food for ever. In the end if one looks very relaxed they succumb, but one must never show impatience, if you do you lose? We have sold to the Chinese for years they are great, because you get used to them and the food is great.

The Russians have been a much maligned population, but Stalin was the worst of all to his people, he almost equaled the Japanese and the Germans in his huge number of atrocities. There has been a chequered past under the Tsars for Russian's, with their sometimes colorful Tsars being memories from the past. Russia is a vast country, there is the frozen wastes of Siberia, now the source of its oil revenues that seem substantial. There is the great plains of central Russia which has the agricultural potential that will someday be realized. The economy of Russia has always been predominately a Dictatorship which is why Stalin was able to get away with what he did, the people were conditioned to disasters and he took full advantage.

Strangely Russia had been developing a very successful middle class known as Kulaks, but Stalin in his madness was determined to wipe them out as a class. They were murdered in their millions for the ideal of a single class, which was what communism was supposed to create. Historically Russia didn't seem to develop along the Western model they seem more Asian, but if and when they do find a way through to develop properly, theirs will be a massive economy. They are very mixed ethnic peoples, but they include the Slavs; and in them they have extremely good workers if they are given a chance.

In spite of the determined effort of communism to wipe out the church, now that, communism is gone the church is coming back out into the open; as strong as ever. The Orthodox Catholic Church reign's supreme in Russia, and all up through Northern Europe, this is quite different from the Roman Catholic Church. The Orthodox Priests were never as aggressive for material wealth; as the Roman church has been through the ages, and still is, but the Muslims seems to have trimmed all religions back as they have grown so fast worldwide.

The communist theory was taught by Karl Marx and his disciple Lenin who were both Jews, but experience has proved that, that type of system cannot work. Even the malleable Chinese have had to modify their approach having found the Govt; cannot be the sole arbiter of human control or effort. When the state contrived to develop a system that guarantees a life from birth to the grave, they took away motivation and developed a type of laziness that was all pervasive. In simple terms the people came to think they need do nothing from birth to the grave, because the state would do everything. Unfortunately what was proved was that such a system created fear from birth to the grave, from the very top there was a constant fear of subversion of one's position in Govt; and the Beauracracy. Stalin ruled by fear but he also lived in fear, both were very real in practice. In such a system one does not know who is plotting to take away the others power, and one needs to be careful at all times what one says or does, life is cheap and one can very easily be the next for execution!

Stalin was the complete ruler by fear, he killed the Kulaks so their lands could be shared out with the peasants under Govt; control, but it also scared hell out of the peasants so they would always be too scared to rebel. He killed his peers in the Govt; again it seemed indiscriminately, but in fact as usual he promoted fear again. The end result was everybody was in fear even Stalin himself. President Roosevelt at Potsdam when the big three met at the near end of WW11 could not really understand Stalin, but he thought he did. Roosevelt was dealing with a mass murderer who was a total cynic, there was no way there could be a meeting of minds, but the American President Roosevelt really tried.

THE NEW WORLD:

The New World to us refers to North America including Canada, Australia and New Zealand; all of these countries have a strong Anglo Saxon background. All were originally settled from the UK. But America soon rebelled and formed their Republic of The United States of America! The rapid growth of the United States led to the civil war, that was won by the Union Army and the future of the country as one country was assured. America the New World attracted immigrants from all over the world; and they were the best class of people looking for opportunity they didn't have at home. The old world taboos were left behind, in the New World everything was possible; and that openness applied in every facet of private and public life. There have been problems such as exposure to criminal elements, the constitution sometime seems to favor the criminals, but the legal system is as fair as can be in spite of some loop holes.

America has become the richest country in the world, we refer here to the infra structure and the military. The financial situation worldwide is now problematic, and it would be difficult to stipulate the strongest currency, although the dollar is still accepted as the strongest. The two world wars bought the USA to full strength and exhausted the pound sterling, the Yen and the Euro are strong currencies, but the Chinese Yuan will when and if it is left to float freely will become strong. The Native peoples so called Red Indians were decimated but have survived and are gaining in numerical strength and rights federally.

Canada to the North of the American continent is often mixed up as just another State of its giant neighbor to the South. Canada is a Monarchy and a strong member of the English Commonwealth! Canada had strong French links and one of its states Quebec, at one stage wanted to secede from the commonwealth. Canada is a huge country but has very hard weather conditions, the Northern states are ice bound in the winter, and the

Australia has never had anything but a Capitalist come Socialist society because her history is only a short period of 220 odd years, and has never been subjected to the economic theories of the past. Australia's first immigrants were criminals from the jails of London, deported to NSW. Since some were convicted of the heinous crimes of stealing a few vegetables to feed their families, it is difficult to know just how bad these convicts were. NSW was with Tasmania the only States that were so blessed with convicts and thus free labor. The real sufferers from the new immigrants seemed to have been the Aborigines, who were treated as vermin that could be, and were killed with impunity. The Aborigines had only a foraging culture, the land was so big they just moved from place to place within certain tribal barriers. The English when they took the country into its Empire, declared the country as having no human habitation, the Aborigines were thought of as a type of animal.

The Australians and the New Zealanders with their island neighbors must be in a trade agreement led by the Americans, if only because of their predominant ethnic Anglo mix, but more properly because they fit. The Australian Continent and its rich mineral resources would make it a valuable contributor to any common trade agreement with America, but it would be good contributors to any common market group. There is also the advantage of education and financial balance. Australia has proven to be strong in spite of the earlier Asian melt down, and at present is still functioning well; in spite of world economic weakness.

New Zealand like Australia was first found and claimed for England by James Cook in 1769, but in that case note was taken that there were native occupiers. Able Tasman (Dutch) first visited the Country in 1642 and he sailed away apparently not liking the sight of vicious looking Maoris; running around poking out their tongues with what appeared to them like carnivorous intent. Tasman sailed away but named the country Niew Zeland, he did not even bother to take botanical samples. After Cook the Settler's started to come out from England, and even some from Australia, probably escaping convicts from NSW. Like Australia there was a two party system now changed to a first past the post with a consolidated majority. NZ had been basically two parties, but had a brief flirtation with Canada's Social Credit political philosophy in 1965, that however was very short lived.

New Zealanders are far more conservative than Australians, but needs to move in tandem with Australia, for as much as the Kiwi's will resist too close a relationship with Australia, the time may come where there s little choice. The economy of NZ is too narrow and its heavy reliance on agriculture and grazing of farm animals has been proven to be weak in the past. The English move into the European Common Market and the loss of markets for its lamb to France, caused NZ a long period of stagnation, it has since got back on track, but the knife's edge was/is fine.

The Pacific Islands will have difficulties as their small economies which are poised so thinly, will be difficult to be able to cost down too ie; reduce the gross production costs. This is why they will have to link with Australia and NZ first and help increase the total GDP as a full pacific grouping. Fiji with its tourist economy may hold up quite well, and its third party production lines may help, but that is problematic. As we see the structure if NZ and the Pacific Islands have a free trade agreement with Australia. Australia will be in the Free trade agreement with the American free trade group.

ISRAEL, MIDDLE EAST & ISLAM:

The Middle East or as it is known in the bible "The Promised Land" is unique in history, it is the land promised by God to the Israelites, way back when Abraham first left his home with his Father and Lot his Nephew just to name a few. God promised Abraham he would be the father of nations, and that he would bring his people to a new home; in the Promised Land.

God told Moses he wasn't going to enter the Promised Land because he had struck the rock when he was looking for water twice, once in anger and this anger had annoyed God. For this reason he would not be allowed to go in with the people, when they entered the Promised Land. God had named Joseph as the successor of Moses and his job was to lead his people over the Jordan River to take over that Promised Land. There were certain restrictions the main one being that he would destroy all of the current inhabitants; because they were so deep in sin, and God did not want his people to become polluted by mixing with them. The story is that Joseph didn't obey God in this and that why the descendants of those left alive, have been there to create so much trouble over the millennia. Right from the start there were problems that plagued Gods' immigrants, the first battle of Jericho was to plan, but the destruction of the Village of Ai was disaster as a family, had to be destroyed for disobedience. Then came the villagers that bluffed their way into servitude to the Jews by claiming to come from afar, and Joseph agreed they could stay. We need not go any further we don't have the space, and this is not the place to discuss Joseph and his leadership in more depth.

The Jews returned to Israel in 1948 when the English relinquished their Israel UN mandate in the face of so many problems. There was a violent reaction from the surrounding Arab Nations that remain hostile until this day, but there is little they have been able to do. The financial support the Israeli Jews have had; and will keep receiving from their many foreign compatriots. (Diaspora) This support is worldwide and will continue, the Israeli Jews are the hammerhead for the advance (creation of Gods' way) and creation of a new system, and they will be in the front line of whatever happens; they have no choice it is their destiny! The six day war that so humiliated the Arabs is still a very fresh memory and one wanders just what would happen if another full scale war were to be initiated now. The West Bank was secured during the short war and there has been fighting in the area ever since. The PLO which was led originally by Yasser Arafat has been unable to arrive at mutual terms with the Israeli Govt; but it's easy to assume there is no real interest in arriving at terms; unless those terms are very much in favor of the Jewish Nation.

The sad truth is we now have the Arabs who as members of the PLO are locked into an untenable situation that is very bad, they have not been able to achieve their goals, and that was to get back Jerusalem and the West Bank. The expansion of the Jewish settlements in Israel including the West Bank; which has exercised many minds in trying to graft a solution together has so far been a grid lock. The interference of Jordan, Syria, and Iran has so far only created more problems; that may eventually create the third world war, but there will be no back down on the Israeli support from abroad. The massive accumulation of funds by the oil rich countries, will never be strong enough to create a force strong enough to destroy Israel; the God given home of the Jews.

The Hamas won the last election quite decisively, and that put that organization at the head of attempts to restore to the Palestinians, claimed land on the West Bank. So far all that has happened is increased confrontation between Hamas and the Jews; the cry of triumph when the Jewish military could not drive Hamas out of anywhere, including the Lebanon was echoed as a success for Hamas. It would seem to us the result is more that the Jewish military needs to be upgraded; and they undoubtedly will be, direct from America? There have been several major events shaping modern Israel, and this situation will continue until the return of Jesus Christ, remember Jesus was a Jew, he will return through them and he will be one of them? His future and his return will be quiet, he will come quietly as he did before and just appear to us, the world is not ready for him yet but it is getting closer. When Jesus Christ does return it will not finish up as him being sacrificed again, he will return in triumph to take over his rightful place; as world leader. The Muslim countries that are most adversarial towards Israel are, Iran (Persia) Syria, Jordan, and Pakistan, the possible future enemies would be Iraqi, Kuwait, Saudi Arabia, and Egypt and Indonesia etc. These possible countries are ones that have commercial or links with America and may not join in any action against Israel, but there is a large Muslim population in these countries that may not be so passive.

The past has been a long period of punishment and sacrifice for all Jews it will continue to be as volatile as ever until the return of Christ and for a while after. It is ordained that Israel will be the continuing centre of fighting as the Arabs try to evict them, but this will be at the Arabs own cost. Unfortunately both the Jews and the Arabs are so very hard headed and self destructive, but this cannot continue indefinitely there has to come a time when a new homeland for the Palestinians is provided. This will have to be in an area other than Israel because there is no way the Arabs will get the Jews out, so the other Arabs will have to find a new homeland for their Palestinian comrades.

There remains much to be understood, concerning the future financial stability of the Oil states, because of the concentrated international effort to find alternatives that is green house gas neutral. In fact there is no way the future flow of Petro Dollars will remain as strong as they are now this is a direct consequence of global warming. This time the resistance is not just price, the big motivation is global, and the goal is to reduce the effect of noxious gas emissions globally. This is global and the resistance worldwide creates a financial effect that is not yet understood, but will control future price hikes such as has happened in the past. The oil after all is God given, the wealth is there and has been extracted with little effort by the lucky countries, but that wealth can just as easily be taken away or reduced. For example if the U.S. does continue to revert to alternative fuels especially nuclear, and the change is successful, there is no reason why they shouldn't succeed, demand will drop dramatically? There is also the other sources such as clean oil, etc! If in total the effect is a drop in demand even as little as 20% as could be the case, then there will be an aggravated drop in value. This drop in value will affect the conditions in the oil countries, especially those who have not got an alternative income source. Not only will the price drop as a result of less demand, but the futures market will collapse?

Countries such as Venezuela that have used their oil revenues as political weapons, and not built into their cash credits an alternative source of income will be in difficulty. Moreover if they have not strengthened their infrastructure to be able to move on and take their countries in new direction post oil, they will be further disadvantaged. This is not a Muslim country we merely quote them as an example, that needs to be a warning to those who would ignore the long term consequences of poor integrity at top level. This scenario is the greatest threat to world peace on the horizon; religion is just a smoke screen! The real reason is bad management by the countries of Islam and they will blame everyone but themselves! They have had a period of excessive affluence; but they have messed up, they were supposed to make their money work as the developed nations have done, but they have not? The conflagration that is on the horizon will be severe and will be blamed on religion, and to a limited extent that may be true, but if we look at the real facts religion has nothing to do with it? The power that comes with a lot of money has thrown the oil countries into future turmoil what should have been a blessing may one day turn out to be a curse?. Power is like a drug has had financial power the Arab countries are no different than the Baby Boomers in the developed countries. Both didn't have knowledge to use their money wisely, and the oil barons are the same they will all pay for their lack of knowledge. This is a replay of when the Moors were driven out of Iberia! The Jews had to be used to create financial stability for the Moors then, the relationship worked well then why not again?

Again the bible tells us, 'for my people die from lack of knowledge,' and we would add, for greed and money is the child of all evil, use both appropriately else the future will be bleak indeed. That is the wisdom of God is it not? Both the Jews and the Chinese are good with money, so what is the end solution he has for this world?

SUMMARY: OF THE COUNTRIES:

The differences between East and West are very stark in the character of their peoples, ie the 'Asian and the Westerner' but in the overall living standards and cultural structures the differences are slight. The biggest difference is in the density of the peoples the Roman Empire at its peak had a total population of 70 million people. But China alone over one hundred and fifty years ago had over 100 million people in its own country. The spread was very wide and the cultural differences were also huge! The Germans and the English for example are of common stock, the Barbarian tribes from the west are common to the Anglo Saxon bloods, and this includes the Germanic Tribes.

The control structure is also a common denominator, with the land being owned by the Aristocracy or the Church and the commoner having little say in their future; or indeed in their everyday lives. Here the Asian and the Westerner are identical!

There was no way that one born as a commoner could elevate themselves above the stature in life to which they are born, which is a reality that survives in the European cultures right up to the present, again Asian and Westerner are the same. The reason the New World countries especially America has flourished, is they have drawn the better quality peoples from the Old World including Asia, and given them opportunities they could never have dreamed of at home.

The Eastern world or in general also the Asians were/are similar in structure, with the peasants having little chance to rise above their place in life. The difference seems to be the lack of respect for human rights, and that applies right up to the present day. Probably because of their huge populations to the Western mind the Asian seem oblivious to human rights, and life can be stamped out like a moth burned in a light. This is especially hard for the New World citizens to comprehend; and creates a fear for all things Asian, but especially Chinese. The Japanese have created a nitch of their own in that their brutality is well documented and they are disliked, but time seems to be mending the rift in western minds anyhow?

Religion and its domination of the human spirit has been the reality that has kept mankind in bondage, through lack of knowledge and at certain stages, just plain cruelty as can be instanced by the Roman Catholic Inquisition. Spain in particular must be considered with some abhorrence for this period of human devastation. One can only wonder if the cruelty of the Spanish; could have been in some way reflected by the Catholic success at driving out the Moorish Muslims. From our reading the Moors were better people than the Catholics were anyhow!

But there have been differing times in all countries and all religions were intolerance and religious persecution has gone hand in hand. Again the New World has led the way in creating freedom to all peoples of all colors and creeds. Admittedly the freedom of the native races and the blacks has been a little backward in happening, but it is happening.

It will be interesting to see if it is possible to one day see religious tolerance for all prevail. Our own thoughts are that first will have to come more education! Only enlightenment will free the spirit and set the people free, and that can only come through knowledge and understanding!

Chapter 3

Money in Practice: Sept 2008.

This chapter is quoted in small numbers say 'one being the active number,' it has been done like this so those with no money knowledge, don't have to be frightened off reading it fully. Some people just because the numbers if extrapolated properly could frighten them off and cause others just too lock up their minds and say this is bulldust. If you would like to get a more specific feel of just how enormous the threat is to the worlds money system, you just need to multiply the simple explanation near the chapters end by say one hundred million times, then for those with a feel for numbers the enormity of the problem is frightening.

It's all like the black hole in space scientist's refer to when they talk about deep space, and like the universe is the orphan of the back hole, the subject of money which will soon be the orphan of Capitalism, is hard to comprehend if put in serious numbers. If you do read and expand the numbers don't worry it's really just a fact of life, what needs to be worried about is the understanding if you do get what we are saying. Just how far the modern world has developed the modern financial systems into an attack on God's teaching, and the effect it will have on Capitalism very soon. The Jews always suffered when they were in deep Sin such as the world is now, and why should the punishment be restricted to the Jews, they have done what we Christians wanted.

In 1929 the world's financial system collapsed and we had a depression worldwide, it took the next 5 - 6 years for the world to show signs of recovery, and WW11 to see the depression really finished. WWI had been a serious disruption of the financial system, the allies had defeated the axis powers, and the repatriation payments levied on Germany had created very difficult conditions in that country? America became a major financial force, but all financial systems then become victims of the depression. Here is a simple example of a study of a Real Estate property in Auckland NZ post depression:

In 1950 a nice home in Auckland city with a well situated block of land was bought for $10,000. The land was valued at $4,000 40% of the value and the house on it $6,000 60% of the value? That same home in the year 2005 after it had been re-valued was sold for $400,000, so growth in value was $390,000, over that 55 year period?

Now let's look at just how those values and costs have been changed within our demand economy all we still have is a simple suburban house. We (The Owners) are now 75 years of age and the house is debt free, it has cost us all up including interest $10,200 and in 2006 the value was $400,000.

The biggest growth has been created via inflation, financial institutional costs, direct and indirect taxation and costs was all that had added to the value. The money to pay for this home from the income of an average worker, who would want this class of home was in 1950 1.2 years of the total gross income, but in 2006 it would take 14 years to pay for the house out of gross income.

The above is just a simple break up, it is not designed as a professional summary, the intent is to show just how the financial taxes and add on costs, have grown and eroded the ordinary persons net income position. This is for those in the new world with ambitions to own their homes.

Now let's have a simple look at how those money changes, have created the artificial position we now have, also related to the position at year's end 1950 & 2005. We have a home that we bought in 1950, and had no debt. We are not computer literate, so we have no access to any search engines etc; to keep up to date with money affairs. We are financially illiterate but we want to do the best we can for our children. Our children are up to 52 YOA and are also poorly versed in computer usage. None of the children have ever been in business so are like their parents, not well versed in modern technology.

In general there is a plethora of so called experts trying to get us to invest in various blue chip and other financial opportunities by borrowing money on our home. What should we be doing? What will be best for our Son, daughter, and four Grandchildren? This has become a very common situation with many families as the parents grow old. Professional advisors have had a wonderful time earning large fees for many years, as people with good equity in their homes, have been pursued to borrow money on those houses, and invest that money in equities?

An army of financial advisors, legal advisors, banks etc; have been created, these are there to help people to use their assets to borrow money. Over the years there is a growing army of investors, who had never done anything speculative in their lives, they are now entering the money markets encouraged by professionals with vested interests! Speculation by investment banks, banks, insurance companies etc; have created a huge investment industry that are the vehicles used to cash out (leverage up) these home assets, and use the money released! The problem is that this lack of knowledge allowed the advisors of whatever ilk to profit disproportionately, the higher up the chain we go the bigger the profits paid to professionals. Paper profits have been transposed into cash bonuses to many sales people and others, who have been the ones actually writing and selling contracts?

Let's try and explain by using another simple flow sequence. Many home owners as the years have gone by have a large equity in those homes. They have been encouraged by professionals to borrow and invest. In fact in America 74% of the population who own their homes have been persuaded to borrow as much as they can and then invest in businesses etc.

The professional earns a fee for directing their clients to invest in various funds proposals. Several other professionals become involved as loans are arranged, and investments are made, all earn fees?

The bank uses money it has borrowed, to lend against the real estate asset this money, which the home owner receives then spends into investments through, again another set of professionals. The bank earns a profit on the loan it has made to the owners by way of fees and interest, and it is implicit in the borrowers investments, since the banks often act as advisors. This is in spite of the banks having vested interest to sell the money invested, because they get commissions and kick backs.

The investment money recipients now use the money on the markets or in its own business. The money may go into many different areas of investment, Shares, Bonds, Options and many other exotic methods of using money. Whatever methods are used to invest the money, there are fees charged and bonuses earned?

There are ways of increasing the value of the money that has been used such as leverage. If there is an investment of $10,000 that may be leveraged, margined (multiplied) etc; up to thirty five times so that $10,000 has now become up to $350,000 for investment purposes. This depends on what type of investment is chosen, and the risk the investor is prepared to take. It's the lack of understanding that is the danger, not that they have not been advised. Greed over comes fear and the apparent bubble may never burst, the profits investors think will forever flow. But sadly Gods book of instructions has warned us all and what he wants us to do is take him seriously and react as we should, and repent these financial sins.

INVESTMENT BANKS, BANKS

INSURANCE ETC:

Banks with a large customer base may have funds they have got on deposit at low cost from their many clients. The bank may have a lot of loans (to home buyers) that it has bought at a certain rate of interest, and the ratio of their loans will be based on a percentage of the valuation they have got from their valuers? Let's assume on these funds the interest paid to the account holders is 2%, and they get from the borrower 7% the spread (profit) is 5%?

They may bundle (sometimes) up those loans and sell them off to bond operators and underwriters, and their (banks) will discount the interest rate or earnings so there is a margin of profit for the buyers of the bonds.

Let's assume a bank has sold off $10M worth of their money into first rated mortgages and they want to cash them out. The average earning rate they have got on those loans is 5% but when they sell them off into bonds they accept only a 2% profit and the bond holders make 3% profit. Those are the agreements that give the money back to the banks so they can sell more mortgages.

The funny thing is the buyers of that bond may be the Investment bank, in which the owner of the original home invested their borrowed money. So is that a circle seems like it is to us? The original owners borrow the money and pays fees to advisor, lawyer, bank, these are the costs. The banks make a profit, the bonds are supposed to make a profit where do those profits come from?

The dealers and brokers trade in so many exotic programs, Currency, Bonds, Derivatives, Options, Shares etc; that's what these big investment houses do they gamble with that money that came from the houses? Just imagine not one house but millions of houses and it's obvious how big these funds have become, but in reality there is nothing there to back them only paper money, in other words Fiat Money?

We need to remember we are making a profit on our house too, because if we assume 3% inflation our home is increasing in value so we are happy as well. To cover the risk the investment bank will spread their investments say 25% real estate, 35% blue chip shares, 20% currency and 20% cash. They may with your permission invest in assets they can margin, or create say a 15 to one margin. This is mainly done in currency trading which can be very dangerous!

If the earnings average is say 15% and the cost of money has been 7% the profits can be huge. If on top of that we can factor in the inflation rate it's all wonderful. What if the cycle goes wrong and instead of inflation we have deflation? It depends on the various economies, if we were looking at 1950 each country's economy was fairly independent, and each reserve bank could manipulate fairly well its own money supply. But now we speak of the World Economy and money is being manipulated at the behest of the major economies in other words Fiat money is being created at the behest of others because the economies are now interdependent.

IN 2002 we thought it all sounded great so as our advisor suggested we borrowed $270,000 with our debt free property as security, and we invested the money also as advised. The housing loan was interest only!

YEAR Y/E 30ᵀᴴ JUNE 2006-7:

We had a net investment income after tax of $90,006

YEAR Y/E 30ᵀᴴ JUNE 2007-8

We had a net investment loss of $142,080, and we had no tax write off.

We still have our property and the block of land is big enough that if we had to we could grow enough fruit, vegetables, chickens and eggs to feed ourselves, but our loan has to be serviced and we are now pensioners, so things look bad? Unless of course our brilliant politicians can fix things for us all?

Many countries in 2005 are interdependent on others and the USA as the engine of commerce is in the forefront. That is changing as the European currency strengthens, (Euro) and China becomes a big producer and creditor to the world? There are countries that aren't wallowing with a mountain of potential disasters within their populations, the ones much at risk are America, Canada, Australia and New Zealand. Be assured there is no way Bush, Obama or anybody else can talk their way out of this lot, they have to find a way to work it out, even the trillion dollar loans spent to save the banks is just a simple band aid. A full cast will soon be needed unless Obama creates a miracle, lets wish him well as he tries to create his first miracle, he will need to produce many more, over the next four years?

As the world contracts there becomes interdependency; and since the USA has been sucking in all of the surplus cash from various country's through its treasury bonds, there is a greater than ever dependency on the American economic stability?

If a 1929 style Great Depression should occur, the values of homes that have been refinanced (Interest only) for money to reinvest will drop; the loans will then be far higher than what the homes are worth, even worse than they are now. Far more ominously is the investments that are now at risk, this is the area that can make or break the near future of the world's finances? Where ever the loans are now held, (investments) they are not what they were originally worth. This means that the investments are now a problem, (ie) like the homes that back them, not worth what they cost, and getting cheaper daily.

This is what has happened to our own investments in the last two years shown above there isn't enough to pay the loans interest only, so what do we do now? Of course we can reduce the margin loans, but even then there won't be enough to service the loan. We can hang out for say two years on savings, but what after that, our pension isn't going to pay for much!

If the USA through its political and financial structure should falter, there would be a worldwide reaction. There would be a sharp reaction in the money markets because of the toxic effect of the overvalued assets held by financial institutions? Incomes will contract and the ability of owners to service their loans will be in jeopardy, because their investments may be in trouble and possibly may not pay the dividends? In other words there will be a cascading effect with none performance all round.

Because banks write off the full value of none performing loans, the effect could/would be catastrophic? This is the real danger to the Capital system of the West, but it's not new just variations. The Roman Empire foundered because its system also failed, but in that case it was a long and lingering failure, from Nero to the end was about 1,350 years. This time it is the world that is at risk but human ingenuity will prevail, and a new system will be created it is only a matter of time. The wealthy nations are going to combine, and in a classic Capitalistic maneuver try to trade out of this massive financial disaster, and it may work one more time.

It is however inevitable Capitalism is on the way to failure, it is only a matter of time. If once again the politicians find a way to rescue the capitalists, there will be another round of corporate risk and human greed, but the next round if there is one will, be shorter and more devastating.

China has reduced its investments in US Treasury Bonds this year to only 5% of the previous year and it wants guarantees for the money. China hasn't yet built its infrastructure so that it has its internal markets in place; it needs another ten years, so does Russia and India?

The world is interdependent as long as there is an economy that is running debtor accounts such as the USA, but once the other nations or the creditor nations convert from export to internal sales, what happens then?

China needs another ten years to build its infrastructure then its own population will consume all they can produce. America, Russia, India could all produce all they need to feed their peoples, so is the future one of isolation who knows? What we do know is there must be a world of common markets if the world is to avoid control by one of the future super powers. Let's be honest America is broke and getting further behind daily.

We hear talk of gold being the salvation of the money system, but how can that be? If the Fiat money is so debased then the conversion rate is relevant. If we assume gold is going to rise to USD2, 000 per ounce, but what will the USD be worth by then 50 cents?

We remember the Roman Emperors starting with Nero who were debasing their currency against the original value, but that took them over 1,350 years to achieve.

Historically Worldwide the peasants were the only ones that could feed the people, under the many and varied world agricultural systems, over the millennia. The only answer is food, we cannot eat gold and we cannot trade it, if there is no money from speculators to buy gold, what is its real value?

Unless we can feed ourselves we will starve, there is many homes that could grow their own food, and the great thing about that there is no tax to pay on that income, because income it surely is.

Comments: Caution: these paragraphs are not meant to be an advisory service in any way, if it helps to create a little understanding, we have done what we want to do.

As we look forward we can see it coming; the collapse of the world's finances, but this won't be a lasting catastrophe, the world finances will eventually be able to weather the storm.

The creation of money in the different countries national banks will however create confusion as money freezes up and business stalls. During the restructure the losses will be very high but will be spread to the small investors, therefore not as obvious but still painful? Just as quickly as the mum and dad markets grew from nothing, now they will shrivel up and waste back to nothing. The loss spread will be very wide because small business will suffer badly. Big business and investment house will sink into mediocrity, and pension's funds will suffer severe losses? This is the serious area because this money is the people's retirement money; unfortunately unscrupulous fund managers care little for the Mums and Dads.

Only Government expenditure will be able to hold the various economies of the countries going into serious decline? The inter dependant link will now become very obvious to all and sundry. The Governments will work together, but the ones that come through with the least damage, will keep to their old selfish way and not help the weak? These are the ones who will be punished as God's will is ignored, all is revealed in his word.

Currency on the world markets: Many of the major world currencies are left to float on the open market; this means they arena't secured back to any type of security, the trading floors will decide the values? The market values will vary according to conditions in different countries, ie the factors that can affect a countries currency value are many, the annual gross domestic product, (GDP) labor outcomes, International Trade Balances, special events good or bad etc? The value will swing up or down against other currencies ie USD/Japanese Yen, currency trading is highly margined and very dangerous even in the hands of experts?

The previous times when in most cases a currency was pegged to the value of gold, countries reserves were denominated in the amount of gold held in its treasury, and the moving value of that gold. The currencies were said to be operating on the gold standard, and could be said to be gold backed. If we assume that we had AUD100, 000 back then when the Aussie Dollar was gold backed, we knew we owned $100,000 but that was backed by gold in the Australian Treasury. As it is now the money is backed by the Government, but has no security, (Fiat money) the value floats to what the currency market values it at. Inflation is the rate by which a country overall financial performance grows or not, after a certain period of time if that country fails to grow it is in recession. If it goes seriously in reverse it is in depression.

Options refer to taking out an option to buy shares in a company. Can in some case be an option to buy a house etc; an option may be agreed to buy most anything. It is a promise or a right to buy something under terms agreed by two or indeed several parties to the option.

The leaders speak about the value of money but money has been undermined, this is very obvious. As the money as set out above in the home example moves around, we the ordinary people can get into real trouble.

Chapter 4

Hope, Faith & Love

One cannot please the lord without an active faith. Faith is the genesis of belief in God, but actions prove that Faith, which is active and pleasing to God. Let us give an example of Faith by expressing none Faith!

The prominent popular father has a bible from which he reads passages to his family, and then gives thanks before the evening meal. But apart from that daily bible reading there is nothing done the Bible is put away and not thought about. The family has no interest what so ever in bible study, and no member including Father understands what he reads, it is just a ritual. The only other time that families Bible is used is when it is carried to church again by their Father on Sunday just to show all of the other church members, just what a pious family we are as we all follow him and our Mother, with our heads suitably bowed into our church.

We sit near the front and all are suitably deferential at all times, because if we don't conform there will be a problem; just as soon as we get back home with Father, this is our none Faith in full view and totally detestable to God. We are not only showing our lack of Faith we are profaning a house of God, is this not sinful, well at least we know we are not walking in Faith. This is visual Faith designed to fool all our companions, but no we are not trying to fool God who is he?

You see we are taking deception into the church as do so many of our Peers it's all a great game, the children know how it works and keep to the rules. It's like they think gee Dad why are we here, the neighbors are all here look at them all lined up like chickens, just like us dad, now aint we good? See that Minister Bloke at the door he looks just as bored as we feel, he's the one that was out front yapping on about something a little while ago. We couldn't understand what he was raving on about; he was so boring why do we come, every Sunday, regular as clock work; and as boring as usual? We hate all of this nonsense, and Mum looks as if she is going to fall asleep, poor old Mum she works all day, and you never give her any peace give her a break why don't you, and hoi why do we have to be punished with all of your bulldust? That father is not doing the right thing his attitude is wrong, and the whole family follows his example and its all negative to God.

That's none Faith and Satan loves it all, he brings it into church and slowly but surely hate grows, but the Genesis of it all is Dad at the dinner table and at church. It's called hypocrisy and is what is destroying our Christian World and our worship! We have nice music to hear and the songs are quite good too specially if those females dress up like they do it's just great!

More importantly for the Nations and the World, this is moral decline and it has been accelerating for years. Most people in the Wealthy west if you ask them how their Faith is think you are referring to their Faith in themselves; they have no idea about Spiritual Faith, the real problem though is that they don't care. The lack of Spiritual Faith indicates a decline in National values, if it is prevalent among a majority of the population. The writer has travelled several countries asking people how their Spiritual Faith is, his small self run survey when he asked how your Faith is. And he always ensured his listeners understood what the question really was, the answers were quite interesting. It should be understood his many travels in America was as a Born Again Christian Missionary giving financial advice to small business people free of charge.

In America mainly among Catholics in eighteen different States including Utah Faith was quite strong and very encouraging, Fiji among Methodists very strong. New Zealand among mainly Presbyterians quite good, Australia among Born Again Christians quite good, but the general public didn't know what was meant, by Spiritual Faith. The Philippines Born Agains and Catholics very strong, the questions were not asked in the several none English speaking Countries he has travelled through, because his desire not to fool himself was strong. Countries in Europe such as Germany and France don't care to answer such a question to someone who does not speak their language. On the whole the Spiritual Faith was in better shape than expected, but had the survey included say Muslims and Hindus, which they were not, the answers may have been far stronger and positive.

The writer is himself very positive towards having a Faith filled Spirit, and tries hard to maintain his own Spiritual Health, but knows well that mental acuity does not replace humility in the search for healthy Faith. One can know the bible well but it has to be known in the heart, one must know immediately if what he/she is doing will please God. If one uses the Bible only as an attachment to display their Christian beliefs, then they are only indulging in self deception and they need to work harder on their own lives.

The basis of that ability to learn and improve is what will propel the self to inspiration, and understanding of God, to love God one must know God and to know God one must understand his word but not as a parrot. To know God one must feel his Spirit working from within, and so when one feels that he knows God truly from the heart, then that Faith is growing and the truth of Spiritual Faith is a victory for self. Then and only then can one have Faith that one has received blessings from God, without having to see the fruit of Faith, one just knows and will walk in the joy and security of God.

Is this a sermon on Faith you ask, no it is not, it is meant to indicate another area of change that must happen in the world as the Global Village concept grows. Spiritual Health is just as important as distribution of the world wealth, and the countries that will succeed in this concept of global cooperation must have all areas of need under control. Love is the vital ingredient to world unity, and there is a sequence of growth that helps achieve the goal. One cannot love self until one knows self this is self explanatory, but the many who don't know self is/are many and growing.

Since the world began there has been nothing but hate; and the ambition that propels hate to maturity, only when that hate is vanquished from the human persona can the peace of God find real root in mankind. Cain killed able in a fit of frustrated rage, his ambition had been to please God he failed! He failed because his heart was wrong when he gave his sacrifice, and because his heart was wrong his sacrifice was rejected. On the other hand Able gave with a good heart with the right attitude, he pleased God and his sacrifice was accepted. Cain then demonstrated his lack of Love etc; he killed his brother and so hate was victorious. We then have two examples of disobedience to Gods will right from the inception of mankind; we were right out of line from the very start.

The next vital ingredient on the path to Agape (God) Love is the love of God, this must rate before the love of self and Family, but again without self Love Agape love is impossible. Next there is Familial and Eros Love the love of Wife and Family finally the love of all including the instruction to Love thy enemy. Anybody can give love to friends and neighbors, but can we love all others that are the challenge is it not? Can we truly love our enemies or do we just pretend?

The ambition to love all good or bad if you have it, will come through the exercise of Spiritual Faith, Gods Spirit will abide within you and love will be assured. The American Founding Fathers when they wrote and approved the American Constitution, knew this well and is why they shaped that document the way they did, this is also why the American State has prospered the way it has. Over the years many abominations have prospered by abusing the civil rights in that American Constitution, one notable example is the Mafia; in spite of the destruction they have spread, they have survived and prospered. Many solid businesses were started with Mafia money and are now strictly law abiding, again the writer refers to his own experience, while resident in New York and Orange County California.

The reason America will continue to flourish is because they have a strong Godly base; that over comes the problems, any country that has achieved what America has, and retained its basic character can be proud of its accomplishments. Russia and China are at a stage of development now that America was back in the early 20s rife with corruption etc. The difference for those two new adherents to the Semi Capitalist growth and to freeing up their economy is they don't have the basic constitution to control the negative influences, that's why we refer to them as the countries to the North of Jerusalem. We need to be clear here we don't know where the North really is, but we do know the negative reality of those two countries as they try to overtake the USA, frankly there is no chance of that happening, but they may do it temporarily while the USA finds its way to the necessary transition, of a new path forward.

Once having found the entrance to the narrow gate of Spiritual Faith, and all other changes needed to convert to a world system compatible with God's will, the four Common Market Groups will be on the path to unity. World Govt; will not interfere with an individual countries independence what will happen is world Govt; will operate like the Federal Govt, but more restricted to central world issues. America, Australia and Canada with their individual States will still have a Federal Govt; but the special issues as noted will be seconded, to World Govt proto cols; which will control the issues that are strictly for International unification. The levels of govt; currently at the State or Provincial levels will be modified, but only to accommodate the World Govt; in proper cooperation to world needs.

The theories as being espoused herein will be quite easy to accommodate within an open society, but one that is even slightly closed, will struggle to conform. A closed society does not easily change even if it wants too, because it must control its population in general; and that type of administration does not develop suddenly into an open society. The Citizen's will find the change to unified effort hard to accept, until they have had time to understand, and that will only happen with the cooperation of their elected leaders?

New Zealand, which has a very small population and has learned how to assimilate with its native race, is an open society par excellence. It has provinces and only two levels of govt; national and local councils this is one country that because it is so open, will have little trouble to adjust. The small highly educated population is a large Island country that has such a diversity of landscape that it is unique in so many ways. The integration of its peoples has been a combination of a highly intelligent native race, (Maoris') and the mainly English newcomers that have developed the land. The Europeans having developed the land used a lot of Maori' labor, but they acquired the land under wrong principles. This was hard on the early Maori' but now they are winning back what was theirs in the first place, but full credit must be given to European development effort.

But it's not the small countries that provide leadership, the usual order of things is that once a system is proved in the small countries, all of the problems are ironed out before being used in the bigger economies, New Zealand is a great development and research country. Once the system is proved as viable for large heavily populated countries, it graduates to the next level and again has to be proved up. For example having planned what the end result is the leaders are looking for, once an example is then ready lets presume NZ is the trial country; and there is going to be a two year prove up period. Then stage two let's say the UK for the second trial period of five years, the UK because this is an old culture much respected by her peers, so stage two is under way. When and if the UK proves viable then the full scale introduction of the entire system is ready to be implemented whenever and wherever it is intended to be developed.

The leading country/s of each group will then agree the system is ready and introduction will be simultaneous. All of the main responsibilities that will be governed by the world Govt; will have been under examination for introduction for some time, and gradually all of the problems and/ or difficulties will be smoothed out. Each Group will also have set up its agreements with the members and will appoint their representatives on the world body; this will be the most difficult part of the entire program. The representative on the world body will be nominated from all countries elected Govt; there must be no direct vote, this would create too much dissension and defeat the goals?

Now that we have established our Faith is growing and it is being nurtured, even as we are elevating ourselves to higher levels of achievement, finally the new world System is ready to be installed for the benefit of all parties. Once the leading economies are established, then the introduction of the new system will be immediate into all of the economies worldwide. Obviously it is vital that the three common groups are settled before all is in readiness, but once the groups are in agreement then that is at least the first stage towards World Gov.

Hope now takes over from Faith, because our Faith is now a confirmed truth even though there is nothing to see. We all know it is ready and operational because God has told us so, it is imperative now we just move on in complete faith and God will make it happen. If we cannot move on then our Faith has failed and the only chance we have now is to hope things will move forward, there is no other way to express our condition, our Spiritual Faith has failed.

We move on in the hope that our plans are going to succeed, we don't give up and let everything we have fought to achieve fail, if we do that we are in real trouble. Some of God's children just cannot walk in Faith, for them all mountains are too high, and they have to modify their walk. It's like the Professor who teaches money affairs and must talk about huge sums of money all day. When one day he suddenly has to commit himself irrevocably to a contract that involves a lot of money he freezes up and cannot sign, he lacks enough Faith to operate at that level. He must reduce the commitment to the level he can move in Faith with, he does not give up he must look for and find his level of Faith, when he finds where he is at he expresses that fact, and tells the contractor what he the contractee can do. He can sign to his level of Faith and hope the rest comes through, in this way his level of comfort as affirmed and his integrity is acceptable to himself.

We all plan and hope that what we want will happen, but only God can decide and what he wants is what will happen. The problem many of us who are aware of how strongly we have been blessed, don't understand that we who have received much, much is expected. When we stop long enough to look at the many around us who have seen so many in our own countries dispossessed, for example the Australian Aborigines, and others from poor countries that have legally and illegally come to live in Australia. The last Australian Govt; was out of touch with the reality of what is called boat people. These are people from poor countries that at great personal risk, buy fares to the Australian coast on leaky dirty old boats embarking from Indonesia.

These unfortunates are only trying to escape from the terrible background they have been unfortunate to be born in. We don't advocate these illegal attempts to breach the immigration laws of any Country, but we do say God does expect a humane approach and a fair hearing, on the reason such people take the horrendous risks they do. Even though they know they are dealing with unscrupulous criminals, they still want to try and find a decent homeland. This is another area that needs to be controlled by world govt; it's not just a matter of the relocation of these unfortunate people. The answer surely is to improve their conditions at home then their troubles will be controllable, and many would be happy then to stay at home.

Many countries have illegal immigrant problems, Europe, America, Australia etc; and a lot of money is spent trying to control the entry points, there has to be a better alternative to how these people are being treated now. What a Spirit of desperation there must be, in people who risk such a dangerous boat trip in soul destroying conditions, and oft times taking young children with them to a land they know only by repute. (Often distorted by criminals) The glossy pictures of the Barrier reef and many other enticements that are used to glamorize Australia are conditions these people crave, yet we locals take for granted.

Perhaps we are now getting into an area of hope that stretches the boundaries of imagination but world govt; may be able to help, by in some was neutralizing these afore said problems. These are problems that have such impact in many countries; we are referring to the country of origin as well as the one of destination. But hope drives so many on when without it many would just give up. If we stop to think, without giving any undue hope, people who exhibit such drive are probably future achievers, if given an opportunity by somebody somewhere. If we look back into the past after WW11 many refugees were taken in and became the best immigrants who have ever found their way down under to Australia and New Zealand. If we honestly look at both Countries on a before and after basis the cultural growth in both is strong, but also unusual. Like America the immigrants have bought their culture with them; and silent assimilation has occurred very naturally.

What a shame that such wealth is not wanted and the world just expands another problem by big ratios and so many suffer. After the Vietnam war when the Americans were finally forced out, so many illegal's found their way to Australia from Vietnam and the look of hope shining on their faces was enough to justify them being given sanctuary. These people have gone on to be fantastic new Australians, especially the children who when they have their own children will just be natural Australians, but the point is that hope so strong separates, the real quality people from those without hope, because the silent one's are the ones who are surely lost.

Many people who came to Australia and New Zealand by boat, under the assisted passage scheme, stayed for a while looked around and after a great deal of whinging went back home, a great number of English immigrants come into that category and were very unpopular. The point was many came with only dreams that were based on a superiority that was already lost. The subjugative concept of Imperialism was over, and the English were just the same as the rest when they arrived. The need to convert dreams to hope was just too much effort; they wanted what they had at home, because this is what gave them hope. That hope was the desire to be the recipients of Imperial privilege, but since that was not a reality any more, they lost all hope and needed to be home in familiar surroundings.

To the many other Northern Europeans who were from countries, then subject to Soviet Union control going home was not an option, they arrived down under with a different attitude they were so full of hope. Hard work changed their hope to real strong Spiritual Faith, and so they were the best immigrants possible. That's why Australia and New Zealand are now wealthy, and rate within the developed world as top producers with all of the facilities imaginable. The USA of course is a Country that led the way to such fantastic opportunities that enabled their new peoples to have such hope, this hope generated energy and so we have the great nation of America; that came into being as a result of Hope Faith and Love.

The new world America, Canada, Australia and New Zealand are great examples of the development of hope, and stands to the rest of the world as good examples of Faith, Hope and Love. This is the new world because these four countries are not polluted with the ancient animosities or hierarchical levels of the past, Europe has been at war constantly for centuries with their peoples always under some type of yoke Feudalism, Agrarianism etc. So these people have for millennia had lack of hope and a type of resignation to the status quo.

This is natural because that's how it was done for thousands of years. The Asian world has always been one that is subjective to a vast majority of the population being in bondage to the few, with very little regard for human life. The Chinese peoples who were so much more advanced by comparison with Europe then suddenly seemed to stultify, what happened. May we suggest the hope was driven from the people and satisfaction descended on the upper classes, leading to a loss of impetus. The loss of Hope created a gulf that slowed down the Asian development and this allowed the Europeans to catch up and pass the Asians. And yet the Europeans have also stultified their peoples so why the difference now. The answer is free education as well as the choice of religions, essentially the New World has forced openness on the old world, and so there has been a burst of hope and thus growth.

The Russian subjugation and Stalin's destruction of its peasant and Kulak peoples also destroyed hope and helped to facilitate the rapid loss of hope for the future. Stalin's destruction of the Kulak class was an action that should not have been tolerated, these after years of fealty to an uncaring Tsarist society created a lifeless society. Only the love for their homeland was enough to inspire the people again, but Stalin's iron grip soon threw the system into chaos once again. Without the ability to create hope the opposite is despair, so after the WW11 the Russian people because they were exhausted sunk back into a mire of despair. The point is that even though Capitalism is on the brink of disaster there is a hope that is very strong, and may allow a transition to a new system without any type of upheaval. Because in the New World

Capitalism is based on a strong hope, with a higher love and Faith quotient than any other nations this USA led Group will be the most successful.

There is little or no attempt herein to understand Israel and the Middle East, that area is best left to the Lord or maybe just left to themselves; to maybe annihilate each other. Their agenda of hate over thousands of years is more than we care to try and understand as we have said Satan is the Father of Hate and that's all we can see over there. The Arabs and the Phoenician's (Lebanese) have contributed greatly to society in the past, but the problems they have now is beyond this book to work with. Israel is the Lords earthly home, and the Jews are his chosen people but that's about all we care to say at this point.

The new Labor Govt; in Australia as an election gimmick had promised to apologize for past abuse, by the original white settlers down to the present perpetuated on the Aboriginals and that was fair. The displacement of children from their parents back then was/is a National shame. The point is that it seemed the right thing to do at the time, the efforts of some were misdirected, but many did what was done in the hope of improvement not as far as we know to commit acts of genocide? The conditions these Native peoples and their children lived in when they were in their natural environment were truly shameful. Unfortunately nothing has changed over the years, possibly conditions are worse with drugs and pedophilia are now more rampant, and horrifying stories have circulated in the press of the mistreatment of children. The apology was when delivered accepted worldwide and the new Prime Minister was lauded in the International media as far seeing, but since then he has become rather controversial here at home, on the odd times he is at home that is.

The Maoris' in New Zealand had through war when the English took control of their country for Queen, Victoria, been wise enough to submit only in return for a Treaty, and Governor Hobson agreed to these mutually agreed terms. The Aborigines in Australia were split up over a huge continent and were easily subdued in fact they offered no resistance because they could not. The English announced the country as empty of human habitation planted their flag and claimed Australia for the English crown. The difference is now seen rather starkly, whereas the Aborigine's have had to fight for even land rights, in NZ it is very different, all rights in the 'Treaty of Waitangi are being implemented in spite of the huge cost'.

'The Treaty of Waitangi gave the Maori tribes strong rights over Land, Fishing rights' etc; at the time just after the Treaty was signed the rights were quickly abused and the agreement ignored. In these latter days however the tribes have pursued their rights persistently and in the end agreements have been reached that has seen cash payments worth many billions of dollars in compensation paid. The Australian Aboriginal's having had no Treaty rights have had to fight for land rights, and only recently have they started to have some land recognized.

The reason for inclusion of these comments in this book is the need to point out that with a World Govt; there would probably receive many claims from dispossessed native people worldwide, wanting fair recompense against their original Imperial occupants. Those colonizers having occupied their land pillaged and took all they could then left, with no compensation paid. A good country that could mount a sound case would be Indonesia seeking retribution from the Dutch or the Philippines against the Spanish. The world court in due course will receive claims from these colonized countries against the colonizers for fair recompense for the pillage of their natural assets.

Chapter 5

Religion

The religious barriers as practiced in the world is not a part of the entry to Heavenly Places, there will be no defining when we are assessed from the book of life, what religion we had practiced while on earth. The assessment will be based on the type of life we had lived good or bad as laid out in the bible, repentance sins and the acceptance of Jesus Christ as our Lord and Savior.

Only the Jewish Tribes are set apart, but then only in allowing for the fact they were the chosen ones, this won't allow them any leniency when they are judged? The Jews will be judged more harshly; because they still lived by the law as originally set out for them, by Moses?

The horrors perpetuated in God's name are all to be taken into account, the inquisition that was inflicted on the people by the Roman Catholics? The bible is clear that in the latter days false leaders will get into roles of leadership in the churches and also worldly places, we wandered just where they finished up, were they to be as part of Satan's hordes? But the beast in revelation we see the worst one is the beast of leadership, these leaders have reveled in the blood of the martyrs (Babylon) and now they will be judged.

The atrocities committed in the name of Allah (God) are not part of what we have seen, but many of those sad wretches were led into their sins by false teaching this will be taken into consideration at the time of judgment. The Teachers (leaders) who preyed on these people will we know be punished according to their guilt. It is a terrible thing to be condemned to becoming part of Satan's Army, because there will be no redemption for those who finish up in that situation. Those serious sinners who are rebirthed even though they have no choice of parents at least have another chance?

We all know the most heinous crime that can be committed is to deny the Holy Spirit, but because we also knew how effective the Holy Spirit is in our own everyday lives, there was nobody who are really believers interested in defaming the Spirit in any way?

The major worldly sects, Christians, Moslems, Buddhists, Animists, Hindu's and even all of the Pagans will be judged according to how they had lived their lives and under what conditions they have lived? What we noticed was that someone who had been raised and lived in the poor world were allowed a leniency not permitted to we who are born in the wealthy countries. People who have been abused and mistreated, the cause will be traced back to the original perpetrators and allowances made, none will be judged unfairly, but using The Lords name in vain is a serious sin?

The background of the Jewish people as the chosen ones is the major belief that has survived over six thousand years. Their history as set out in the Old Testament and studied by the Christians are a part of the Christian Bible. This record is not necessarily as practiced by the Jews! The reason they are the chosen ones is theirs is the basic example of law; the Lord gave the world through Moses, which applied until the time of Christ. That law is now coupled to the teaching of Christ which is Love, this teaching enforces not replaces the law. If a follower of Christ has love they live by the Jewish laws quite naturally. It needs to be remembered that originally the Christians were a Jewish sect. St Paul was the one who was the most dominant among the Apostles, in planting the first churches in Asia in the first century AD?

The original Christian church was the one now known as the Orthodox Catholic Church, they were dominant for the first, a little over 300 years? The Roman Catholic Church in those first years was helped financially and by the supply of priests, gradually the main strength changed from the Orthodox to the Roman church. In 320 AD the Emperor Constantine from the new Eastern Roman capital in Constantinople accepted all of the Christian Catholics, as the official religion of the Roman Empire. This was done though when he was close to the end of his life? His mother Helena was an early convert to the new religion! The problem becomes one of where and when, Constantine was in the East, but the West was controlled still from Rome. The Roman Catholics were far more aggressive than the Eastern Orthodox Catholics, and so there was a split and the support from the East for the West was cancelled.

From the start the spread of the new religion was dynamic and took hold throughout the Western and Eastern Roman Empires. The various Popes throughout the ages have been good, bad, and indifferent, but the ambition to control the world was constant. The East was the starting ground of Christianity, but it started as just another Jewish sect. The work of St Paul was the momentum that set the new Jewish Faith up, but it was his Jewish persecutors that forced him to go to Rome as a prisoner to claim justice from the Emperor. Paul had claimed to be a born Roman and as such had the right to claim his birthright and that was to be judged in Rome by one of his peers.

ST Paul and St Peter were both executed in Rome but over the years the persecution of the Christians was on a very big scale. Emperor Nero having contrived to allow fires to destroy a large part of Rome, used that as a way to divert the blame from himself to the new sect? He then used his accusations as the reason to kill thousands of Christians by feeding them to Lions, which had been deliberately starved before being set loose, so they would kill and eat Christians in the Coliseum in Rome? The other method Nero used was to have his slaves pour boiling tar over his victims and listen to their screams. The people soon got sick of Nero's persecution of the Christians, and attendance at the Emporium fell of dramatically.

In the early days only the priests and church leaders were permitted to study church doctrines, but the priest were often only the younger Sons of the landed aristocracy with no church teaching of any sort except attending weekly Mass. Many Church advantages were granted to the aristocrats, in the expectation the church would inherit the estates in their final will and Testament. There are examples of Priests taking the furniture and even bedding of the poor on the death of a Parishioner as a fee, to speed the deceased through purgatory. Even though the deceased's family would be left destitute, the families Priest claimed he had to confiscate the chattels, since they were now church owned?   Most of the land was owned by the church and the aristocracy! The cultivation of the land was done by peasants under the feudal system! In this environment the peasants were expected to work the land, and provide a share to the landowners whether the church or the aristocracy were the land lords. The peasants were expected to attend church and be totally subservient to their landlords; it was rare for people to rise above their station in life? The church inherited enormous tracts of land from the wills left by the aristocrats, and the wealth of the church quickly became greater than the state?

As the centuries went by the church landholdings increased tremendously, therefore more and more peasants became subservient in every way to the church. The inquisition which permeated the church in the dark ages can only be described as horrific, even wanting to learn the teachings of the bible and wanting to know was heresy, no one ever questioned the church or its agents, (Priests etc) that was a sin punishable by death on the rack or similar horrible torture to the death. Very few ever, during the age of the Inquisition had the courage to stand up against the authority of the church or its agents, because to do so was to invite a horrible death. Those who did so was normally burned to death at the stake as heretics, it was claimed the church had to clean out all heretics. Joan of Arc was a famous heretic burned to death for loving her Country, and leading the army of France against the hated English, she was caught and executed.

When Luther nailed his thesis on the church door at Wittenberg, he opened the way for what would become Protestantism. Henry the 8th when he took over the church in England was the genesis of the Anglican Faith. The following centuries during which, starting from Elizabeth 1/ the English created their Empire they spread their Faith or Protestantism, in its many forms throughout the English colonies during that Imperial era.! The Scotts and Irish objected to the English church, and the wars fought were many and life destroying for as long time, especially in the lifetime of Elizabeth. Mary Queen of Scotts was a Catholic, next in line after Elizabeth 1/ she died for her schemes against the Elizabethan crown, but she died with dignity proclaiming her innocence.

The Christians and Muslims wars (Christian Crusades) were first promoted by the Popes who feared the Muslim penetration into their flocks, as they spread throughout Europe. The Muslims conversely were just as determined to protect and preserve their own followers. The main interest story that came down to the modern ages was from the Crusades. And the leading story from then was the battle between Richard the Lion Heart King of England, and Saladin the leader of the Muslim armies? These two warriors and their armies battled each other and in the end really destroyed each other? King John, Richard's brother took the crown of England, and Saladin retired under a cloud of criticism and controversy? Apart from their religion the other advantage the English took with them throughout their Empire was the political system, which had matured with time and experience, and all of the countries colonized by the English became predominantly protestant countries.

The Spanish, in South and Central America, and the Philippines took their Catholic Faith with them and forced the natives to convert to Catholicism, but failed to inject political stability. The Dutch in Indonesia and the French in several countries never created any successful cultures to anywhere near the level such as the English did? The Portuguese in Brazil were diabolical in their persecution of the Natives and were also quick to enforce Catholicism on their new subjects. The Americans rebelled and broke away from the English and where supported in the East by the French. Canada stayed within the empire but Quebec is still strongly French but Canada has remained as one nation. Quebec looked and asked for permission to separate off from Canada and become a separate nation, but that was refused? There is still a part of Canada, where French is the Language and the French leanings are very strong, but again it is a protestant country.

The biggest change in all of the various faiths is that the people now know what they believe in? They have their books and the spread of education, has meant the churches are under more scrutiny than they have ever been through in the past? The problem the Catholic Church has had in the latter years, if we think about it bodes badly for the past when ignorance of the people was the norm. The power of the Priest was absolute and the peasants didn't't dare to question the authority of the church leadership. The Bible tells us that in the latter day's false teachers will arise; it would appear to us that false teachers have been an important part of the spiritual teachings from the time of Christ. We must therefore assume from that, the bible is referring to latter days as starting from the time of Christ? The world has built up such a diversity of teachings it becomes more confusing for the various teachings to be understood by its followers. The leaders however keep getting more and more ambitious! The ambition seems to be to build more and more bigger churches, the problem is whether these huge enterprises are for God's or mans glory?

The problem of extremes as being perpetuated by Muslim extremists is not new; the war that America must battle on behalf of democracy has become headlines in the daily news. But again it appears if we are honest; the attempt to democratize the world using the CIA appears to be exported third party terrorism? The negative impact is exploited by the terrorist organizations, the more horrible the sins they commit the more news worthy they are? In this current time of Terrorism there is the visual phenomenon of world war, but the protagonists claim to be doing the work of God. We must therefore assume there are two God's taught, one of hate (Satan and his demonic army) and the other of Love. (Christ and his army of Love) we are not allowed to judge who belongs where, (vengeance is mine saith the Lord) but most of us who cling to our own thoughts think we know, but do we? Are we really able to see into our own hearts; and know if we are walking in the footsteps of Christ?

The modern media is proving to be a double edged sword through how religion is treated. The media pounces on anything they can find to demonize any and all philosophies and those of any creed. The problem is the media is rarely fair and balanced. America leads the way in the public recognition by politicians of their beliefs, it is normal for meetings to be opened in prayer, the question is do those prayers go beyond the ceilings to reach out to God in Heaven. America is a Godly country, but it is plagued by those who hate them and would bring them down, we are referring to citizens of America who live within their country and yet seek to do their own country and its citizen's harm.

The media is relentless in following through atrocities committed in the name of any religious teachings and trying to show the world what is happening. This is not meant to indicate that other crime with of none religious background is ignored, it is not. The problem is that the perpetrators of these religious based atrocities glory in their crimes, and think that their agendas are being enhanced by such media attention. There is a need to know what is going on in the Lords name, but the horrible reality is that such attention encourages more and more crimes against humanity to be committed? Recent public executions shown on T/V did nothing to help the Muslim cause just the opposite; they cultivated hate from people so they became themselves the emissaries of hate.

Nearing the end of the Second World War and while in the South Pacific the Japanese in desperation, encouraged their pilots to fly suicide planes into the battleships of the USA Navy; when they could not compete with the Americans? The Japanese Navy was largely destroyed by the Americans, and so these suicide planes were a desperate last effort that was urged on the Japanese flyers, and that was suicide? This analogy of the destruction of the Japanese fleet seems in the Western mind to be retribution for Pearl Harbor, right or wrong it seems the Americans took vengeance. Our Western minds see that fleet destruction as fair, but what does God think?

The wars in the Middle East has created suicide bombers who deliberately strap explosives onto their bodies, and try to set those bombs off where maximum damage to human life can be done? These men and women, who are programmed by their leaders to commit such foolish acts with the promise of heavenly reward, seem so silly to normal persons. The hatred of the Jews who have retained land taken during the six day war is an enduring problem, as is the division of Jerusalem? The acts of Barbarism by Arab and Lebanese (Phoenicians) Muslims will not rectify any problems it will only create an equal but opposite Barbarism. This is the hate of Satan not the Love of Christ; both emotions are growth orientated and expand rapidly if properly cultivated. But to any genuine Christian the thought of propagating Satan is sickening, yet sadly even if unintentionally that's is what we do and seem set to continue, unless God steers us on a better course.

The site of the Muslim Temple is now claimed to be sitting on the place that is claimed to be where the original temple built by Solomon was sited. Then another temple was built by King Herod, and created another problem that seemingly cannot be fixed? Because Jerusalem is sacred to the Jews, Muslims and Christians it is a flash point in the Middle East how that will be resolved if ever, only the Lord knows how and when? What we do know is that in Gods timing all things will come together for those that love him unreservedly and with repentance for our sins. In our eyes the only country with real influence that has God as its mentor the USA, this is why we feel the future common market that will be the result of American faith is the one that will prosper.

We know that Israel is the strategic country from God's point of view. When the English cancelled its mandate of responsibility to manage Israel, and handed it over to the Jews in 1948, they fulfilled Bible prophecy, but also set up a problem that is now stronger than ever. With the help of financial aid from Diaspora Jews whom have been spread out through the world and American Jews in particular, Israel has become the major power in the Middle East? America has been and is the patron of Israel, and this creates problems in so many areas,

Egypt and Saudi Arabia are so far, neutral but most of the Arabian countries are potential aggressors which would join a consortium with whom war could erupt at any time with Israel? This neutrality has been won by the Americans, but they have accepted the Dictatorship that is Saudi Arabia, nor is it sure how long Egypt will remain neutral what happens if both of those countries change in the future when alternative fuels change the financial horizon. Saudi Arabia has the world's biggest reserves and Iraqi has the second biggest reserves, where will they be when the world reliance on oil diminishes and their incomes are suddenly at risk. The games they have been playing and putting the world at risk will rebound on them shortly as the world is determined to find alternatives to their oil, with renewable energy sources.

The world wide spread of people committed to the Muslim faith has created a front for terrorists, in Heaven genuine practicing Muslims are treated the same as everyone else. Those that falsely claim to be Muslims and use that as a front for their cruel and wrong schemes are among those immediately condemned to the ranks of Satan's army; from there no Salvation is possible. The foolish innocents who fall victim to such wicked, mostly men, are judged according to the lives' they lived before becoming mixed up with terrorists. Ours is a loving and forgiving God, but there are stipulations such as, Repentance and the acceptance of Christ as a part of the Trinity, but there are many men created interpretations?

The position of Israeli's is sacred to God, they are his chosen people, they were created to do a job one they have done admirably, and all in Heaven recognize that. The USA seems to have been as far as possible, quite a good vehicle to demonstrate love as Christ was sent to demonstrate; with his sacrifice on the cross. The weakness in the USA is human nature and the evil that invades any open society such as that one, but God is the creator of all things and therefore ensures the majority applies. Unlike the rules of democracy God is a Dictator he has decided what happens and his rules are immutable, those who don't know the Bible don't know God the Father that is a simple fact.

The return of Christ will be accompanied by the defeat of Satan's spiritual forces and the same defeat of his followers on earth. The defeat of the evil Spirits will change the situation on earth and the influence Satan's followers, is expected to change the dynamics of the earth's final war, which will be spear headed by the USA block and Israel. This lessoning influence of Satan's army will mean there is less in numbers to attack and keep people in bondage, as the bondage is reduced, so will the numbers who are earthly followers of Satan be reduced. Christ's control and mentoring of his followers will ensure the victory, even the numbers will ensure Satan will be quickly defeated.

It needs to be understood that India has a heritage that includes being a part of the British Empire, in fact was known as the Jewel in the crown of the British Empire. India will play a similar part in the USA block as the world moves into four viable but separate blocks. India is by far the biggest democracy in the world and its natural for them to link up with the wealthiest or perhaps more appropriately the most influential. The heritage left by the English, democratic parliament, an English speaking minority, but still large in number of English speaking people, and the start of an education system, give India big advantages. India has a difficult religious situation several hundred different sects abound. In this area the British had little success! There was no way the British, could or even wanted to interfere with the Indian Caste System, and the same system seems set to help the graduated Indian development of a superior society, in a huge population second only to China

The separation of Pakistan by the breaking off of a large part of this sub continent did separate the Muslim's but has not fixed the problem with the Kashmir area which both countries claim as being part of their territory? The big problem with the Indian Hindu's still seem to simmer beneath the surface; we see it as a shame to have such huge and un necessary division? The time approaches more quickly than most understand when the country that is India will become just as influential as China, and in fact will be a counterbalance to China. The future with China and Russia in Common Agreement will be balanced by India and the USA in Common Agreement, just as Europe North, West and South then including Africa will bring population and financial balance. The only stand out is America with its mighty military and magnificent space achievements.

The British Empire has left a heritage as it was meant to do in the Lords Will. The English language and its Parliamentary system, democracy, and protestant religion will create the opening for the growth of what will be the USA Block. Malaysia, India, New Zealand, India, are all strong in those English advantages.

Most countries in the SEATO block and the second most important language Spanish is spoken in Mexico, South and Central America are big populations that will be in the USA block, but these countries are strongly Roman Catholic and will remain so for the present anyhow. The second language in America is Spanish speaking and has the Latin's with its pigeon Spanish as the number two language. Latin's are a large, part of the American population, whether they be legal or illegal immigrants the result is Spanish influence in America and with them the Catholic Church.

We all tend to forget the money movement is worldwide and the effect is accumulative the undermining of the system as shown starts with homes, but then carries on into the investment funds. The truth is the investment funds are now way out of their true value, and that combined with being linked to home values being under threat means the system is failing. This is not meant to be a prophecy of doom what we are saying it may not happen for another two hundred years, but it will happen and quite soon. That final upheaval will indicate the return of Christ is really very close, and finally religion will all come together, for Satan or for Christ. It is only then that we will get religious unity, because then all will see and know Christ on earth.

Chapter 6

From 1900-2010

America is the country in the eye of the coming storm, but this is a young country really a part of the new world with Canada, Australia and New Zealand, and is the country the world is looking at to lead the way in weathering the storm. It is possibly true that no other country in history has reached the heights of splendor that America has. It is true however the time of testing is getting very close; as the financial burdens she has carried excluding the billions spent on a military and security systems, puts her financial viability at risk.

The financial support from the twenty most wealthy countries of the world may be enough to keep the financial systems intact, but we don't believe in what has been attempted. China will surely be looking to see if there are loop holes that can be beneficial to them, and the Russians also are interested onlookers. Both countries have expressed surprise at the weakness that has been shown in the Capitalist system, but not surprisingly both hope the problems can be overcome.

The financial crisis is very deep and cannot be bought into any hope of recovery without Govt; assistance, and such assistance can only be short term. There is a fundamental flaw in the Capitalist system as at now, we can win some battles but we cannot win the war. The new American President is preparing to push over $800B into the economy creating he says 4,000,000 jobs, that's really great but it's not the full answer. It will cost a huge amount of money to fix the total underlying system that has created the potential disaster that has occurred.

The System has been ripped off mainly by financial institutions Directors and overpaid contracted CEOs, for many years. All have enjoyed the apparent affluence, but now the time has come or is near when the bills must be paid. The American economy that has carried the developed world forward since

1942 is now in a state of financial chaos, and the rest of the world especially Europe and all other developed economies must help, if there is to be a recovery. If they don't they will suffer with the rest of the world as a severe depression develops, one that will be far worse than 1929 and longer lasting. Ironically there is no Hitler rabble rousing Germany this time, there will be no war to take us out, the only way this time is to trade through the total mess that will take from 5-12 years just to get the debts into balance.

One of the biggest problems is the sheer size of the American administration which has created a bumbling giant! The inter Govt depts.; are so intertwined, that so often they are confused by their own duplication of work, too often this confusion is destructive and retards rather than drives forward, to achieve the progressive aims of the Govt.

THE GREAT DEPRESSION OF 1929: THE ALLIES:

- The effect of the Great Depression starting from the Stock Market crash on the 29th Oct 1929, took varying lengths of time in different countries to recover.
- The Recession of 1987-1992 and again the recovery period, from the working man's ability to understand is examined.
- The Stock Market Collapse of 2008 and the future that will follow, is also examined.

The globalization to a world village concept is well underway and free trade groups are ever more important, in the near future of mankind. The Common Markets that will develop between the major groups; will clearly define the future, but the Middle East with its historic animosities will never be able to create an effective group. The presence of Israel is the catalyst, which forever divides and inhibits them to militaristic activities. Israel with its strong connections to the USA and world support from Diaspora Jews, is a combination her unfriendly neighbors cannot beat? Nor will they ever be in a position to destroy Israel that is after all, their oft stated intention.

The Great Depression started with the American stock market collapse the so called black Tuesday. This collapse was the lowest point of the problems that had been progressively felt during the previous few years, while The President grappled with the warning signs, as the markets wavered within quite a small ratio of movement, then completely collapsed. The effects very quickly spread too many parts of the rest of the world! The President had tried to take hands off approach, he had wanted to leave the stock market to find its own level, (value) this policy was a disaster, and the direct cause of the stock market collapse?

The next President; was very effective in the gradual improvement of conditions in the USA, but WW11 was the vehicle that really pulled the world out of the depression. Pearl Harbor was the catalyst that bought America into the world war, it was the only country that has had true benefits from the two world wars in the end. That attack awakened the sleeping U.S. giant, and globally she has never looked back until 2008! Even though the Soviet Union created and propagated the illusion of being an equal, if not superior system, this was a short lived illusion; that was shattered with the collapse of Communism? The illusion that was created by the Soviets may have accelerated the American effort that created this current situation of being unassailable in two areas. Military and Space!

There are many dark secrets hidden within the various archives of special American Govt; agencies; we know that secrets are vital to security, but there is a need to recognize the truth. The public should be allowed to know why they are there, and for what very good world safety reasons? The President was confident of his Countries capacity to increase productivity, and it was quickly obvious that his confidence was well founded? The supply of war aid by America, to England and Russia, as well as equipping herself in the Pacific and the European war, showed by just by how big a margin the Japanese planners were wrong, in their basic calculations of the war projections for productive readiness of the Americans? They as well as the Germans had no idea what the true capacity of the USA was, until their real potential was released, and in the end created the power that was to so completely decimate the Axis countries.

The brilliance of the Lend lease system formulated in the USA finally without any doubt, helped to suborn the UK to a minor international position in the future, as its Empire crumbled. This loan system which worked so well; was the vehicle that eventually made America the leading world Nation, and it financed the war effort? WW11 changed the world pattern forever, the change was coming anyhow, but suddenly the depression was over, and the heat of war started in earnest. The production lines of the U.S.A. was so impressive, that its problematic that even the Americans understood what they had, until the truth was demonstrated. It needs to be understood though it was not only the material advantage; it was also the spirit of this young nation, which helped the Allies to carry everything before them.

The attack on the beaches at Normandy, and the clever subterfuge by the English, was what kept the German forces unsure of where the attack was going to be. This was a spectacular success! The English on several occasions were able to completely fool the Germans; about their real strength, another time was at El Alamein, when their army finally drove back the panzer divisions, by having previously created clever subterfuge about their real power or lack of it. The Germans were fooled into splitting their defense forces on the shores of France; so their total of 60 armored divisions were split three ways, had the Allies not achieved that trick their 37 divisions may have faced the full German military power? This may have delayed the invasion and the landing may have been beaten back!

The rapidity with which the Allies advanced once they had a foothold on Europe was spectacular, but there were differences on how the war was to be progressed, as the Allies were planning the strategy on how to fight on through Italy then on to Germany. The English were well aware of possible future events they wanted to invade Sicily, and then transfer the attack across to Northern Europe to beat the Russians to the main prize. 'Berlin'!

U.S. policy condemned the Northern Europeans into Russia's brutal grasp! The English could not convince the Americans, of the threat that Russia represented to world peace! Because of the English distrust of Russia, for them the main attraction was Europe and Berlin. Taking Italy first was not as the English had wanted, by getting into Northern Europe first; the entry to Berlin before the Russians by the Allies, in English minds was assured?

By leaving the way clear for the Russians to get to Berlin first, future problems with the Soviet Union was guaranteed, as Russian forces ruthlessly moved forward. The Russian military exacted on the Germans in vengeance for what had been inflicted on their civilians by the marauding Germans, as they had invaded Russia initially. The German technique of blitz Kreig had been just as successful initially in Russia, as they had been in the invasion of Europe. But like Napoleon's forces before them, once they got to Moscow they were stopped, and then turned around in their first humiliating back down of the entire war. They were left to face the winter cold and the disaster that followed was inevitable, as the Russians counter attacked with a vengeance! After gaining a foothold by taking Sicily and then cutting across to Northern Europe, the English had hoped to forestall Russia's ambitions to overrun countries like Hungary, Yugoslavia etc; the American Commander had insisted that Italy be taken first? This allowed the Russians to take Berlin and thus create the problems that followed! Once the Russians got into Berlin they surrounded the city, and then tightened their hold until they had completely annihilated the final resistance, of the German forces in their own Capital City. Right to the end the Germans would not capitulate!

Russia did not feel the effect of the Great Depression, but this was largely because of the low standard of living in that country anyhow? The English aim was to create a safety valve against Russia, but also against possible descent into another recession, after the war was over? They had a natural suspicion of Communism, but more specifically they never trusted Russia, they instinctively knew that once the war was over there would be problems with them! The English had a very real feeling that there was going to be a new war with Russia and they were right, the cold war that followed after the armistice pervaded all of the European countries that Russia had taken over in their forward rush. The so called Iron Curtain was drawn down on Europe, and stayed there until the Russians lifted it many years later.

England had come out of the depression quite early, and was on her way back onto the Gold Standard by 1934. The repatriation for WW1 that was due to England, took all German gold reserves; the horrendous cost of WW1 almost bankrupted both Countries? Germany had to convert to Fiat Finance (means value as dictated or backed by a countries federal bank) to allow its lack of gold to be overcome? The German Leaders sense of his own destiny was really responding to the need of his people's; and their sense of hopelessness, he was a light in the dark to them, their new hope and they followed him blindly? That light took Germany into its darkest days ever, but 'He' did lift the country out of depression, and much of the rest of the world with them! The English message after their Leader returned from his meeting in Munich with German Leader was, (Peace in our time) this could not be so and another who was a war lord by nature could see the truth? The English belatedly began gearing to a war time economy, but it was too late the Germans were ready to take Austria and Chekoslavakia first; and then all of Western Europe, the rest is History? Blitz Kreig in Poland demonstrated just how advanced the German war machine was, and how far behind the Allies were?   For the Germans the depression was well over before 1939! For the Allies England and France came out of the depression in a rush, but the USA not until eighteen months later? France was too late anyhow, as she was quickly overrun by Germany. France then had to rely on England to stand alone, and supply residence for their 'General Leader'. But the French resistance was very tenacious; and kept up a constant fight against the occupying Germans, for the entire war.

The drop in production in the USA after the Wall St collapse had been extremely high! The construction industry was down to nothing, agriculture was almost as bad, and industry was down by 84%? The funds were available for business, but the lack of money in the hands of the working classes created an imbalance, there was no money to buy the products produced anyhow? Business people foolish enough to keep producing their products, found their inventory sitting on the shelves and wasting? France was later in coming out of the Great Depression; not until after 1936 did that country start to recover, by that time the need to prepare for war was there, it was actually too late? The USA finally came out of depression completely in 1940, and into that country's amazing full war production in 1941! The Americans very quickly showed they were the ones that set the bench mark to the rest of the world, none could match them? The Presidents manipulations; and attempts to play Russia into the status of friend was mistake! Only the English could see the duplicity of Russia, but their continual crying wolf was to no avail. Russia's Leader was always a dark malevolent man, and his ability to fool the American President was surprising, probably it was more that he saw and understood what he wanted too not what was, 'the true monster within'! The American honestly, and the Russian cynically tried to work together, but that in the end was hopeless. The Russian Leader was totally negative towards the Allies and always was, once the war had been turned around his contempt showed clearly! This was the cause of much frustration to the English, and their aim militarily to thrust from Sicily across to Northern Europe fell on deaf ears! As far as the Americans were concerned, they were more attuned to the Russians at that time, and so it remained until the end of the war? The Americans even tried to exclude the English from some of their meetings with the Russians, but in general this was unsuccessful, the three leaders were operating on different agendas.

In the early part of the recovery phase during the Great Depression, America was tending towards isolationism through the medium of increased tariffs! The retaliation by countries that depended on export trade was to implant higher tariffs into their own systems, but this method of recovery was difficult for everyone? Russia was looking toward the expansion of Communism! The English were trying to hold on to English Imperialism as best they could! The Americans could see the end result of the war would be the confirmation of their world financial superiority, as America became the world's controlling trade nation? It is often a surprise the extent of America's external trade, but that trade keeps the world moving as countries need that trade to balance their accounts. Maybe more accurately put is the world needed the American consumption to keep everyone moving, whereas the U.S. could have done without a lot of the imported products she bought. The U.S. T/Bonds is the instrument that balances world trade and is very clever, a true financial innovation!

Countries like Canada with its high dependence on primary industry suffered greatly; and its great prairies became desolated and abandoned. Australia was probably one of the worst hit countries in the world. The demand for wool and wool products fell dramatically, as did all that countries products. At one point the unemployed in Australia rose to 32% by 1931-32, and created an enormous amount of misery? New Zealand was in a position similar to Australia and suffered just as much! Monetary problems and recessions have been quite prevalent in the USA for many years pre 1929 and unless better controls are found, there are as yet no real solutions. Recessions will continue to be an unfortunate part of trying to find the balance so that money flows evenly; through the American and therefore the world's money system, because this is still far from resolved? The tinkering with the economy whether fiscal or monetary, will continue for as long as we have banks being the interpreters of Govt policy, this is because many politicians fear the consequences of bank failure? Until better methods of control are found in the USA, there will be the continuous cycles of boom and bust as Govts; try to balance their budgets to match election promises? The cynicism towards politician's promises by the electorate is starting to have some impact, as media commentators start regurgitating those promises at the next election? Politicians will have to start being more truthful about what they can or cannot do, when asking to be re elected as the next term comes near! What we are saying is the end of the current election campaign, is the start of the next one!

Capitalism has proved its inability to adjust to changing money movements, repeatedly the USA with its total commitment to this system, has persistently demonstrated the weakness that we think proves the system does not work. The artificial use of money through inflation and other idiosyncrasies, and dishonesty by Directors etc; has seen the barstedisation of Capitalism. Is there any difference between the accumulation of power through money or through Politics, both eventually disadvantage the working classes? Socialism is a system of controls through Govt and Business which tends to favor big Business and big Govt; in this way the system becomes cumbersome, and difficult to work with? A conglomerate that is controlled by bureaucrats; and the weaknesses therein again disinherit the workers, and small business, this leads to a total lack of confidence. The electorate as a whole loses confidence, but when key sectors start to fail they cannot recover because there is no confidence over all. For example when retail sales begin to go into a slump its really bad, but when food retail sales, slump then there is little chance of a quick recovery; because food is the last sector people can forsake.

All of the Axis powers under rated the huge potential of the USA! The Germans dreamed of world domination, with Germany at the top? The common bond between the Germans and the Japanese, is the inherent belief in their racial superiority? The Japanese see her Asian neighbors as all inferior beings to themselves, and the Germans see the entire world as inferior to themselves. The Italian's were only in the war in the hope to gain advantage from her association with Germany, and her Dictators dreams of expanded empire, 'he wanted to control all of the countries on the Mediterranean? The problem was he had to take out the British fleet first, quite a dream for a little fat man'. The Italian Leader had dreams of recreating the past glory of the Roman Empire, controlled from Rome! Even the lifting of the Italian economy out of depression, did not enthuse the people, in their alliance with the Germans. The Italian Leader seemed to have forgotten that the Germans were historic enemies of ancient Rome? The old Western Roman Empire borders, was a constant source of conflict to Rome and the reason was the Germanic Hordes. The Italians have never found a bonding with the Germans, just the opposite; consequently the Italians were considered by the Allies to be inferior fighting men, which of course is foolish. There was no enthusiasm by Italians to fight for or with their historic enemy, the Huns of the West. The Italian military had no taste for the German Leader, and his German hordes! 'The Germans and eventually the Italian Leader himself, got carried away with memories of past glory, and for a brief period the public responded to the rhetoric that sounded very persuasive, to the Italian and German people'. This is why the Italian mainland was quickly defeated by the allies, mainly the English eighth army, but still the delay was long enough to allow the Russians to entrench themselves, and for their military to be first to Berlin.

Russian forces as the English had feared took Northern Europe, and created the conditions for Stalin to consolidate those countries forcibly into the Soviet Union. The American Leader did not recognize the malevolent nature of the Russian; and his commitment to world domination of his political philosophy Communism. The Russian Leader had been quite close to one of the founders of Communism, and he was in competition with another leader for outright domination of Russia. The final winner in the race to control Russia was a Georgian by birth, and strangely was educated in the ministry, although he did rebel and leave that training without giving any notice?

The German people much as they have tried to disassociate themselves from the Nazi Regime after WW11, and the fear of retribution once again was imminent, there is something in the German character that allows such brutes to gain control! Much as they appear just as Anglo as the English the truth is they are very different, they are totally German, just as the Japanese are brutally Japanese. It is just that the Japanese are Asian and renowned for brutality, but again historically so are the Germans of yore. They are just as brutal in every way, but they are Europeans and therein lies the difference in acceptability, or that's how it seems. Having said that there is no doubt the Japanese are unique, they have no peers when it comes to sheer brutality.

The innate American kindness as a people was and is mistaken as a weakness by Europeans and Asians, but when finally bought to acceptance of war they proved themselves as aggressive, as any other nation. But Americans are slower to anger and more inclined to quickly forgive, they are not a brutal people they are just the opposite. However the sinister nature of some of the American pseudo govt; agencies does create an intense dislike by many against the Americans. They are perceived by many as treacherous and this may be quite true, they are after all a Capitalist Democracy, trying to build a Democratic Capitalist Empire. They wanted to build up that Empire with Nations that choose to be part of their system, not ones that are forced to be a subject Nation is true, and what creates the misconception. This is a different approach to colonialism, but in the end the target really is financial colonialism. The coercion practiced by the likes of their sub Govt agencies has been, and is destructive to America's world image, plus of course jealousy of a country that has been so successful? The image of American Tourists has also been negative to the American persona? Loud mouth Americans was once the favorite way to describe Americans, especially down under, it was particularly so in NZ. The Kiwi fighting men were not pleased to come home from the war, to find so many half breed Yanks added to their families, fathered by Americans on leave while the Kiwi's had been away in Europe fighting?

The antagonism was quite natural and in the case of NZ has only just started to fade, as these mothers & the children have grown to adult hood, and the children have now left the family nest. Kiwis don't forgive easily unlike their Australian cousins; who have of course more reason to forgive, and embrace those loud mouthed Americans. However most sensible Australian's and New Zealander's know alliance with the Americans is vital, because both countries are surrounded by Asian countries that would quickly swallow both up, if they got the slightest chance. Banks bear the blame for taking advantage of foolish politicians as politicians stuff things up, by playing with the levers of economic policy, to facilitate required outcomes for political advantage at the next election. Until better methods of control are found in the USA, there will be the cycles of boom and bust as govts; try to balance their budgets to match election promises? Politicians will have to start being more truthful about what they can or cannot do, when asking to be re elected as the next term comes near, of course we realize many don't know much anyhow, nor ever will! What we are saying is the end of any current election campaign is the start of the next one, due at terms end, and the scribes have their notebooks out already! The recent election of the first cross bred Black/White President is momentous for the world not just America, If a colored can win in America it can be so anywhere! It was in South Africa that the first black man of stature to reach that goal triumphed! However He was/is in a class of his own, that black man is unique in human history he was a politician par excellence, and will be remembered for many years to come as a really unique Statesman with world respect, probably more accurately put with world Love and admiration. No other man in history has sunk to such revilement (except perhaps Spartacus) then raised to such heights, Spartacus never reached the heights, but he did make huge sacrifice and was loved as was/is that South African has reached?

Again none of these systems are acceptable to God and the reasons have been expressed earlier, but the signs are beginning to show of what the future will be, we need to look back at the systems of the past. All were closer to God's requirements than present day atrocities that are accepted as modern needs, that match up to the new world industrial needs. The much revered German Adenauer's many years of Public Service reached its glorious heights after the war and he was a Statesman of world stature who led his country in its greatest time of need. Germany came from the position of being a universal pariah, to respect with of course a lot of help from American money, they had received much the same benefits as Japan received.

In the early part of the recovery phase during the Great Depression, America was tending towards isolationism through the medium of increased tariffs! The retaliation by countries that depended on export trade was to implant higher tariffs into their own systems, but this method of recovery was difficult for everyone? The peoples of the nations that had been in depression mode were trying to withdraw their funds from banks, and banks were not lending. The funds held by banks were being withdrawn and the effect was so severe, they (Banks) started to fail and the panic started. One of the big issues was interest only loans; these had become very popular and meant that when interest rates started to increase, the costs impacted on borrowers, causing them to be unable to service loans?

The interest rates over the years previous to the depression had not been a major factor creating high inflation, but the equity in homes was being curtailed by the interest only loans? In short people were merely borrowing the houses and creating no equity, so that there was nothing to fall back on when the depression got fully underway? The number of homes being repossessed was very high, and created a situation of families wandering the highways with literally nothing, but what they could carry as assets? Families fell apart as some married women left unemployed husbands for single men with jobs, in the hope of finding some security. Daughters and Wives drifted into casual prostitution in an effort to feed families, after husbands had left them and gone wandering the highways in the search for work. It was only as work began to expand slowly that this disastrous threat to public morals was bought into check, largely through the efforts and successes of their new President. This President's popularity soared as the Depression started to fade from view, but even so it wasn't until the attack on Pearl Harbor, and the war declaration was approved in Congress then announced by that President, did real growth extinguish all lasting effects from what was known as The Great Depression. Since then many theories have proliferated as to the causes and how to protect against recessions have been many, the great theoretician Keynes advocated Govt; intervention and his theories still retain some adherents, but the Lords teaching in the book of Deuteronomy, was do not move the boundary markers is still the truth. Shifting the boundary markers creates theft from ones neighbors, Capitalism is notorious it is in direct conflict with Gods expressed will? In Deuteronomy we are told and thou shall not shift the boundary markers, which is a very clear instruction. The system that is a part of Capitalism shifts the markers daily hourly and by the minute. How then can we think we have a system that will last, it cannot because God says it is dishonest. None of the three philosophies are honest in the context meant by our maker, when he warns us don't shift the boundary markers, and we do so as a matter of daily business, more it is built into the human ideal of possible ways to control financial collapse.

We are deep in Sin and in defiance of our Father Gods instructions, we will like the Jews of old, all be punished at some future time, that is a simple fact. We are merely relating here what we read and understand God is saying to us in his holy book, and we relate it here just as simply. We agree the Bible is full of symbolism and prophecy etc; but what we are referring to here is none of those let off excuses, they are a simple direct instruction to the Jews, and thou shall not move the boundary markers. The agrarian system of the past seems fairer than now, but a whole book could be written on the differing systems over the many centuries, and of course why they would not fit into the book we have now written. The removal of money from legal tender replaced by plastic tender will fix many problems of the now, but there is much more than money, that needs to be rectified in our modern world. Our bible reading seems to be saying we are living in an age that is reaching obsolescence and change is near? The difficulty for practicing Christians will be the mark of Satan 666 and the belief that all will be branded if we want to be part of the new way. The Christian is specifically warned not to accept that satanic branding. They are also instructed they must take the mark of God! When these things happen we are told that those who don't have the number 666 branded on them won't be allowed to trade. This is the time when the believer who claims to believe will have to make a choice, we would caution though those that do choose 666 will be destroyed with Satan's flock.

GERMANY AND JAPAN THE AXIS POWERS:

As money accumulates and shifts from the consumer to the producer, the dynamics of supply and demand changes. The drop in relative values, also change dramatically! This is what happened with Japan when its planners looked at relative world GDPs? The difference between themselves a country barely affected by the Depression, and many other countries badly affected such as America, Germany, France and the UK etc when analyzed a false impression was given. Before the depression the GDP ratio between America and Japan was seven to one in favor of America. At the depression's peak that ratio had dropped to two to one in favor of the USA!

But Japan was already on a war production basis which maximized her GDP, and created illusory ambitions for her planners in the South Pacific, or Axis Powers dreams of World domination? The dramatic change in the U.S.A. was the shift to a clear demand economy, and the result was immediate. The sale of war bonds soared and the population got right behind their Govt; they were not supporting the English or anyone else, they did the right thing for mankind, they helped to destroy the Lunatics that were trying to dominate mankind. Sadly they could not deal with the Russian Leader, he was one of the big three, and for a while a great man on the world stage. Both of the main Axis powers never understood the huge potential of the USA!

The German Leader would have linked up with Italy and his fellow lunatic in Spain, and then they would have argued over how they were going to divide up the America's and Mexico. The Hun's would have taken the North and Mexico, and the Jap's would have taken the South and Central, and the world would have been plunged back into the dark ages. Finally they would have got back to China, Russia and Manchuria, and then there would be a complete subjugation to the monsters. Sadly it is probable that the Latin countries Germany and Japan would have been complicit in the murder of billions in Asia alone. And the Africans including Egypt would have been annihilated, but the Middle East countries would have done well. Israel of course would never have existed! For us all of this demonstrates the hand of God at work! The Italian's were in the war in the hope to gain advantage from her association with Germany, and her Dictators dreams of expanded empire? The Italian Leader had dreams of recreating the past glory of the Roman Empire, controlled from Rome! Even the lifting of the Italian economy out of depression, did not enthuse the people, in their alliance with the Germans. The Italian Leader seemed to have forgotten that the Germans were historic enemies of ancient Rome? The old Western Roman Empire borders, was a constant source of conflict to Rome and the reason was the Germanic Hordes.

Always throughout history there has been supply and demand that is created by differing circumstances or needs. The French during their revolution cut off the heads of the Aristocrats, and left a void among consumers; who had been buying their products? This left an opportunity for Napoleon to mop up the manpower and transfer them to the military. In other words the switch in the demand centre was political and an advantage to Napoleon, and his ambitions through his war machine to dominate Europe, he appeared as if he was a hero in time of need? It took years to depose him and even when they did, he made a comeback that was only terminated with one last major battle at Waterloo, with the English forces commanded by the urbane, but highly effective Duke of Wellington.

The Nation had been in severe depression the people were starving, this is what led to the uprising in the first place. Napoleon is still aggrandized because of his administrative skill and war genius! He mesmerized the French, but what is more important is the background that allowed that situation to grow? Yes there were Royalists, Revolutionists etc; and war situations, but the basis of it all was financial need and hunger! At the time of the French Revolution, the French peasants were living in terrible circumstances, and finally violently revolted! The Royal family namely Louis 16th and Marie Antoinette were aware of the problems, but had no idea how to correct things, they were enmeshed in palace intrigues that in the end spelt their doom.

The German Leader did the same in Germany refused to keep paying repatriation to the victors of WW1; and switched to heavy industry creating his war machine. He was able to force his will by creating the demand for labor, in the military and in industry. The reality is the same, the depression was over! The German Leader was almost a Messiah to the German people the mighty Fuehrer had arrived, and he exploited his advantage to the full? As the Chancellor he had control of the Treasury and the Central Bank, he merely created the money he needed to finance his venture, and killed any who would complain. The German people had suffered such severe deprivation because of war repatriation, the country couldn't pay.

The German Leader using his mesmerizing speaking ability was able to create production through his war machine! Germany came straight out of the Depression servicing the military and police forces as well as war production? Under normal conditions the German Leader would not have succeeded! What he did was much the same as Napoleon had done before him, turned his country into a giant war machine? The Great Depression in Germany was over; Germans reacted by dedicating themselves to their Leader! It still seems strange that such a great people could totally subjugate themselves to that one man, they almost lifted him up to the status of a God? The last vestiges of the Great Depression vanished, as various countries transferred their industrial capacity into war gearing. The greatest mistake made by the various dictators through the years, has been the relative gearing of their target countries? Japan which did not suffer greatly from the Great Depression badly miscalculated the capacity of the USA to respond to the lead held by the Axis Powers! The Great Depression had created a vortex in the world finances, that none had the knowledge to handle. It was only the Great World War that created the demand situation that plunged the entire world on a course of massive production then demand inflation. After the war was finally over, the demand was firstly just to feed the people, then to clothe and house them, was unprecedented. The demand inflation was enormous and out of control, this is the main period through which a new generation of financial adolescents grew up. Then there was the huge growth of uneducated Mum and Dad investors, until we finally have the enormous mess we now have worldwide.

If understood from that context as it was seen by the Japanese, it was quite feasible they could defeat the USA in the Pacific and on the American homeland. By the time of the outbreak of WW11 the Axis powers had amassed a huge military machine, but the need for oil, pushed the German Leader to attack Russia in spite of the peace accord. The oil in the Caucasus was the real aim, both Germany and Japan suffered from fuel shortages nearing the end of the war. Only 60 miles separated the Germans from Oil in his attempt to push the English back to the Suez Canal, and it was the skill of the English General that halted the English retreat, and finally won the victory at El Alamein. Had the Germans succeeded to getting to the Suez and oil supplies the outcome in the Middle East may have been very different.

Had that happened the war would have dragged on longer, but there is no doubt in the end the Allies would have won somehow. It was natural for the Japanese to assume the Germans would help to soak up their apparent productive difference of only two to one against the Americans. The reality was that American gearing to a war economy changed the dynamics, so that the Axis powers in both war theatres were eventually outclassed? It needs also to be remembered that Japan without the resources of the countries they were fighting to dominate in the pacific, is an island nation reliant on the import of all of her minerals, from countries such as Australia. The Americans had been negotiating their ban on Japan for materials and frozen funds to be released, the Americans refused Japanese requests so Japan attacked at Pearl Harbor. The Japanese had struck a stunning blow and for a while had the advantage, the smashing victory for the U.S at Midway crippled the Japanese fleet and was the start of the end.

It is debatable what the American Leader and the English Leader both knew before the Japanese attack at Pearl Harbor, that it was coming! Both were very intelligent men but the Americans would not have been so supportive had there been no Pearl Harbor. This was the catalyst that changed the course of the war and ended all of the War Lords dreams of world domination. The period 1914 – 1945 is one that in world history is best forgotten yet never will be for very good reasons. It was the time of the ascendancy of America to world domination, and the period during which domination by the British Empire expired.

THE 1987-1992 RECESSION:

In 1987 the stock market declined suddenly and banks were at risk, once again. The housing industry in the USA went into steep decline, as borrowers failed to service loans, which were very high and expensive. The S&L loans were under threat and foreclosures were again very high, throughout America! This problem was mostly contained within America; some of the world banks had problems, although it was handed quietly and no massive loss of confidence occurred. The problem had started with the stock exchange in New York closing down very heavily, and creating serious waves in Australia there were ripples in Australia with one of the major banks close to serious trouble! After the initial big and then with the continuing drops on the Stock Exchange, money diverted to commercial real estate loans, but interest rates were very high, in Australia one bank was quoting 25% and still not lending? This period was presided over by a Republican President and included the Dessert Storm period? The Election of a Democrat President to the White House seemed t0 have quieted down the fuss on the markets in 1992, but money was still very tight.

Dessert Storm was an opportunity missed, instead of taking over from, and ousting Saadam Hussein thus possibly stabilizing Iraqi, the Americans accepted an agreement with the Dictator and went home? This was to be a bad mistake as the years following allowed terrorism to flourish, and terrorists began to feel they were immune from American retaliation? In the end all that really happened was that Saadam Hussein over played his hand and finished up on the gallows, dead, this was the bill for his many atrocities.

To borrow money was very hard even on well leveraged Commercial Real Estate, whether asking for loans in New York, London, Switzerland or anywhere else? Even with strong equity, high interest and perfect repayment background there was no money around for commercial loans? The big investment firms on Wall Street, the big banks and the insurance companies were not lending to anyone.

This writer had a contract to raise USD500 million at this time for a client, he travelled all over the world and failed, there was nothing wrong with the assets we had wanted to borrow against there was just no money on offer to my client anyhow. The only offer we received was from the New York Mafia, which his client declined to take. The meeting with the Mafia heads was held in Palm Springs and the agent fees were to be paid immediately but reduced by 70%, the agent's full commission was to be paid to the Mafia on settlement. The agent was happy to go along with the deal, he would have received USD15Million immediately the contract to lend was signed, but sadly his Australian developer client refused the money as being too dangerous. Sadly but interestingly; the money could not be raised at that time, from all major money market countries. The client went broke; he was ripped off by an Australian Merchant bank and his Receivers for about AUD450 Million.

The drop in value was as calculated quite normal, in the market place at between 30-40% on valuations only six months old, which was why lending stopped? There was a strong uncertainty of what real values were and naturally the lenders all took fright and closed shop? All of the investment banks and major banks on Wall Street were approached, but no money was available. On this occasion there was plenty of money in the hands of the consumers, but little in the hands of small Business. This meant reverse situation demand inflation, created by insufficient products for sale. Values shot up money started flowing from the consumer to the investment banks, the stream became a river and the American economy came into balance with a grand flourish. The new Democrat President is credited then as being a good financial strategist for the USA? We respectfully suggest it was more that he was the right man in the right place, as the natural flow reversed itself to his very great advantage. The Recession continued until late 1992 during this time commercial property and business funding worldwide was hard to find, and remained so until two years into the Democrat Presidents Years. After he was elected in 1992, there followed a period of quite sound financial years; with external stability (no recession).

As noted above we believe the change was in spite of him, not because of! The financial institutions and the solvency industry cooperate to create huge profits, as public companies are ripped off by their Directors and the solvency experts (so called) step in to rip off the creditors and the shareholders. Between1987-1992 there was a wonderful opportunity for merchant banks, which were able to step in and buy good assets up for next to nothing, top performing commercial assets were sacrificed and developers were sacrificed. We are not advocating a case for greedy developers; we are saying the big sharks got eaten up by even bigger sharks. The biggest Australian merchant banks had really flourished during this period and have continued on using strategies sharpened during this period, their top staff earned enormous bonuses, but the position in 2008 is in reverse.

The hatred that was growing in the Middle East and being nurtured in Pakistan and Afghanistan, against anything American became extremely obvious, during the Democrat White House administration. The softly, softly approach of the new Democratic President and his later public persona, was taken as the example of Western culture that was so at odds with the Muslim culture. While The President made a good job of bringing financial stability to his country, and balanced the budget, he came to symbolize the accelerated moral decline that was then taken as the Western norm? This in turn created ideal conditions for Osama bin Laden and his ilk to develop and nurture hatred of all things Western! The President was aware of the growing problem with Bin Laden, but could do nothing the problem was left to his successor?

It matters not whether we refer to those with a Phoenician or Arabic ethnic background; the rapid growth of the Muslim faith even in Lebanon makes Democracy in danger of becoming but a dream? Living in Sydney Australia we know of Muslim men who never work, but have several live in women and many children. The women draw the various pensions due to them and their many children, and they all live together in beautiful homes. It seems to us the Australian Govt; is doing a good job of nurturing the Muslim faith, because they are growing large families that the secular people are not, and therefore cannot afford.

The question we ask is does it matter once alternative fuel sources are found what the Middle East does! We think what they believe is relevant only to Israel? The threat of nuclear attack via a long range missile will surely moderate that threat! The real threat it seems is some crazy terrorist setting off a nuclear bomb, yet we ask is that not hard for them to achieve? We are told the cost of the two bombs used against Japan was prohibitive even for a country to fund. The more we look at the Star wars concept as instigated by the then President, the more important that program should be initiated becomes! But it seems that was a dream that came to nothing because of the huge cost; at least we hear no more of it here down under. The period being discussed was before the growth of China and India as major producers in the world market place. The collapse of the Tiger economies (SEA) in the eighties, and their rapid re growth demonstrated the versatility of the Pacific Rim countries to recover. The emergence of China with a steady 10% annual compounding growth and India not far behind, has changed the dynamics of the worlds Debtor, Creditor nation's relationships. China is now the world's biggest Creditor Nation and looks set to grow even more. In terms of Creditor lead times, this may not be so dramatic because the size of annual export sales by China and final surpluses, means the credits allowed are really not so high, when considered in relation to total credit granted? It's the true Capitalist approach huge volume low price, fine net margins but because of the sheer volume great profit. Those communists are stickin it too the capitalists real good!

In 1945 America was the world's biggest creditor and trade (Lender) nation now this is reversed and she is the world's biggest debtor (borrower) nation what a reversal in only sixty years? The years ahead were difficult from 1992, but eventually under the Democrats the good times returned but we think it was only illusory, and building up to the big bang we now have? The point is as the worlds wealthy countries come together for common policy what happens to the poor countries once again. If we take an example of Sierra Leone the poorest Nation on earth, with vast mineral resources and racked by war, what happens there, nothing we presume?

Russia has gone from bust to boom, as their Leader's are forced to be realistic, and cut back the capital race with America! The American Presidents derogatory taunts and challenge to tear down that wall and Evil Empire forced the final show down that caused the collapse of the Soviet Union? The changes that the Russian Leader admitted had to be made; were anathema to is politbureau, but he had no choice. He was challenged for his position by another leader who turned out to be a drunk, who resigned in favor of an ex KGB chief. Wealth had come to Russia now in the shape of oil wells in Siberia, the frozen wastes of Russia, and their economy has become sound, although troubled by massive tax avoidance. The original break with between China and Russia was the start of the collapse of true communism! The defection of Yugoslavia was another body blow to Russia and their acolytes, but those men are all dead now and the change over to a type of Socialism come Capitalism is well underway? Russia and China resemble America in the early 20th century plagued by criminals and gangs, but instead of booze now there is drug's? There appears to be a full generation lost to the drug culture, inherited from the Hippy era! The reign of the drug lords will not be so easily dominate the economies of these two countries for long, the niceties of the American Constitution that tends to protect gangsters in the U.S is not a part of the Laws of Asia. Instant execution is common, with or without the sanction of the Law, in Asia that's not a problem!

We have heard it espoused by one of the Harvard intellectual elite that the drug supply could be stopped quickly, if the powers in control wanted to see drug use stopped. But it serves as a good cover for the real objective, which is war on a continuing basis and the financial flows that result from that military machine, only America of course could even contemplate such a scenario. That is for Academia to believe, but we don't quite agree with such a simplistic view, there are too many negatives, that are not balanced in the theories espoused. The system of the U.S of cash through its treasury bonds being used to ensure the world money flows including the wealthy countries, could soon crumble if viability of this system fails.

THE PERIOD PRE 2008:

The President retaliated strongly after the attack on the twin towers in New York perhaps too heavily and possibly foolishly! He immediately sent extra forces into Afghanistan against the Taliban, not only to oust them but to find the base of Al Qaeda concentration and oust them? How real is all of this search and kill, and the payments of billions of dollars to these countries? The President of Pakistan and Saddam Hussein were both recipients of American largesse and both were failures or were they? Both of these men were supposed to be allies of the U.S, and both received massive amounts of money but were of no benefit to America in the long run. Hussein was a running sore as he escalated his regime to that of being a total and cruel Dictator, it seemed the Pakistan President did nothing of any real value. He was good at tickling American ears with Muslim platitudes!

We the common people stand back in astonishment and watch as the world convulses to acts of barbarity unequalled in history, and propagated by the world at war. The problem now is we can sit in our living rooms, and watch these acts of horror, as they are inflicted on the victims! It seems the Generals are accountable, but it actually appears as if the enemy is not. Our question here is who is at war and who are the real beneficiaries of this barbarity? We know there are Terrorists running around everywhere claiming Jihad or holy war, but how do they benefit except dying as Martyrs for some holy cause. Do these people really worship the same God as others, or do they have a different God? They use the Old Testament and worship the same God as the Jews do, but they have their Koran and like the Mormons worship their own book the Muslims have their book of Muhammad or something like that? But then they spoil it all by murdering each other, it's just all, so very strange to us and we don't understand?

The President by taking America on a unilateral course and ignoring the veto in the United Nations, going heavily into two war zones con-currently put his Presidency at risk of being the most unpopular President ever! There was no need to wait on a popularity vote in the United Nations, and of course as the mightiest Nation ever on earth, America and its President has no need of popularity, (but it helps with the people at home) but even America stumbles when it stands alone, adrift from the less than Mighty. One can feel a little sympathy for The President, he was indignant and took the reins as he was advised to do, but it is not the first time the American Public has changed its mind. It did not take long before he was being questioned, he won re election and then sunk to record lows in his popularity, but such is life in the White House and politics.

In the UK the originally very popular labor Prime Minister of the UK; saw his mandate to govern slip disastrously, as England joined the so called 'Group of the willing'? The UK contributed the largest force after the USA as a sign of its support, but this was loudly decried in the English Parliament? England's days of pushing its weight around are truly over, even if the Politician's don't know that the people quickly made their disapproval obvious. The English people if not their politicians are sick of war, they have had centuries of it and just want peace now. Their Empire is gone, thanks to the Germans in large part, and their Royalty have grown distant not the Queen, but her Husband and Off Spring, have lost their way. The UK has no advantage now from participating in any wars she has no production war machine of substance to service, and no longer needs be concerned about her prestige. The silly show of power by England instigated by the Iron Lady, when she held on to the Falkland Islands was the last gasps of a lost Empire. But little squabbles like that is not a problem, it's just some sort of a joke really. But getting into a war of substance with a President with poor judgment is just not on, and the English Prime Minister was shown that, in no way were the people going to accept that? The waning power of the Bank of England is we feel another evidence of a once mighty Empire, and that no longer is debated.

The failure of the Americans to support the English and the French, when they tried to hold onto the Suez Canal, should have cut any final allegiance to the USA. It seems the Americans could see Japan and Germany as more important as future allies than England and France, and the loss of face to England seemed irrelevant to the USA at that time. We believe this because Japan and Germany were the defeated enemy in WW11, and yet received huge financial support; Britain and France received little help, and at that time of need (Suez) were opposed.

The Australian Leader lost his next election in a land slide to the Labor Party led by a Beauracrats who became the new Prime Minister. The Prime Minister even lost his own seat that he had held for over twenty years? To Australians it did seem that their Prime Minister had become more enamored of the President than was necessary. He seemed to have lost touch with Australian conservative views; and over proud of his closeness to the US President, and the UK Prime Minister. The memoirs of the ex Coalition Treasurer seems to confirm that the old Leader had became addicted to having the power and prestige of being the Australian Prime Minister, and over stayed his welcome. It seems a great shame because Australia lost the chance to have what may have been a great Prime Minister in the ex Treasurer, but we will never know now?

The emotional impact of the attacks on America in 9/11 created an atmosphere of vengeance that was ill conceived! It was not that the attack on Iraqi was so bad; the point was more that it was poorly planned and badly carried out, in the initial stages? The latter stage known as the surge seems to have bought the war back into balance, but the idea of a Middle East country becoming Democratic seems at best strange. This is a country with a civilization thousands of year's old, anti Jewish and just as hard headed as any of the other Middle Eastern countries? The different Muslim and Kurdish needs make it hard to conceive of an Iraqi dedicated to a democratic future, guided by the Americans. It is easier to believe in another Dictator arising and harvesting a big crop of Oil and American dollars that will just be a repeat of Iraqi

It seems very much as though it is time to move into the now; not live in the past, the Middle East is a receding oil power it is vital now to move on. The future is not with Middle East oil it's with renewable energy, such as Compressed Air, Solar, and Wind etc. Vested interests in the White House driving the world towards massive profits for oil companies, and oil countries are finished, and by the grace of God will stay finished. What we mean by finished, is in the regions ability to hold the world to ransom, with oil prices the world just cannot afford to pay, and yet they can and did charge. Oil should never have been left to private development, without controls; there should have been a limit on the profits available to investing shareholders. Oil companies should have been scrutinized and held responsible, as should the countries that exploited Gods products of plenty, because they used his blessings to hold the world to ransom.

Seldom before has so much been expected of one man as is expected of the new colored President, the world waits and wonders whether he can achieve what is expected of him? In America great numbers of people have invested in him, millions of small contributions have come in via his networking system? This gives him an enormous public expectancy, more than any other previous American President. In his Fathers native Kenya and Indonesia where he once lived, great things are expected of him! The blacks of America will expect to be treated better than the whites, why not he is their President? The whole world waits to see how well he carries through on his promises. But what problems does he have to deal with that we ordinary people can try to understand, what we do understand is his promises seem almost silly and impossible to fulfill? First there is the balancing of the budget from a negative half a trillion dollar deficit, in the last financial year. (#2007-8) Then there is the problem with housing foreclosures, and the promises to fund medical insurance, using the same type of policies available to the Congress and the Senators. This guarantee of medical insurance for all an election promise seems to us very strange! Why did the Democrat Presidents wife fail with her attempt to do this when she was in the White House, working with her Husband?

The falling stock market has never been so seriously sick before, and must have the financial doctors trying to mend them! Because 74% of ordinary working Americans have borrowed on their homes, and invested in business etc; and are now looking at losses, there are serious problems ahead? These losses have been created by cash flows through to the workers being negative, and business suffering as a result. But what is more important is the long term effect on the ordinary American family, and the drop in value of the main family asset the family home. This has been created by a readjustment in true values, but unfortunately the numbers have clashed, because of the crash of borrowers over leveraged. There is the big drop in the value of the homes, but more importantly the inability to service loans, by the people who have been over leveraged, and then the ability to service these high ratio loans has failed. This has thrown the next sector at risk and those are the borrowers who have invested their loans, they have also over leveraged in the desire to invest as much money as possible. To service the interest only loans they need the investments to perform and pay dividends, this is a tactic that is on the verge of failing. There is fear developing and that is now two sectors in trouble, but if the public doesn't spend, then in reality there are three sectors in trouble.

We hear so much about Govt; efforts to throw money at and rectify the problem, it just won't work? So this is the circle we have now and it's not going to go away easily. First we have the people who are just poor and been dispossessed, next are the investors whose homes are the next at risk, then we have the businesses that need the public to spend. Sadly it's a circle of pain, and it is only the Govt that can give answers, but even they will be struggling to halt the ascending problems. They cannot just throw money at the banks, that's like giving money to a person with a gambling problem. The money must be used in cash flow businesses, that are creative and cash flow productive, ie renewable energy is cash flow positive. The cash flow comes from money not paid to the oil companies?

The great majority of the American investors 64%, are those who have leveraged their homes to the maximum, and now have to make good (service) on their investments. Their loans are interest only and they have no equity, what they now have is investments in loss making investments. If the unearned income drops via lack of dividends from investments, doesn't come this will mean a drastic fall in tax revenues. And if the income from these investments drop into a loss situation how does that affect the future revenue, not immediately but in the years ahead. It seems there is the effect of foreclosures on home owners, but what of the drop in values caused by the overall loss. This surely will work its way through the economy unless there are alternatives, and do the alternatives create stability, or will it be just another band aid for another twenty years. Before the Great Depression interest only housing loans were endemic and a part of the problem, but now it's far worse. Huge numbers of people have borrowed money from the big investment groups to invest, and then leveraged their investments at high ratios. Much of this money has been borrowed off the huge investment banks, and then invested by the borrowers back through those same banks. Initially the returns on those investments were sufficient to service loans, and make grand profits? But when part of the loan has been margined even as low as five times, and are lost the repayment on calls, will be hard and probably impossible to meet! The five times leverage effectively more than doubles the loan total, which is fine when one is winning, but a disaster when on a losing streak.

The winners are the brokers, lawyers, agents and all of the others on the peripheral; these people have been paid fees sometimes huge amounts? These costs are factored into the accumulated losses, and cannot be recovered they are the hidden costs, that will be paid by the tax payers, or/and the ordinary investors in the New World? These people have of course invested in themselves which is not unusual, but nobody cares about them they had the high life for quite a while, many have spent so high that they are now in debt themselves. We see grand houses, private jets all now being sold for a fraction of the value, so the winners are once again the solvency specialists, and those who have the cash. Before the Great Depression there was the growth of interest only loans that were a problem, in 2008 the position is far worse. The Wells Fargo Group started up the interest only loans again in 2001, but by 2004- 63% of all housing loans were interest only? People were borrowing as much as they could scrape together, so they could invest in the never ending boom times! Now that it's all gone bust what is to happen! The human experience and lessons from the past are ignored, but this time it is worse than ever. Admittedly there is more experience to deal with what is happening, but do we go from boom to bust now? Probably, because the human memory is so short, we forget the past and dream of the future, which is great, but becomes a danger when the time of bust arrives?

It seems the world Govts have come together, well at least the top twenty have, the aim being to spend the way out of trouble. It would seem to us we are on the brink of change, America has no money to spend unless they trade their way through via India and China. The Chinese are now the ones with the large debtor accounts; they are the world's largest debtor nation? The USA is the world's biggest creditor nation at ten trillion dollars so what is to happen? The USA is still the biggest consumer Nation, but they need to stop buying oil and start to use their own resources. The world relies on the Americans to keep consuming and buying, but they will not because they cannot, and it doesn't matter how much Congress primes the pump, because the people are frightened. We have now reached the perfect balance; America owes too much money if she doesn't pay only the creditors get hurt, so China beware!

Our Australian Prime Minister is rushing around telling us the govt; has to pump more money into our economy, and we presume the rest of the developed world is doing just the same. But what does that mean, doesn't that mean letting the genie of inflation out of the bottle again? No we are told now is different it's a matter of international need! May we suggest that it is a case of catch up and to ensure our homes goes back painlessly to past values? Three years of 10% inflation will bring homes back to their old value, and hopefully all will be forgotten, it's a perfect answer and there will be no tax problems. So quietly the determination to control inflation will be forgotten; and in this way Capitalism will be saved, in fact the free world will be saved hmhm?

The biggest industry in America the Automobile manufacturers are in trouble and losing billions monthly. The new President has stated that's one of his priories to bail them out. But if the Americans start to squeeze down on free trade they will be the first to suffer, could we imagine the reverse happening. What happens if creditor nations start to tighten their credit conditions and they gear down! What happens if China for example demands a reduction in its debtor accounts before it continues trading, or threatens to discontinue trading and demands reduction of its debtor accounts. That's not likely we know that, but it is interesting to speculate, on who has the financial power now? If the Americans decide not to buy from their debtor countries via tariffs etc ie GATT all over again, and then the creditor countries cannot buy from them. It surely follows the countries who are large creditors will want to be paid out, and the money won't be there unless its fiat money? Crikey we have the Romans all over again, deliberate reduction in the value of money? The only way is to increase the value of world trade and how do we do that, the only way is via inflation? But that will further disadvantage the poor nations especially Africa! China and India are already doing in Africa what the Western Countries did for years worldwide, exploiting the disadvantaged and natives of many countries? America may have created a new form of colonialism control by way of money, be assured the Asians will grab the opportunity that is there, they already have?

Now we get back to the new American President, he will be expected to look after the Africans as well as his own Afro-Americans. Here in Australia we are expecting him to support us, but why should he, is there not a full plate for him already? It was nice he had so many individual supporters sending in their $20-30-40 or even $50, but they will be all there expecting him to create miracles. What his biggest problem will be is if he does not create those individual miracles, they will feel let down and become rebellious.

Then there will be his deeply Socialist Elite who will be expecting great things, they will be waving their banners and looking for favors right from the start? This President will have a longer honeymoon period than most, but it will end and then the usual rubbish will start to emerge of course from the right, but that is only to be expected. This may be a different color President, but he is still only a man and can only achieve what a man can, and it doesn't matter if they are black or white. His great communication skills are going to be well tested right from the start. His depth of commitment to the overall population, or his preference for the Socialist left will quickly show up? The new President is an intellectual and a highly gifted speaker, but none really know his true agenda! HIs administration will be plagued by infighting and a series of opinions, from all his advisors. It is interesting that the new Foreign Secretary who supposedly had no credentials as a foreign diplomat, or he so accused in her run for the Presidency, should now be the Foreign affairs representative for her nemesis.

AMERICA;

American growing power and the gradual decline of the English Commonwealth of Nations was a light that had been well ignited by the end of WW1. WW11 merely cemented sped up, and completed the process! The UK infrastructure was slipping into obsolescence and its Empire was beginning to disintegrate. The UK was old and feeling its age, its foundations were mired in the hierarchical past the use by date was close! The USA was young and vibrant and beginning to flourish from its superior structure, such as its unique Constitution, and its financial system was already in the process of flourishing worldwide. The money has been spent to create the most powerful nation, that has ever been here on earth and the most progressive, has that money been well spent? Our instinctive answer is yes, but our brains tell us no there are far better uses they could have been had for that money, but hey we don't know just what they really did, get out of their Space program for example? The true champions of democratic capitalism had arrived and would eventually overwhelm all other systems. The American desire to control through a combination of superior strengths, intertwined with diplomacy had never been tried before. The activities of the CIA and its interference in many countries affairs, was sometimes worse than the direct domination by the Imperial powers of the past. The back door approach to control through an administration caught in a financial net was a great theory, but its many failures serve to show it doesn't always work. The trouble is the type of leader this throws up is basically dishonest, that is to their people and eventually their backers. Through Govt; sub agencies like the CIA is the theory to create a certain type of voluntary colonialism, that in theory is very smart, but in practice very expensive. Mainly because the elevation of subordinated control through man, is difficult to synchronize to the needs of the people, just as Imperial controls had been inflexible, so the control from centralized finance didn't meet the needs of the people. The huge sums of American money became sustenance to a variety of Dictators, most of whom abused their benefactors the 'American Goliath' eventually?

Many examples can be given to list attempts to undermine left wing Govt; in favor of right wing opponents apparently friendly to the USA. Many times the results of such interference were a disaster resulting in the loss of many lives ie; Chile is just one example of mistaken support, leading to the installation of a despotic Dictator, Saddam Hussein was another. The memories of these human monsters live on and are a stain on the American Nation, in that its leaders could understand and enforce internally its own constitution and use it to frame freedom for their nation, yet seek to condemn others to penury, through the support of malevolent Dictators in their efforts to promote Financial Imperialism?

The American Nation and its primacy as the only Super Power, after the general collapse of the Soviet Union is looked at on the basis of future events, when without a doubt other powers will achieve financial Super Power status. America as the world's financial engine will find its big State deficits, affecting the Federal budget; this will force the Feds to support the States, to the cost of the Federal balance in its internal accounts. At the same time the individual States will have to rein in their budgets, just as all of the other Federal Govt; departments will have to do. It's tough times ahead but that's not new! The American future as the world's financial engine controlled through its Treasury Bonds; seems to be in danger of being eclipsed by the growth of strength in China, and the European Common Market. The ability to create an effective answer to the much vaunted T Bonds; is what will be needed to challenge USA financial primacy, or conversely the collapse of the T/Bonds.

These bonds are the vehicle that allows countries to keep their surpluses earning an income at little if any risk, they are part of the American system that keeps the surplus funds or even vital deposit funds that must be kept in

American currency, for purchases such as Oil earning a return? The major thing is however that America keeps the world working! America with its massive consumption really keeps the world trade in balance, all countries Australia included needs to know the Americans are there to consume what they can't sell elsewhere. It's what is called a back up market they buy, but at the cheapest prices than others can get and their spoiled consumers; buy at the best retail prices that are available worldwide. It's the American T/bonds that keep's all of this interesting manipulation in balance; the clever Jews have done it again! America's new President has pledged to balance the Federal budget etc; and this will be a major challenge in America over the next four years. Their President Elect among his many campaign promises has said, he will balance the budget within his first term, that promise will be watched with interest. American Politicians proclaim loudly the cost of the war in Iraqi, the real effect on their cash flow is never examined or explained to us in any depth.

The gross cost of the war is quoted as USD10B per month, that's the cost to the Government. How much contra is there in military i.e. wages etc that would be in the fixed costs and what amount goes into their GDP; and as such recycled through the economy? Nor is the total numbers of people employed in the military clarified to us people, without the military the ratio of unemployed in the USA would be far higher? We know the $10B figure is still the real cost we are only asking if there are any set offs, in view of the American economy really being on a war footing all of the time, which makes war cost part of their normal GDP. The war machine it seems to us under writes American financial power as well as real war etc; if this system fails then we will have the biggest depression ever? A lot of the money comes from US Treasury Bonds; these bonds suck up all individual surplus funds from countries such as Japan, and are the engines of war! Are the surplus funds of the oil producing countries such as OPEC; also sucked into the T/Bonds and does this money fund the same war machine in Iraqi and Afghanistan. All countries buying oil must keep the value equal to current purchases in American dollars, within their National Account Reserves. Many countries would like to hold their oil reserve funds in the European Euro, if this was allowed how would such change impact on American credits as those funds are withdrawn, and converted to another currency? This we feel is the great unsaid, add to this NASA with its huge funding and labor needs! The intellectual profit from the space program is huge and largely secret, when if ever, is there to be a monetary return on this expenditure? We refer here to the need to service the money used to build this fantastic program, what has been achieved is wondrous, but is there a cash yield to the public purse or is this never to be? It could be there are accrued benefits that we of the public will never see, such as special metals developed for the NASA space program, our only concern is the secrets not be stolen nothing more._

The USA prestige from the time Kennedy challenged his scientific community to land man on the moon, has grown like a mushroom and seems set to continue in this manner. No activity can exist solely on its previous prestigious success, surely great financial reward is on the agenda in some way, or is it just that the political prestige of sending space craft to the great unknown is all that is needed. If the money had been spent on the starving millions instead of space, would that be more in Gods will than the fantastic costs on a program that certainly proves American superiority, but perhaps questions the humane truth._The cost of Medical care in America is of increasing concern to them, as the Federal Government tries to work out a program to insure the entire population, at an affordable cost? This means that American superiority in the financial arena is being severely tested, that assumes superiority is correct and not now a fallacy? This will be certainly so since the new President has promised insurance for all, maybe his wife is going to be the same as Hillary Clinton and be the promoter of her Husband's promise of coverage for all?_We assume that the urgency evoked by President bringing together of the twenty Nations is indicative of weakness. The difference in the Presidents attitudes when it comes to the need of help in the financial world balance is stark; he has shown humility that has not been a symptom of his Presidency in fact just the opposite. The President had a very arrogant attitude in the arena of war when dealing with the UN, and his entirely different approach toward financial independence now seems very revealing.

It is interesting here in Australia, our new Prime Minister seems to be dealing with this financial emergency, he doesn't seem to trust his Treasurer to do the job. Or maybe he is like our last Prime Minister and just wants to be a part of the American recovery miracle._To us the facts are obvious, America is so far ahead in its Military and Space program, but is now being forced to recognize its financial weakness. If this were not so the previous President would display that same arrogance as he did previously, when he had all of the power. America is now exposed, in simple jargon, the Rolls Royce that is the USA has had to call on a fleet of small car owners to help? We wish them all well, but there is a hell of a big job ahead to fix up the mess, as we have written earlier it will take at least three years, to get the confidence of the American Public back.

This cooperation is the only way the world financial system will survive to go another round, but again this will be another battle won not the war, the war for the survival of Capitalism would still be far from won. How long it will survive is what we simple people want to know? The rot that is beginning to show and will get worse is obvious, and only a new system can save our modern society, so it can continue to do the job that is required by God, equality for all men worldwide. We are not here referring to the IMF which is not powerful enough to do such a big job, if that is the vehicle of the future it will have to be revamped. It will also have to get serious money from the world community if the IMF is to be able to do something, and it will also have to get political support also worldwide. The American Space and Military, has created a huge intellectual knowledge base, which cannot be challenged even when other super powers emerge and merge. Of what use is this advantage if it is rejected by the majority of their voting public, this vulnerability was demonstrated with first the Vietnam and now the Iraqi wars. It means the USA is the nation that is pre eminent in Space and War, but do these costly ventures continue at the same level, in spite of the huge foreign debt?

The USA with its war machine could obliterate mankind, and it is a deterrent to others, but is such enormous power is really so necessary? Columbia is already moving towards being within the American orbit, and that country has great potential, if it escapes from its bondage to the drug cartels. There has been a strong effort by the Govt; to escape from drug bondage, and an equally strong effort to work towards linking to the U.S, as effectively as they can. Countries like Venezuela with its leftist President will realize where its true future is, when the new system emerges and the question of political manipulation; is no longer feasible. Their President is trying to form an alliance with Russia, but what he is really doing is twisting the American nose. South Americans are not natural allies for the Russians, and any agreements forged won't last beyond him unless he achieves a Dictatorship. The Argentine and Uruguay have common bonds in the European mix to their peoples such as Germans escaping retribution after WW11. Argentina has vast land resources and large peasant (Peon) class and Uruguay has an educated class, and has the academic elite of South America. The sadness of those countries was its bondage to poor Govt; such as the Peron years and then later The Generals. Uruguay has also suffered from poor Govt; over the recent years, and its people have suffered almost as badly, but truthfully all of South and Central America have been victims.

Ever since they were discovered by Columbus, those countries have been pillaged by the Spanish and the Portuguese, much to the benefit of the English. The English let the others do the work, and then simply stole the fruit of their work! I know we are like a broken record, but let the Americans take the example of the English, and not let others steal their property. Free trade at present seems like an unlikely benefit to America, one would even wonder, how long before a policy of isolation develops in that country.

America is dominant in several world areas. She has the greatest war machine ever, far superior to any other group of nations. She is dominant in her space program and the secrets gleaned there from are apparently immense.

But of course experience has shown the cost of isolation is too high to really be an option towards world recovery the opposite seems to apply as examples from the Great Depression shows? America has the capacity to produce its own consumer products, and within her own free market we have mentioned herein, needs no help from Russia and China, this is a reality and needs to be analyzed. The attraction of these two countries is the cheap cost of consumer products and contra trade, but the negative in reality seems to be very strong and growing as they become more powerful. China needs the Americans so they can build their own infrastructure, once that is in place they have a huge internal market and they will be back to where they were originally, but with a healthy wealthy population. Our comments here apply equally to Russia, although Russia is earning their money from oil and gas sold to Europe, but she has a huge agricultural future, and large mineral resources which she will have the money to develop.

The market spread within the American block which will include Central and South America, will be large enough to be self contained. The Star Wars shelter over America (or the threat of one) and her satellites will be enough of a deterrent to force peace, in spite of the Russian Chinese threat, and size? The aim is for the four Groups to be self contained in all ways; this is what we believe is the way of the future we know that, but by the same way of thinking the need is to see the world secured, so that there is safety for mankind. There can be no way to be secured from the strength of nature, but the point is when disaster does strike the entire world is there to help. The fear of course is from the rogue Muslim states, especially Pakistan with its nuclear capacity, but how real is that, is it really just a smoke screen to keep the American Public quiet?

India with its huge population also needs to improve the living standard of its peoples, but they will need to work with the USA to improve their lot. The Indian Anglo heritage will be an advantage to India in the future. India and South East Asia could come together as a common market could all be linked to the USA block. Japan and South Korea may retain their links with the American block, the financial muscle created within that block, will for the present still be the world's most effective financial system.

Capitalism will fail just as did communism, and a new world monetary system will emerge that is more equitable. Capitalism has proved its inability to spread the world's wealth fairly, even as Communism failed to utilize the creativity of human being's. Socialism while probably the fairest system at present, does not get the trickledown effect, needed to spread the wealth fully worldwide. The phrase "to spread the wealth" created a sensation during the American elections, when spoken by their future President on the election husting's this is quite a shift for the Americans. The abuse of money and the possibility that Socialism may create a more equitable, monetary spread is just another dream. The Bible tells us false teachers will abound in the latter days and in this context Socialism is just another false teaching, unable to fairly spread the wealth on a worldwide basis? That falseness is not just in the human spiritual condition, it relates to all of human affairs. Anything that is negative to God's word and has Satan's influence, and retards any growth that is positive towards God; and his desire for his children's, welfare must be changed.

Only God can and will create the monetary system of the future which will be fair and equitable, free from human ambition and geared to free, the poor countries from commercial rape and plunder, by the various methods created and perpetuated by man. The only poor on this earth will be lazy and slothful people who are condemned to their own failure in their lives', they alone are the ones who will be poor in Spirit and in material possessions, in the future heaven on earth?

We note with interest that India has now been granted certain rights within their nuclear needs by the USA. This cooperation will grow and India will become the Jewel in the American Free Trade Group, when that structure is eventually developed. It is our sincere hope that the Indian improvement in the living standards of all its peoples; will mature well in a future group linked to the U.S.A. The cost of the war machine that is the USA, and a large component of its GDP will continue, but China and Russia will also have huge military budgets. The USA Treasury Bonds at present the engine of American Financial superiority, and world trade will falter, as challenges emerge from the Common Market Euro.

The Chinese currency will also be very strong if not the strongest currency, the Bible tells us the lender is master of the borrower, this seems to us as natural, but it is reinforced by the Bible, so must have sound current truth, as we look at the world's financial morass. It is easy to say the U.S treasury bonds will falter, but at present they are vital to world trade, unless and until an alternative is found they cannot founder; the world cannot allow that to happen. When anyone looks at the real function of those T/Bonds they are amazing, but it needs a strong America to secure them, not one that may fail and thus not really be able to back those securities. It is the huge American consumption that is the other ingredient that backs the T/Bonds! America not only sweeps the world of excess money it takes up all excess production, and sells that to its voracious population. The old saying was, if

America sneezes the rest of the world get real sick, it doesn't apply so much now, but it is still an important part of world affairs!

The worlds wealthy nations will lose their edge, but the education that their peoples possess, will mean they will have the advantage for possibly the entire 21st century, but changes during this period will be huge. The fact that human life is more valued in certain countries will also affect the world, the lack of regard for human life will be greatest in the countries to the North of Jerusalem, (In Bible jargon) Russia and China!

These two countries are the main challenges to USA financial supremacy as the American infrastructure ages, but the change in world trading patterns need to be understood before large funds are spent in the U.S.A. The worlds changing needs, must be catered for before the American infrastructure is up dated, but this is vital in the near future? It seems to us the USA. as the most advanced technological country must develop its infrastructure to encompass that other countries needs for the new century, not the old needs, that type of infrastructure should be left to the newly developing countries? These huge changes are coming and the conspicuous per capita consumption of the USA will evolve slowly downward as it must. This downward spiral will mean a change in world trade, not necessarily a loss in the overall conditions of the American people. The truth is America must evolve within its own group, not in tandem with countries that mean the USA harm. And those that mean the USA harm are growing in number, sadly those are the facts when one has so much there are many that would take much, and give nothing in return. But it is wise to remember that war is an integral part of the U.S. economy! America must turn to its more reliable friends such as

The UK, Mexico, India, Canada, Australia and New Zealand, South East Asia etc; its future friends on its own continent such as South and Central America, and possible friends such as Japan and South Korea. It is hard for some of us to ever again trust Japan, Pearl Harbor and the twenty years of development hidden underground, precludes a future with Japan, to many of us who remember their past activities well? The Samurai past that is still of much pride to the Japanese is hard for all others to understand. It is this background that has cultivated an ideal of Japanese superiority, that sets Japan apart and the future difficult to assess. The lack of minerals both motivates and controls Japan, the need of sound sources to guarantee their needs, but the inclination to brutality is very strong within their culture and therefore distrusted. The emergence of more Super Powers will mean the USA must live within its Federal budgets, and especially must not rely on debtor nations such as China to in any way help carry the foreign debt.

Unfortunately the American methodology for world domination has created a lot of negatives, especially in Africa and South America. American

World domination has been successful, but the direct and indirect costs have been very high. The CIA has become a world leader in creating confusion, from which they want to benefit America. Far too often the goals have backfired, and what has been created is neither beneficial to America; or the target country they have been in the process of disabling, for various reasons? Chile is a good example, the leftist Govt; of Allende was undermined in favor of Pinochet, who murdered so many of his own people in his mad need, shared by many Dictators, to try and guarantee their continuing control, this was neither beneficial to Chile nor America.

The Soviet Union during the Cold War (so called) was also of very much interest to the AIC; but this was countered by the interest by the Russian KGB in America, both pseudo Govt; organizations caused a lot of drama within their security activities on behalf of their two Govts. Both competed for influence and both operated outside the law, in their own and any other country they were trying to subjugate in some way. The USA will continue as the strongest supporter of Israel and will ensure its territorial integrity against its Arabic, and other close neighbors. The European block encompassing all European State's which will never integrate totally because of cultural differences?

But the economic success will hold this group together and expand it headed by Germany and France! As we examined different philosophies and moved back and forward between countries much was happening. America had been the main beneficiary of the Second World War; her culture was being exported all over the world. Unfortunately much of what was sent from America to the world at large, was destructive not constructive? The movie industry had been a major method of taking the American ideas to the world, and yet strangely the movies didn't't really depict the true American? Americans are a decent and naturally peace loving people; the problem is the same for them as any other dominant culture throughout history? Everything they do as a nation is closely scrutinized, and criticized, we refer to the people not necessarily the leaders! Now it is far worse; the new medium of communication is in full swing, and Satan's hordes were really taking control in the spiritual battle. WWI had set America up as a major financial force, but her industrial power had not yet been released, WWII would achieve that.

The world in awe then watched the tussle with the Russians, and then suddenly America was alone at the top, because the competition had collapsed. The Second World War was an enormous setback for England and its Empire. The terrible war in Europe was devastating; and until the Americans joined the war after being attacked at Pearl Harbor, defeat was possible? England after the Germans over ran France stood alone! When the

Americans entered the war, they entered two main theatres at the same time; Europe and the South Pacific? Strategically after the war Germany was seen as the major ally for America as the bulwark with Russia in the West and Japan was the ally in the South? In those days the threat of communism was a major fear in the USA, and their anti Communist Senator, could see communists under every bed.

This period in the USA is one in which the fear of Russia, and its ambitions worldwide was in epidemic proportions. For a while it seemed as if the threat of communism would develop everywhere and especially the South Pacific up into Asia. The genesis of this fear was the fact that Russia was not affected by the great depression, this seemed to validate the superiority of Marxist Communism. Everything McCarthy did was giving Communism a validity, that never existed until he started to see them under his bed, and proceeded to make an utter nit wit of himself, in the American Senate. Because of the American financial support and the maintenance of American Military in West and South, both Japan and Germany, emerged quite quickly as major economic forces while England sunk in a mountain of debt; leaving her Empire exposed in every area, and her overall situation became one of a second rate power. The reality was that the American monetary system was now the world's engine; with England no longer a Super Power. After WWII, only the USA and Russia were considered to be super powers, and the difference between the political systems of these two super powers was really stark.

The Germans and the Japanese having unleashed the mighty productive capacity that is the USA, were eventually overwhelmed? The great winner from that war was America; the great loser monetarily, and in its colonial possessions was England! The philosophy of buying capital assets, (Home consumer products on credit) and seeing those assets grow in value thus reducing the debt ratio, was creating illusory paper value? Gradually as those assets were used as securities the value of assets shifted as securities; with borrowings shifted from real assets to shares, bonds, insurance and a host of other semi tangible assets? This financial philosophy would fire demand and create big markets, but how long would it take for such funding, to catch up with itself? The other problem was greed as the ratios of investors grow in the western world, so the money flowing into the capital markets engorge themselves?

The profits are siphoned off as large company's show huge profits on paper, and big contracts are awarded to top executives for their so called paper profits? These profits will one day top out and another world depression will ensue, it's logical if we spend what isn't real the paper will run out? The behavior of company executives towards their work, first by them destroying public companies and losing big wads of their shareholders money. Then when they are cashing out their preferential saleable shares and retiring with huge wealth, The idea is to regulate the net returns of their public companies, so the Directors get a big feed first then out of the little bit left the shareholders get a dividend. The assets are revalued and this strengthens the balance sheet, so that the backing for shares held appears sound, but are only so on paper.

These Executives will one day be judged by God when he asks them, well fellas so what did you do for your fellow man? Their answer must be we cheated and stole from our neighbors, we don't even know how to spell the words love thy neighbor, we are so sorry Father. And God will say it is so sad my friend, but I know you not, now on behalf of my own children we return you to your real Father Satan. It is he you have worshipped now it is he, you will be returned too, goodbye stranger. The wealthy countries will see their real estate values decline, as the newly developing countries start to take up a greater share of the world's wealth? This decline in value will affect the size of the American financial markets, and the financial power will shift from the USA to Asia, Europe and Russia? The USA will still dominate in that it will have the world's largest military, and will have a sphere of influence of its own?

It will also have those T/Bonds so what will happen, when like the Romans long ago and the English yesterday, the Americans have their turn and go broke. Well there is always a section 10 they can go into and to hell with everyone else! It is seen as an advantage for the USA if she no longer has to be the world's policeman. The main change will be the moral and personal freedom that does not have the same importance to the upcoming super powers. NATO will be the new policeman for the New World and Europe, with a larger contribution from Europe? The Lord has warned the Jews in his word, that what the world is doing now in financial terms is not in his will! Yet they are the architects of the USA financial system, which has been so successful, according to worldly assessment, but a total failure according to the bible?

Stranger still Karl Marx was a Jew and he sure stuffed us all up, the father of communism, we should have sent him off to buggery (Hell on Earth) before he got started, and caused so many problems. For the above reasons we with Prophetic leanings feel the whole method of USA deficit financing will eventually blow itself out? We are taught that when the American's foreign debts in the shape of treasury bonds exceed $15 Trillion the whole structure will implode. The USA will face an international call on its treasury bonds, which it must refuse to meet because it cannot honor those bonds? The USA will freeze the bonds and will isolate itself from all but its closest allies! The so called success of Democratic Capitalism cannot last, because of the unequal distribution of world resources. The efforts of the USA to create a democracy in Afghanistan will fail the cost in the end will be too high. America must accept that the ethnic and religious mix is not conducive to democracy and in the end really, why bother? The importance of the Middle East to the world will diminish as the USA develops and sells energy alternatives. This change alone will diminish world tension and the suspicions that exist naturally in the Middle East. None of them the Arab/Muslim States nor Israel will ever find peace this is preordained, and reasons go way back to Joshua's original entering of the promised land, and his failure to do the Lords will.

Only if the responsibility can be siphoned off to a third party will there be a semblance of a little success in Afghanistan, if they can accept this as a goal America should cut and leave, it is a Muslim country why don't we just leave it to them to sort out. The love or rapprochement with Muslim to Muslim should be left to them, America is a Christian Country and anathema to most Muslims except the few who are USA citizens, and have no alternative than to conform to American Law. The tendency for the Americans to isolate themselves will be strong, but recognition that the world has diminished to a global village will force all parties to join one of the three different blocks? In 1990-91 Iraqi headed by its Dictator attacked and was in the process of taking full occupation of one of its oil rich neighbors Kuwait? Hussein had been at war with his neighbor Iran for almost ten years, and at one point had a close alliance with America, which failed? The Americans headed by its President, decided to defend the integral territorial rights of Kuwait and sent in an attack force to push Iraqi back to its own borders? This short war was known as Desert Storm and quickly succeeded in its aims! The American forces didn't't pursue the Iraqi's and were satisfied to have agreement from Hussein, not to pursue any further territorial ambitions towards Kuwait?

Terrorism has been spawned as a result of the hated American power; as the satanic forces really started to flex their muscle, but we ask who the Terrorists are. Strong suspicion falls on third parties and American Govt; agencies as perhaps guilty for Terrorism as they exert unreasonable influence on unstable countries. American economic power is too strong for these terrorists to get international support; but it does create an America at war. This era has been greatly increased under the American President! It is suggested by an American Professor Academic, based at Harvard University in Massachusetts, that America could be the greatest Terrorist country of all time, but we aren't skilled enough to support that suggestion as true or false. Finally that Harvard Professor suggests the Western ability to apply natural integrity should be applied when looking at who the real Terrorists are; his prognostication are indeed interesting, but he aims no accusations against American integrity, he only suggest we think about it and believe our own conclusions? Our own conclusion is yes the U.S is the greatest terrorist organization of all time. The CIA was implicated in the over throw of President Allende the leftist prime minister of Chile, in favor of Pinochet whose brutal regime was an indictment on AIC activity? Thousands of Chilean dissenters against Pinochet just vanished during the night just taken from their beds never to be seen again over the years. Many stories are told by families of Fathers being woken by the state police at night taken away never to be seen again? The Pinochet regime became famous for its brutality and in later years the attempts to bring Pinochet to justice at The Hague, was only frustrated by that old dictator being allowed to leave England and return to Chile. In Chile he was able to escape justice until his death of natural causes (old age) another brutal Dictator who was never punished? An ex UK Prime Minister was a supporter of Pinochet and was instrumental in allowing him out of Britain to die in his bed back in Chile!

The episode that became known as the Bay of Pigs was when the CIA tried to set up a military secret invasion of Cuba in an attempt to remove Cuba's Leader only one who thought it was a secret was The President. An American Colonel was the facilitator, who had the responsibility to set up and train the force of 15,000 Cuban refugees in Guatemala all were Cuban's keen to see the Cuban Leader removed? The necessary funding was raised through the CIA and later in an American Senate investigation, the authority of the Colonel for the funding use was a source of contention that was an embarrassment to the President? The whole invasion was a dismal failure and it appeared as if the Colonel was the scapegoat, a responsibility he seemed to accept, presumably to protect his mentor The President?

Funded by the flood of income from other investment currencies into the American bond market, creates the real engine that is the USA financial strength. The Japanese had enormous funds to invest; the oil rich countries were suddenly afloat with U.S. Dollars for which the main investment vehicle was the US Treasury Bonds. A lot of these surplus monies especially the Japanese Yen were spent on a land boom, all of a sudden the boom collapsed and money invested outside of treasury bonds lost value. The Japanese were heavy investors in many countries buying up real estate projects. The downturn in many economies left them with poor yielding and even loss investments? Their attempts to sell often left them with heavy losses against the original costs, the reduction in values forced them to sell and recover as much as they could, but the losses they suffered in some cases were very heavy?

War is now brought into the living rooms of all people who have a T/V and the atrocities are seen by one and all. The difficulty for the Western Countries, but especially America is the activities of the military are so closely scrutinized by their own public? This creates a quick public reaction to war, and the generals now have to cater to what they know will happen, when and what their troops do when their activities are shown in living rooms across the nation? American Generals are deeply concerned at their exposure, since they are involved in so many war arenas!

The war on Terrorism has no boundaries and American Embassies need to be closely guarded. The USA is deeply entangled in the Iraqi and Afghanistan wars and there is turmoil in their country, as to how they are to get out of their continuous wars. It's true that the USA military is the greatest the world has ever seen, but people get sick of war, even though the production of war material is a strong part of the American GDP? The military also employs a lot of people and if it was not there, America's effectiveness as the world's police man would be reduced. This in turn releases knowledge that can be vital here on earth as we progress to an ever smaller world as the Global Village concept grows, in spite of not because of politicians. It is the scientific community that will be more influential than politicians in shaping the Global Village. The USA with its very advanced program learned through its Space program has already yielded much knowledge and gives that country a huge advantage, but the other potential Super Powers will be doing as much as they can to improve their own knowledge. This includes through stealing secrets from the USA! The relationship between Israel and America with its block of associated countries will get ever stronger as the democratic process as practiced in the USA, spreads to her allies? The more America and her Allies become independent of outside or third party costs, so their problems will contract and those problems move more towards the other Super Power blocks? The NATO forces will be strengthened and better financed, and there will be a fairer share of the costs carried by all NATO members including America. The nuclear shield as constructed to cover the USA and certain allies will need to be funded, and agreements will be made also to share that cost, but perhaps that was/is just a Reagan dream, he ran his country into huge deficits but is still eulogized for his ability to tell his people what he was doing. Reagan was the great communicator and is still remembered for his ability to talk down, we suppose that's what his reputation means, the skill to talk down in simple language

We recognize that the principles of the American Constitution is Superior to any other, but like any other great country has problems, that spoils ideals? Democratic Capitalism as practiced in the USA is the best there is on earth, but it is far from God's ideal. What is acceptable is that the people have political freedom; but their system of finance tends to create voluntary bondage, and is the extreme weakness of Democratic Capitalism? Until one system reigns supreme on earth and has the ability to create a Godly world based on Love, then problems will continue! Only the Godly system based on Love can unite the world and only when Satan is destroyed, and his army defeated is there the possibility of world unity. First the economies of the world must be bought into balance, and then the total freedom of all mankind into a close knit village will be able to be created? The USA block of Allies will be the ones that will lead the way towards that ideal, but they are far from being able to do it all alone? The USA because of its human rights that is written into its constitution remains the leading light, the light on the hill in bible parlance; this is the advantage that propels that country forward? The reason for so many countries interested to join the American block will be the changing world situation, and the trust that their constitution engenders to others.

IRAQI:

There was an attack on the famous landmark buildings in New York known as the Twin Towers, when four planes on commercial flights were hijacked and rammed into the Towers. Another plane was flown into the Pentagon with the total loss of innocent lives of over 3200 people. A fourth plane aimed at another site was stopped by some of the passengers, when they overcame the terrorists. The terrorists were found to all be from Saudi Arabia. The President declared war on all terrorists and America was at war world wide. There was then the chase to catch the leaders of the group that had committed the attack on the USA. The name of the organization was determined as a Terror group named Al Qaeda and its leader is Osama Bin Laden. The country that at that time gave refuge to this group of Terrorists was Afghanistan? This country at the time was headed by a theocracy "The Taliban" which is an extreme Muslim Group!

The USA sent billions of US dollars to the President of Pakistan, presumably buying his support to catch Bin Laden and his followers, this was another AIC failure. Iraqi because its leader was thought to still have expansionary ambitions, and was believed to have connections to terrorists and to provide a safe haven, was a target of American retribution? It was also believed Iraqi had WMD (nuclear weapons of mass destruction) that were hidden beyond the ability of UN inspectors to find. The Americans tried unsuccessfully to get full support from the United Nations; they called for a coalition of countries to join them in a military invasion of Iraqi? The French and the Germans among the Europeans in the UN Security Council were strongly against the attack of Iraqi and voted for Veto, but the American war cabinet and its President decided they would go to war, with the support of its willing partners, and the UN was hopeless in the Presidential advisors collective view anyhow?

England was the biggest supporter of the American invasion of Iraqi but the English Prime Minister had a very difficult time from then on with his parliament and eventually retired. A coalition was formed (the coalition of the willing) and Iraqi was quickly beaten. No weapons of mass destruction were ever found and the peace proved worse than the war? Saadam Hussein's military machine was dismantled and the members of his military dismissed, this was the basic source of the terrorists that arose in defiance of the Coalition? The intensity of the terrorist activity was such that the initial victory appeared to be teetering on an edge dangerously close to a defeat for the allied forces, headed by the USA.

The American President decided to send in more marines to the war zone and this added force, (The Surge) proved to be the catalyst that bought the hope of victory and the possibility of a stable Iraqi, as a democratic partner to America in the Middle East? The cost of the war in Iraqi to the American tax payer is quoted at USD10B per month, but the cost of defeat will be much heavier. The true net cost is not known as the expenses are calculated on the basis of fixed not variable costs! Costs such as military wages etc; have to be paid anyhow, the weapon's are part of the American GDP and we cannot know the true cost. The hot spots of Shiites, Sunni and Kurds with all vying for the oil riches it is difficult to for its new government to mediate and satisfy all parties, the killing of Muslim by Muslim is hard for other people's to understand especially by none Muslims. They are different sects, but they are all human beings not just animals to kill it seems just for sheer pleasure or is it just a form of lust, killing lust?

GERMANY & FRANCE:

The European common market lead by especially France and Germany begins to flex their muscle as the Euro begins to strengthen! Then there begins a move for greater political union, and the common financial and political market of Europe begins to emerge as a reality. The financial muscle of the American dollar begins to be a little less dominant, but still the engine of the world. The Germans and the French are far more exposed to the reality of Muslims in their countries population and thus political base, so the move away from American hegemony grows apace?

In the past the Anglo Countries, have been blessed by God during the World Wars; the Anglo Christian countries lost comparatively few lives in the horrific battles and other atrocities that took place. We look at the millions lost in the world wars, the Anglo Countries by comparison lost few lives, the cost to the Jews, Russians, Germans, Chinese, Japanese and others were horrific.

KOREA & VIETNAM:

The Americans using technology that had been developed by the Germans with swept wing F86 jets were able to overcome the Russian Migs; but these American Jets were not available when the war started. This war was the first one in which pure jets did battle. It was well into the war before the Americans began to get the advantage over the Russians? The Americans were reluctant entrants to the Korean War; they initially were looking only to bring out American Nationals stranded in South Korea, but finished up fully involved. The enemy lost over 810 planes during the Korean War, the American losses was 79 planes; the ratio was as much because of the pilot skills as planes?

This was the first and last war during which jet planes were used in single or air to air combat. Since then missiles have been the main air combat war vehicles, surface to air. The forcing back of the North Korean's to their own side of the 38th parallel was finally achieved and credit must go to the Americans for their work in this war zone? The Korean War is known as the forgotten war because the North and South lines are now well recognized; the 38th parallel is now apparently safe?

The Vietnam War was in every way a human disaster; sadly there were terrible consequences for all in the end. The modern history of the Vietnam has been a sad one with occupation by the French who were finally pushed out. The Communist North wanted to take over the Nationalist South, and the Americans not wanting to see the growth of communism in the area, decided to back the regime in the South? The activities of the Viet Cong were always difficult for the American forces to deal with! The difficulty was to identify the enemy from the friends, and American efforts were continually frustrated by penetration of the Viet Cong sympathizes, into the villages of the South.

The efforts to defoliate the heavy bush using chemicals then known as Agent Orange, was eventually a disaster as the troops and the Vietnamese were to suffer from the sprays? The pictures of villagers and their children being terribly killed and dying in spite of the American best efforts, created problems with the American Public? President Johnston was so vilified he didn't't seek reelection, but retired when the next election came up!

The public was enraged at some of the media reports coming back from Vietnam. From this time on the media bought war into the living rooms of the world, and there was condemnation of all the troops as they returned from active service. The abhorrence to this war was worldwide, and it was not only the Americans that were so severely treated when they got home? Australian and New Zealand returning troops were vilified just as badly as their American peers were.

The over run of Saigon by the Northern forces was a period of embarrassment as the Americans and its allies tried to get out of the city before being captured! Many of the South Vietnamese needed to be got out because of their work with the Allies; it was a time of sheer frustration for everybody?

The Vietnamese war was a loss of prestige to America, but the fear of communist growth because of that loss never eventuated, in time Vietnam became an accredited customer to and with the USA? It had been thought that future wars would be won in the air, with air to air combat and the attack of ground forces from the sophisticated war machine in the air that was America's pride. The Vietnam conflict proved this not to be so, with all of their air machines the Vietcong managed to defeat the mightiest military machine in the world? But to be really fair it was in the end really public opinion that prevailed, and ended a war that was being fought on the screens of T/Vs in lounge rooms worldwide?

CHINA & RUSSIA:

The real fear is the emergence of the Chinese from their self inflicted isolation of many years, the sheer size of the population of that country and the size of their GDP as it grows internally and externally, must cause the USA concern? Obviously there will be plans afoot within USA policy to contain these threats, but they cannot do it alone and only India has the right structure to stand with America, this is becoming very obvious to us now. We assume and hope that behind the scenes this is being worked on. China will strengthen itself financially, by becoming an industrial giant aided by its huge labor force. It's on the Chinese agenda to increase its own space program activity; it has declared its intention towards developing a space program of its own. The Chinese will go it alone with its space and nuclear program; as usual it is essential that the USA has its security program operating at top efficiency! The theft of secrets at top level is the cheapest way to catch up to America; it is a fact after all, that the leader opens the way for all that would follow, look at Great Britain with its industrial revolution!

The huge population of China means that as the living conditions of its people improve, so will the economy or gross domestic product, (GDP) must grow to cater for that extra huge need. The Chinese and the Russians will find it expedient for both their countries to join together in a common block, and surrounding nations will be invited to join this huge land mass block. This in the Bible is the area referred to as the North, and the one that creates such disagreement with Bible Scholars? These two nations don't need war or inflation to keep their gross domestic product growing; they have the growing understanding and need of their peoples pushing them? The improvement in their peasant populations living conditions, creates a huge internal growth future for their GDP? On the other hand both Countries need to earn the funds to finance their internal growth. This means that at this stage their world trade is vital. For this reason the USA with its disproportionate per capita consumption is vital to China and the world, but in a decade China will be self sufficient with an internal market that has improved its buying power?

There is no way the Chinese Russian conglomerate could neutralize American military and space power, the problem is the continuing cost of this advantage? Can America continue on to carry the cost structure it does, while others run free under this umbrella. Germany has grown conspicuously strong once again, but still has American troops within her borders for her protection. The Japanese still has an American force stationed in their country, as they have flourished commercially, how long does this continue or do those two countries pay a repatriation fee to the Americans. Russia and China with their growing monetary spread surely must rate special attention, as both race towards financial strength, both after all are potential threats to American waning financial power. These are now the other countries that will race ahead of America, in the ratios of the trading credits and debit, when the financial balance is under scrutiny.

China has now become the production and trading giant of the world with its huge annual surpluses, the slow down we have worldwide at present, will only be a temporary blip on those Chinese surpluses that makes up the Chinese credit accounts especially to America. Americans are by a long way the biggest per capita consumers of the world's products, they draw in and consumer products from all over the world, long may they be so blessed. But we think some of that consumerism will soon begin to slow down, as the effects of the current or future financial crisis, begins to bite into all investing American's average incomes? Russia will again raise itself to Super Power status, on a far more stable status than when it was at that level previously. The new Russia will have a far more stable political and financial base, and has over 15,000 nuclear warheads in its arsenal, as well as a large military at its disposal, although it is all aging and unless development continues will eventually lessen its deterrent effectiveness. Russia would like to reform the old Soviet Union, but many of those former colleague States, are moving towards linking up with Western Europe. The political fortunes of the European Common Market, is not as successful as their financial union! NATO will be the military force trying to ensure a peaceful future and must eventually take over as the world's police men, taking over the role from the USA, and the ECM must pay its fair share of the cost, as must the Russians and Chinese?

It is naturally of concern to the Russian's that they are being surrounded by the rapidly expanding NATO membership. The difficulty will be how they deal with what they see as the threat to their security, posed by country's formally part of the Soviet Union now becoming part of NATO. The only real answer is for Russia to itself join NATO an abhorrent idea, but is that not so, ie an answer? But eventually NATO must to be really effective, and become a real organization for world peace. China historically has had a system that has little value for human rights, this is probably because their population is so big, and whatever the reason it is difficult for us in the West to understand that apparent cruelty. The effort to fit more equitably into a new world may change this attitude if only a little! One will often hear Western visitors to China, express distaste for how the poorer classes are treated, and the apparent lack of sexual morality of any type. We need to remember that China isn't a Christian Country, although Russia is, but they don't labor under the condemnation of Sin, as espoused and understood in most western countries. Russia has suffered heavily under Stalin, and the whole communist structure, that systematically denied all human rights. But it could be, they are more successful than the Chinese at improving the human rights of their many faceted population, (which has a strong Orthodox Christian background) they have within the Russian boundaries as they are now. Russia is still a huge country uncommitted to a Western view, it is interesting to note though that communist attempts to destroy Christianity failed, and the church is beginning to flourish once again.

China will spend huge amounts of money on its infrastructure; this should enable the benefits of its dynamic growth to filter down, to its huge Peasant population! Because of its huge trade surplus and its large debtor accounts, the Chinese will first build up its infrastructure, but when completed they will hopefully then surge ahead with their internal GDP. The big problem is their history which has never had a big middle class; the Chinese have never been strong on creating benefits; for their low class mainly comprising peasants. The modern world naturally produces a split in the population to different classes, urban dwellers and peasants, all classes will stimulate improvement in their own conditions, but again all classes will produce their percentage of misfits. Already there is a wealthy class emerging that is the upper or privileged class, these people would normally consist of the better educated, business and the political elite!

Russia has huge uncultivated land areas available for agriculture, and has the peasant population to develop that land mass, Stalin in his madness destroyed what was actually a burgeoning middle class, (Kulaks) but the very strong Russian Spirit will carry the day and their middle class will rise again, it's only a matter of time and the construction of the necessary infrastructure. Alternative fuels may yet be a big winner for Russia, but they also need the people to regain confidence, the proliferation of the criminal classes is strong, but then so it was also in the USA in their early stages of development, still is but at a lower level. China has perhaps the best way for them at present to deal with its growing criminal classes and that seems to be swift execution. Many Asian countries have their own unique criminal classes that are a scourge and have existed for centuries. China and Japan both produce these clans in abundance, but so do the other Asian countries, perhaps they are not quite so visible or well documented in countries such as India and South East Asia etc.

The President of Russia seems to have been a leader in the KGB at some time in the past, but he has been successful in bringing his country back from the abyss to financial maturity at last, after the silly antics of his predecessor. The oil strike in Siberia has been a big help on the Russian journey to maturity money fixes many failures at whatever level, if available when needed. Russia is very much back as an integral part of the world community, and its move to democracy could have been broken with the recent financial collapse, in America, but they seem to have stabilized. It would seem that being a part of the world community is more important than seeing Capitalism fail. Unfortunately the Russian legal infrastructure seems to have been inadequate to control the dramatic profits to be made, by dodgy entrepreneurs.

Fortunes have been made, but tax controls have been inadequate to see the state gets a fair share of the loot. We express this in the criminal vernacular, since it seems criminals were the ones who benefitted most, from the Russian new found wealth. There can be no trickle down share to the masses if all profits stay with the business promoters. Dazzling profits were made and kept, very little found its way to Govt; coffers. But then when Putin reacted he was accused of using KGB; tactics as well as being complicit in the murder of a Russian enemy of his, in the UK; maybe he was but how does that affect world affairs?

The consumption realities will change whatever the cost mix becomes! China and Russia will eventually not need American trade, as they are able to increase their internal consumption, and the ability to trickle down the new wealth they will have to share. But that's assuming the Govt; and the wealthy do want to share! Stalin's despotic regime was enforced brutally and once enslaved none escaped until Mr. Gorbachev announced the failure of the Soviet Union, and the taking down of the Berlin Wall. That edifice not only kept Germans separated, but symbolized Soviet Power! The resulting changeover of Russian Presidents further bought Russia into foolish disrepute as one of them demonstrated his drunken episodes for the world to see. The new President has changed all of that and bought respectability to his country that was badly needed.

The resulting Re united Germany although expected to experience great financial difficulty was able to create another German miracle, and we now see that country with France at the fore front of the European Common Market. This is an indication of German resourcefulness, but the far seeing Adenauer was the father figure; that guided his country back to being a major economy, after the disaster that was WW11. The biggest problem will be with Russia and China, but they also must recognize there is no alternative as the world keeps contracting. This is when a world Parliament will be agreed to by the three major common groups. A World Leader will eventually emerge who will really be an agent of Satan, and then the final conflict will be getting very near. At present we have a type of world domination by the United States powered by its monetary system! Post WW II, it became obvious that the previous relationship with the then Soviet Union was not workable and quickly deteriorated? What was called the Iron Curtain became a reality, which vanished when the illusion of communist power became a dead emblem of the past. The fall of the Berlin wall from the era of Stalin, Khrushchev, Brezhnev etc was gone as was communism!

The future will change American dominance as we see China, India and South East Asia become powerful in their use of their big low cost labor populations? The block including Russia and China will be very strong, and this time the union between these two countries will succeed, unlike the previous attempt that was doomed to failure from the start? The politicians of both countries will understand the need for each to support the other, and the suspicion engendered previously by political vanity and greed will be protected against? The astute Chinese and the aggressive Russians will create an enormous political and military force. Both Countries fail the measure for human rights as recognized in the West at present and this will only improve as its citizen demand better freedoms. Because this block is the one referred to in the bible as the North, that move to freedom will be restricted by the lack of respect in both countries, for human endeavor and freedom? From the start China and India will exploit Africa, and the mineral wealth won't be fairly distributed to the countries from which they extract these resources? The African's will finally realize how they are being exploited, and will demand the cancellation of unfair contracts. With the help of the Europeans fair contracts will be set up, and the resources used for the benefit of the African people?

The Soviet Union had also become a super power, but the atrocities inflicted on the people of that group of countries, specifically Russia was overwhelming. Approximately 27 million people from the Soviet Union had died and gone to heaven the brutality of the Soviet Dictator 27 million victim was unbelievable, contrasted with the German Dictator 50 million victim's two monsters. The Chinese had also suffered greatly under the onslaught of the Japanese, starting in 1931-38 the bitterness between the Japanese, Chinese and the Koreans are akin to the ethnic problems in Yugoslavia. The Japanese see the other two peoples as racially inferior, and really practiced a type of ethnic cleansing? It will take many generations for the Koreans, and the Chinese to rise above their hatred for the Japanese, if ever!

The Soviet Union was one of the major beneficiaries of Stalin's demise if he had left a little earlier it would have been better, even better had he never been born. Stalin was a mass murderer who got off for his misdemeanors, where as he should have been drawn and quartered in Public, as some small retribution to the millions he killed. Russia with its Chinese ally looked as if they were poised to become a strong contender for world domination, but in the end their system failed. China and Russia have changed to a type of Social, Criminal Capitalism, tax exempt, but that is only the start of evolving as a new order engulfs the world and the Global Village concept is propagated. This new order will facilitate major changes for good and for bad, the bad, will be a restriction of privacy as all become prisoner's to the concept of big brother in control. Both countries have problems allowing their peoples political freedom, and both are still brutal regimes. The problem they have now is their people are becoming aware of the greater social justice enjoyed by the democracies, and will want to see their own social conditions improved. The big test is India which is the world's biggest Democratic Capitalist Country, the way that country adjusts and improves the conditions for their huge population is going to be an example that the Chino/Russians won't be able to ignore, if India is successful, with as usual American help? The world will change as China, India and the S.E.A.T.O countries start to take their place as producers and administrators of the world? As the world diversifies its source of energy, there will be a change in capital flows!

NATO as a world police man in the place of America will create a great opportunity for the world to come together, but will be difficult to achieve? Russia in particular will be hard to convince to the idea that it should be in the

NATO Alliance because it has its own nuclear arsenal but will be convinced in time? China with its emergence as a Super Power will be a major producer to the world, but its own population will have the need of a huge gross domestic product, that will inhibit China's world sales? At present we have a type of world domination by the United States powered by its monetary system! Post WW II, it became obvious that the previous relationship with the then Soviet Union was not workable and quickly deteriorated? What was called the Iron Curtain became a reality, which vanished when the illusion of communist power became a dead emblem of the past. The fall of the Berlin wall from the era of Dictators Etc was gone as was communism!

The future will change American dominance as we see China, India and South East Asia become powerful in their use of their big low cost labor populations? The Soviet communist system set out to match and defeat the Democrat Capitalist system in every way, including Outer Space, Economic Development and Nuclear Weaponry. We were aware there was no possible hope that this could be achieved; long before it actually happened the eventual collapse of communism was obvious? The death of Joseph in 1953 was the first event that loosened the grip of the Dictatorship, on the Soviet leadership. The emergence of the ebullient President, as the General Secretary of the Soviet Union, was greeted as a possible advantage in the USA and the Western World, but then anything was better than the malevolent stare of his predecessor?

The growth of Chinese communism was destined to be more effective than Russia; because of the different methods employed to fight for its growth, no other Nation is as well equipped to accept the concept of Communism, but even there that philosophy eventually failed. The communists in China had to defeat the Nationalist, which they did; but in the process the Nationalists shifted to Taiwan and set up a separate country. This is still a thorn to the communists and the relationship between Taiwan; Mainland China & America is to be stilted for years as the USA supports the Nationalist Chinese breakaway state? The split between China and Russia, the two main and founding engines of two differing communist ideologies, was caused by problems between the two dictators, Stalin and Mao Se Tung. The two countries will come together in the future because they will need each other, and a more sensible leadership will emerge within the both to create an alliance? The rest of the world's unaligned countries will move to join different alliances! The point is, as the world comes together in different alliances, we know we are moving towards the coming of a world dictator, who will preside over the world for a time? The destruction of this dictatorship is prophesied to come quite quickly, the bible is clear on the events that will precede the second coming, it is then we know the coming of Christ is near?

The face-off between Soviet Russia on the one side, and the USA, England and France on the other over the division of Berlin was the first serious confrontation between East and West, post WW11 Russia lost. Berlin after WW11 was divided between the occupying powers, Russia, America, England and France, but Russia had wanted to take full control of Berlin. Berlin was able to be isolated by the Russian area, and in an attempt to gain control of Berlin, the powers in Moscow decided to block off all access to the three other nations? This was referred to as the Berlin blockade and lasted for twelve months. The blockade was broken by the aerial support of the Berliner's by the three powers. (Mainly America) The airlift was an achievement of logistics and planes of amazing proportion. Only America could have achieved such an aerial assault, Russia finally relented and lifted the blockade, but only because the propaganda that was beneficial to America became great, as the rest of the world looked on in amazement?

The understanding that the world is policed by an independent body, will not seriously offend the sensitivities of pride that are so important to large countries. Many will continue to see the separating of Police responsibility to an independent body as intrusion on their sovereignty, and they may well be right. But sacrifices will have to be made, and it will be safer to be on the inside looking out than the outside looking in, this is the conundrum that needs to be settled by big countries, or small countries with arrogant Govt. The average level of personal prosperity in China will rise dramatically, because of the change in the peasant population's perception, of how the rest of the world lives; they will want to have improved prosperity as well? The ability of the internet to cross all borders will teach the peasants how much they are missing, and they will rebel unless they are given better conditions? The communist dictator Fidel Castro was anathema to the USA, and the AIC was able to warn their President, that Soviet missiles were being installed in Cuba? This was able to be confirmed via satellite, it was confirmed that a flotilla of Russia merchant boats were on the way to Cuba carrying missiles, then the argument (negotiations) began.

The President ordered a blockade of Cuba by the USA Navy and warned, the then General Secretary of the Soviet Union that his merchant marine fleet would be destroyed. At the time it was not realized in the West that there were four nuclear armed Russian submarines, in the area with orders for their commanders to attack America with nuclear missiles, if they deemed it necessary? The near tragedy was averted but only by the Grace of God! The submerged submariners endured great hard ship, as their commanders tried to decide what to do? Contact with Moscow had been severed and only the orders issued when the subs were sent out on their missions were known. None of the four Commanders could contact each other, for fear the breaking of silence would lead to them, and their crews being destroyed. At that time those Russian Commanders with their nuclear armed torpedoes, was the slim difference between those two major nuclear powers, and catastrophic nuclear attack.

The world waited in tense horror as the face of between the two leaders grew to fever pitch, and then all were relieved when the Russian Merchant boats stopped and turned around. This turned out to be a great media propaganda event for the American President, from then his reputation was made as a solid politician who could and would defend the American way of life? The fall of Russia's General Secretary was not very long in coming; his politburo members were not impressed with that and other exhibitions of poor judgment by their leader? The American President went on to become a real hero, but this is not unusual when a popular leader is assassinated. We do know though that his extra curricula activities were really unwise for his future after death, in Gods agenda nobody is treated as special, all must answer for their life activities? MM soon after his death speculation has always been rife as to her Relationship with JFK, the spectacle of her singing a birthday message for his birthday has been strong fuel, to suggest a stronger than passing acquaintance between the two. Speculation was also directed against his brother as being a close friend to MM, but truthfully who knows and really who cares.

Hungary a country that had been subordinated to the Soviet Union at the end of WWII decided it was going to break its links with Soviet Russia. The brutally of the Russian military subjugation of that attempt by Hungary, was an indication that breaking away from the Soviet Union at that time was not an option? The strength of the military force sent into Hungary was a signal to all other countries in the Soviet sphere, that breaking away would not be tolerated? The brutality of the Soviets was a real surprise to the rest of the world and once again the Soviets were condemned worldwide! The jousting with America at times has appeared a game that both countries enjoyed, but in the end the clear superiority of the Americans ended the silly game, between those two great world powers.

JAPAN:

Japan's GDP is second only to the USA by value, but this country has labored over recent years as other Asian countries have grown, particularly the ones known as the tiger economies in Sth East Asia. The Loyalty of Japan to any group of countries would always be suspect; its habit of war without warning, and the twenty years of preparation for its attack on America at Pearl Harbor, leave's Japan as the country we all love to distrust. Japan is a country small in land size, but big in a population that is highly malleable by its leaders, it must rely on all of its mineral supplies from abroad. The success of Japan as a militaristic people much akin to the Germans is something hard for the Anglo minds to understand. The total commitment to an Emperor who is considered a God, and ancient ideas something similar to the code of honor once practiced by the European knights of medieval times, somehow cloaks Japan in a mysterious mantel all of their own, but their innate manners cannot cancel their brutal past. The idea the Japanese have been tamed by the Americans with two nuclear bombs, is an idea propagated for world consumption, but not to be digested by their own people.

Japanese leaders dreamed of world domination not just the South Pacific, their war with Russia then Manchuria and sudden attack on Shanghai, was/ is indicative of Japanese war morality she has none. The brutality exhibited by the Japanese to the Russians, Koreans and the Chinese without even mentioning the brutality exhibited in the South Pacific, creates an image of Japan that is very unflattering. We need remember that Japanese brutality, and not just brush aside that part of the Japanese character that enables them to swing from apparent docility since their defeat in WW11, to the brutality in their character that lurks just beneath the surface. Japan is a small island country with a big malleable population, that can be manipulated however or whenever their leaders want to change course. Even the Japanese internal control of its own people requires complete subservience to the leaders. The Japanese as a race have been indoctrinated to consider themselves superior, and the result is that members of our society, who are old enough to remember, feel just the opposite and that Japan doesn't belong in any league of nations that wants to create equality for all. The same could be said for the Germans, but somehow there is a difference, the Germans were susceptible because of the severity of their exposure to the depression. The Japanese on the other hand didn't experience the depression, they reached for domination because of their home land has needs for minerals they tried to redress through military conquest, the brutality they exhibited is part of their natural thought pattern, the Germans also had leaders that were brutal, but it is true the people responded.

It was natural for the Japanese to assume the Germans would help to soak up the apparent productive difference of only two to one. The reality was that American gearing to a war economy changed the dynamics, so that the Axis powers in both war theatres were quickly outclassed? It needs also to be remembered, that Japan without the resources of the countries they were going to dominate in the pacific, is an island nation reliant on the import of all of her minerals, from countries such as Australia. The sweep south from

Japan put the Philippines first in line for take over and on the way back, one of the staging posts for the attack on the Japanese homeland. Who knows what Japan has this time may have hatched somewhere not in the mountains this time, but in some hidden computer system that they may have developed? Perhaps they have figured out how to get into the American systems and can send off missiles without authority, sound silly, yes it does? We only mean that as an example of possible Japanese duplicity, or what happens if the Japanese could lock up all computer systems excluding their own, there would be chaos while they came up with some Pearl Harbor style attack, we believe it's in the Japanese, genes the art of deception. The example that must never be forgotten was the rape of Nanking in 1937-38! The perpetrators of that horrendous event are lionized in Japan, quite in contrast to Germany where there is shame for their leaders despicable past.

We note though the English and their American Allies never had the numbers to lose that the Chinese did, and their populations would never accede to such a destruction of the military and its civil population. The Japanese slaughter of Chinese in Shanghai was horrific, the Japanese proclaimed the Chinese as inferior beings and they were justified to slaughter them by the thousands? The Shanghai slaughter has never been forgotten nor forgiven by the Chinese, the future relations between Japan and China will be tainted by the rape and pillage of Chinese cities, committed by the Japanese during that period, for centuries to come? The Japanese memory however doesn't seem to react to their past atrocities, the children of those Japanese back in 1945 are a different generation, that seem puzzled at any claims they are a barbaric people. The current generation seems perplexed at other countries that have suffered at the hands of their forebears, but the arrogance has never vanished from their persona.

The attitude of the Japanese to the Koreans is the same; the Koreans are seen as being inferior to the Japanese. The Korean conflict which started in 1950 when The North Koreans tried to conquer South Korea was a war that was conducted under the auspices of the United Nations, predominantly by the Americans? The North Koreans were almost victorious even without help which was given; by the intervention of communist Chinese troops and then later by Russian jet fighter aircraft was a big help to the North Koreans?

EUROPE:

Europe has the difficulty of having so many age old cultures that are difficult to bring together and that will always be a problem. Without France and Germany being the unifying force it would be difficult for the European

Community to keep going ahead. We only have to look at a country like Yugoslavia that after the death of Marshall Tito has been a shattering symbol. The reality is that historically these nations have been unable to coexist, but it's now very much in the interest of the main countries in Western Europe to keep the total market community in harmony? The success of the Euro in the combined market is the catalyst that will keep the community viable! The breakup of Yugoslavia after the death of Tito has been latter day ethnic cleansing, as Mr. Milosevic tried to eliminate the Muslims, but his actions were just as brutal as all Dictators who seem to relish mass murder. Most of the present country's that are part of the more affluent world and can do so, will start to work toward a greater move towards clean energy? By the end of the 21st Century the move towards renewable energy will be well established in the developed West. Large parts of the emerging world will be well on the way towards the use of natural energy as well? The technology learned from the American space program makes greater knowledge available to the world's scientists, but at a cost? What is needed is to improve knowledge that allows the world to progress in its path to the more effective use of the world's natural resources, the Americans have that knowledge?

INDIA:

India the great sub continent will become a strategic Allie of the USA! This will be vital, as will the link to the UK, Israel, and Australia. India has the second biggest population in the world after China, and has a nuclear capability. With closer links to the USA and the UK its population will benefit, unlike the previous experience with the UK. There will be huge growth in India's economy, as the peoples begin to produce and receive the benefits of the Indian links to the USA, but the benefits will be reciprocal? The USA in the Spiritual world is way ahead of any other of the major economies! This was a position created by their founding fathers, and is why their constitution is the way it is, in that it guarantees certain rights such as the Fifth Amendment, that is a shelter from self incrimination. We have the sleeping giants China and India, plus the millions in all other Asian Countries, (Indochina) that are keen to improve their economies and their peoples living conditions. They have wakened and the potential size of their economies is huge.

India is the World's largest democracy; and is an Asian Country with an enormous labor base, with the advantage of a large English-speaking part of their population, and the Westminster Political system? China is flexing its industrial muscle and what a muscle it is! The high growth rates remind us of the time when Japan and Germany were exactly the same, but look what they are now, with American help? For example India will gain enormous benefits from some type of union with America, but the reverse applies also.

The same advantage applies to South East Asia, England, in general and the USA will dominate in the South of the American continent. England is a natural ally as is Australia. NZ and Canada all are originally Anglo countries as was the USA. South and Central America and Mexico these are formerly Spanish and will ally with the USA. The West will be dominated by Germany and France with their European allies, the latter's alliance with Africa will create world balance and fairer access to the minerals of Africa. India also with its huge population has an even more instant problem with its peasant's, because of that country's low average income for the peasants! The same applies in South East Asia, and again the peasants will have to be given the hope of better living conditions! Pakistan as a Muslim country will find it harder to enter one of the three blocks that will emerge; probably Russian/China will be its best chance of participation within one of the three blocks but again its Muslim and needs to be in that block? Another major confrontation was with the USA over Cuba, again Russia lost.

AFRICA:

Africa will be exploited by the Chinese and the Indians, contracts will be taken out in which the exploiting countries undervalue the resources; they will take out of Africa? This will be because of poor business understanding by the African leaders, and why the change of direction is needed? Africa will be treated fairly by the Europeans; this will be of great benefit to Africa and Europe. Even at present the contracts being taken out by the Chinese are exploitive and unfair, Africa will eventually cancel all such agreements especially with China? India will be more restrained because of its relationship with the USA, but will also be exploitive in Africa; it is only because of the changing world environment that these situations must change? All of the wealthy nations have exploited the underdeveloped and poor countries in the past, it is only because of the new concept of the global village, is the world in the process of big changes. The African Continent in time will be allied to Europe and will be properly treated as equals, as the African leaders mature. Shackles (unfair contracts) being set in place by India and China will be shaken off, because the agreements that are being set up are unfair!

Africa is the last continent destined for economic real growth; but its politicians will have to show stability and responsibility to their own people that's never been there before, this continent will be the hardest of all to improve its people's standard of living, but it will happen. Because it is the last to develop the future union is hard to see but again it will happen because it's God's Will? There is a changing pattern in the world; no longer is it seen that physical occupation is necessary for world domination; this could have been achieved by market and economic domination, America has tried for that and failed! Memories of Idi Amin, and the violent death of Patrice Lumumba of the Congo and many others and the slaughter of thousand of their peoples have us all wondering what the future for Africa is, and how long before there begins to be improvement for their starving and medical problems, not to mention financial management?

WORLD AFFAIRS:

The world alliances will change dramatically over the 21st Century, as the world moves towards change. At present the need for oil is controlling world affairs, but the development of alternative energy will change the pressures, structures will be dramatic dramatically, because of changing world priorities! The countries with the very large populations will become the productive engines of the world. The world's monetary systems will change and economic progress will develop, because of this dramatic change. In the future there will be three super powers, and four world common trade blocks? The Middle East will still be the world's flash point and a pariah in Western eyes we cannot make any comment because we know of their wonderful past? But we look with some jaundice opinions at their extremist associations now and find it hard in our western hearts to wish them well! Meanwhile Israel which will retain her close ties with America!

The change in the world's energy materials and the ability to reduce the costs will be large and this energy source isn't controlled by the avaricious few. But solar, wind, and hydro will be more cost effective than they were when they were first beginning to be explored as alternatives to oil and coal? The fluctuating values of oil which holds the world periodically to ransom, and drains the wealth from the West to the oils countries, is something that has to be brought under control. The President of Venezuela is a good example of oil riches gone mad, his stupid antics don't bode well in the long term for his country, and his flirtation with Russia is perhaps an indication of another Dictator drunk with power, his country would be better serviced by some one more intelligent.

We have only outlined the major blocks in this writing because it would be a major book to set out all of the alliances that we see developing in the future? We are herein referring to three major blocks in which all of the countries will be in one or the other, the four blocks are definite but the alliances are just too diverse to set out here! The exception is the Middle East the world's trouble spot from early bible times, this will continue just as Israel will continue to be the focus as the home of God's chosen people? These bordering countries will never be able to form a union, and Israel will always be the recipient of the surrounding countries animosity and hatred? The population of the world will be stabilized with ten billion souls and that will be the population when Christ takes control of the world. This figure will be reduced by the number of souls condemned and destroyed, after having been condemned to Satan's army.

Canada, Australia & New Zealand:

Countries like Canada with its high dependence on primary industry suffered greatly from the depression, its great prairies became desolated and abandoned. The Canadian support for the mother country England was as strong as the rest of its siblings Australia and New Zealand, quick and unreservedly. The four Western Provinces of Canada that are dependent on Wheat crops saw their incomes drop dramatically by around 90% and the Maritime Province went into depression in the early twenties. The prices earned for grain before the depression was $1.60 bushel but when the depression took hold the price was down to 28 cents per bushel. Immigration was down dramatically by 85% and deportation and death was up slightly due to harsh conditions. Bank of Canada was set up in 1934 and The Canadian Broadcasting was first bought on air in 1932. Richard Bennet a Conservative was elected Prime Minister when he capitalized on a mistake made by McKenzie King in 1930. His period of power was unremarkable and he lost the election to McKenzie King in 1937, and then proved himself far more capable than Mr. Bennet. Housing and Industry had suffered badly with an 85% drop in output there was just no demand, no potential customers had any money?

The white Australia policy held back the flood gates for a while, but once that policy was cancelled the floodgates to Australia was opened. The Snowy River Hydro scheme bought big numbers of immigrants to Australia, at its peak around 100,000 per year, from many countries and many vocations in life. The big money being paid for labor on the Snowy meant that some could set themselves up for life, just by spending a sound saving period working there. As is always the case some started with nothing and ended up the same way, gambling and boozing took their earnings as fast as they reached pay day. In Australia the Aborigines got no benefit from those boom times, they were still being treated as vermin that in most case were expendable, and had no rights they were not even considered as real Australians. Mixed breed children were removed from their parents in the belief the State could raise them better, thus they had the stolen generation. Finally after many years, the new Govt; gained worldwide accolades, for its much feted public apology to the Aboriginal people. This act was much more vaunted because of the previous Liberal Govt persistent refusal to apologize. The new Prime Minister gained a Political coup with his promise and accomplishment of that apology. Australia as a country is very successful, not because of but seemingly in spite of its politicians, this seems a fair assessment of the political quality of the country. There is enormous mineral wealth in that country, and Western Australia has experienced a great bonanza, created by astute hard working men and women, ironically Japan has been Australia's best customer for quite some time, but will eventually be supplanted by the Chinese insatiable need for minerals.

New Zealand was in a position similar to Australia and suffered just as much! The far smaller land mass and its small population did slightly help but very little. It was from this time Kiwi Farmers earned their reputation of being able to carry on under any condition, because with a pair of pliers and some fencing wire they could fix almost anything, and in truth the reputation was well earned because it was true. The NZ contribution of troops going to war in defense of the mother country was disproportionate to the countries size, per capita it sent the highest ratio of its men to war for the defense of the British Empire. For the first time a full battalion of Native Kiwi's, Maoris' fought side by side with their own countrymen and Australians.

After WW11 Maoris' were an essential part of the labor force in NZ that catered to the high demand from overseas for NZ food products. It was also a period when returned soldiers of all creeds, but especially those of a Maori heritage received help to rehabilitate themselves, and were able to fit into city life. Most had left to go to war from country areas, but on the return wanted to become urbanized which they were to achieve with Govt; assistance. Maoris' quickly proved their value as great workers; and they were very successfully absorbed into the Kiwi work force.

Back then from 1950 onwards, the demand from Australia for Maori contract workers was very high, travel costs and accommodation was offered and many Maoris' did come to Australia and stayed. The irony was/is that the NZ Maori was accepted without any problems, and integrated into the country as just more immigrants, (albeit without the need of Passports) where as their own Aboriginals were rejected there must have been sound reasons and there was. The author of this book was one of those Maori immigrants, but prefers not to comment on Aboriginal problems; beyond saying there was/is little compatibility between these two native races. Maoris' by nature are a militaristic very aggressive people, whereas the Australian Aboriginal is very passive, and as a race has a history dating further back than the NZ Maori. The Maoris' who has wandered in from who knows where in this world, some six to seven hundred years ago to NZ, and decimated the original inhabitants the Morioris. This is just a blip in time compared to the Australian Aboriginal, who some say have been in Australia for at least one hundred thousand years.

The writer remembers the time in NZ where wool was so valuable, children could make good money wandering around farms picking wool off barbed wire fences, and selling this wool to the brokers, again this is a memory from the past for this writer. There were blips on financial developments, (recessions) but so far none as serious as back in 1929 when the worlds systems failed; but it must happen eventually if only because such artificial growth, must eventually over run itself? We have a system that forces all people to steal off each other and thus keep expanding our sins, those Americans have done it again. They are not satisfied with sending themselves broke, they want to bankrupt us as well,

.Whether they want to admit it or not Muslims are committed to a different end result, they want to see the Muslims with Theological worldwide control and their efforts will not stop until that goal is achieved. We have heard it suggested that the Muslims want to dominate peacefully, certainly Australia seems to be encouraging their Muslim peoples to grow its population, as they pay multi benefits to big families with several breeding females, one male and lots of children all supported by the State. Several European countries are reaping the harvest of disloyalty by their Muslim Citizens as young male Muslims prove to be hazardous, as they claim discrimination against themselves in many guises, we prefer to look at reality, more that it is discrimination in reverse. A recent problem in a beach area of NSW Australia; proved the penchant for young Muslims to gang together and want to challenge the norms of their new home land. The reality of loyalty to their religion first, above that towards their new country, is distasteful to most Australians, who cannot abide the habit of ganging up by young Lebanese Muslims. The example of young Pakistanis in England is also discouraging to Australians who are prepared to speak up, and fear the future when similar atrocities may develop in Australia. Australians are proud of their reputation of giving everybody a fair go, but the young Lebanese Muslims youths are stretching their luck in this regard. Further the spectacle of some of the Muslim Sheiks speaking of Aussies females as meat, doesn't bode well for the future in fact it is sowing this type of bad seeds, that will grow and create a future backlash. Many of these young men come from violent backgrounds, but this begins to pall as an excuse as resentment grows. We need to stress we are not anti Muslim, we are very pro Australian, and don't want imported problems, we don't want to see more and more problems growing and excuses being made.

The Australians in particular became closer to the Americans after their help in pushing back the Japanese, after Darwin was attacked and the Sydney Harbor was infiltrated by mini submarines? The American General shifted his headquarters to Australia and was accompanied by quite a large military force! This created what became the start of a closer relationship between Australia and the USA. For a time after WWII, Australia and NZ were low cost producers; the using of discarded USA military equipment was a feature of that period? Many of those early entrepreneurs, got their start using or buying and selling this discarded machinery? The funny part however, is that now the very big industries in some of these countries are sport? These activities are great, but produce nothing towards the gross domestic product of these various sport-mad countries? Tourism has the biggest future in these wealthy countries apart from of course mineral extraction, Australia and New Zealand no longer see the world through the eyes of meat lambs in NZ and wool in Australia.

The great plains of Canada, Argentina, Russia, Mongolia etc, will all be being harvested with crops for bio fuel, but the world need for food will be so increased by the better world conditions for the peasants classes, that agriculture will be paramount? Efficient producers such as NZ and Australia will be hampered until an answer can be found for the methane created by sheep and cattle, if it can? This closeness has got stronger as the years have gone by, Australia has been a supporter whenever and wherever the Americans have been, in one of the many American war zones? The truth is that Australia and New Zealand are countries that have been originally peopled by small Native populations, and Anglo Saxons, and are really deep in an Asian dominated area of the world? The basically Anglo countries such as the USA and the UK are natural supporters, for these two countries in the South Pacific.

The many Islands in the South Pacific such as Fiji, Western Samoa, and Tonga etc; will link up more closely with Australia and New Zealand and as such, be part of the USA block and common market? For a time after WWII, Australia and NZ were low cost producers; the using of discarded USA military equipment was a feature of that period? Many of those early entrepreneurs got their start using or buying and selling this discarded machinery? The retired American General was bought out of retirement, and placed in control of the entire military operation in the South Pacific. At that time in the South Pacific the Philippines was under Japanese invasion, and was looking as if it would be over run as it eventually was? The General was forced to withdraw his main force as best he could, but he left a force of about 75,000 mixed Philippine and American troops under the control of an American General, behind? This force was unable to hold out and was defeated by the Japanese. The General when he left the Philippines assured them he would return and he did when his forces retook The Philippines?

New Zealand being further away was not so impacted by American salvation and retained its closer ties with Mother England. The New Zealanders have never been as close to the USA as Australian's are. This was because the UK was seen as the major market for NZ frozen lamb especially after WW11 when food for the English market was badly needed? For several years the fear of the English joining the European Common Market was of great concern in NZ, and an alternative market didn't't seem possible? After the UK did join the fears of market loss in NZ become a problem, the production of lamb was considerably reduced! New Zealand suffered greatly from 1974-1992 before that country began to revive itself. Several meat works owned by English firms were closed down; even some famer owned works were closed. Big tracts of land once used for growing fat lamb are now planted in radiate pine, and NZ is a large supplier of pine logs and a large producer of pine lumber? The growth of radiate pine forests in competitive countries such as Australia and Chile seems to be creating tough competition for this product, New Zealand is a long way from world markets and freight costs are high?

The post-war impact was strong in both countries in that their capacity to produce food for England was desperately needed; both countries enjoyed a period of high growth and prosperity? Many large English companies had major holdings down-under and were quick to harness their advantages; producing all kinds of goods for their home markets? The NZ fat lamb industry quickly became a large supplier of frozen lambs to the UK, and the indigenous Maori workers were important in this semi skilled work. Initially the Maoris' were seen by their White employers as "cheap labor", this was largely in the fields of Shearing, Slaughtering, Driving and Roadwork's? This strategy didn't't work because of the high level of over employment, which forced labor costs up without much effort from the employees. After a period the Union movement took over and their success was helped by that same labor situation. The Freezing Workers, and Wharf Union's, then spearheaded the good conditions enjoyed by that class of workers? The wool industry in Australia and to a lesser extent in New Zealand created a dramatic increase in the value of the annual wool clips; the demand for shearers and slaughter men in both countries was very high? Australia regularly imported these skilled workers from New Zealand, with the employers paying all relocation costs!

It was becoming obvious the American absorption of the worlds surplus funds via its US Treasury Bonds, meant that America was sucking up all of the worlds excess capital. It was also obvious that the world's financial system was changing; debt funding was gaining in popularity with citizens of the world, especially in Australia, NZ, Canada and the USA. (The new world) The notion of the "free world" became an interesting idea to us in a small country like New Zealand.

Kiwis are a very creative people, because they are a small population their ingenuity stands out, and they have done well in this complex world we now inhabit. Many of the worlds wealthy are immigrating to NZ as they seek a hide away from a world going crazy, economically, politically, socially etc. NZ and its isolation are at last getting an advantage from being so far away from a world system in decline. To compete in any and every way Kiwi's must be innovative as they truly are, just ask any Kiwi they will tell you they are unique. They can plunder their Australian cousins with total immunity; just ask an Aussie they will tell you what a nuisance their cousins on the other side of the ditch are. But don't any of you Wogs criticize us on either side of that bloody Tasman or we will want you to go home.

How, we down under have asked, did the world's large western economies see their citizens as free; if they were enslaved to debt? It was obvious the creation of a consumer population all geared to debt was not in biblical teaching; the world is heading away from sound money doctrine. Those American done it ya no, got us Antipodeans in so much debt we now have to actually work, where as once only our darkies really worked they had too. But they are big and strong that's their destiny hard work, and long may that be so?

Chapter 7

Geographic changes,
Common Markets:

There are dramatic changes occurring in the USA as her position changes for the English speaking minority, but its neighbor Pakistan and Kashmir is a problem. There will be dramatic changes, the financial map must change. The USA with its huge foreign debt cannot change quickly enough to balance out the creditor Nation that will become China. But we know the effect of the lender, borrower scenario, God tells us this in his Bible, and we must learn to live with but also to embrace what he is doing, because he is in the process of doing it now in his own timing?

The demise of the Soviet Union as a political identity was quite a shock in the Western World. The financial difficulty that Russia as the head of the former Soviet Union found itself in was exacerbated, by acceleration of the American capital expenditure under President Reagan. The Soviets tried to match the USA but collapsed in financial distress. The Soviets had surprised the world when it was the first to launch a space satellite, "Sputnik" but the challenge by The President for the American's to be first on the moon was a staggering success. When The President authorized the Nuclear Shield over the USA; the challenge to the Soviets was what finally hastened the destruction of the Russian financial viability. At the same time The President presided over record current account deficits, he helped bankrupt the Soviets, but he also set the USA on the path to record foreign debt?

The weakness in the Russian version of communism was demonstrated with their inability to meet their various forward production plans. The guarantees of The State sponsored security for life destroyed incentive! This was particularly well demonstrated on the huge state owned farms, where budgets were so far behind predictions. One of the highlights of the American President visit to Berlin, (which is still remembered and often quoted) was when he stood at the Brandenburg gate, and in his speech said Mr tear down that wall. He was referring to the wall built, to keep East and West Germany separated; it was not long after that when they ordered the removal of the Berlin Wall.

Russia will harness its energy resources in both oil and their agriculture capacity, by the harnessing of its huge unused land resources for bio fuels. Russia has ambitions to again achieve super power status, and will fight to control its black sea ports, that will be surrounded if both Georgia and the Ukraine join NATO. To us it seemed natural for Russia to object to the countries on either side of her only deep sea port, becoming members of NATO. Because Russia has such a huge number of nuclear war heads at the ready it's easy to see the anxiety of the countries that were a part of the Soviet Union, Russia won't stand by without some type of retaliation. Russia and China for their own protection must create common alliance with other surrounding Asian countries. We therefore see Russia, China and other Asian countries in alliance, that's the Northern Common Market Group in Bible parlance.

Eastern Europe will combine with Western and Northern Europe to become a large Common Market Community Block. The African continent will link up with the Europeans this will be the second of the three world groups. Europe with its old cultures that link back to the various Barbarian tribes of yore, as well as a large part of the old Roman Western Empire. The further link up to Africa will cover some of the area which was once a part of the Roman Eastern Empire, never the less all of the cultures will find it very difficult to form into a common bond. Africa is reputed to be the cradle of humanity, Europe is the consolidation of many cultures, and at present all of these countries have strong Muslim influence. The future will see just how well that diverse group will work together within the proposed common market, but we think it will be a very successful cooperative group, and they will be in the middle protected from the Russians and Chinese, to create an effective group. This Chino/Russian Common Market Group will be the largest in both land mass and population, but it will also be the one that will have the most difficulty creating a human quality of life, that the world and God will find acceptable?

India, England, Japan, Sth Korea, Australia, New Zealand, Canada, the Philippines, Taiwan, Mexico, India, Central and South America and SEATO will link up to a common market with the USA. This will be the most dynamic Common Market Grouping of the three, and also the one that will find it easiest to settle down to world centralized Govt; within which the real big brother concept will have finally found its way. This is a disparate group and is grouped more for compatibility than for common heritage. Japan and Sth Korea are the two members that are there because it is hard to see them fitting in elsewhere. Japan in particular is hated by the Russians and China would find Japan hard to stomach. Sth Korea conversely will have trouble working within Russia and China, their attitude from the past when both supported Nth Korea, will be difficult to see as part of any other than the American Group. England is another that will be out of place and yet not really they are the progenitors of the common Anglo Saxon heritage; that predisposes them to this third group.

The Middle East will be the centre of continuing turmoil as it has been since early biblical times. Israel will continue to be closely linked to America, and part of Group three, but it is in the centre of hostile nations and always will be disadvantaged. From the entry to the Promised Land by Joshua and the wandering Jewish nation, this area has been the most contentious of any in the world. From 1948 the Arabs and the Lebanese Muslims have decried the presence of this Jewish State; this attitude will never change until the return of Christ and the banishment of Satan from his position as the king of the world. Satan in his guise as a world leader will be of course the much trumpeted Anti Christ! Israel will flourish prior to Christ's return and the air of expectancy within the Christian world will permeate all areas of the Christian world. It matters not where in the world one lives in; as most of the world's peoples, await this so momentous event. This return of the Christian founder will excite peoples of Faith who adhere to Christ's teachings, no matter where in the world they live.

The biggest change in the modern world is communication, which is now instant. Personal Computers and the Internet has guaranteed that anyone who wants information on almost any subject, can immediately find out what they need to know about anything, that is of interest worldwide. The search engines available to one and all means we don't have to go to Libraries to study up past or present world affairs, all that needs to be done is check in on a search engine ie Google, Yahoo, and MSN etc.

The world is becoming smaller as prophesied and the Global Village concept is fast becoming a reality, China and India with their huge low cost labor forces, have become what Japan and Germany once were, the low cost producers of the world. This phase has now changed and both those countries Germany and Japan have become more quality producers. Both of these two countries were supported by the USA financially, as they fought to recover from severe wartime damage. The USA have their own agenda they were/are looking for acolytes to secure them in the West and the South, this importance to the well being of America, has given Germany and Japan a very quick recovery from the internal destruction during WW11.

Germany and Japan have as their main strength for recovery, a hard working highly disciplined and educated work force. Chinese and Indian populations are huge, their foreign trade is vital, but they also have the need to improve the life styles or conditions of their own peoples, and in so doing create enormous internal markets. Jesus has told us the poor we would always have amongst us, this meant the lazy and none productive peoples would always be with us, and they would always be poor. What was not meant was that we would have starving millions, in countries while others live in better conditions. The concept of the wealthy country's earning large amounts of interest off poor countries, are anathema to the Lord's request, that we live in love one for each other.

Until there is a more equal distribution of the worlds natural wealth there cannot be a godly reconciliation between all peoples. In the Lords eyes it is an abomination to see starving millions especially in the African Continent, but also in many other areas ie South America from Mexico to Chile, India, China, SEA, etc. What is serious sin is for the wealthy nations to profit by the starving millions, and the sight of the poor countries being charged interest by the wealthy, is really the worst of Sin in God's sight.

We see the future of China, India, and South America being on the verge of improvement. Russian economic change powered by their oil resources and the obvious other advantages that are emerging, will catapult this country back to Super Power status. Huge oil reserves have been discovered in Russian Siberia and the vast expanses of the Russian plains is an untouched natural resource that will be bought into production for the growing of bio fuels .The nuclear arsenal still held by Russia is huge; some 15,000 nuclear heads, the reason for the Soviet Union collapse and Russia's loss of status was economic not military.

The countries of Europe will strengthen as Germany and France, lead the way for the many other surrounding nations ie Europe, Western, Eastern and Southern will come together in union their peoples will benefit, and living conditions will improve. There are still huge difficulties in Europe, mainly culture and language that will continue to cause problems. As noted in the book of Daniel, the feet of the golden statue had toes of clay and feet of iron, this signifies that difficulty or as we understand it incompatibility of these diverse countries and cultures. This future consolidation is far beyond anything achieved in the past, certainly more countries are involved than those indicated in the golden statue of Babylonian fame.

The main continent that lags behind is Africa the cradle of mankind; this is the main area that is slowest to improve. Over many years African Chief's were the ones who delivered up captives for sale to the slavers, thus being destructive to their own people. The record of leaders in Africa has not been conducive to creating confidence to investors, but the Chinese and Indians will be more aggressive in their approach to extracting the minerals in Africa. The problem will be whether good contracts are negotiated and if they are, whether the wealth will filter down to benefit the African peoples.

In the Lords scheme of things though, financial benefits will eventually filter through worldwide, and an equal distribution of the world's wealth will be created. There will however always be that difference between the energetic being wealthy, and the poverty of the lazy and slovenly. To achieve this improved status for the countries that lag behind, does not mean the poor countries will be elevated to the level enjoyed now by the industrial world. What will happen are the emerging nations will improve upwards, but the wealthy nations will have to slip backwards, here in simple terms is what must happen? If we take one hundred as being the present indicator for the wealthy nations, and fifty as representing the emerging nations then twenty as being the poor nations, only when all nations are on eighty will the Lords Will be near to satisfied. From that point all can grow back to one hundred in tandems, this will bring without turmoil equality for all, not upset promulgated through war. Terrorism and the human condition will be   greatly improved because of the Spiritual growth of the many, which will create worldwide peace, and Gods Kingdom on earth as a reality

The world consolidated domestic product will obviously be huge and hard to imagine at this time, but there will be a dramatic change in the method of international trade. Money will not be the method of trade a method of trade tied to exchange between nations; will be possible as the systems of computer controls become ever more sophisticated. Accumulated lazy wealth to none productive areas will change, but the initiative to individuals will still be available. Cash as such will no longer be legal tender all exchange will be by credit transfer; this will start in the wealthy nations and gradually filter down, as the other nations improve the conditions of their populations. This transfer method of trade is already being used ie electronic transfer from point A to Point B, the computer strength to coordinate these none money flows are available. The computers to control plastic money once this method is legal and cash is cancelled, so the billions of people change over to plastic tender will be completed.

Trade will flow smoothly with no money being used, but there will be a central body amongst the trading blocks, USA, Russia/China and European blocks. Then and only then can a world dictator appear, he will come from one of the blocks and he will be Godless. Then the Spiritual battle will be joined in earnest, and the conditions will be near for the return of the Lord

Jesus Christ to claim his Kingdom. This anti Christ will be the President of the world parliament, but may not emerge for quite some time, what we are saying is the machinery will be in place for the anti Christ to take over and he will, but only for a very short time.

As a result of the meltdown in the financial markets, there will be millions of homes in the new world on which the owners will owe more than what their homes are worth. The income from the investments these owners have made may not perform, but the USA will be the main victim of this situation, followed closely by Canada and eventually Australia. New Zealand may be a candidate for financial meltdown, but Kiwis are not as exposed as the other three countries. Australia and New Zealand are very exposed to the commodities markets, but their markets in Asia should remain secure. If the markets for Asian products collapse, though this will trickle through to Australia's commodities supplies. NZ with its low cost agriculture may come through, but there will be a period of severe strain on their economy.

America with its huge foreign debt needs to see a change in its structure. The role of being the world's police men and defending its democratic capitalist system will become too expensive; the wars America is fighting will suck their economy dry. America will retain its superiority in the military, but will bring its foreign accounts into surplus, by reducing its buying of oil, reduction in foreign aid and a greater export account earned from its technological advantages, gained from its huge space program technology. What this great power has gained from its space program is what sets it so far out in front of all other countries, which of course is why the other nations will keep trying to steal her secrets.

The Chinese will have a space program of her own, but the pressures of its internal needs will slow her down. The cost of her military is of course a direct cost but at the same time creates a huge use of labor. The war machine creates an internal money flow that bolsters the economy; one wanders what America would do without her war machine as a huge part of her gross domestic product. As China's population becomes more educated to understand world conditions, "the same applies to India and South East Asia" the demand from her people will increase at home. This will slow her development of the space technology, and her need to spend heavily on her local population will accelerate. So they will try ever harder to steal the secrets from the USA.

The New World America, Australia, Canada, and New Zealand, has the largest percentage of home ownership among their population's and so will be the country's most directly affected. The American economy will be the most grievously damaged, and may have to face international loss of confidence in their money. If the foreign investors are able to, they may want to withdraw their investments in UST Bonds. America won't be in a position to redeem those bonds so the world will go into a severe depression just as bad as 1929, but this time will be of a longer duration. This will be the main instrument that the Lord will use to change the world's economy, and it will also be the instrument that will leave the way open for an evil world dictator to emerge. Only the return of Jesus Christ will be able to keep the Anti Christ under control, this is why he will return at this time, and he will but this time in triumph, even if still born of a women.

There will be no war, or nuclear attack the collapse of the world's finances is the only instrument, that will bring the world to its knees. The world's politicians will look on in horror as their Governments collapse, but of whatever persuasion they are, there will be nothing that anyone can do. The industrial advantage will move to Asia, just as it started in England then passed to Germany, the USA and Japan in the near future will move to Asia. This time the spread of countries involved will be far more than in any time in the past. The New World will still have superiority in the number of its educated citizens, there is no doubt the workers of America are of a very high standard, that's why it achieved the prominence it did. Australia is on the same path now taking in immigrants from all corners of the globe and reaping the benefits from that policy. There is however no previous industrial giant that can match Asia, since there is almost 50% of the world's population in this area, once it really awakes there will be a new world order. But for the New World to be dominated by the North will not be tolerated by our God in Heaven.

Covert operations within the CIA have been two edged for America. The work in Iran for and on behalf of the Shah of Persia was effective. The surveillance and warning to The President that Russia was installing nuclear weapons on Cuba was a face down, that appeared very dangerous to world peace until Khrushchev was forced to back down, and the Soviet ships were turned around, this was a CIA triumph. The small army of so called contras which ended at the Bay of Pigs in Cuba was a public relations and military disaster. The U2 episode when the Russians shot down the spy plane over its territory and Colonel Powers the pilot was coerced to confess his real mission were a disaster. The CIA in America, MI6 in the UK and the KGB in Russia are security vehicles or spy organizations that are foremost in their countries security activities, the AIC has at times had very big budgets to do their work.

The need to protect her interests will get ever greater as the competing nations try hard to sabotage American security and ever more the CIA and other secret organizations of the USA will proliferate. There would be nothing worse for America and her allies, than to know the American Space created secrets have been stolen and are being freely distributed, in a world that is totally alien to the democratic way of life. There is no doubt the American heritage is the best there is on Gods earth, the problem is to preserve that way of life, but to bring it into order so that it begins to conform to Gods will more accurately.

In Gods agenda, the expectations on America is high, much has been give so much is expected. Americans who really believe in their country are a pleasure to behold and as we moved across that great country there was so much to admire. Having said that we spirits had to admit there was much that had to be done, what we knew was the USA was for its sheer size a great country. The new financial system that emerges will dictate the political structure, but whatever evolves will be in line with God's word.

The sequence of events that will happen as the world develops. A Godly system shall be.

- The development of the global village by natural means not by war, God will guide our politicians as they try to find the path.
- A cashless society for the general population followed by the same change in the method of legal tender in the commercial world.
- The recognition of the three Common Market areas that will be formalized by the introduction of a world central Govt:
- The procedures that will be developed so the world Govt; can be truly successful.
- That central Govt; will control, Crime, International monetary control, Military Security, the election of the world delegates etc.
- Each country will have representatives according to their GDP and the spread that creates that GDP.

These are the vital areas that will be the start of evolving to a new world political control system, and all will be accomplished without war.

Chapter 8

Gods Kingdom

In trying to understand what the world is all about and how we are to achieve Utopia, the first thing we need to understand is the difference between a world dominated by Satan and his demons, and what the future will be like when Christ reigns on earth. The Christian Bible has two parts the old and the New Testament! The Old Testament is a record of the Jews and confirms they are the chosen people! The reason they are the chosen people they were set apart to demonstrate the Will of God. The Patriarchs Abraham, Isaac and Jacob are all examples of God's Will. The Jewish people have demonstrated the Law of God and thus his Will. Jesus Christ came to fulfill the law not cancel it; the law is as relevant now as it ever was.

When Christ died on the cross he was demonstrating his bowing to the Will of the Father, but more importantly he was demonstrating the Love of God. The Bible therefore is the guide book of the Will and the Love of our Father, our Creator, this is unchangeable. When Moses wrote the first five books of the bible he was inspired by God, but so were all the other books, some are more effective than others, but all are inspired of God. The first book for example speaks of creation, but Moses does not tell us whether each day of creation is a day as we know it or a day in Gods world. We know that Gods world has no time, so each day could have been a thousand years or even a million years, even we in his Army don't know. The Lords agenda is known to him only, none of us knows just what his timing is, anybody who says differently and claims to know is wrong. The Bible is only the instruction book we need to study and understand, none can know God if they don't know his will for his creation, the Bible explains all we need to know?

When Alexander built Alexandria it was to his own glory, and still is remembered in honor of Alexander.

And so it has been with all war lords, they have only ever been interested in glorifying themselves. In some instances they have tried to claim what they were doing was to Gods Glory, Stalin is said to have tried to fall back on his early training in the ministry when Russia was attacked by Hitler. Stalin was a demonic monster responsible for over twenty seven million deaths of his own people during the revolution and WWII. Hitler was reputed to be inclined towards a belief in what he was doing was pre ordained by his Gods mind, we don't know who his God was. It is said that Hitler's belief was taken from the music of Wagner, after he came from a musical evening of listening to that composer. Suddenly Hitler proclaimed that the Jews worshipped a different God than the rest of the world and should be destroyed.

Napoleon was a brilliant administrator, what a shame that brilliance could not have been used for the good of all Nations in Europe, and Egypt a country he had wanted to claim. Napoleon rise and rampage through Europe was brilliant as a man of war, but how much could he have achieved as a man of peace, none will ever know. Winston Churchill was a war lord a hero to the English and rightly so, but as a man of peace he was in most ways a failure. So many wars down through the ages in the name of God or Allah, but always man elevate himself and so we can see the difference. When we defeat one of Satan's Demons in defense of one of our own children that means that demon is finished it is destroyed there are no failures accepted. The demonic spirit is like a candle if you blow out the light the candle is nothing, its life is gone. So it is when we beat a demon the demon was the light it went out and so is gone finished Satan cannot relight the fire, that demon is no more. Satan is the Father of all the abominations that it is possible to imagine: Hate, Lies, Murder, Jealousy, Adultery etc and all are negative actions. Christ is the Father of Love, Marriage, Faith Hope, etc and all positive emotions; let us first think what life would be without any of the Negatives that Satan creates.

First off the Demonic Army we have all of the various demons that specialize in the various sins. Let's imagine if there was no hate on earth. Hate is the opposite of Love so if we had no hate the dominating emotion would be love. From that we know that Love is the most powerful force and will dominate in the future Gods earthly Kingdom. If we had no hate we would have no wars, because the hate generated would not be possible, but how can that be achieved, what is the genesis of Hate? Ambition and all other negative energy creates a lot of the negative vibes that then convert gradually to hate, in most circumstances hate is a growing cancer that has its genesis from within, until it reaches the human extreme which is hate.

But if that ambition etc energy had been channeled into creating Love the difference is extreme. If Love is the foundation of what is again ambition, but now as the desire for positive energy what we then have is the opposite in every way, thus in all things we have opposites. Satan generates hate so he is the father of negative energy we express his quality as hate. Christ is the creator of all things positive so he is the father of Love or all things positive. Man as he progresses is growing ever fonder of Satan's way of life, and this has been so since Cain killed Able (after Adam and Eve were ejected from the Garden of Eden) because of Jealousy, from that time Satan has been in control. This is why Satan has to be finally banished from Earth and Christ must take control, but the final battle must be fought even though the battle at Calvary was a win for Christ; that was only the first example of the battle. Any battle has to be prepared, and this is what is happening as the evil beings are rejected from Heaven, and the only way left to them is Satanic.

The Spirits that are accepted into Christ's army are the superior beings; this quite naturally creates a superior army. The return of Spirits to the world gives those who haven't been quite good enough to enter heaven are given another chance, but they get no chance to pollute those who have been approved. We who choose to work with our families as I did myself, are considered to be the elite of warriors and as such are given every encouragement to be trained for the final battle. As time goes by the both armies are growing, but Satan does not have the facilities to train his horde, and they remain what we on earth would see as illiterate louts. These are the types who were the brown shirts in Hitler's army and were rejected from his main forces; even the evil ones know the difference of good from bad, they don't see their energy in the same way the believers in Love do, because they enjoy their ambition which is for evil. The other advantage Christ's army has is there is no attrition so the training is accumulative, and effective for the soldiers of our army; but Satan's army are suffering losses continuously even now. With the Salvation of our own loved ones every time there is a victory means another Demon destroyed never to return, destruction is the demonic price of failure, and hence we have even there the fostering of hate!

If Love was the natural Human emotion there would be no starving millions, because all would want to share, the wealthy would share with the poor world. If there was no lying and killing there would be trust and from that would come confidence, of all mankind one to the other. There would be no stealing so there would be an openness one to the other. Adultery will be the hardest sin to control, but with love as a basis of civilization that would also be abolished. This is the basis of the spiritual wars when the demons that promote those sins are defeated, and then the sins will become controlled. When Christ's army reigns supreme with him then no longer is there a spiritual battle. Christ will be in control; there will no war and therefore no mass killing as well as little murder. The energy wasted on wars will be diverted for the good of mankind, and there will be no racial problems. Nationalism will still be part of the human experience, but it will all be constructive, competition and healthy. As the world becomes smaller and like a big village, so there will be a inter breeding of the races that will reduce racial tension. The National identity although still dominant will be less aggressive, any aggression will be taken out through games and athletic competition, it is in this none war arena that the inter race conflict will be played out, not killing and bloodshed. Healthy competition is the hope for the transference to a world economy based on love!

We accept that there will always be the minority that will be unable to live by Godly rules, but these people are abominations and will be dealt with as we are shown in the Bible, God's book of life. The complex human institutions will no longer be needed because there will be no need for jails etc. Hospitals will be very few because sickness will be unusual and not really needed. Because people are so healthy there will be a huge growth in sports, but there will not be the hero worship of the super sports people, and that will be because such worship will be diverted to God and the Salvation. This primary emotion will automatically remove the tendency of mankind to worship sports idols, film stars etc; all such Hero worship will be reserved for the Savior. The future timing is still only known to our Father in Heaven, only he knows when and how some of these final earth shattering events will take place. We in the Lords army only know what we are listed to do and on that we are very clear, we are to destroy Satan's army and in the process we are cleansing mankind eventually, in fact the process is already well and truly started.

The book of Daniel's prophecy will be seen to be true. For example the European Nations have been consistently proved to be culturally incompatible as signified with the Golden Statue built by King Nebuchadnezzar, the toes of Clay and the Feet of Iron cannot blend. Europe is blending ok financially, but the future will show their inability to blend politically.

The apparent blood thirsty tone of the Book of Revelation is strongly towards the Spiritual Battle, but there is no doubt end times is going to see a lot of physical death as well. However the four horsemen for example are a Spiritual example, not the death of earth people at that time. The Beast is also spiritual and not part of the apparent bloodletting that people see as an abomination, and is so scary for people to accept. There have been various ideas on earth by theologians who have seen the beast as Catholic, but others see it as Muslim etc. We know that neither is correct that beast is religion as a whole, and the abuse by all of the multitudes of the leaders of the many denominations is that beast. There are so many leaders who have abused their flocks in so many ways and have taken advantage in every way, money, power and sex etc. In so many ways the ordinary people have been abused by the beast over thousands of years, this is why we are getting close to the apex of Satanism, that system is the Spiritual system, and that is operational now.

If we look at the Roman Catholics their origins are in Rome, planted by St Paul who was imprisoned in Rome. He started by having meetings in his prison, his jailors were sympathetic to his teachings, and thus he planted the first house church in Rome the ancestor of many more. St Peter came to Rome too so both were church planters in Rome. Both were executed in Rome, but the work they did went on to become the Roman Catholic Church. Prior to being sent to Rome to plead his case before the Emperor Paul was the main one responsible for planting the seven churches in Asia, so the antecedents of the Orthodox church is clearly seen as a result of Paul's work..

The Western Roman Catholic Church was for the first 300 plus years supported by the Eastern Catholic Orthodox Church, both financially and with the supply of missionaries, to help establish the church in Rome. The Western Catholic Church became the official church of the Roman Empire, when it was accepted by the Emperor Constantine near the end of his life. This was done from the new Capital adopted by Constantine; he was the one who was the builder of Constantinople in present day Istanbul in Turkey. It was said that Constantine early in his career when going into battle, had a vision that he would be victorious in battle that day. He was as he believed he was foretold totally victorious, so from that day forth his troops wore a Christian flag into battle wherever they fought. Constantine's mother Helene was an early convert to Christianity was being abused, as the years have gone by the greater the abuse or changes, in what she was supposed to have done.

The genesis of Protestantism was by Luther when he nailed his thesis on the church door at Wittenberg in Germany that has been the start of an enormous proliferation of different sects worldwide. The break away from the Pope by Henry the 8th and the formation of the independent Church of England, helped accelerate the Protestants. His daughter Elizabeth the 1st was the main Royal to perpetuate the Church of England, her reign can only be described as spectacular. The growth of the British Empire meant the spread of the various off shoots from the English Church.

Muslims have had an equally spectacular growth worldwide, and the followers of the various different sects number the same as the Roman Catholics. The sects in India are just amazing in numbers and the problems between the Hindu's and Muslim's are horrific. All of these major religions are headed for a future bonded as one, when Christ arrives to take his place at the head of his church.

The teaching in Revelation referring to the beast is referring to the Christian Faith. Since the time of St Paul the teachings of Christ have been abused and emasculated. By the time John wrote Revelation on Patmos it was near the end of the first century. By this time Christ had been crucified for almost seventy years. His teachings and the rest of what became the Christian Bible was already abused. From the start of the Old Testament even the Jews were in rebellion, when they had just come out of Egypt, and while Moses was up on the Mount Sinai the Jews were in rebellion. Moses own brother and his Sister Miriam were both complicit in building the Golden Bull, this cannot be just brushed aside, it's symbolic of human rebellion hence the beast.

A good example of how the church used up the Aristocracy was Richard the lion Heart of England; and his Crusades into the Holy Lands as they were then known. Richard and Saladin the Muslim autocrat faced up in war and really exhausted each other. Richard for his part at the point of consummation of his battles turned away; and pulled back much to the disgust of his knights. Saladin after the Christian withdrawal was treated with disdain by his followers, and retired into disgrace.

Under the ancient feudal system the peasants worked the land for the land owners and the church were the major land owners as they were left aristocratic estates left to the church in the final wills and Testaments of the wealthy. The sales of symbols of many characters was once a thriving industry in medieval times, the sales of articles to hasten ones path through purgatory is a humorous story on its own.

Summary

The questions we have posed herein are those who have no access to inside information would ask. Over the last seventy years the writer has seen a lot of changes, and has often marveled at how quickly mankind can forget what has happened in the past, and will struggle on making the same silly mistakes. Humans have developed such a diverse brain yet never really seem to learn very much, it just seems somehow we are born to forget tragedy.

The world has gone through the 20th century, it has been a most momentous period during which two world wars, and a worldwide depression and numerous financial recessions have been inflicted on, or affected the entire world in many ways. The scale of deaths was unprecedented in world history, and it is doubtful such a scale of conflicts and human deaths will ever be exceeded, unless nuclear war should break out which could totally annihilate mankind.

America has risen from just another young nation, to possibly the greatest one ever! England had continued her mighty way, but exhausted by war sank to the ranks of mediocrity, but retained her Monarchy with all of its traditions. The Germans outdid themselves in their ability for self destruction followed by feats of recovery only they could achieve.

There has been the attempted total genocide of the Jewish race, but they returned to their homeland en mass, Israel. One of the lost tribes was found, living in Africa, and as colored as any normal African! The Jews were not wanted in Israel by the surrounding Arab States, but a military confrontation was fought between Jews and Arabs, which led to a route of the Arabs. The period ended with the Palestinians being stateless, and living in atrocious conditions, in horrible camps on the West Bank of Israel.

Several Dictators arose who were responsible for the mass rape and murder of hundreds of millions of men women and children. Germany,

Russia, Cambodia and others were among those befouled by such monsters! The populations of the Asian countries reached staggering numbers and still growing, but other nations find their peoples getting steadily less.

Obviously the biggest difficulty in store for those ambitious to see World Govt; become an integral part of the world structure, that all may benefit is the religious divisions that separate us all. We know that Religion must not be a part of World Govt control that would be none workable, because religion has been the focus of hatred and ambition in mankind that is evil since creation. The freedom of religion is a plank that must be recognized, and kept under the control of National not World Govt. It has been recognized that all countries will retain their territorial integrity in any future World Parliament, but areas that would benefit from world control, is what will be within the scope of that world organization.

An acceptable formula that could be enacted to cover the need of all countries will be difficult, far harder than any financial or any other obstacle. Satan will do his very best to fore stall any chance of success but in the end he will be defeated. The writer finds himself at some odds with his own Christian Faith, but has a strong belief that what is best will prevail if only because Gods Will must be satisfied, and at this level he will steer the way through. The people of the world we are most interested in are the poor countries, and we see them as one of the vital reasons that the world must succeed, in its struggle to find fairness for all.

The truth is that man has reached the level of mental development, that wars and all attendant evil should be controllable. There can be no valid reason for a repeat of the humungous horrors of the 20th century, if there is it will be because man has self destructed and given the planet back to the insects. This is quite possible if a nuclear holocaust is triggered somewhere, somehow in this crazy world.

Chapter 9

The World as One: The years 2100 to 2200

It's the end of the 22nd century and mankind is finally all working in unity within the Common Market Groups. The world is at peace, but has not found full world unity there are still occasional wars that flare up which have to be put down. But the entire world inclusive of the four Group Parliament's are now ready to reach out to each other and perhaps come together in a world unified, to working within a world parliament. The sins of mankind are undiminished but enormously improved from the 20th century especially in the areas of money; the cashless society has made a big difference to the treasury incomes of the nations of the world. But despite the improvement as always the ingenuity of man has kept sin as a major platform in the ways of the world, and there has been little difference in the level of negative human attitudes. The unity within the groups has hugely improved the lives of the poor people of the world, but it hasn't eradicated the poor entirely, which of course it never will. The number of the naturally slothful and lazy people ensures the poor are always with us, but the Bible has warned us we will always have them know so we know this is an ill us will be with that forever.

The success of tax control and all sources of revenue for the governments have been great for the treasuries of the world, but there has been loopholes exploited as expected. There are smart accountants and financiers; who as expected would have found ways to be creative, but they would never again be as effective as they were prior to the groups working in unity, and the cashless society becoming a reality. These loopholes will be closed when the world financial system that is foreseen, is finally fully in place. Politicians now have to be far more accountable to their constituents for everything they do, even in Russia and China with their now more educated population, egalitarianism is now the common denominator of all countries' big and small.

The still dominant countries are Russia and China, Germany and France, America and the United Kingdom. The Muslims have found their way back to their former glory as they were in the 14th and 15th centuries, but for them there is no clear leadership. The Middle East Countries are very strong, but Indonesia with their big population is very important in the Muslim economies, all are doing well, but Indonesia is out of control with its annual population growth rate. But that is a problem for the Muslim's world; the other groups are not involved. India has been the big success story of the 21st and 22nd centuries' and they are now working with SEA on massive production schedules. They are replacing China which now has its production capacity absorbed by the needs of its own peoples. The Indian untouchables are now a major production force, as is SEA and the Americas!

Israel is still the dominant military force in the Middle East, but peace agreements have been hammered out, and the inter religious hostility is not now so severe although there will never be a time when Israel can relax. However the Jews are now very sure the Messiah is due, and the Christians are sure the return of Christ is near. That confidence is warranted because the tribulation has already happened and much as predicted in the book of Revelation has come true.

The economies of the four groups has allowed a far more equitable distribution of the worlds natural resources, and Africa working with the Europeans is on the verge of starting to thrive. China's peasant class are far better off than they were in the early 21st century, but now at the end of the 22nd century China and its huge mass of people are doing well. Russia has developed differently, their population has expanded and the Kulak class is back now having developed the Russian natural resources. Both Russia and China have flourished Russia with the use of its natural resource, and China with its large Labor resource. Both have worked well together, but both still have problems with the freedoms of democracy, they prefer to stay with a type of mixture between all of the groups in the entire world at large. In this way they have developed a philosophy that is unique to their own society and economy, and it is working well. Theirs is the only way such a huge mass of people can be controlled! India has managed its growth and their huge population quite well, now that Pakistan creates no problems all is quiet on the sub continent!

Communications have changed dramatically as the internet is now all pervasive and is taken for granted, as a facility enjoyed by all. The home computer is now all pervasive, but totally different than it was in 2,000 it has been miniaturized so that most wear their computer in a ring on any finger. There is no longer any need for a monitor, and the picture can be seen instantly just in front of the operator, in any position they want. Voice control is now the method computer management which makes IT the tool of all mankind. Many just use their mobile phones, but these are very different now, the most advanced models are linked to their operator's thoughts, so we have thought and /or voice control. The people now have a huge amount of information at their disposal, but the need for education is ever more obvious as information is bought to a parallel with understanding. This has led to a highly educated system, but at the same time the people must now evolve on a parallel with govt; invasive thought control?

All travel has become quick easy and cheap, as fuel resources are more equitably shared and used. The main fuel used in cars is now compressed air, the cars are quite expensive, but the fuel is very cheap. Public transport is now exhaustively used but again these facilities have evolved as much as private transport. Renewable fuel is now over 50% of the energy resources used, and most homes have their own power source, with their surplus being transferred to the local power grid.

Most of the operations on all animal farms use animal methane for their power source, and again any surpluses are transferred to the local power grid. The OPEC nations still sell their fossil fuels, but they don't have the power to force prices up at will, at the same time trading in power on the World stock exchange is forbidden. Cars are now able to travel on water in the air and run on roads, most are fueled with compressed air, with a few using gas and other green fuels. Compressed air is a major propellant and the ability of cars to fly; has eased the road congestion in major cities worldwide, Los Angeles, Beijing, London, Berlin etc.

The giant media organizations have faltered as the major movers have lost their founders, and the resulting heirs have lost the original drive. The media has now become better controlled as more authenticity is controlled by law. The media still have the freedom of the press, but they must now be able to prove up what they are sending out to the public if and when they are challenged. Their source of information is still kept private, but the financial cost of false reporting is now very expensive.

The global problems are in the process of being improved, the gas emissions are now controlled, but the need now is to fix the huge hole that is claimed to be up there. Now is the time when that great hole so called has to be proved up. It is now muted that man is trying to achieve is to change the course of the natural climatic changes that have occurred over the last one million years; it's a big job and may be an impossible task? The scientific community can no longer trumpet the hole in the stratosphere, because the politicians are demanding proof and answers now.

The real failure has been religion, the mix throughout the world has not been effective as the priests etc fail to create unity, and in fact see the problems exacerbated. In the previous chapters as we have set out what we see is the situation if the World now achieves full unity for Economic Common Market Groups, with a world Parliament. It is time now to take the final step and look into the future for what will happen in what the Bible calls end times? Going forward in these writings we are not trying to be prophetic, we are just commenting from the book of Revelation, which really is not so hard to understand, now we are really in the end times.

The time of the great tribulation has happened and all true believers who were still waiting on earth for this great event to happen, have finally been taken up and are now with their Father in Heaven. This is made clear in the book of Revelation as all of the saved ones gather around the Lords throne and give thanks. The book of Revelation is obviously a symbolic look into the future when the right times in Gods Will has finally arrived. The symbolism of Revelation is horrific but the true believers have no need to fear, only those who reject the Trinity, need to be in fear. There will be tremendous loss of spiritual life within Satan' ranks, but the end is near and those in the fight who are in the armies of Christ will be saved immediately so they cannot lose.

The tribulation that had been waited on for so long was sudden and emphatic! Many people who all thought would be certain to be taken were left! Many who were thought to be no hopers were taken, so the religious world was in total confusion? There were many who were accusing each other of sins and many who had begun to lose their way, while there were now many new followers coming to the truth of Spiritual truth daily. But at the same time many still reject the truth of Christ and fight on against anything that can be seen as the coming of Christ, they still refuse to recognize God and his family of man? Fear in the ranks of these lost beings is now profound, as they sense the inevitable, but cannot change their obsession with sin and are therefore lost souls. The book of Daniel warned us all that a great block shall fall on the worlds regimes and erase all of the world systems that have come before, and the new World system shall arise? That great block of stone represents the new world that shall be led by the Lamb of God and shall prevail forever as the Government of all Mankind. It is now close to falling on the world, and the promised rule of Christ is near.

The world is in turmoil as it has been for millennia the four groups are working together well, but the tension worldwide is increasingly hostile, all because of religious dispute. The many religions of mankind are in dispute, the Roman Catholic Church has long been in decay as it struggles to erase the memories of sexual immorality; within the churches. Woman Priests have been ordained, but that hasn't stopped the Pedophilia and Homosexuality that has plagued the ministry for almost 200 years that we know of, but probably 2,000 that we don't know of. The religious strangle hold on the people, which were once held and manipulated by the leaders of all denominations is under threat. Finally after so long creating confusion within the great bulk of the people, the day of reckoning is nigh!

There have been many new advances in Medical, Information and health improvement has been tremendous, with fewer hospitals now needed as most healing can be controlled by general practitioners. Space travel has become affordable to many more people, but a new planet for the world occupation by humans has not yet been selected although Mars is still favored. Astronomy is still postulating the enormity of the universes, and the claim that the universe will one day self destruct is now more insistent. Food enough to feed all Peoples is now being produced, but the use of home gardens is now prodigious worldwide. Stem Cell advances have been effective and a legal formula for their use is in place. Travel is now very cheap to all parts of the globe by air, but the internet is now so personal there is no longer any need to travel to be with family, except the young still need that physical contact. Science is charging ahead with new inventions of real use being an almost daily occurrence. Religion has gotten more disorganized than ever, and is still the main source of hatred within the human condition. Global gas emissions have been brought under control, and there is progress within science towards healing the hole in the ozone layer. The world population is now almost ten billion, but the explosion has been brought under control and future is growth neutral.

The Beast of Revelation is religion, and the false leadership which is leading mankind in all the wrong directions is now understood, but nothing has yet been done. Religious Leaders have aspired to political influence and this has been very destructive, in that it is tearing the people's loyalties apart and tension is now higher than ever worldwide. Because every country in the world has a mixture of worshippers, there are many different denominations cults etc; tension is growing ever worse; finally the conditions are right for the return of the Savior. The false leaders that the Bible has predicted is a phenomenon peculiar to all religions and cults, as Science (Evolution) competes with Religion (Creation) and the leaders are ever more false to their various flocks.

We need to look into the book of revelation to understand what the future events, will be and what will be happening in the very near future. The Christians have been waiting for the return of Jesus Christ from the time he left over 2.2 millennia ago. But the time is now near, because world conditions are right.

Just as his people the Jew's would not accept him when he first came; they will do the same again unless the proof is obvious, they still live by God's Laws so they need legal proof. But this time there will be no doubt, Christ will come at the head of his Spiritual army and all who are not blinded will see and believe in him this time. It is at this time the final choice will be there for the population of the world too choose, between Christ and the Enemy led by Satan. Both will be at the head of their Spiritual armies, and this time full battle will be done, and the final victory claimed.

The book of Revelation will now come to full maturity and all that is prophesied therein will come to reality, as the two armies meet for the final clash. Satan's hate will battle with Christ's love for supremacy; and it will be both a material war and a Spiritual one at the same time. The letters to the seven churches in Asia give us the warning of what God expects of us who are his children. The warnings are very clear, the most auspicious one is the letter to the Laodicea's who are neither hot nor cold and are look warm, he threatens to spit them out of his mouth. We need to study the letters that were fairly new when the book of Revelation was written, from them we will learn what was already happening in churches that were founded by Paul. Paul had within the last sixty years set up those churches yet all were in need of advice when Revelation was written, only fifty years later.

The Four Bests that rise up and worship God as he sits on the throne of heaven, and the twenty four Elders represent all of mankind who have died and are believers in the Father God. In the name of the living dead, they worship and give thanks, and they will do this on behalf of all saved children of God, forever and ever as the prayers float up and are heard.

Then the book of Gods   is offered to be opened, and none but The Lamb of God, Jesus Christ is able to open the book after he has taken it from the hand of God. The lambs stand before God as he was when he was bought down from the cross of crucifixion, and only he is able to open the book, because in all time he is the only one who is worthy. And the lamb had the seven Spirits of God on him, and the four beasts and the elders all fell down before the Lamb to worship and praise him. And as they worshipped the Lamb in this way they professed he had the seven wisdoms of God, these are to be the future Kings and Priests on earth and all will pay homage to Christ the Lord.

Millions of Angels were above the throne and the worshippers, of and were, in worship of God. And they all sang in a loud voice proclaiming Jesus, blessed is he the Lamb who is the Son of God and will rule the earth forever.

- Then the Lamb starts to open the seven seals and the first one is the white horse which represents the Spiritual and Physical armies of God as they ready for the final battle with the hosts of Satan. This rider is the leader of the good army the army of God.
- The next seal is the red horse and it will go forth and create dissension among all of the people on earth and they shall become confused, but they must be one or the other, none who have the Laodicea's mind shall survive, they will die in confusion. This rider will defeat confusion and ensure the children of God know their own minds and repent unto the savior.
- The third seal is opened and the black horse is revealed, he will bring justice to all mankind good or bad right or wrong. This rider will ensure that followers of **Satan know their own will they will follow Satan and the followers of Jesus Christ will follow Christ. This rider will ensure all is fair and correctly achieved, he is justice.**

The End.

Ten short stories

Written by
Vincent, (Winty) H Stephens

Rugby Trials:
1948 (#62)

Break a boys Spirit, be a bloody idiot.

Winty had been chosen at his Seddon Tech Memorial College for the North Island Schoolboy Rep trials! He was so excited he had, had a terrible time settling into college, and to be chosen as a rep in the game he loved was beyond his wildest dreams, he was ecstatic. The college coach had been so complimentary telling Winty he was a natural, and should make college rugby captain by year eleven. The game he had said was more than just brawn, it also needed brains and Winty had a footie brain, such compliments Winty was starved for, he was so demoralized.

Since coming to College there had been a series of disasters, it had started when he was second in the entry exams! Teachers and Parents had loudly claimed he must have cheated, this had been proved wrong by producing previous exam results, from his primary school! There was a history of academic achievement as a youngster, but when he got to College that all stopped now he was treated as the local clown! Winty normally loved to compete at anything, but at college this trait he had which had always been strong was quickly quelled!

Then on the day he had started the other kids would not sit next to him in the form room because he was a cheat so claimed by their parents, and confirmed by the teachers? The only one of the teachers who treated Winty with any semblance of respect was the Math's teacher, but then Winty always had a math's brain, respect would have been for that reason only?

He had on his first day at physical education been ridiculed in front of his class peers as inferior, because all natives were physically and mentally inferior to Whites? This was claimed by Mr. Rees the phys-ed teacher! Winty had been bought up to the front of the class and after being told to remove his singlet, Rees demonstrated with a ruler why he was inferior to his class mates physically? Then Rees had, using the same ruler showed by the shape of Winty's head why he was mentally inferior, as well and had no capacity to think like the other White Kids? This Rees claimed was why it was a travesty for Stephens to be allowed to sit in the presence of whites; Niger's said Rees should never be allowed to sit when whites are in the room. Stephens should therefore not be in the top stream class as he was? This had been accompanied by sniggers from the class who were asking questions, mostly as to how Stephens could have cheated and why!

All of this Winty had to endure while beginning to for the first time in his life feel totally inferior, he had always been praised as superior! It did not take long to kill Winty's self respect, and he hated them all for what they were doing to him! Jimpy Powell the A grade form teacher, took electrical science and Winty hated him and his classes, Winty's brain just closed down and he was demoralized! Jimpy made it very plain he did not really think any Maori could learn his subject anyhow it would be a waste for a Maori to be taught in his classes. Winty could have told Jimpy he had no wish to be a dumb arse electrician anyhow; college was for Winty a nightmare.

It was compulsory that the students do work practice, Winty was sent to a lawyer's office to apply. This was done by the College office and that turned out to be a nightmare as well. When Winty went in and told the receptionist why he was there, he heard her say to someone out back Seddon College has sent a Maori for work practice, what do I do boss? Ring that smart arse at their office and ask him what the big idea is sending us a Nigger, and tell them don't ever send anymore Niggers here? Oh and tell that Nigger to piss off case we don't take Niggers here, they stink! Winty slunk out of there like a dog that has been kicked, and he never went back into another office for years. Years later he was invited into the fancy office at Kiwi Bacon in Christchurch and greeted like a man not a stinkin Nigger, but the memory of that day lingers on right up until the present day.

Anyhow the trials were being played; Winty's specialist position was in the centers, coming in to dummy half when the play called for it. Winty had been sitting waiting for his turn to have a run, and after about an hour he said to the coach, when do I get a run coach? You aint never gonna get a run in any team I coach you little Nigger Basted said the Coach! Even if you were not a cheat you still will never play in any team that I have anything to do with, now piss of you little black basted, I hate you fuckin niggers. They should have killed the lot of you years ago then we would not be having the trouble we are having now, go on piss off, I say. Winty left the field and swore he would never play any sport ever again, even though especially Rugby he loved the game, he was really heartbroken that day.

He was even offered to become a member at Titirangi Golf Club a most prestigious club and a great offer but he refused. He had been playing Cricket and Softball, as well as being a Champion on a Horse, but he even gave all of that up, no more for me he thought no one will ever speak to me like that again. Years later in the army at Papakura he was amazed and amused when the trainers were teaching and explained why the Maori physique is superior to the white man, touché Rees you old prick he thought.

The Boner: 73

The Mutton season was over, it was June 1954 most of the Maoris from the North had left and Vince was making arrangements to leave. He had been living with his old friend and Mentor Mike Gaulton (Bighead) in one of the meat companies two room army style barracks. The Man and the Youth had developed a strong bond and Mike had taken Vince under his wing teaching him many tricks of the meat industry. Mike was acknowledged to be the best meat producer in the Southland Otago area; and his exploits with a knife doing any sort of meat work plus his strength were legendary. The day before Vince was due to leave and travel North, Bighead said, "I have been authorized by the company to employ a learner beef boner, would you like to take it on, I know you will be able to do it without any problem, but the season will go for another two months can you stay longer"?

Of course Vince was delighted and was also quite certain he would become a contract boner very quickly all he said was, "when do I start"?

The learning was very quick Mike was a very good teacher, and Vince was already showing good promise as a future top producer, although nowhere near as strong as Mike, he made up for that by being very quick. The usual time that it took to reach tally the others in the team had told Vince was two months, so you will be a contractor by time the season ends. Vince made no comment but privately thought this will take me a week to learn, what are they on about?

Vince had started on the Monday morning and there were four contract boners including Mike, but Mike was the only one that cut high numbers daily. The contract rate was 100 quarters of beef a day, but Mike did 200 per day, all of the others only did the 100 to qualify for their contract. The pay was so much per quarter of beef and then penalty rates for bulls and overweight steers.

214

It was fortunate for Vince that Mike had taught him many tricks of the game on the first two days, because on the third day Mike cut his arm badly fooling around with the knife, and had to go off work! On that Day Vince had cut 70 quarters and was learning quickly, when Mike came back with his arm all stitched up, he asked Vince when he would do tally or 100 quarters?

Yeah well on Friday I will do a 100 and the week after that I will do the same as you, which drew a big laugh, between the two friends.

On the next day Thursday Vince cut 90 quarters and now quite openly told the other boners e would cut the full tally the next day.

Boning was always considered a plumb job and only locals were employed because they stayed back after the Maori teams, had gone back North to be with their families. Mike was a Delhi or Yugoslav so Vince was the only Maori. There was quite an interest in whether Vince would get tally so quickly, most of the other boners were feeling foolish for having said it took two months to become a contractor and here it was being done by a nineteen YOA Youth within a week, only Mike thought it was funny.

The big day had arrived and Vince was going for tally, one for one with the contractors, and at smoko he was two ahead of the others so it looked real simple, he had two less to do than the others to reach tally.

Mike had come to work to see the final, but he knew there was a trap coming; a real test for any learner. Vinces last quarters were coming out, and a big cheer went up, on the rails was two of the biggest toughest Bulls most of them had ever seen. Eight of the hardest quarters one could ever hope to see, they were all being paid double rates, but normally they also took twice as long to cut and process, Vince was really in the gun now.

By the time he had boned four of those quarters the rest of the team had caught up, another two and they were ahead, it looked bad, would Vince beat the clock or not. With a final burst of energy Vince made it by five minutes, the 100 was done, he was last to finish but he had made it in one week.

For that day's work Vince was paid for 108 quarters counting the bulls at double rate, but more importantly he was now a tally boner, he never cut less than 108 quarters from that day forward and as he promised within the first month he was matching Mike one for one.

It was several years later when at his own factory Vince had a young man working for him who considered himself the best ever with a knife, but he had never seen his boss really bone, Vince had a policy of never showing the others up for being slow. They were doing their best and if he showed them he believed they would lose heart and not try so hard to be fast. One morning Vince came into work in a bad mood and they started on about racing so in that frame of mind he agreed to race.

Two sheep were selected and the young bloke went first, when he finished his sheep in 39 seconds he was so excited and claiming he had won already. Vince did his in that shitty mood and his time was 32 seconds, it broke Johns heart and he never tried again to be as fast, in fact Vince had to speak to him about being too slow.

What Vince did was foolish, bad tempers don't make friends.

Paying the Wages: 74

Payday again at Vinads, and Vince had to put it all together make up the wages, pick up the cash from the bank what a bloody bore that was. When the business started and there was only five to be paid it was easy, Vince would take of his white coat wash his hands and go down to the National Bank in Hereford St; then he would work out how much money was needed go in and get it, then just drive back to work and pay the men. But it was getting harder and harder now there were over twenty men and it was harder to work out who got paid what? Goodness he even had a wages book now and he had to work it all out, bugger the tax in those days it was their own problem, and there was no bloody GST either.

Payday was always a drama because Vince used to be the only boner when Vinads started, so while he went off to the bank the boning line stopped and the men went onto other less productive jobs. Then when he got down to the bank he was always annoyed at the attitude of the bank tellers and their superior attitude, which he had bought on himself by being so casual, never dressed adequately and often covered with blood.

This one particular day Vince had arrived at the bank flustered and late as usual, and when he got to the counter, all of the bank staff ignored him they were busy having their own conversations and couldn't be concerned about that jerk who wasted their time every week.

Vince waited impatiently for about 15 minutes, but then having lost his temper he let out a bellow, where is the manager, I want to see the manager right now.

One of the girls casually walked over and asked with a slight smirk on her face said, "Can I help you at all"?

"No you can't I want the manager I am tired of trying to work with you damn flunkies, get me the manager I have a complaint"? Vince snarled.

"I am so sorry but the manager is too busy he doesn't see customers like you he is too busy," smirked our young girl.

"Well you had better get him real quick because if you don't I will kick up such a fuss, he will come alright and then I will give him too busy to see me alright be warned," all said very loudly.

All of a sudden a man emerged and wanted to know what the fuss is all about, and could he help because he was the manager.

"Well first I come here every week to pick up wages and every week I am messed around by you and your staff I want it fixed not just today but every week, now what are you going to do?" Vince asked.

"Oh I don't think I have ever spoken to you and our girls are very polite here I know that for sure you must be mistaken," said Mr. Manager with a smart arse smile.

"Are you the manager because if you are these girls represent you and when they treat me like shit they are doing it for you so yes I have spoken to you. Now you can fix it or there will be one almighty fuss in your lousy bank, you and your staff are nitwits now how much longer must I wait to get my wages cheque cashed"? It was all getting very nasty and Vince was in no mood to be fucked around by a second rate bank manager.

"I find your attitude obnoxious Mr. Stephens why do you have to be so nasty these are only girls here and you can't be too hard on them now can we"? Said with a smarmy smile.

"You had better have a look at my account right now, because any more shit from you and I will cancel my account and go elsewhere. I will also go to your head office in Wellington and tell them what a dick manager they have in Christchurch now how would you like that Mr. Manager?"

Having gone away and come back the manager, now looking very sheepish said, "I am so sorry Mr. Stephens your account is a good one and we need to look after you can I promise you that in future there will be no problems with our staff! He said.

"Yeah that's fine now while you are here a want a $20,000 overdraft can you set that up for me please and the sooner the better. Oh the Northern Building Society will guarantee me just give them a ring.

"That's fine Mr. Stephens and if you ever have trouble again give me a ring it will be fixed immediately. You see we don't often see Maoris who are business people they are usually laborers and no good with money so we are very careful when it comes to your race you see they don't pay their bills and we have a lot of trouble with them." As an afterthought he suddenly asked, "You are a Maori aren't you"?

"No actually I am Chinese can't you see the eyes and the yellow skin," Vince now replied with a nasty smirk, "can't you see what breed I am for goodness sake".

The Salesman for Vinads: 72

Having bought a small factory equipped with a full set of old machines, it was now time to look for sales and the only one around was Vince, he was salesman, producer, driver etc; he was alone, but not for long. The previous firm had left the phones on and on the morning the plant was taken over, there was a call from a major hotel asking for the previous meat firm. Vince took the call and finished up getting his first order. He had taken the customer off the other firm, he kept it for many years and it was one of the best hotel orders in Christchurch. Because Vince had once been the foreman-salesman for the only two wholesale meat firms in Christchurch, he knew all of the various buyers from Hotels, Hospitals, Govt. buyers, Manufacturers and Retail Butchers shops in that City of only 300,000 people. It was for this reason the growth of his company Vinads Wholesale Meats Ltd was so successful very quickly.

The first call was to the biggest pie manufacturer in the South Island at that time, but Vince had known the owners for many years, and was friendly with the 'Father and Son', Owners. Vince walked into the factory and asked for a share of the orders for pie meat; and they agreed to give him an order for 500kgs per day six days a week. How they asked had Vince managed to buy the old factory from the previous owner. Vince told them the truth that they had almost begged him to buy it and he had got it for next to nothing fully equipped! Their response was how stupid can you be, they will rue the day you are the worst one they could have sold too, they have financed their own opposition far better for them had they burned the place down.

The next call was to one of the major bacon, ham and smallgoods manufacturers in NZ they have large factories in every province. They were one of the few firms Vince didn't know, but he wanted to prove he could break ground for himself so they were a good target for him to learn with.

At that time this was the biggest and smartest office Vince had ever been in so it was a little intimidating, but he was determined not to be stopped. As he walked up to the reception he was plagued by memories of the office he had gone into as a student, and he had been treated with scorn for being a stinking Maori, he was trembling at the knees. On being invited into the Managing Directors office, he was greeted enthusiastically for being a Maori who was having a go, by the MD. This man was to be a friend for many years to come, and he explained he had been raised and educated in an area dominated by Maoris, so he had the greatest respect for all things Maori. He promised that Vince would get an order, and he was true to his word, and order was received for one tonne of boneless mutton every week from that time forward.

Vince was going well as his own salesman, he had to hire five men immediately to fill the orders he had so far won, and he had only been in business for two days.

The next client he called on refused to give him an order for 12 months, but when he did it was a very good one. The following successes were a series of Hotels and Restaurants, he was especially well received by the Chinese Restaurant owners who all placed orders.

Vinads had been manufacturing bacon and ham, but went out of production at the request of one of his old bosses who was more a friend than a boss. Vince's sales had penetrated so deeply that he had threatened the other firm's viability.

Within 12 months Vinads had won the Hospital Boards orders for their seven major hospitals, again this was because he knew all of the Dietitians, they had received his contracted offer and persuaded their board to accept the new supplier.

The next client won was the major NZ International Airline, but all they bought back in those halcyon days for airline cuisine was Fillet Steak and Land Loin Chops, it's a bit different than what they serve up now, all sorts of tasteless hash.

The two biggest manufacturers of frozen food were Watties and Birds Eye, Vince had orders from both although the Birds Eye order was the big one, some 600 tonnes per year and that was only half of their order.

In the meantime another plant had been bought and was operating in Auckland equally well.

The Auckland Hospital Board was won by contract another 15 major hospitals, and again hotels and restaurants were numerous in placing orders with Vince.

The Govt contracts for the Navy Base at Devonport, the Airforce at Whenuapai as well as the Army at Papakura were all contracts won by Vince very quickly.

By this time Vinads had become the second of two major private meat companies in NZ; now far swamping the competitors in Christchurch they were now very small by comparison and they were all so glad to see Vinads easing up its tight grip on the Christchurch market place.

The competition in Auckland were not so sanguine their acceptance of this newcomer was very different than Christchurch, the intent was to ruin Vinads and chase them back to where they came from, although amusingly Vince was an Aucklander.

Within three years Vince had won sales that dominated both Auckland and Christchurch and in 2008 terms would be over $1M per week from a start of nothing. It was only in Christchurch that he won so easily in Auckland he had had to fight all the way against very cunning competitors. Vince's boast as a young man he was a meat salesman par excellence.

Buying a workshop in Auckland: 75

Vince his Wife and two Sons had left Christchurch on Holiday, and had finally arrived in Auckland after several detours on the way including going to visit friends in Nelson. Vince had left his business in Christchurch at a time of severe difficulty because of insufficient space as well as a problem with obtaining supplies. Because of the size of the business he had now created, he had to do something, but he had no idea what. When he arrived in Auckland he could see immediately there were large supplies of beef cattle, Auckland is a beef province, Canterbury is a sheep province, and Vinads needed big supplies of beef. Having looked around the whole town Vince decided he needed to set up a new branch of Vinads in Auckland, so he started to look around to find a shop with as big a work space as possible.

There were lots of butcher shops for sale in Auckland, but he needed one of a particular size and that wasn't easy, finally after a lot of hassle he found one that was as near as possible to what he needed in Takapuna. It was big enough to have a staff of about five running a boning line, but the meat had to go straight to Hastings daily in a frozen truck in the hope it froze at least partially on the way.

Barry Kipa Vince's Cousin joined the company as its first apprentice, and quickly proved his natural ability with a knife and making smallgoods. The shop in the normal sense was big, but for what Vince wanted was tiny, those days of cramming all of the work in such a small space was a night mare. Vince then started to look for real processing premises, in which a real copy of the Christchurch plant could be set up as a matter of urgency.

An unused factory was found at Whenuapai; it had been a Chicken processing plant and was ideal for what was needed, with terrific facilities and plenty of freezing space. It was owned by Fletcher Holdings and was a property left over from one of their takeovers, Vince offered $25,000 but they just laughed and said they would just leave it sit there until somebody sensible came along. In the end He had to pay $100,000 for the place, but it was still very cheap because it included 20 acres of prime land. The family company Stephens Contractors spent a lot of money doing the premises up, about $30,000 which Vince paid for with a share issue in his company. The premises in Auckland were now far superior to the ones in Christchurch; it was about ten times bigger and better equipped.

Now that the real base for Vinads had been shifted to Auckland, a lot of Vinces time had to be spent there, the business really flourished and the shop in Takapuna as well as the Factory in Whenuapai was really passing out a challenge to all of the local firms just as had been done in Christchurch. The boning lines now required two full time boners in Auckland, and new equipment imported from Germany gave Vinads the capacity to process smallgoods on a scale commensurate with the biggest public owned meat firms in the city. Vince had done all of this while being unaware of the turmoil he had created in the opposition firms, he had only thought of it in the same terms as Christchurch, there plenty of business to go around, but that's not how the local Auckland firms viewed the position. What they could see was an invasion by a Southern firm into the Auckland market and they were very upset about the situation. What Vince saw was himself coming home and he had every right to be there, which was quite true, the problem was he was taking the lion's share of the local trade and Vinads was looking very competitive in all areas of the industry. He had even had an argument with the meat workers union and won, this alone proved his danger to all of his opposition, they had hoped the unions would break Vinads instead they made the company even stronger.

Without realizing what he had done, Vince has turned Vinads into the biggest private meat business in NZ, the only other that could compete for size was one in Hastings that had also managed to grow big on the same scale as Vinads. We need to be careful here we are not referring to freezing works that are owned by Farmers Coops or foreign ones owned from the UK. These are export meat works, built to take advantage of NZ ability to grow cheap animals for slaughter and export to the world, these are a different category to what Vinads was competing in, the local market so successfully and causing a lot of angst for others in the same industry.

It was a very hard battle between Vinads and its rivals, but Vinads had such a cheap cost structure and was well managed, that the opposition could make no impact at all on them they took on all comers and won easily. What Vinads didn't have was a good administration and whats more didn't know how to put one in place. This was the Achilles heel and what became a real problem as the company grew so big.

Vinads had a shop for genuine continental smallgoods, one for frozen meals, 16 retail butchers shops, two wholesale meat factories all that Vince had bought in his quest to make Vinads a well balanced business. On the practical side he succeeded and his work was all in place except an efficient administration, there were no companies in Christchurch or Auckland that could beat his record of buying assets at knock down prices and turning them into thriving businesses. The only problem became one of having too many assets, and a sprawling business out of control.

Ngapuhi Meats Auckland: 78

Vinads had been offered a chance to buy 13 meat shops in many of the main suburbs of Auckland city and because his retail division was only three shops he was looking at it closely.

The butcher shops were owned by Wally Morris through his grocery chain Shoprite stores and were all immediately beside one of his groceries. Shoprite was one of the earliest no frills grocery chains in Auckland and Wally had decided they weren't able to run butcher shops so he wanted Vinads to take them over for no cost except paying a rent for the floor space.

Although Vince was no retail butcher, in the sense that he had never actually run a sole butcher shop he was well aware of what was needed, but with the shops he was finally getting on over his head. The need to control theft of money and meat and even shop supplies were suddenly added to an overstretched poor administration, the shops were a disaster from the start.

The retail shops were set off into another company Ngapuhi meats, which was the tribe into which Vince had been born, and the new company was 100% owned by Vinads Auckland Ltd; in its turn 100% owned by Vinads Christchurch. The shops were never managed properly because Vince never appointed a retail manager; he just preferred to run them himself which in itself was indicative of his lack of administrative knowledge. All except one in Grey Lynn were nice looking shops, and all being beside Shoprite high customer flow stores should have been a raging success. The Takapuna shop which had been the one Vinads had purchased first; after the new factory was built just a normal shop it was added to the Shoprite ones and managed by Vince personally.

The time Vince could give to managing his shops was minimal, most of the time he was busy straightening out problems with his very big retail business. His idea of managing Ngapuhi Meats was to perhaps go around and visit his managers once a month just to see if they were doing all right which of course they were, every one of them were stealing money from the cash registers except his Sister Aloma who managed one of the stores.

When the realization that Ngapuhi Meats was losing big amounts of money came Vince settled down and concentrated on the rogue shops but he couldn't find the main cause of the problems. He devised profit and loss week sheets, he did costing's but still there was a money drain he couldn't find, there was a major leak somewhere, but it was really well hidden. On the face of it the shops were all making profits, but Vince's instincts were very strong that there was something wrong. Not having a background in retail Vince should have understood the need to appoint a manager straight away, he had actually done this but that hadn't worked either. The manager he appointed was the person he had bought the Takapuna shop off, but in retrospect he was an older man and probably spent most of his time sitting at home with his wife drinking coffee. Then Vince decided to do a shop audit, all the stock was assessed and to Vince surprise he found that every shop had a large debtor list, how can this be he asked these are retail shops why have they all got debtors? His manager told him that many Maoris shopped at Ngapuhi Meats but most demanded credit because they were related to Vince, they were all of Ngapuhi Tribe and as such were entitled to free meat.

Vince went into a rage, how stupid he stormed that no one asked me who they were entitled to give credit too. The only credit customers were buyers through the wholesale division and they must be buying for a business and be able to pass a credit application. All retail credit was cancelled immediately and the Maoris all stopped coming, they would not pay they said that Stephens had everything from the white man's world he should share with his brothers. Vince found it amusing that it was always those who did nothing and were lazy who wanted to share, everything they had there were other reasons why he never trusted Maoris again and never wanted to be part of the Maori Race.

Although a big reason for losses in the shops had been found, another was still to come. By this time it had become obvious there was a problem in the overall Vinads business structure, it had become a large integrated business but there was still something wrong. Now that Vince was aware and had started hunting it wasn't long before he found the fault. The distribution manager had a brother driving one of the delivery vans, and between them they were selling meat from the factory to the shops on a COD basis. They had their own delivery book, and they would do a COD docket then they would share the cash each day of what they got from Ngapuhi Meats and any others who wanted to buy on a cash basis.

Vince had found out what they were doing but that was only the start, he found they had linked up with an outside team of wholesale butchers who had decided to send Vinads broke, they were loading out from the freezers at night and in terms of 2008 values over two million dollars worth of frozen stock had been stolen.

The culprits were caught red handed by the police and got eighteen months jail for stealing, but what good was that o Vinads. Vinads lost its insurance claim because the thefts were committed by their own staff.

Shearing on the Hanson's Farm 1951 (# 33)

Farming for Hanson's like all farm Labor was poorly paid and creating problems! Winty had made it plain he was dissatisfied, and for that reason he was not interested in staying, he would be leaving unless better wages were paid. Arthur and his Brother Ernie Hanson; had got together and came back with an offer. That if Winty could learn to shear sheep he was to be given the job to do their sheep. He would be given time off from farm labor, and could go to a shearing shed to learn, but he would have to learn quickly because together they had 5,000 sheep to be shorn; and they could only hold up by one month. For shearing they would pay Winty the full rate, he would have to work at his current rate for the full year, but only do the milking while he was shearing. As a learner it would take Winty a month to shear the total flock, and it was a big challenge; while Winty would make money out of the offer, it was a tough ask. The Hanson Brothers would have their flocks shorn without the usual difficulty finding shearing teams that travelled the area to do their sheep, and the Hanson's would have to supply the shed hands including a fleecy. Winty was still only 16 YOA, but shearing was like slaughtering really heavy work, which he was used too!

It was a compliment to Winty that the Brothers thought Winty could do the job, but they were well aware he had been a contract slaughterman at age 15; so they had no doubt he would be able to shear the flock as they wanted. On the other hand Winty was jubilant; this was the chance he wanted to learn another contract job! If he wanted he could leave immediately he had finished the Hanson flocks, and join one of the contract teams. His own integrity would not allow that; he knew that he would have to stay for the agreed four years, so knowing fully what it all meant, he agreed to the offer and he did all they had asked for.

Winty was sent to work with a shearing team, and given a learners stand to work on straight away. As usual with learners the shed foreman was supposed to teach the learners, and he did do that, but after only the first day announced that Winty would be able to shear at least 100 per day in a week, and would be up to 150 per day very quickly. It was a five man team he was learning with, and as usual mostly Maoris' four of the five shearers were Maoris, one shearer and all of the shed hands were Pakeha's. Back in the 1950s there was a big shortage of all workers, but particularly shearers and meat contractors were in very short supply. It was only Winty's luck he was starting his working life at such a time, a worker could shift from job to job at will.

Winty only stayed with the shearing team for a week, his teacher announcing he didn't need any more learning, just time to increase his speed and that would come naturally. So it was back to the Hanson's, milking cows morning and night then shearing during the day, for Winty it was a triumph. As agreed he was to be paid for his farm work at full rate, and he would be paid full rate per hundred, for shearing the Hanson flock. He started the shearing on a solo stand as soon as he arrived back at the farm, and within a fortnight was shearing two hundred sheep per seven hour day. The normal hours in a shearing shed is nine hours, so effectively Winty was probably able to shear 250 on a full day. When he was years later shearing in Australia, he was only able to shear 200 in nine hours. Shearing is far harder in Australia, the sheep rarely get wet whereas in NZ they get washed almost daily. The result is the wool in NZ is not as good, this is only because they are bred for meat, and as such the wool is not as fine. The Australian Merino sheep bred for wool, plus no water to soften the fleece, plus the dirt and biddy bids, make the Australian flock very tough to shear or slaughter.

Shearing the Hanson flocks became within two weeks quite easy, the early period as a meat Contractor on full tally, allowed Winty to adjust to the heavy work very quickly; his body adjusted to the work with no effort. The reality is that shearing is a challenge to all who would take the job up, what is needed is a very strong back, the full day is spent bent almost double while at the same time holding a fully grown sheep between ones knees. The entire flock of over 5,000 sheep were finished within six weeks, and the fees were paid to Winty as an extra above the his farm wages so he was satisfied to stay. He finished out another three years working on the farm, which he loved doing, then shearing the flock as well as crutching, (Cleaning the tail area for stale hardened shit) it is a period of his life he always remembers as the happiest in his life.

A new Ariel Motorbike:
1951 # (34)

Truth and bravado are distant cousins, one must always know the difference and keep hand in hand with truth its far safer that way.

Winty had started with an old Ariel motor bike he had bought for 25 pound (fifty dollars) which he had used to learn to ride, and to get his first license granted. In 1951 a youth could get a full license at the age of fifteen, so having a motor bike license at 15 YOA was not unusual. Winty's motor bike had been used for about six months; and he had even had it when he first started working on the Hanson farm. It was a noisy old single cylinder 500 cc, a 1932 model and just to kick it over took a superhuman effort. It actually looked like one of the bikes used during WW11 for sending courier riders with messages, and even then looked precarious to ride. The Hanson only Son's Wife had come home with their first baby; and Winty's nocturnal habits was waking the baby with that noisy old bike. It would be banging away and very noisy as is natural for a single cylinder bike, this was aggravated by Winty's coming and going at all hours of the night. The complaints were voiced very cautiously because they didn't want Winty to leave; they liked him but not his noisy old bike.

Winty was getting sick of that old bike anyhow, so he gave it to his uncle George Kipa and then went shopping for a new one for himself! After checking out all the models available at that time, Norton, Triumph 500 ccs etc; he settled on another Ariel, the glamour bike of the time the 1000 cc four square motor with all the mod cons etc. What a wonderful day it was when he picked that bike up brand new from the shop, there was only one problem; Winty was not a good rider and never became one. He never did get to be a really good rider, because he was too cautious on those two wheels, he could handle the tar sealed roads ok but not the unsealed country roads.

The day he picked his new bike up he rode it for about 10 miles then going around a corner struck an oil slick on the road, and he and his bike went for a slide on the road and crashed. Luckily he had all the safety gear on his bike, so in spite of the accident there was no damage to the bike, but there was a big dent in Winty's pride. Feeling rather foolish in front of the crowd that had quickly gathered, Winty picked himself and his bike up; and continued on his journey back to his job at Helensville.

He never told anyone what had happened, but he never forgot that momentous first trip on his fancy new bike, and he never fell, of it again during the five years he had that bike. He travelled from Auckland to the Bluff twice and up to Cape Reinga once, before he finally sold it by offering it as first prize in a raffle at the Ocean Beach Meat works. Winty paid $640 dollars for that bike, and when he raffled it off he got over $700 dollars for it, after all of the travel he had done on it, so it worked out to be a bargain.

The Hanson's were delighted with the new bike, the motor being a four cylinder just sounded like a big cat purring, and the baby never woke again much to the delight of his parents. The old single banger which used to be at top speed when it reached 60 MPH was gone, but the new bike which couldn't be put into top gear at less than 100 MPH had arrived. Winty rarely got that bike into top gear, he never got the confidence to want to travel at speeds over 100 MPH, but he did once try to see what the top speed was. The bike still hadn't reached top speed at 130 MPH, so he gave up and was content to travel mostly in fourth gear, but he never rode at more than 110 MPH or about 150 KPH.

His family especially Mum Stephens were really upset when she saw that bike the first time. Mum had heard so many stories about temporary Kiwis, because of so many fatal bike accidents, she was so upset she went out and bought a very nice Ford Car. She hoped to get Winty to give up the bike and use the car all of the time, but it was not to be because she died soon after.

Mum never knew that in spite of his easy going manner with his bike, he knew if he rode foolishly it could be a death machine; so he always treated it with the greatest respect that one accident the day he bought the bike was enough for him. No matter how much he loved that fancy bike, it could never take the place of his horse Kino so sadly killed. Winty was not going to allow that bike to kill him, a horse at full gallop was safe but a motor bike at 110 MPH was definitely not something to fall off.

Over the five years he owned and rode that bike, Winty was always full of rubbish about how fast he rode it, but the honest truth was he was too frightened of it to ride it foolishly, a bit of bullshit was one thing, but actually doing foolish things was quite another. When he thinks back and remembers it is with a cynical grin he remembers the bravado with which he boasted about that bike, the truth was just the opposite to the silly talk; he was really frightened of the bloody thing, which was the real reason he sold it in the end.

Ping Pong Champion:
1947 # no 15

So who is going to face the champ tonight? Na not me too tired, she looks to fit to me!

Clare at the time we are referring to here had two children Richard and Granville; and she was the family Ping Pong Champion. This was in 1946 not long after Murray and Darby had returned from the war in Europe, and everybody was young and full of energy. She was a young wife often bored, just staying home with her two babies, and just a small house to look after, although back then the home meant a lot more work than modern homes with all the mod cons. We all lived together Mum, and the two boys in one room, Winty, Jerry and George's Brother Theo in another and George and Clare in the other. This was when we were living at 37 Sale St Freemans Bay, before one of the children burned the place down, while playing with matches. Aunty Lil, her husband Wally and her two children lived next door at number 35 Sale St; they were related by the marriage of Mum to Dad Stephens. Mum was the only Maori the rest were all Pakehas' part of a large extended family, most of who had settled in the North Auckland area, when their English ancestors arrived in NZ.

There were no electrical appliances back then, the wood fueled stove was kept going every night by covering the remaining coals with ash, before going to bed. There was a wood fueled copper that had to be lit to boil the water each day, to wash the clothes and baby's nappies. And that same copper was used to heat the water for baths for the women; the men went down the road to the council showers, for which they paid three pence. There was no fridge, T/V, telephone, or car and the pubs closed at 6 pm every night, so beer drinking parties at home were quite frequent, about once a month.

The parties were riotous events George Kipa was always asked to sing solo his theme song Peter Fraser, and Anne if they could get her to dance it did a great hula version.

The house fronted on to Sale St and there was a verandah which ran right across the front, and at the end there were steps down to the street. There was a narrow walkway between 35 & 37 Sale St and both used the stairs as the only access, and there were very small front areas between the houses and the street below. The area would have been one of the first developed in Auckland, and for the time those houses would have been considered quite modern. There were separate flush toilets, but a shared wash house and bathroom, a large part of Auckland back then was not sewered, so we were fairly modern. The coal man came every week to deliver the weeks supply of coal, and he was a very busy man; he delivered to every house in the area. How well he can be remembered, climbing those stairs with that full coal sack on his back, and emptying it into the coal box out in the back yard. The only electricity we used was for the lights, which were used to light every room as needed.

The Kitchen was the room in which everything was held as well as eating, and there was a small pantry set just apart from the kitchen in a kind of alcove. That main room was used for card games, parties, and Ping Pong, oh the stories that table could tell if it could talk. The table was undersized and so was the room; for Ping Pong, but they played on it very well especially Clare. There was room for about five spectators to sit and watch; which Mum always did and so did Winty when he was at home, which was seldom.

Clare had a funny style she didn't palm the bat, but held it with the third and fourth fingers on one side of the handle and her thumb on the other, as a result the bat was pointing down not across. It is an unusual style but those who master that way are great defensive players as Clare was, very few shots got past her no matter how hard they were played.

Everybody lined up to beat Clare, and some of them such as Theo and Murray were good players, but she used to beat all comers alike, much to their frustration. Murray hated to be beaten especially by his own sister, hard as he tried Clare would stand there just sending the ball back until the opponents failed, and in the end they always did. Clare must have learned to play at home with her family when she was just a young girl, but where ever it was she was very good!

The parties, cards and Ping pong went on for years, Clare had Walter, Murray and Sonia there at Sale St, and after the family shifted she had Denis, Barry and Steven, in all a wonderful family. We would bet that none of her children would have been able to beat the ping pong champion of Sales St City.

However most good things come to an end, Winty came home late one night and when he tried to get in the front door, so as to his room it wouldn't open. There seemed to be something funny, so he went next door to ask Aunty Lil and was told the family was gone, the house had been burnt down.

Uncle George's work (Hellabys) had supplied them with a home out at their farm, and they were already shifted, they had nothing to take it was all consumed in the fire. The only things that were saved were the children, and they were all that mattered. So there it was the good times were over, no more cards, parties or ping pong, but Clare remained to this day the family champion at 37 Sales St City.

Cards and Gambling;
1949 # 16

I bet one penny and now I put you up one penny you betcha!

It was Friday night and the card sharps were ready to play, this was a common event most weeks. Generally the players were Clare, George, (sometimes) Mum, Thelma, Murray, Winty, Darby, Dawn Alma and many others. The games played were Pontoon (Blackjack) Slippery Sam and Poker. The card games carried on for as long as they players wanted to play, but the games were often changed especially if Winty wasn't playing. Only six players could play so it was quite often that there were several onlookers, and Winty would as the youngest have to sit out. Poker was the fairly safe game and Slippery Sam the most dangerous, in terms of win or loses of money. In Slippery Sam three cards are dealt to each player, and they back their hand against the next card turned up by the banker ie; If the player is holding three suits and the bank turns up one of the fourth suits the bank wins. Or if the bank turns up one of the suits and the card is bigger than the player's suit held again bank wins. Obviously in this game if player has a prodigious memory; and remembers the cards that have gone, he will win because he knows when the bank is weak. Winty always wanted to play Slippery Sam, but the others would only play when they happened to forget Winty's advantage, his memory for numbers. Winty could quote the cards that had been played, and therefore what must be being held by the bank. Pontoon is another memory game rarely played when Winty was around, that is where the players have to get 21 points, and are again betting against the bank. But Poker was the game played 90% of the time.

Poker was Mums game and she just loved to play, even if her Youngsters joked around with her. Most of the bets would be one shilling (ten cents) minimum and quite often in the several pounds, (two dollars) but if Mum was the first to bet she would bet one penny, and if she had a real good hand she would bet three pence. And if anyone wanted to play she would when her bet again come round again, she would bet another one penny etc. It was Ok if no one had a good hand, but many times when one of the big betters such as Thelma or Murray had a really good hand, and Mum was spoiling with her pennies, tempers were often close to the surface. Old Mum didn't give a damn, she would say I raise you one penny, whoever was trying to bet. Poor old Mum they would almost cry as she spoiled their winning hands, and they won only Mums pennies. And if she should win with her penny bets she would count it all, and stack the money in front of her with a big cackle of delight.

Mum Stephens in her last years really loved playing cards, she would sit for hours by herself during the day, playing her patience or different card games. Then when her youngsters came at nights or weekends to play their money games, she was the first one sitting at the table waiting to start. In the evenings when the games got to be too much and she had to rest, she would get up toddle of to bed to get her rest. Then as soon as she got up in the morning she would expect to be given a seat in the game straight away. Mum didn't and wouldn't have to wait like one of the others; she was the boss and was allowed a seat immediately. The games had between six and four players, if there were less than four then the game was ended. If more than six which was quite normal in the evenings, then the extras had to sit and watch. Some players didn't arrive until late, knowing they wouldn't get a seat until about two in the morning anyhow. This was why the games went on and on, some like Thelma and Murray were addicted, and would play on with little sleep for many long hours.

The other game they played which was to Winty's advantage, the gamblers would, make up their race horse bets before each race on Saturday. Winty would take the bets and quote the odds he was paying, on each horse. Then he would work out the bets he was going to hold and set off the others, with a local bookie who operated out of the dairy shop at the end of Sale St.

It was great fun Winty was by then twelve years of age, and had run away from the Browne's for the last time. The men were all home from the war, and all were making good wages from a booming economy, they even had a taxi driver and his girl friend, who used to come and play cards and bet on the horses. These two were Pakehas' and Winty never did work out where they came from, nor he did he care their money was good.

Saturdays whenever the races were on was a big day for Winty, he would sell the Turf Digest and pencils outside the Ellerslie racetrack in the morning, then ride his bike home to start taking bets from the second of eight races.

When the races were on at Avondale he didn't sell race books, just stayed home to take bets.

Murray, Owen, and Thelma were good for decent bets say ten quid, (twenty dollars) Aunty Clare or Anne ten shillings. Mum well she stepped out big time and would bet sixpence. But if they had a sure thing, that was it she really bet up large ten pence, but for that she wanted two to one minimum. Winty always gave her the odds she wanted, but he couldn't set her off like the others, the bookie would have said, are you crazy go away kid?

T G I F*

*Thank God I'm Frank

A Memoir

by

Frank Gutowski

with

Monika R. Smith

iUniverse, Inc.

Bloomington, Indiana

TGIF*
*Thank God I'm Frank

iUniverse books may be ordered through booksellers or by contacting:

iUniverse
1663 Liberty Drive
Bloomington, IN 47403
www.iuniverse.com
1-800-Authors (1-800-288-4677)

ISBN: 978-1-4502-9884-1 (dj)
ISBN: 978-1-4502-9885-8 (ebook)
ISBN: 978-1-4620-0602-1 (sc)

Printed in the United States of America

iUniverse rev. date: 3/10/2011

In Memoriam

Willy Finnegan, SJ

Teacher, Mentor, Friend

FRANK'S EPIGRAPHS

Credo

My sense of God is my sense of wonderment about the universe.
(A. Einstein)

Motto

A.M.D.G.

Modus Operandi

When a job is once begun,
never leave it till it's done.
Be it large or be it small,
Do it well, or not all.

Mantra

I am a child of the Depression!

Exhortation

Be sweet, kind, and good.

ACKNOWLEDGEMENTS

My life as it is would not have been were it not for many others. That includes all those who have gone into eternity: most of my family and friends now reside there.

Even the insistence of numerous bridge partners, urging me to write a memoir, has diminished in recent years as many of them also moved on to another life.

Those currently in my life are most of all my children: their desire to know is as much stimulus as it is reason, cause, and encouragement to carry this project out.

The technicalities and details of producing these pages lie with my best friend, one time wife, buddy, pal and alter ego. As my scribe extraordinaire, Monika puts my words on paper. She also adds her own two cents when she is so inclined, and does so in her own voice.

There are and will be many others involved in the overall process which will lead to the eventual or possible printed product and its distribution. I thank them now for future efforts and for all time.

Lastly, I thank those who provided the occasions that promoted my life from ordinary through careful molding into the extraordinary person I had the grace to become and am. Their understanding, interpretation and application of the principles of Christian love imbue my being. Truly, their rationale, if not their ultimate actions, prompts my writing now.

INTRODUCTION

In three parts

Part 1. It's fall. The late summer sun of the first millennium year is warming my windowpanes. Its light penetrates brightly and the many plants and leafy growths I have assembled on the sill are stretching and reaching high and higher to bask in its warmth. At times, earlier, a strawberry appeared. Tomatoes have gone from yellow flower to greenish pink in this confined indoor space. Flowers and greenery abound. It would seem that I have acquired a green thumb.

My big reclining chair sits close to this small, limited but lush rain forest. I like the dancing sunrays entering my enclave as much as I love the music emanating from my exquisite stereo system, fed by my enormous CD collection. I spend much of my time reading, solving cross word puzzles, enjoying the music filling my atmosphere when sports or other TV fare are not engaging me.

I exercise with daily walks of up to three miles or so. I have three different paths of varying lengths, the longer include a park bench rest stop. I don't like cold and relish heat, but only rain, sleet or ice keep me from my routine.

I enjoy playing bridge as much and as often as I can, some weeks daily. I have taught bridge to various groups both in the neighborhood and at the local senior center. As a matter of fact, I have a class there again this fall. There are regular bridge games there in which I participate, there are other regular games at the country club, or at my groups' various homes. I often substitute for an indisposed fourth.

While I don't tutor regularly any more, at times I return to help a student because old referrals die slowly and calls continue. I'm volunteering my teaching skills and using them at the city's GED center where I teach physics and math in an adult learning program. I read newspapers recorded for broadcasting to the visually impaired. Till not too long ago, I also volunteered to assist families in need with their budgeting and bill paying, but after the last client passed away, I stopped this activity.

I am now in my eighties. I am long retired but busier and more active than ever. For being eighty something, I am doing well health-wise all around. No medications, no infirmities. My artificial hips serve me well. I am convinced this is my earthly reward from my Heavenly Father. Job well done, malice toward none. Like Erickson's last stage, integrity is mine.

Over the years, family, friends and those who have heard some of my life's story and especially the difficulties I encountered, suggested I write it all down.

It has been a unique life. A life in service to others and for others: it has been my best effort to be Christ-like. I was most vehemently condemned by those who claim to spread and promote Christ's message on earth, in the name of both their Society and the Pope whom they serve. My mortal life descended into hell. It is no wonder that a loving God now rewards my waning days: come, faithful servant, enjoy the fruits of thy labor.

My "sin" was that of blind obedience. Had I not obeyed and exhorted others to obey, this story would not be. I took seriously the vow of obedience I had made. I obeyed what I had been taught. I obeyed my superiors. Above all, I obeyed my conscience which had been so finely honed in trained practice, to never ask why but to just jump high.

2

Till now, I had neither time nor inclination to sit sequestered and secluded banging a typewriter to the tune of memories filled with sadness and pain amidst the joy of now. This is no longer true. What has changed is Monika's offer to put it all on her computer and thereby save me the tedious typing I abhor. Like in the old days when I had a secretary, I am dictating once again. The words are reflecting from the screen before being committed to paper. Her enthusiasm fuels mine. I proof-read the results, I critique and criticize. Little keys are all that needs to be pushed to correct and change what needs to be improved. None of this re-typing from scratch that I had dreaded! Progress is swift.

Part 2. Famous last words. I should have added that, whereas progress is swift in mechanical execution, time is the element that eludes the best laid plans of mice and men.

What had begun with soaring enthusiasm became not a lesser priority, but a victim of circumstance. Then again, Thoreau took eight years and produced seven drafts to write Walden, so there's hope for this venture.

First it was my diminished desire to attend bi-monthly symphony performances with an occasional opera added here and there. Next, an increased desire to enjoy the comforts of my humble home with books and music everywhere superseded any wish to drive long distances. My outside activities became more exclusively daylight oriented.

Once again, God intervened: the memoir-ish effort needed to be speeded up and moved along. I had to undergo some surgery for a complex hernia. The lengthy recovery occasioned a renewed and quite intense effort to progress on what had been lying fallow all too long. I was able and Monika willing to put in endless hours in dictating, transcribing, rereading and editing. Late 2007. We did some of it. It's the editing that needs me most.

Thereafter, it was our intention to spend intermittent weeks pursuing the completion of this, my "Apologia pro vita mea". Our good intentions suffered a set back when I was instructed to stop driving later that year. We spent hours on the phone. I filled in gaps Monika had found. I answered questions she had. And, I reviewed the stages and ages of my existence.

For a while, I used the adult bus service to get to the senior center; I didn't like it. I soon stopped and restricted myself to the privately arranged bridge games with my long term partners. It is incredible to learn how independence is tied to four wheels and horsepower. Not driving meant becoming somewhat dependent on both my daughters, Leila and Nadja, who became my life lines and support in countless ways. They carried me to doctors and dentists, to the bank and various stores. At times they indicated their displeasure with my housekeeping by arriving with brooms and buckets and, to my dismay, scrubbing everything in sight or discarding carefully assembled treasure like a month's worth of the local newspapers, catalogs and ads. They meant well. I liked it best when Nadja baked for me. I relish the plethora of baked goods arriving with her. I devour them slowly and savor every bite. Of late she's got something else in the oven that's due around my next birthday. A boy!

In July 2008 I received my death sentence. An aneurysm was discovered on my aorta. The prognosis for surgical intervention was dismal at best and exacerbated when considering my chronological age. I therefore decided to forego any operation. AMDG.

I have till now lived each and every day to its fullest. It is my intention to continue to live every moment fully, and to continue to do so in my own home. I will NOT consider moving anywhere. Monika has offered countless times to share home and hearth. My doctor wants me to seriously consider increased care, especially as I am losing my short term memory. I don't see it; I think I am perfectly able to care for myself within some limitations, but far from requiring outside assistance. Everything important is in order: my will designates Rob as my executor but I changed that to Steve because Rob is now living in Germany. I hope it's legal. My financial affairs now consist of one checking account from which I withdraw my monthly needs or wants, or give an occasional gift-mostly to the kids. Monika has power of attorney; she's had it for years, ready to use if and as needed. These days she does use it as my bill paying has become erratic. I have willed my remains to the state anatomical division to use as they see fit. If any ashes come back, they are to go to Monika to eventually be mixed with hers…and disposed of along with hers according to her wishes. I have a living will, and I am not to be resuscitated. I have accepted Meals on Wheels because my doctor insisted on it. It's Winter.

Christmas was a nice time with Steve and his little daughter Noluenn at Leila's house. The little one is so joyful, and I am happy to see her. I hear nothing from family. My nephew Bob's daughter sent a Christmas card, so did her mother, and so did my niece Rita. As a matter of fact, Rita writes and sends cards now and then. It's been a long time since I actually saw her. None of Rose's kids have kept up with me, and I don't know what happened to Joe's son Jim Gutowski. To the best of my knowledge, they're all around the Detroit area. Rita has a live in boy friend, and I am glad that after she spent most of her youth in the convent, she's found contentment in her retirement years. I find it hard to believe that the little girl I knew when I left for seminary will herself soon be 78. She calls now and then and that pleases me.

I understand that there is to be a birthday celebration at Leila's house on January 25th. I will be 90. I used to plan to live to be 100, but as of late I have lost that desire. Maybe it has something to do with knowing that in all likelihood I won't make it.

Totally unlike me, I've been nagging. I am nagging Monika to hurry and finish typing up all my dictation and her notes. We're nearing the end of the memoir writing project, but there's a lot of editing to be done because Monika writes run-on German sentences that require pruning and separating into their logical parts. I was, after all, trained to use words both to their full effect and to their best advantage.

My need to express myself succinctly and astutely suffers palpably until I've honed each sentence to perfection. Time is of the essence because I don't know how much time I have left. I did manage to hit 90 three weeks ago!

My thoughts have begun to turn to my final days and wishes. I don't expect much of anything, I don't even want anything. I want to die in my apartment and do not wish to move or be moved or removed. I do want a little time set aside to be remembered by my friends, most definitely my bridge buddies of long duration. It would be nice if my former confreres in the Society would see fit to give me a blessed send off….but I expect nothing from them. I expect my kids to respect these last wishes to the best of their ability. Monika will know what to do, she does so instinctively most of the time. We're truly one.

When she brought me flowers this morning for Valentine's Day, Monika suggested that starting later this month and continuing till whenever, we devote ourselves to nothing but the completion of this effort by sequestering ourselves at her home in Fleeton for however long it will take us. As I have repeatedly said, I really want this project finished. I said it, I told her so, and I mean it. I'll mail her all these recent scribbles tomorrow in one of the self addressed stamped envelopes she's provided. Carpe Diem!

This evening, Monika called to suggest logistics and time frames. The starting date of our final marathon is to be February 28th. Monika will pick me up that morning, and I will have a little overnight bag packed for a week or so. First we go see Nadja's baby whom I've not seen, from there we have lunch and then we will hit the road to Fleeton where we will work till we're done. Monika promised to drive to Richmond for my bi-weekly bridge games which are now my major enjoyment and interaction with the world around me, and the friends with whom I play are my treasures. Tonight I feel very tired and heavy but I will go downstairs to throw all of this into the mail box before hitting the sack. Saturday we'll continue. I'll write another introductory paragraph. The last one at long last? Let's hope so.

Part 3. (AMDG).

PREFACE

Frank journeyed to his eternal reward on February 24th, 2009. A month earlier, on January 25th, 2009 we had celebrated his 90th birthday.

Frank was no longer the feisty jut-jawed man of God as Jeremy Main had described him in Money magazine some 30 years earlier. He had become fragile; an aura of serenity surrounded him. His long term memory was sharp and clear. His short term memory, or its consistent decline over time, worried him almost as much as it worried all of us.

For him, it presented frequent frustration. For us, it gave grave concern about his continued independence. He dreaded its intimated loss and implied, inevitable, relocation. We had begun to prepare for the certainty of such an eventuality.

God intervened. He took Frank home just as he teetered on the precipice of dependence while yet in his home: self sufficient, serene, satisfied and content.

For years, Frank had been encouraged by all who knew him well to pen his memoir. Frank was a great writer of concise scientific or academic material. He dreaded the thought of anything of this nature although the memoir idea appealed to him. He started a notebook, he wrote on the backs of old correspondence and technical forms. He assembled a lot of pertinent background information such as the defunct Project Themus, the court case, and folder upon folder documenting his struggles. He had the transcripts of the JCU hearings and the Money panel sessions. He had documents and notes on what when where why who and how. His writing included no reference notes; I can only conclude he dictated solely from memory. I myself did look up a few things just to make sure….and found only the spelling of the erstwhile Father General amiss…..and he was Polish!

Years ago, we had begun to work on the memoir together. We started to decide how to arrange it: what to include or emphasize or around what part of his life he would center the entire effort. I had typed, he had corrected, I had made some corrections on my laptop based on his editing, but never went back to thoroughly read page after type written page…..and finally my computer died in the interim and this is a new one Frank never saw.

I realized if we didn't finish this now at once together, it may become never. When we talked on the evening of Monday, February 23rd, I told Frank I'd be driving near his place the next morning but he declined a visit because of the early hour I had indicated. He did agree to have me pick him up the following Saturday and, after visiting Nadja and the baby, to come home with me so we could finish this project once and for all. He just wanted to make sure I would carry him to Richmond for any scheduled bridge games while our writing and editing efforts were being carried out. At this point, bridge was every other Thursday.

We had an exceptionally long talk that Monday. Like during several lengthy conversations in recent days, Frank was in super form. It seemed as if the concerns he himself had about remembering the here and now and yesterday had become moot. He was his old self, 100%. Plus.

We ended the conversation with, "It's only Monday night! We'll talk several times between now and then regarding any details!" We talked nearly every day. Each conversation ended with "I love you, Frank!" "I love you too, honey!"

I had no idea that this was to become the last conversation we would have on this planet. And yet, the tremendous resurgence of energy, lucidity, memory, and eagerness should have been a clue. I'd experienced this with my aunt Terka the day before she passed away, with my dad, and as well with a good friend. The final hurrah!?!

When I learned of Frank's death, however expected to be sudden but not considered as possible in any immediate or real time, I had just returned from the early morning shopping trip I'd mentioned to Frank the night before. It was late Tuesday morning. Meals On Wheels discovered the warm body, breakfast coffee in the pot. He had taken his sheets to the laundry room to wash them earlier that morning. He was nearly fully dressed, a shoe came off when his spirit departed a collapsing body.

Devastated, the stages of grief tumbled about me in a chaotic jumble. Emotions raged. By the end of the day I'd drunk a half bottle of rum with diet coke to numb myself on the one hand and to allow free reign to the torrents of tears gushing from my eyes, and flooding my face.

I was so glad that there would be no need for relocation, so glad that any suffering was brief, so relieved that he was well and I was utterly certain that a loving Father held him close and would do so henceforth. I cried as much because I was now alone as for his passing.

The ins and outs of family, estate, liquidation and disposition followed. Grief so intense needs time to dissipate and be integrated. No one really thought all that clearly for a while. Once they did, life went on. I spent my weeks trying to disengage myself from the morass of depressive feelings inundating my every fiber and thought. I never knew how tough tough can be: Frank had been my life, my breath, my love and my best friend.

When I first met Frank, at age 23, he was the father and brother I missed so very much. For a while, he was my husband and lover. For most of my adult life, he was my true and devoted best friend. Without him, I feel like a wandering stranger in a no-mans land where everything was familiar and routine and nothing made any sense.

9

The rallying point for me was my grandson David Anthony's baptism: déjà vu. Frank had baptized both Nadja and Stephan. And here we were, assembled around a baptismal font celebrating a life that had surged as Frank's ebbed.

Driving home I determined that I would gather all the fragments of our past memoir writing endeavors, and construct the whole that Frank wanted complete. I am ashamed to not have done so sooner, I have no excuse. I am totally convinced Frank is right here, now, to make sure I finally get all that we'd begun at long last really done.

As the weeks became months, Frank's ashes were returned to me. It was then that I began to attempt to fulfill his expressed final wishes. There had to be some small memorial event, and a mass, preferably one that would recognize his contribution to the Society and his unfailing love and life for what it encompassed.

Since I had studied at Loyola College, I had maintained contact with faculty and students. Among them, and a most dear and beloved friend, was Bill Sneck, SJ. By coincidence, Bill had been in the Detroit Province during the final year of Frank's residence and subsequent sabbatical leave and thus knew of him.

Earlier, Bill had introduced me to Frank Kaminski SJ at the retreat house on the Potomac (Faulkner, MD) who kindly gave me some guidance in dealing with Frank's imminently dangerous condition. Unable to reach Frank, I emailed Bill to let him know I was about to drive to Durham, NC and knew that the small chapel next to Central North Carolina University was run by Jesuits from the Maryland Province. Indeed, Bill replied and got me in contact with Ray Donaldson SJ at Holy Cross Church in Durham.

At the time, I did not realize that the parish had relocated into an absolutely beautiful new and modern church. It was there that I met Ray in person with my request to give Frank the proper send off into eternal life, closure that I needed a lot more than the soul that was already enjoying its heavenly place for quite a while but still in need to have a Jesuit reconciliation.

In spite of a heavy schedule made even tighter by impending diocesan meetings, Ray agreed to meet me on the following Saturday morning for a Eucharist honoring Frank's life and memory in fulfillment of one of his few wishes indicated on Valentine's Day.

It was an inspiring, beautiful, heart warming and perfect celebration. Frank's ashes were surrounded by flowers arranged by Ray. Ray moved furniture, books, lectern and candles. Most importantly, Ray gave a sermon that Frank would have truly appreciated, that Frank would have not only approved of but would have relished with the kind of quiet shy smile any praise directed at his person evoked in Frank.

Later, Bill would remind me that times had now changed. I wonder; I maintain that it's the Provinces that are different: I dutifully informed the Detroit Province of Frank's passing. It did not utter a single word of comfort in my hours of loss and sorrow.

As cold as Christian charity? Obviously, not everywhere. I am and will remain grateful to Father Kaminski, and especially to Fathers Sneck and Donaldson for their understanding, empathy, kindness and true love.

The second part of Frank's request for a little memorial was a little more difficult to carry out. At first, Leila offered her home as she had done for Frank's birthday at the beginning of the year. We all agreed to wait till Rob would be here from Germany. That set the date for October. Then suddenly, after a lot of to do and emails, the kids said they wanted no one but themselves in attendance. I knew myself obligated to fulfill Frank's wishes that included his dear bridge partners. Finally, the kind administrator of the Senior Center of Richmond stepped up and offered to host a luncheon in Frank's memory shortly before Christmas 2009. Ten months after his death, at last, his wishes were about to be completely fulfilled.

Frank now sits on the piano in my living room. Someday, our spirits will again be in the same dwelling place, the same location. Even so, for now, I know he's with me 24/7. We talk regularly. It's very much like Billy Graham's assurance to Nancy Reagan after she asked if she'd be with Ronnie once again. I fully expect to be with Frank. And now, it's high time that I carry out this writing project because Frank will otherwise chide me with: "when a job is once begun, never leave it till it's done." And so I will. It's Frank's birthday!

Fleeton, January 25th, 2010

From the Ordinary

I

"**H**ey kid!"

I heard the sound coming across the grassy ground towards me as I walked, carrying a small bundle.

It was moving day. We were moving into the house dad had bought on Helen Avenue, 6555 to be precise, right near the intersection of Harper and Van Dyke. Detroit.

And what a house! To me it was just great. I would have a large room shared with my brother Joe on the second floor. Mom and dad had their bedroom downstairs off the kitchen separated by the bathroom from my three sisters' room. A large homey kitchen, dining room and front room completed the floor plan. There was also a basement. And a furnace, too. Also in the basement were a water heater, storage closets, pantries and larders for provisions, and a huge work space that soon would hold the tools and interests of my oldest brother, Leo.

"Hey kid!"

Again the same voice. What?

I looked and saw a boy near the fence. Throughout my life, this voice and vision remained as the earliest memory of my

13

life though I do no recall exactly how old I was when we moved to our home.

"Hey kid!"

I did not understand what he was saying.

His words had a strange sound to my ears. I knew no English. My language until then was exclusively Polish. My parents were immigrants and I was –by a considerable margin- the youngest of six.

II

Czarist Russia was not a good place for a young Polish man. Poland's turbulent history and repeated divisions had cast the Gutowski family into the eastern-most sector and thereby under czarist rule. Work was difficult to get and joining the army of the oppressor was anathema. Few options existed.

There were the mines, the sea, fields and military. If you were not physically situated on land that had been yours but which you now merely tilled for the ruling powers, you had no access to land. If you were too far removed from the sea to see a possible merchant ship escape, you were prevented from that means of gaining sustenance for survival. There was the military, but no self-effacing Pole would consider serving a regime that stood for the exploitation and cruel domination of his home-land. The drudgery of darkness in mine shafts tunneling deeply into the earth remained the only option.

Young John Gutowski worked in the mines. He was sturdy, he was strong. His mind was elsewhere, his dreams propelled his pick. His thoughts were of America.

The lure of America was irresistible. Many had gone there, including people John knew. Men, women, children, families all headed toward a land that promised work, freedom, possibility and an end to the never ending terror imposed by the far away regime's local representatives.

Some adventurous young fellows like himself, young and strong, not burdened by family responsibilities, free and unencumbered, had also gone abroad. It might also be possible for him, he learned. Save money, pay certain official representatives to provide passage together with any and all adherent legalities, and it was assured. All it took was money. John went to work.

He scrimped and saved every penny. At last, somewhere in his later mid-teens, he had managed to put the stipulated sum together. With joyful eagerness, he approached the broker-middle man who would make the arrangements. It was a heady, breathless time for the young spirit like he had never experienced before. The New World beckoned. The departure date drew closer. But John was not to be among the emigrants heading for a better life. The szcsedyi/Shyster had not delivered but instead absconded with John's money.

What a shock it was to learn he had been cheated! His money gone, his dreams shattered, his hopes replaced by disappointment. He rallied quickly from the bitter lesson learned. He would not be defeated and certainly not cheated a second time. Undaunted and stubbornly focused on his goal, John proceeded.

Once more he slaved in the darkness he had hoped to have left behind. In his mind's eye the shining light of life in America was brighter than ever, stocked mightily with each stroke of his pick, with each bucket of coal loaded into the lorry, with each putrid breath of black dust.

John had not yet seen 15 years of life at the time he was so cruelly taken advantage of by the unscrupulously thieving con artist. Now, not much older but light years wiser, he once again was ready to depart. This time he made certain that the exchange was equitable: money for passage, ticket for zlotys right then and there. He began the journey to a new life while not quite sixteen years old.

I know nothing about his journey, I know no more about is arrival. I imagine he must have gone to Ellis Island with thousands of other immigrants from everywhere. His was a time when Germans tried to escape from Bismarck's regimentation and conscriptions. When Jews tried to escape Pogroms all throughout the Ashkenazi

15

belt stretching from the Ukraine to Poland and through and along the Eastern borders of the Austro-Hungarian Empire. Masses of people came. The stream of immigrants was endless, their masses legion.

One John Gutowski, Polish, from Russia, departed from Bremen on the steam ship "Braunschweig" and arrived on April 15, 1895 on Ellis Island where his name is recorded. The ship's manifest listed his age as 18: he always said he had to make sure he'd be considered old enough to travel alone.

John next found himself in southwestern Pennsylvania, possibly West Virginia, but definitely in mining country. He was skilled, he was able. He was young and he was strong. Industry needed coal, John knew how to extract it. Is this all there was? John knew better. His dreams were alive and well again, ready to be attained.

The industries demanding the coal culled from both deep in the bowels of the earth and scraped from its never to heal crust where located further north. Some of those areas seemed more promising than others appeared to be. John considered a move, weighed it against his ambitions and opted for change and challenge.

His Polish roots were deeply embedded in John's heart and soul. The love for his homeland and longing for its traditions and people played a big deciding role in his thoughts. Many of the areas he considered as potentially worthwhile dwelling places also had developing and already existing Polish communities. He could have the best of both worlds. American Freedom in the midst of Poland's atmosphere. The now nearly twenty-year old selected Detroit.

Around the turn of the last century, around 1900, John Gutowski set out for Detroit, Michigan. He found foundries operating to meet the demands of heavy industrial machinery. He found a fledgling automobile industry with big plans and great potential. He found jobs aplenty for a strapping young solid fellow eager to put his shoulder to the grindstones of fortune and opportunity. And he did well.

His social life centered around the Polish community and its churches. At some time, one of his sisters had also come to

Detroit and settled there. Hers was a family of both immigrants and acquired after her arrival. And she looked out for brother John along with her own Grabowski family obligations.

III

Unlike John, Susi had grown up in Detroit. She had been raised as the only child of her parents. She had become theirs not by natural birth but through adoption. Susi was born in the German part of Poland, her heritage spoke of German affiliations but no concrete relationships were ever ascertained at a later point, leaving many unanswered questions.

When Susi came to her parents' loving home, she came along with trunks of finery and riches. Lace clothing, embroidered linens, and more. It was as if she had been given a magnificent dowry at the tender age of birth.

Susi's parents felt no need or want as they embarked for the New World with Susi's inheritance, possibly speeded along in their departure by the very sources of this wealth and well-being. It was not a deep dark secret that Susi's progenitor had been a straying noble eager to erase the evidence of his philandering, and that her mother was, no matter her heritage or background also a possible financially contributing party to that which had occurred. It would be a secret never known or uncovered, but a wonderful tale told repeatedly. Moreover, a tale with the substance of having provided for a young woman till she married and went off to create her own hearth and home.

Susi's circumstances and the economics surrounding her heritage allowed for a gentility not usually found in the hard working blue collar immigrant neighborhoods. While her formal education in matters scholastic and academic was minimal, Susi's love for the finer social and cultural things in life became part of the legacy bestowed on her off-spring. Her interests were echoed in the love of music, traditions and customs engendered early on especially in the tastes and likes of Joe and Frank, and later in Leo's daughter Rita who surely was equally endowed through her mother Helen.

Accomplished domesticity was Susi's work in life. She raised simple living to an art form in her quiet, non-obtrusive and non-assertive way. The daily travails of a household with six children ran effortlessly and smoothly. She is remembered fondly, lovingly, as being there always without drawing attention to herself. She was what is generally associated with the Southern Belle: a steel-strong iron Magnolia filled with gentle softness, her husband's true partner in life and in love, in the midst of a struggling immigrant town.

Creating a home for John and any blessed bundles that might be theirs was her aim. It is what she had been prepared for, and what she intended to carry out. She cooked, washed, sewed and cleaned. She knit and preserved. Pickles, Sauerkraut, eggs in big jars and Kielbasa hanging in rings, smoked and dry. She was the incarnation of Proverbs' Virtuous Woman and saw her role as such. The strength and comfort of her husband, mother to his children, and the twinkle of happiness in his eye – Susi's days were full.

Susi's life centered around time with friends and family. She was a devout Catholic and engaged in the activities of the local parish. There was little time for less physically or more intellectually demanding pursuits: she could hardly read English, and was limited to Polish print. Susi had been educated formally only long enough to fully participate in the Sacraments: Penance, Eucharist, Confirmation and then, finally, with John at her side, Martrimony.

While there was an abundance of love inside our home, life outside the bosom of my immediate family taught me later while a member of the Society that actually I grew up in cultural and intellectual poverty. How relative things can be! My memories will not tarnish.

The first of the hoped for blessed bundles arrived in early April, 1905. Leo Gutowski entered this world. It was only fifteen months later when his sister Rose arrived in June 1906 and not much time elapsed till brother Joseph saw the light of day. Helen came next (not to be confused later with Leo's wife Helen) and

18

when Theresa arrived in 1912, both Susi and John decided five children made a wonderful family to raise and enjoy.

Because they were devout and practicing Catholics, John and Susi turned to the Rhythm method of birth control. They counted days and heeded calendars, and lived their loving lives accordingly while watching their children grow. They were just about to send the youngest off to first grade at the local parochial school when Susi's belly grew once more. John had not only miscalculated, but had mistakenly believed the opposite of what was correct. He thereby inverted the fertile and infertile periods.

On January 25th, 1919, I arrived lustily screaming into the bosom of love, warmth and a Polish celebration. Frankie had arrived. I was baptized Frank, with no middle name, and began the life of a little Polish kid in the midst of a Polish neighborhood of which I have absolutely no knowledge or recollection except for that fateful day when we moved, prior to my starting school, to Helen Avenue. It was sometime around 1925 I think.

"Hey kid!"

In my family, only I was still a little kid on this moving day.

IV

Because my siblings were all considerably older than I and, moreover, close in age to each other, I was rarely a peer among them. Instead, I was the baby. I was cuddled, coddled and carried, especially by my sister Rose nearly 13 years my senior. The five older Gutowski children were already young adults when and where my memory begins.

When we moved to Helen Avenue, my brother Leo, born in 1905, was already around 20. I have no recollection if he was living with us, or if so, where he slept. I do remember that he had a workshop in the basement where he carried out miscellaneous projects such as woodworking and building various things, including a crystal set. It was my first encounter with that wonderful invention, and one I was to put to good use many years later.

It must have been around this time that Leo married Helen. He was working for a lumber company, a job he held life-long till his retirement raising two children over many years. In that period he had worked himself up to the position of THE manager of the concern. I certainly do recall that the two had their own home, a duplex, purchased with my father's help in 1929, and lost in the crash of that year when the other tenants' lost job became their own misfortune in making payments impossible without the rental income. They moved.

Leo and Helen had two children, a son and a daughter. The son developed MS and his life's path was forever changed. Had it not been for his mother's devotion, he would not have attained what he did, including two wonderful children who survive father and grandparents, accomplished and independent in their own lives. The daughter's life detoured through years of convent life, teaching and performing music to subsequent years as a psychiatric social worker from which she is now retired herself, enjoying a late blooming relationship. She's my niece Rita. As I write, Leo and Helen have left this world long ago to go to their eternal rewards.

Rose might have been my nanny. She carried me around like a live doll when I was little, played with me, spoiled me, cared for me and did for me. Her steadfast affection was to be mine throughout my life, in times of turmoil and troubles yet unforeseen, never wavering, through periods of grief and when other siblings were more concerned with appearance than substance.

She was working for a furrier when she met Paul, and her marriage to someone of German origin was not especially welcomed in a very ethnocentric family. But, persevere she did and four children sprouted from the union of Paul and Rose Mierzwa. Two daughters flanked by two sons, each in turn later on married with families that presented Rose and Paul with over a dozen beautiful grandchildren to love and enjoy life long. Rose outlived Paul by many years after his life ended in a nursing home to which she went with daily devotion. Eventually, in her high eighties, Rose's life drew to a close in similar surroundings, much loved by all and deeply mourned. Her mind and memory had gone long before her earthly existence ended.

Joe got a job in the gas company in the City of Hamtramk. His bilingual abilities were a requirement in that nearly totally Polish city within a city. More than any of my older siblings, it was Joe who read much and enjoyed music and stage performances. Thanks to his work, we had a gas refrigerator, a gas furnace, a gas hot water heater and of course, gas to cook with, including even a second stove in the basement whose function was canning foods and producing beer. (More on that later).

Joe served in the Army and was stationed in Italy, but I never heard about whether or not he saw any combat, or other actual action of any kind while he was there. Maybe that was because when he returned, I was no longer at home. He did marry Ann, his long time sweetheart, when he came back, and both raised a son who himself married late in life, long after both Joe and Ann had passed away.

My sister Helen never married. She held a variety of office positions, ultimately working for the railroad. In the early sixties, she fell and broke her hip. The treatment process uncovered cancer. The once jolly and ebullient 200 pound woman dwindled to an emaciated 60 pound skeleton before God called her home, but not until she had given me detailed instructions about what she wanted said about herself in the eulogy I would deliver when I officiated at her burial.

Theresa was next to me in age, though already in school when I arrived in this world. Like Helen, she remained unmarried and also like both Helen as well as Joe who married after service, she lived at home as long as my mother was alive. Theresa was fun. She was always fun: as a child, as a young woman, and in old age.

And Theresa could drink....she among all my siblings inherited my father's love of Vodka, no matter what time of day.

And no matter how drunk, she retained her happy disposition until sleep would overcome her consciousness.

Theresa too worked for the railroad. She, unlike my other siblings, was moved away from the Detroit area and spent some years in Baltimore and Huntington, WVa, witnessing some of the mergers which the B&O and C&O suffered in the process of becoming part of the CSX system. Her retirement guaranteed, she returned to Detroit. For a while, she lived with a young male couple in Lansing, where she was sort of "housemother". In that role, she gave legitimacy to an otherwise unacceptable liaison long before the advent of gay rights. Her joie de vivre exuded happiness to all, her sense of humor made life's travails bearable, she added a certain "je ne sais quoi" that has never been replaced since her sad, untimely passing too soon in life. Anytime would have been too soon to lose Theresa.

Of course my siblings appear in my own recollected life, but their assured place needed a little more space than my so very different life affords them. Like my parents, their influence on me at a young age was substantial. I took something from each one and each one offered me something I have taken with me throughout my own life as a treasure from my very beginning. I remember much starting with the Helen Avenue days. I especially remember:

"Hey kid!"

And now, to me.

V

There were lots of kids, and we played a lot. These were the days when none of the fun, games, or entertainment we sought was provided by electronics or the media. We made our own. We played ball and we ran around. We did all manner of things little kids will do when left to be creatively unencumbered by outside influence or resource.

Our games changed with the seasons, and with each season our ages changed the games. There was swimming at the YMCA and movies on week-ends, especially on rainy ones. There were empty boxes to be turned into various imaginary structures our imagination then made use of, there were trees to be climbed, and balls to be chased, kicked, or hit with a bat.

Even when school settled us into well behaved, uniformed little boys and girls at St. Thomas the Apostle parochial school, presided over by the Sister of St. Joseph of the Third Order of St. Francis, our week-ends and free times continued the pattern we'd begun in our younger years.

We walked to school. There were no buses to this neighborhood place of learning attached to our parish church. On week ends I followed the same path, first only with my mother, who took me to Mass early in the day, and on Sundays, with the whole family as we would attend Mass en masse.

There were eight grades in the school, taking us to high school age and preparing us for a world beyond our immediate parochial horizons and neighborhood outlooks. Our activities were reflected in our free time. While we were once content with randomly frolicking about, we now had acquired greater skills with balls, and we began to segregate our interests by sex.

The less we now saw of the girls who had until recently been just one of us, the greater our interest in and fondness for their presence. By 8th grade, it had become obvious that they were growing breasts and we were not. We learned games in which we could continue to both participate. Pinochle on our front steps was one of these. Another one of these took place in an old abandoned neighborhood barn.

Up in its loft, we had our occasional poker games, strip poker. Shy, curious, our yet slumbering slowly awakening prurient interests jumped to full alert and life. Socks, shoes, a scarf, a cardigan…. maybe a boy's shirt….I still remember our eagerness, our warm and rapid breath, our bulging eyes and our satisfaction to know we had won our hand. Either we lacked skill, time or were too frightened: we never played long enough or well enough to see even the smallest glimpse of flesh of either boy or girl.

And by then I knew what I was looking for: it was boobs. I sought soft, warm, pendulous boobs. I had seen them. I had been embraced by them. I knew the feel and smell of them. Of course I was no stalker, had stalking even been a term that then connoted what it does today? My voyeurism was direct, innocent, and practical.

Saturdays were house cleaning days, a task to be complete when my dad got home for the Sunday. It was Helen's job to scrub the kitchen floor. It didn't take me long to discover that if I volunteered to wipe dry what she had washed and rinsed, I would be behind her clearly able to be watching the thin cotton of her housedress modestly shield the mounds of female form engulfed by my interested imagination.

I have no idea or recollection how many occasions of card playing or floor washing actually happened. Was it a regular event or a sometime happening? Surely the floor was done frequently. Were our barn exploits ever discovered? I know not now.

What stands out is that these are the first two memories and the only two memories I have of something sexually related prior to high school. Later, I would form perceptions at the Y pool to which then were added a third memory. What happened most immediately was my first sexual arousal in the form of an uninvited erection.

I was, after all, from the moment I was born, destined by my mother, to become a priest. Such a blessing, this baby late in life! Such a blessing, to have a priest in the family! Such an honor for both (him and his family)! A guaranteed place in heaven for the mother of such a one!

And mother was undeterred to get me there: taking me to mass, keeping me close, expressing her wishful intentions like a mantra I then called or had learned to call litany. The die of my life was cast amidst my budding baby teeth and formed ceaselessly thereafter like the honing and tempering of a fine steel blade.

It is now some seventy-five plus years since those days and I recall only snatches here and there. I do not recall what I thought or felt to have my life thus decided for me: at a young age one accepts without question or thought, and simply does. Independence and initiative come with maturity, self determination follows, and so do some resentments and rebelliousness.

There are two events that now, with 20/20 adult hindsight, make me wonder about what went on in my thoughts back then, and whether I might have responded physiologically: it seemed as if I blatantly reacted over pressures that my tender years might have perceived as threatening.

The first relates to asserting myself by making decisions unheard of for one in fourth grade, and based on my own reasoning and logic as a result of observation.

In fourth grade, we could continue to study Polish which had been both taught in school and spoken at home till then. Or, we could drop it and concentrate on English. I decided to drop it without parental approval or consideration. I saw my older siblings partake of an English speaking world where Polish had no place. They read English newspapers and magazines; they had friends who spoke no Polish at all, and they spoke English at home, among themselves and to me. I reasoned that that was the way to go to get somewhere in the future and acted accordingly.

The second event was an illness that might have been a reaction to pressures. I developed St. Vitus' dance or Chorea, now called Singleton's Chorea to differentiate it from the devastating Huntington's. I twitched, I shook. I was ordered to bed and the family doctor came for house visits for the duration of the illness which was lengthy. I nevertheless did not lose scholastic ground and caught up with school work: I had skipped a grade earlier, even repeating now would not have been a set back.

Our family doctor was a lady. She was kind and gentle. She examined me from head to toe as I lay in bed. I believe I was about eleven, in sixth grade. My little penis stood at attention when she gently touched it, pushing back the un-circumcised foreskin. O God what a smelly mess: no one had ever shown or taught me proper hygiene regarding this appendage not removed. Whatever

25

cleanliness there had been was purely accidental, spontaneous in the swimming pool or unrelated in the bath-tub rub. It had been kept totally unmentionable. Of course from then on I became meticulously clean. There was a bonus: it felt GOOD.

Recollecting this incident reminds me also that when we went swimming at the Y, boys only, no suits were worn. It was then that I learned that penises came in various sizes and that mine was pretty small. I learned that I could make my penis bigger by pressing it against the pool wall.

I don't recall how or when I learned it could get stiff, and at no time did I advert to anything sexual or sexually stimulating. I did not connect my penis' action as at all related to anything even remotely sexual.

I had received absolutely NO sex instruction. I didn't know how I got any of my subsequent knowledge. I do not recall that my brothers shared any of their information with me. It would be much later that I finally learned things in class, at a time when everything was associated with sin and evil, the devil, immorality, and base behaviors far beneath a vowed Jesuit.

The years on Helen Avenue moved along, often a blur of jumbled pictures in my mind. Basically, I was a good little boy. I was a good kid. I was a good student. I recall no memorable trauma, no unhappiness. My parents did not fight, there was no violence. They were quiet, kind, loving and sweet, to each other and to each of us. Mother took care of the house, dad worked and supported us. We kids helped and did what we were told to do: school at first, and then, one by one off to work.

I recall a loving family, a family in which the members shared and cared, laughed and joked and enjoyed each other, did things together, and were there for each other. This was how it was when I was little, as I got older, and I like to think also after I left home. My sister's kids continued the traditions of Sunday family dinners or get-togethers as long as they all lived near each other and their mother, my sister Rose, was alive well into the 1990's: going to any of their homes was going home just as it had been with mom and dad.

My own memories of school vacations and family vacations include both the ordinary and the special. Special was going to a wedding in Alpena where we spent better than a week among relatives I do not recall. Ordinary get-togethers included the Chmura's and the Grabowski's, the former my dad's sister, the latter good friends. Or was it the other way around? With cousins real or believed we fished and rowed, we ran through fields and played games kids play on holiday away from their customary haunts.

VI

Life was good. For me, anyway. I was a happy go lucky kid. Just an ordinary run of the mill working class offspring of immigrant parents settled in a major city engaged in being productive and upwardly mobile and trying to gain financial security.

I loved life, and I loved my family. I especially liked any time dad and I could spend together which was a rare treat given his long hours and hard work. There was one thing I did regularly with him: I helped dad make beer in the basement. These were prohibition days.

Outside, the depression raged. Unemployment was staggering. Poverty was rampant, and hardest hit were the working class immigrants toiling in the factories that prepared goods consumed by the rich and well to do. Detroit during the depression was depressed. Whole city blocks would find no one employed. "Brother, can you spare a dime?" wasn't just some slogan, it WAS. Dad never missed a day of work; we never lacked anything we needed. And to assure this, we concocted booze. In our basement!

We brewed beer. Dad would bottle it, someone would come to the door, hand him money and he would hand out a bagged bottle. Or two, or three or? Empties came back to be refilled, a great recycling scheme of brown glass before thinking green had become fashionable.

On various days, mostly week-ends, dad would bring home with him an assortment of men he knew from work or the neighborhood. The motley crew would remain confined to the basement where ribald jokes resounded amidst the chug-a-lugging of home brew. Home brew kept our home fires burning: dad supplied his boss who kept his supplier happily employed.

Those who know me well, well, actually, they don't even have to know me well in order to have heard me say repeatedly what has become a life-phrase for me whenever I need to decide to spend, save, evaluate any money related matter: I am a child of the depression.

The depression colors my every thought in how I relate to money. My "kids" have heard it so often, it's a family joke. "Dad's downstairs, just wait, one of the first things he'll tell you is that he was a child of the depression". This was a comment my 30something daughter made to friends who helped her move while I guarded the half loaded truck parked curb-side.

I may have been a child of the depression, but what I rarely consider is that we were not poor, we were what was then middle class. We owned what was available to the average households of the time. We had a little more than many others. Dad did well.

The depression affected us: dad lost his savings. He also lost investment property on which no rental income was possible from destitute tenants whereupon he couldn't make the mortgage. It grieved and angered him, but he also got over it. What we ourselves needed remained ours to use and enjoy. We weathered the crash and its aftermath. I remember it well: it influenced me as when it came time to consider my choice of high school. After having one grade after another successfully completed, I found myself ready to graduate from St. Thomas the Apostle and my thoughts turned to "where next?"

Most of the neighborhood kids would go to Eastern High School, but Sister Nemesia (I remember her well!) had mentioned she thought other schools, more academically challenging and of better reputation, might be considered for me as I would move toward my priestly mission goal in life. These considerations included a lot of decisions and responsibilities for a thirteen year old, but were just another challenge for me. I always thrived on challenge.

I investigated the options, and considered another public school to which I applied. I took entrance and scholarship exams to several high schools including those run by the Christian Brothers and another order I can't recall now. And, I was offered a one year scholarship which would be renewable, to UoD High School, THE high school, far across town where the rich folks lived, the best there was. I accepted. Another chapter along the way to meet mom's expectations was about to unfold.

It was the last summer in the neighborhood as I had come to know it. I did not realize that attending another school far away would change my entire life, my relationships with kids I had known since before my first school day, the games, the friends, the whole atmosphere that was as much me as I was it. I was looking toward the future, the opportunities, the knowledge, and the learning. I also looked toward the cost and means: how I would get back and forth across town, how I would continue beyond that one definite first year of scholarship funds, and so much more. I knew I could and would. "How" became mere logistics that had to be worked out.

The Preparatory High School of the University of Detroit was across town. It was prestigious. It was highly respected. Its faculty was the best of the best. The most educated of the educated. The most elite of the elite and esteemed like none other. It was run by the Society of Jesus, or Jesuits for short.

I knew nothing of Jesuits. I knew nothing of their lofty reputation or goals. I was a kid from a working class neighborhood commuting with my thumb across town, the so called other side of the tracks. I had seen the neighborhood where the school was located when dad drove me around the area: manicured lawns, huge houses, elegant people climbing in and out of elegant cars. I liked it. I might not belong now, but I would…someday. Aspiration preceded perspiration as I embarked on my Freshman year.

At this point in my life I had made and carried out a considerable number of very serious decisions. Serious and considerable for anyone. More so for a 13 year old. I had decided to drop Polish in 4th grade, now I decided which high school with an eye on my future. I had just graduated from 8th grade at age 13.

I made decisions that indicated independence, self determination and walking to the beat of my own drummer. Maybe this is part of the territory that comes with being the youngest. The molds that train, constrain and form were as worn out as my parents must have been tired of raising yet another little one. They had done it all with the five older ones, following each other like graduated organ pipes. By the time when Frankie decided to drop the Polish language, and to seek a school apart from what was commonly done by other kids who went to the local neighborhood high school and mostly joined the work force before completing it, it was accepted more with a resigned shrug indicating: "if he can manage financially, then let's let him" than it had been with any of my older siblings.

VII

University of Detroit High School and Academy, as it is now known, had just moved to its present campus on Cambridge off Seven Mile Road when I started my Freshman year in the fall of 1931. Originally founded in 1877 at the request of the local Bishop, it had been both distinguished from the University of Detroit itself, and been accredited by the University of Michigan. I don't know if it already had North Central accreditation at that time, or if indeed North Central accreditation already existed.

There have been many changes in the world, the church and the Society since those days. Nevertheless, if the school had a concise mission statement then as it has now, it certainly would not have differed from the present. This was, after all, the time which provided the foundation that became the cradle for the thought formation and later ascendancy of one Pedro Arrupe. Eventually, as Father General of the Society, Arrupe would give voice to what was to be taking place as a result of what was happening in the teaching of my here and now. The formation of future "Men for

Others", we would use all we learned for the greater benefit of all. At this very time, it was the Austrian Polish Ledochowski who had been at the Society's helm for two dozen or so years. We were but the seed bed for the future.

The current mission statement speaks of the school's commitment to providing the highest quality Jesuit high school education, its desire to collaborate with parents in challenging students beyond the mere scholasticism to reflective and committed service in faith and for justice in an atmosphere of learning and spiritual development for the individual within community.

When I arrived scared, tired, and weary on that first school day, none of the above mattered to me in the least. I wanted a good education. I wanted a great education. I wanted to live like the people in the houses around the school and up the road with their curving drive-ways, manicured lawns, and smiling people in big expensive cars. This would be my ticket to get there, to study and do well, and to become somebody of importance or at least someone with money. The priest idea was still there but had become a given in my life; it was so frequently reinforced, that at this point I ignored thinking of it. I certainly did not connect it to UoD High School and where I would go as a result of attending it.

Just now, right now, this very first day of school, I was more concerned with how I would get back and forth. I stood on the street for quite a while before my thumb caught a ride. I knew the way home would be no simpler. Moreover, I was fully aware that this would be the start of four years of getting up extra early to make sure I would arrive on time no matter the duration of my thumb's success, and later, on the way home the time was equally long if not quite as critical. I was, after all, vi-a-vis the rest of the student body just a kid from the other side of the tracks. Tolerated, not welcome. Allowed but not accepted. I also was certain of my desire to blend in and become part of the majority.

I was never late. I never missed a day because I had no ride. I did have some adventures. After a while, men going to work

31

would stop often enough that I developed regulars. That was great: they got to know me and I them, though we spoke little. We did develop some sort of trust and expectations, being there on time, no extra favors or demands, expressed gratitude. The adventures consisted of overt homosexual advances from which I instinctively recoiled. (Am I homophobic? I don't think so. The distaste of those few instances, however, is with me yet).

As my life had been thus far, so my high school years proceeded without any major memories, traumas, illnesses or happenings. I was not aware of the politics which would soon plunge the world into war. I did not feel the negative effects of the depression. The home brew we continued to make for my dad's friends and co-workers was constant with or without prohibition, and is credited with assuring my father's on-going employment.

My brother Leo was married and gone, I knew he had had a son and a daughter but they were little tykes of little interest to a high-school student. My sister Rose got married in those years, and had her first son: I remember clearly that I was asked to watch him while the family went to Christmas Midnight Mass during my senior year. Jerry screamed the entire time they were gone, non-stop. I had no idea what to do. Poor kid.

I was a student of good average ability. I recall no driving ambition, nor abject dislike of anything that was required, demanded or suggested. The distance of the commute made it difficult to participate in some extra curricular activities, but I was also small in size, and so found myself in the bantam foot ball group which was formed among the upper class students who did not make the football team in their first two years. One might call it the JV team while Varsity was the thing to play.

I followed the ordinary course of study prescribed. I spent a lot of time in the library. When it became clear I needed a job to continue past my scholarship term, the good Fathers assigned me there to keep me with my class. It was what one might today call a work study program. Undoubtedly, my circumstances influenced me. I became somewhat of a loner.

I was no longer one of the kids in the neighborhood. Not only had we all gotten older, but I no longer participated in the daily life experienced by the group I had forsaken in my quest for better educational preparation. I was too busy with work and commuting time to allow much association with classmates before, during, or after school. I lived at too great a distance to foster relationships or participate in some of the get-togethers my classmates held.

Of course there were exceptions. I did visit the homes of some classmates and was impressed by their life style as compared to mine. We weren't poor; we did well within our own part of town, our immediate immigrant neighborhood. But now I saw a new world that was far more complex, detailed and acquisitive than I had fathomed from the outside.

The manicured lawns extended into marble foyers and unto oriental rugs. The smiling people held delicate martini glasses and did not slug down boiler makers. The music wafting through large rooms was live as family members tickled the ivories. It was all overwhelming. My senses filled with smells and sounds and visions.

I did not realize that all I perceived was not highly unusual, but that many, not necessarily affluent or wealthy people, had pianos and drank little. Or, that where ever homes were on the continuum from simple to extravagant, it was the character and value of the residents within that mattered. I was young and impressionable, and what I saw was desirable. I had never felt economically deprived, now I felt culturally and intellectually deprived.

My parents, bless them, lived and loved and worked. Their own backgrounds had not included time or interest in more refined things life offered, even when it was of no cost and free. Their reading was confined to the Polish paper delivered to our door. My siblings included an English newspaper with this no-assortment of printed matter. There were no books and only occasional magazines. There was no interest in them and no reference to either their availability or existence. The radio was on the Polish station which catered to Polish polkas and the like that linked the hearts to home. There were no discussions of anything significant or anything interesting. There was nothing intellectually stimulating, personally invigorating or mentally challenging and culturally expanding. What I had grown up to understand from and about my mother's interests was totally church centered whether in music, lesson, worship or association. Polish Catholic. Our culture and tradition; it's what made us neither special nor unique.

For the first time, I felt poor, but in a totally different sense than poverty was experienced by the effects of the depression. Mistakenly, all my life I have said that I was a child of the Depression when I reflect on my early years. Now I realize my impoverishment was cerebral, and the cure was available with enough elbow grease and desire. Oddly, now that I am an octogenarian I realize how much like my father I really was or am. A young man with a dream, knowledge to turn this dream into a reality, a vision of what and how it can be, effort and tenacity to pursue it, and lastly, motivation and determination to fulfill it. Back then, I was merely a kid who was eager to proceed.

Enter brother Joe. Joe and I had shared bedrooms upstairs for as long as I can remember, certainly for as long as Leo was gone and that had to be at least four years considering his little Bob was three and Rita in her first year of life. Joe was working for the Hamtramck gas-company by day, and interested in many other things outside of work.

From Joe I learned my love of classical music. Joe had a radio that played the great composers I'd not paid attention to before. Not only did he enjoy the music he listened to, he knew about it and could talk about it. I was all ears. I vaguely remember attending some performances with him, but really don't recall just what or where they were. In retrospect, they could have been free, out doors, in some park, on a Sunday afternoon. I also recall the many melodies that had accompanied the films I had seen. Before "talkies" were the regular venue.

Joe read a lot. He subscribed to the Saturday Evening Post, the only magazine received regularly at our house. He took me places though I recall the going more than I do why we went and where. While I had lots to study, I read even more: everything and anything I could get. Education, effort and desire would take me places. As dad said, this is America.

My eagerness and application did not go unnoticed. Intellectual curiosity and learning are the hallmarks of the Jesuits in whose environment I had placed myself. It didn't take long for some of the Fathers to note the little Polish kid's academic performance, consistent in its strong average, and the diligence and interest with which he pursued his studies.

I loved learning, I was curious and studious, and I was eager to please when it meant my tuition payments depended on me. The idea of possibly considering a later joining of the order was presented somewhere during my Sophomore year. It dovetailed my mother's instilled aspirations for my life. Priesthood. If it was to be thus, than why not the best, the elite, the Jesuits?

VIII

The University of Detroit High School was and is a Jesuit institution. Its traditions, educational style and philosophical premise are rooted in the teaching of St. Ignatius of Loyola, founder of the Order. Like all Jesuit institutions, it follows certain methods and aims in accordance with the purposes and aims of the Society Ignatius formed. The reputation of the order precedes it worldwide: academic excellence and superior scholasticism in a unique atmosphere of learning, challenge, reflection, commitment, as well as personal and spiritual development.

Few have not heard of the Society's reputation. Few are not impressed by the methods and means used to attain stated goals. Many laud the what, why, when, how and where of the society's works, even more people approve. Yet, there are those who absolutely decry the order, its members, founders, generals, outlooks, perspectives, including the mere existence of the Society of Jesus for as many reasons as there are dissenters. Rarely does a discussion of the Society not evoke some emotion, be it pro or con. Catholic or not, Christian or not, the Jesuits elicit emotions that one take a stand either with them or against them. The "Black Pope" (the presiding Father General of the Society in Rome) and the Pope are often seen as opposing forces.

It all began in the middle of the 16th Century. Ignatius of Loyola, a Basque soldier wounded in battle, was recovering at his ancestral castle, devouring any reading matter accessible to him. His selections were limited: mostly spiritual and religious material was all that was available to him. Reading of the life of Christ and the saints, he had a spiritual renaissance and the time to ponder his life's purposeful mission within God's world as he waited for the healing of battle torn flesh. While the body mended, he committed heart and soul to God.

Guided by Benedictines and participating in various religious experiences finally took Ignatius to a cave near Barcelona called Manresa, where he began to collect his thoughts more formally. It was about 1522. Ignatius was about 31 years of age. Ignatius had found his life's purpose. The Spiritual Exercises had been drafted into shape and would, after numerous revisions, shape the lives of thousands for centuries.

Ignatius' thoughts turned to the "hows and wheres" of his mission: he knew that what he wanted to do is be a force for good in the name of God Jesus both spiritually and practically. He knew of others who would share his zeal and commitment. Eventually he turned to Paris, and there he assembled a small cadre of men who were likewise eager to pursue the greater good and to become engaged, one and all, for the greater glory of God. (Ad Majorem Dei Gloriam=AMDG).

Six men joined Ignatius to vow chastity and poverty before God. They dedicated themselves as a group in a little church on Paris' Montmartre in August 1543. It had taken

Ignatius a dozen years to turn dream into reality. He was 43. The Company of Jesus as it was called was born. Its greatest missionary, Francis Xavier, had become commissioned for action.

Ignatius was a soldier. What he knew was military. What he had experienced were order, regimentation, discipline, and blind obedience to commands, leading and following, and the importance of knowledge to determine a course for guiding principles, values, actions and intentions.

Ignatius understood human nature and the needs that propel men to action. He therefore fostered a strong sense of identity, the sense of affiliation provided by community, and well defined meaning or purpose of action among his group. Not unlike the musketeers, this Parisian band of brigands believed that they were all for One (God) and one for all.

Around these men dedicating life and limb to God, the world was undergoing turmoil and change. Their time of arrival was optimal, the fields for their labor fertile in a world falling fallow in faith. It was a time of major change and upheaval. The magnificent and the horrible happened next to the memorable and the best forgotten. The slaughter of Indians for the glory of God was not the least among the latter.

What was considered fact based on knowledge one day was disproven on the next. Columbus had discovered the New World in 1492, the year after what probably was Ignatius' birth year. He was quickly followed by John Cabot, Vasco da Gama and Amerigo Vespucci. The race for expansion, discovery and colonization had begun. Among them: DeSoto discovered the Mississippi River, Cortes conquered Mexico, Balboa discovered the Pacific Ocean and Magellan circumvented the globe. The atrocities they and others committed while calling on the name of God in reality were for their lust to loot gold.

There was a growing sense of nationalism and secularism in Europe, and with it a decline of the papacy's influence. The Borgia Pope and his brood did little to inspire confidence in the sanctity of the Holy See with their devious and murderous exploits, yet St. Peter's buildings were soon to be erected under the watchful eye of Donato Bramante.

Art reached heretofore unknown heights not only in its works, but the astounding number of major artists in a relatively brief span of time: Michelangelo and DaVinci, Rafael and Titian, Bellini and Cellini, are but a few. Further north, Bosch, Duerer, Holbein and Gruenewald were engaged in their life's art work.

Palestrina composed music that would earn him the reputation of the Catholic Church's first great musician. Lass, Willaert and Senfl composed Masses, motets and madrigals. The genre of the German *LIED* was born.

Science would demonstrate factually that long held truths were false: Copernicus was hard at work threatening the order of the Ptolomeic universe. In the wings awaiting birth were Tycho Brahe, Keppler and Galileo. The world as it had been known till then would never be the same again.

Erasmus and More were among those who re-examined scripture and subsequently espoused humanism which gave fodder to the reformers. Rabelais' humanism and humor found popularity in Gargantua and Pantagruel. The thoughts of man had been awakened in rebirth, it was the Renaissance Age and men would now live life fully thinking. The Church's days were numbered if it did not open its eyes with an approving nod to what was going on around it scientifically, artistically, culturally and socially.

The mighty rulers strengthened their positions lest they be swept up in tides unwelcome. Charles V inherited the vast Habsburg lands that, thanks to fruitious marriages, had united Spain, the Netherlands, Italian kingdoms, Bohemia, Austria and lands adjacent under this one consecrated Holy Roman Emperor. Henry VIII sat on his Tudor throne fostering kinship with the Emperor, seeking an heir and rationalizing faith so his beliefs would suit his lust. The king of France fretted both about appeasing the Emperor and the King, and how to maximize the benefits from his English and Scottish relationships.

There was a ferment that did not only include the bedrock of the Protestant Reformers, but the entire scope of man's knowledge was about to be invalidated. The Renaissance had reached heights that would cause it to topple from its own weight of excesses to a rationalism resounding as a call to arms in the works of the great reformers. Calvin, Zwingli, Knox and others fired the flames of their own politically hued slant on Protestantism in the shadow of Luther whose thoughts on Jewish inferiority would someday be fodder for the Nazi proponents of the final solution.

It was a heady time of fascinating change. It was chaotic and in need of order. Ignatius saw the church under siege, beleaguered by its own frailties, and attacked by many in its surroundings. He had been forced to abandon his hopes to convert the infidels in the Holy Land, and his hopes to fight the Turks ended when they broke through Christendom's door at Mohacs. The Pope had sent help there. Too late. Now, the Pope needed an Army. The Company of Jesus was at his service.

Ignatius had chosen the term company because as a military man, he liked military terms which best expressed his intentions. His society of men would be the Pope's Army in face of the enemies of Christendom near and far, responding to the Pope's call and command without notice or hesitation. A fourth vow would be added to those of chastity, poverty and obedience: a vow of fealty and allegiance to the Bishop of Rome who would be working side by side with the Society's General headquartered in the Eternal City.

In time, the term "Company" would be permanently replaced by the now familiar "Society". In time, too, the various study regiments, the meaning, purpose, work and missions, as well as the identity of being a Jesuit amidst a community of like-minded Jesuits was honed to the manner in which it has continued for centuries. Among all the study and work, the Spiritual Exercises which too had undergone numerous revisions, remained the outstanding and principal sign of that it meant to be a Jesuit.

Ignatius' own early training as a young man at court and as well his life experiences and exposure, suggested prescribing a course of study that would prepare men to fight not with their swords, but with a rapier sharp intellect and wit.

Later credited with stemming the tide or Protestantism and regaining some of the lost souls and territories for the Church, it was the finely trained minds that were the success tool of the Society. If Christianity was under siege, then the army was poised to fight. How well this was done was visibly two fold: by the numbers of men who chose to become members of the Society of Jesus, and how far and wide their influence would go. Empress Maria Theresa called on the Jesuits to re-Catholicize a then protestant Austria.

A hallmark of the Jesuit modus operandi was to use everything at one's disposal that could be practically and intellectually incorporated into the promulgation of faith. To Peter Canisius that meant gaining access to what then was media: printers and publishers who would provide the vehicle for the literary defense of the Truth. He entered Germany with two other Jesuits. When he left thirty years later, there were over 1,100.

The missionaries abroad adapted themselves to local color and tradition. Unlike their predecessors who preached that outside of the church there was no salvation, Jesuits saw local beliefs as only somewhat erroneous in need of correction to the One True Faith. They became adept at adapting to being like the natives, whether in Africa, India, China, or Japan. Francis Xavier, one of the original six, was incredibly vastly traveled given the time in which he lived. Others accompanied him and followed. All were not equally welcome at all times. Jesuit martyrs abound.

Jesuits also became a force that at times put the Pope in untenable political positions, such as in South America where the Jesuits' efforts to empower indigenous Indian populations so enraged the Spanish and Portuguese colonists of Brazil, Paraguay, Uruguay and Argentina among others, that the pressure put on the Pope finally caused him to disband the Society and thereby halt its efforts and works. Had it not been for Catherine the Great who harbored Jesuits during their Diaspora, encouraging their works within Russia, and thereby assuring the order's existence, there might no longer be a Society today.

Whether the intellect of a Bellarmine, or the missionary zeal of a Marquette, Jesuits worldwide had become a globally recognized force that shaped the minds of generations in its institutions of higher learning. It was this atmosphere that permeated University of Detroit Jesuit High School. It was here that I found the stimulus of what I was looking for in life, the challenge to go after it, the support to carry it out, and the motivation to keep going.

Ignatius and all his Society of Jesus had become, was, and is and stood for, found itself into the heart of one little Freshman boy. If my historical vignette is briefly included here, it's because it all made such an enormous impact on me then and thereafter. There was status, there was identity. There was belonging, community aspiration and the chance to let perspiration make it all come true for a little Polish kid from the other side of the tracks.

IX

My high school years passed quickly. I worked in the library, thumbed my way, studied much, hard and daily. I had little time for activities outside of work and school, but school had a brighter side with drama, football and other activities that took place outside of classroom activity.

I cannot recall any major events. Year in year out the routine varied little, the subject matter changed and my intellectual curiosity grew, my interests were piqued and my knowledge of both books and the world increased. With them also did my desire to follow in the path my mother had encouraged without fail: to become a priest. I was now certain that that meant in service as a member of the Society of Jesus. I decided I wanted to become a Jesuit.

It was my senior year, a year in my life when many things would change or be set in motion. I submitted the necessary application materials as prompted by one of the older priests whose task it was to identify potential candidates. I had no other plans for myself. I assumed it was a given that I would be going to Milford and the Novitiate. There was no Plan B.

At home, things were as they always had been: mother busy, sisters Helen and Therese and brother Joe working; brother Leo now the father of two, and sister Rose had given birth to Jerry. I was home very little, and if or when, then my schedule and dad's continued to conflict in such a way, that we spent little if any time together.

He would leave for work as I was arriving at home. He would be asleep when I left for school. I knew he'd come home when I smelled mom's cooking. Dad would eat a full dinner after a long night's work in the auto-body foundry: pork chops and Sauerkraut, potatoes, bread, lots of beer and a few shots vodka. Exhausted and full, he'd be in bed before I got downstairs. It had been like this all through my high school years, except for Sundays when we went to church with the family dinner afterwards. We saw little of each other. It was the same this spring of 1936.

Everyone was proud of me when I became the first member of the family to have a high school diploma. All the family attended my graduation. We celebrated and I enjoyed both my achievement and recognition. I hadn't heard from the Society, but I was confident that I would be accepted. It was a good time, an optimistic time, and a carefree time.

I spent time with some of the young people in the neighborhood, with my family, and did the things young people did in those days during the summer school holiday. I do recall one time walking a girl home after seeing a movie. My arm slid around her waist, and slowly moved up her side brushing against the side of her breast. But before I reached far enough to be certain of touching, I withdrew hand and arm and remember feeling both awed and guilty at the same time. This would become the sum total of any experience I had with the opposite sex, at age 17, for the next thirty plus years.

This summer, Dad took some time off, and we painted the house together. The warm long summer days were an ideal time to take care of all this. It gave dad and me some great time together, something we'd never had before. Dad always worked hard: whatever it was, on the job or now painting. His motto, "when a job is once begun, never leave it till its done, be it large or be it small do it well or not at all," drones in my ears even yet, some seventy years later.

Once painting was done for the day, dad would ask me to come and sit with him for a while. We talked as I watched him consume a bottle of vodka, and, once done, stagger off to bed to sleep. He wasn't a loud or violent drunk, he was a quiet man with his quiet bottle, hard working, hard drinking. Theresa learned it from him. Much later, I discovered that so had I.

It was only a couple of weeks after the house painting was done and dad had returned to his regular work week when Detroit was gripped by an extremely wicked heat wave. While the city sweltered along with its residents, the men in factories were particularly miserable. No one spoke of risk or the need for drinking water. The foundry ovens spewed their flames, their heat-breath flooded the air with no relief, escape or end.

John Gutowski collapsed of a heat stroke in the midst of the heat wave. He was rushed to the hospital, never regained consciousness, and was dead the next day. Dad was 56. It was July, 1936.

The family gathered for the Polish funeral that was to follow. The same Jesuit from UoD High School who had encouraged my application to the Society came to the wake. He announced to all gathered in grief that the Society had agreed to accept me as a candidate for the Novitiate to begin at Milford in August. I was to start preparations immediately.

Now this many years later, I realize how tactless he was in the hour of my family's debilitating grief. Incredibly insensitive and tactless.

While my mother, sisters and brothers, were still in shock at the loss of our father, I turned my thoughts to what was ahead: my life's work. I was to now embark on it in earnest. So focused

43

was I, that I did not notice the looks of shock and disbelief on my siblings who felt I was mom's strength and support and should not leave her at this delicate time. I learned this much later. Had someone confronted me, things might have been different. At the time, I was oblivious to all about me and my mind was already miles away.

My trunk with specified clothing, and what ever else I was to bring along, stood ready. Each article had been carefully marked with my name on labels that were hand sewn into an inconspicuous place. The list had been specific about what was expected, there was no deviation from the required, contraband was forbidden. I deviated for the first time: amidst my things was a crystal set from brother, Leo. I would spend many illicit hours under my bed listening to the forbidden outside world in the months to come.

And so, one beautiful August day, I kissed mom good bye and went off to become a Novice, to Milford, and to life in the Society. Little Frankie became Francis. Since I had chosen Aloysius for my confirmation name, I now used it as a middle initial as no middle name was on my birth certificate. I officially entered the Society on September 1, 1936.

At Milford, and henceforth and forever, I would be Francis A. Gutowski, SJ. It sounded really good to me. My hopes and dreams would now become realities.

FORMED AND MOLDED

I

Milford was (is) in southern Ohio, on the outskirts of Cincinnati. I am not sure why that particular location was chosen for a Jesuit novitiate, but I learned later that it fit the general concept of both location and institution of what then was considered to be the ideal primary indoctrination point. Certainly it did provide both the isolation from the modern world plus the access to a university faculty to provide us with the instruction necessary for our formation. That may have been the rationale for locating there. Or, maybe it was a donation of land for Jesuit use. After all, while we were to be kept away from secular corruptive influences, our guardians were certainly not desirous of separating themselves from the customary life style they'd acquired. It was also shortly after the Great Depression: Jesuits no less than the rest of the country had learned to cut back, to curtail, to do without and sacrifice accustomed niceties when their income sources became depleted. In some cases those houses better off assisted those in dire straights while weathering the storms of nation wide hardship.

The terrain surrounding Cincinnati is one of rolling hills through which the Ohio River forges its way westward toward the

Mississippi. Milford lies amidst these hills: in fact, the Novitiate was situated on top of a hill, a relatively recent addition to a hardy landscape that blended nature with function.

Erected in 1925 to accommodate the overflow and increase of budding Jesuits, it was a formidable structure amidst a rugged terrain. There was nothing bucolic or pastoral about either the grounds or the building. They represented the Jesuit spirit of actively doing with fierce determination. While nature surrounding house and grounds had been largely tamed by 1936, this was but a physical manifestation of how our own spirits were here to be equally "broken in," or "tamed," and would then be harnessed –"formed"- in service to execute the work of Christ. Hence came its title, House of Formation. Here we were to be formed into soldiers of Christ for the Pope's Army according to Ignatius' military model.

The buildings had been specifically designed and built to be a Jesuit Novitiate. The grounds were secluded enough to sequester the aspirants sufficiently from all things worldly and mundane, but yet were sufficiently accessible to allow any one of us to take a bus for dental, medical, or other necessary appointments for the 20+ odd miles to town. We had ball fields and tennis courts available to exercise on grounds lovingly kept by a number of Jesuit Brothers, who also attended to the keeping of the buildings and the kitchen where our meals were prepared.

II

In August, 1936, a group of thirty eight young men arrived on two separate arrival dates to begin their induction into a new life. They were about to be educated for service, prepared for religious life and trained for the rigors of the Society of Jesus. Eventually they would become commissioned in service to the Holy See, soldiers in the Pope's Army. "Camp" Milford was Basic Training 101.

Much material exists on Jesuit training and education. For my writing here suffice it to say that we Jesuits are trained, educated, and prepared with infinitesimal care to detail to and for both worlds: that of the spirit and the one in which we are currently planted. We furthermore learned early on that it is not our will but God's will in the person of our immediate superiors that rules. Our years to be finely honed into the corps best able to serve Christ, Church and Pope would be long and arduous. When we are at long last done with studies and finally ordained, we get yet another dose of spiritual inoculation to boost our immunity to worldly corruption before we are released into its midst to perform our future functions.

I am writing to recollect my own experiences, my own feelings and reactions and not a description or critique of Jesuit formation or education. To me, what I experienced simply is or was. I am not about to judge long post facto that which I now at 82 think might have been a better way to live as a 17 year old. Or, how I would have adjusted, changed, rethought and formulated some aspects of the 19 years I spent as a student. It is always amazing to me what clarity of vision the dullest lenses of old age provide when judging the fog-shrouded specters of our pasts. I don't want to look through their haze: instead, I look at old snapshots focused clearly in my memory bank.

There is no question that, when I look at 17 year olds today, I question the sanity of a society willing to accept these kids so naïve as we were, and yet so worldly wise as we were not, back then. What kind of men would we have been had we lived life and then entered? Some have, but I don't know them well enough or just never asked. Would we have entered had we lived Life? Some surely would have and have. And in my group, would we not have been cannon fodder instead of living life even to the degree we lived it? There are some who served country first and when safely returned, came to serve God second.

None of that really matters now, that was then and this is now. If we are decent human beings, which we most certainly were and are, we do the best we can with what we have or know at the time. The Jesuits did for themselves and theirs: as best as they knew how and sincerely believed.

III

Here I was. I found myself feeling frightened, eager, apprehensive and proud. I was among the chosen. This was my ticket away from intellectual poverty, ethnic identity, Polish perspective, manner, language, and food. What I had begun as my single-minded sole purpose while in fourth grade when I refused to continue bi-lingual studies, I now carried further. I was on my way going MY way!

My fears were overwhelmed by my determination. Often, in the weeks, months and years to follow, when my body and mind ached from discipline and demand, that determination is what kept me going, doing, achieving. And in those moments when my will weakened, my pride took over as my brother Joe's words echoed in my mind: "You'll be back, you won't make it!" By damn, yes I would.

Although I was never in the military, there is a certain similarity between boot camp and the start of Jesuit training. Ignatius' soldierly life is reflected in our beginnings. We are first of all completely disoriented in order to then become re-oriented with desirable input.

We spent the first few weeks settling into our quarters, and getting used to bells ringing for every thought and action from morning till night. We made bodily readjustments to hours of prayer, kneeling, meditating, and contemplating.

Our own little quarters were alcoves partitioned with ply wood and curtained to separate us from the next person. Our lives were mostly communal. Our camaraderie was melded in likeness not forged of differences. All of us were kids who entered a life like kids today go to summer camp. We were new, fresh, scared, young, eager and apprehensive. First of all, we were kids.

We learned we were not to smoke our cigarettes nor retain any money in our possession, as we learned to denounce property. Cleverly, according to good catholic rationalization, we did not smoke our own cigarettes, we smoked those of the next fellow who

48

then smoked ours, neither of us smoking those we had ourselves. The same applied to money: we could not use any, but who said we could not use that of our neighbor freely exchanged?

It didn't take us long to discover that we became aware of residents in our tower. Ah, bats in the belfry. And what kind of mischief might a bunch of teenage boys devise with this knowledge? The game of bat-minton! We took our tennis rackets and batted bats. The poor creatures we knew to avoid any object were no match for the air rushing through the webbing on its way toward their fragile bodies. We weren't mean spirited or nasty. We were young kids needing some outlets for being young. Our consciences had not yet been formed to discern that what was appropriate joy for us was in conflict with life sustaining importance for bats. That came much later. For now, fun is what mattered!

The gleeful days were short lived. We quickly began the first of two thirty day retreats. The second would complete our years of Jesuit training many years hence: this first experience of Ignatius' Exercises was very much like six weeks of basic: total disorientation and reorientation. Who we were gave way to the spirit in us, the burning love for Christ, devotion to His mother, and the dedication to our order.

Anyone who has ever made an Ignatian retreat, whether in its full thirty day or reduced time, knows that there is a specific sequence: creation and ourselves in it, the duality of good and bad ending in stringent self-examinations, contrition and amends, the life of Christ from baptism to works to passion and death to resurrection until, sending the Holy Spirit to strengthen, we are ready to see the world anew fired with love of Christ and eager to do His will: What have I done for Christ? What am I doing for Christ? What will I do for Christ? The answers are the journey that lies ahead; the path, however has been forged.

Our studies now began in earnest. We were college level students. Our professors were formally attached to Xavier University in Cincinnati, and as such our course of studies was accredited and approved with that University's setting though we never set foot into its classrooms. No wonder: most of our readings were religiously influenced, our studies overshadowed by what we were being formed into rather than who we might become.

We lived by the bell. Literally: bells told us when to rise, when to pray, when to eat, where to be and what to do with whom, how. "Why" did not exist. We never asked why, the life discouraged asking why of both ourselves and others. (Many years later, I would say: "first do as I say, then and only then you can ask "why?"").

The rhythm of daily life was a constant: periods of silence, periods of prayer. We both meditated and contemplated. We studied and read. We ate, slept and recreated. Bells sounded for each period. The days themselves followed one upon the other, their differences the particular day's saintly life commemorated, then Sunday with more time for recreation and less for class.

We saw no newspapers. There was yet not television and had there been, we would have had none of it. When I finished the first two years, Austria had been, in March 1938, annexed as part of Germany. I knew it then because there, quietly under my bed, I heard what the world far far away shuddered to hear, as close to me as the precious crystal set Leo had given me. I did it my way, once again.

My own militaristic experience was to follow in the footsteps of Ignatius, to be a rugged individual molded in the form of an Ignatian soldier-scholar, ready to take up arms for Christ, ready to sacrifice life and limb for Him in the name of the Society, masculine, combative, and competitive.

Years later, an article about me referred to my combative Jimmy Cagney-esque manner: it can be traced to those first two years of Novitiate when every fiber in me was pulled and stretched to a new shape or form in conformity to be part of the fabric that was the cloth from which a Jesuit was cut. Years later, I wondered if back then it was more like the dough from which we were stamped like "Spritz" cookies: all for one, one for all, more alike than two peas in a pod. We'd been kneaded into a firm mass placed on an assembly line extruding identical shapes that remained malleable and resilient enough for continued and additional imprinting and shaping. When we weren't studying, we engaged in sports. I loved football. Later, I was to coach it. Much later, the injuries I had sustained turned into arthritis. Then, they destroyed my athletic aspirations amidst excruciating pain. Not now: now I lived totally unaware what I would learn later to be or become a psycho-social principle. We were trained to become a part of a group, an elite group. There was no space for individuals.

Our bell-regulated life was without outside interference dedicated to common purpose within a uniform framework. The latter extended to our quieted and cassock-cloaked apparition. It made the novitiate a powerful re-enforcer of life-style goals and ideals. In single file, we were black lines swooshing silently toward the chapel doors, refectory, or classroom. As a group, we were young, eager, subdued and serious. The individual did his share within the collective. The whole provided the support from which emanated the motivation of the individual, and on and on.

It cannot be said enough nor emphasized sufficiently: formation really meant FORMATION. We were being formed. Not by studies or thought or consciously participating decisions, but rather by routine, ritual and repetition. Our formal studies were not as enlightening as the warm glow of community and belonging that imbued us with the feeling of Jesuit strength. Who we were individually had become incidental. Who we had become mattered to us in the moment: now. It mattered for the future. We were Jesuits.

We had been trained and accustomed to living in obedience. We responded like Pavlov's dog's salivary glands: the cadences of our daily lives and the pealing of the bell-reminders set off instant and automatic responses to what was known to be expected at that particular moment without question and without fail. Most of us had survived this first phase; a few had left: one as early as when our retreat got under way in the first month. He was but 16, the only person younger than myself.

Once we completed the first two years, we no longer were colts in need of breaking in. We had become as yearlings ready to be put through the paces that were the next phase of our training. We would now pursue college work in earnest as we left Novitiate for Juniorate.

IV

Externally, few things changed as we progressed. We continued at Milford, simply leaving one part of the building for another. Just as the Juniors did not associate with us earlier, so we did not associate with the next batch of Novices. We knew and felt that we had cleared a huge number of hurdles to get to Juniorate, and indeed we had.

Actually, little changed other than that we were no longer the recruits awaiting induction. We could look down upon (we were on the upper levels, separated within the building) the newcomers quaking in wake of their future knowing full well how we had felt just 24 months earlier. Now we had a great sense of being superior, older, wiser, and that certain air one gets from the experience of having been there and done that. We were now full-fledged recruits, cadets, if you will; candidates yet in our quest of being fully commissioned in service.

Our transformation thus far had been basically internal: submission of will, aflame with love for Christ, bursting with desire to serve, instant automatic response to the beck and call of what is basic to Jesuit life: Unquestioned prompt obedience always. [Ironically, it was that firmly inculcated sense of obedience that would eventually turn to bite me].

Milford, however, continued to be Milford. Its location was little affected by an economy recovering from the Depression, a Holocaust gaining momentum, a war about to plunge the world into a decade of chaos, or anything else that was going on anywhere. If Milford the town wasn't worldly wise, Milford the Jesuit Formation House was even less so. 1938 was a good, quiet, positive and nice year for a young man who had just made it through step one, and was ready to start step two with three not far behind. (At the same time, Austria had welcomed Hitler and the Wehrmacht would soon goose step into Poland as I learned from my crystal set).

College had now begun in earnest: the years when both undergraduate and graduate work would lead to extensive studies of the humanities and classics, the kind of well rounded education for which the Jesuits were (are) famous in their colleges and universities. We were on our way to become well grounded in diversified fields, solidly based in both orthodoxy and antiquity. Aristotle and Augustine; Aquinas and Ambrose. Math, science, and literature; Language and Philosophy.

Languages consisted of sufficient Latin to the degree that it became the language of instruction in the years of both Philosophy and Theology. Ancient Greek, of course, was its close second. And then there were the modern languages: French and German were added to prepare for future study paths to be decided at a later date.

We were consciously aware that our proscribed path now went from forming to learning, from training to educating. For us it was obediently doing as we were told, performing as best we could, and the fact that this period of our formation shifted from being drilled in blind obedience to academic learning went unnoticed as to actual differences. Yet differences did exist: the military drill and command of religious content remained but gave way to include preparation for a competitive and argumentative society. Debate was encouraged. Assertiveness was cultivated in Latin language exercises. We attempted to substantiate the number of angels dancing on the head of a pin or the validity of Socratic discourse and Platonic platitudes. It was important to be knowledgeable and articulate.

Eventually, we would be cast into a world in which the Devil was on constant attack, and we had to be vigilantly prepared

53

to out-talk, out-reason, out-wit, and disarm him at every turn with a well prepared arsenal of knowledge, language, discernment, spirituality, faith and fervor. Much like in rabbinical circles, we were honed to razor sharpness in our verbal acuity and ability to defend, attack and smite the enemy of our belief. Our tongues had to become sword-edged and razor-sharp as did the pens in our hands producing our writings. During our various academic courses and later in philosophy, the scheduled staged syllogisms were to be the proving ground.

Ad Majorem Dei Gloriam! For the greater glory of God we were in the fight against evil till the death, but better yet, we were prepared to vanquish it in Christ's name. Ours would be to banish heresy and sin, to spread God's word and extend His embracing arms to wider influence and greater numbers.

We had plenty of models to emulate: primary among them was Francis Xavier. Work in China, Japan, among American Indians and elsewhere left martyrs in its wake. Martyrs were not something from an ancient time: Jesuits kept a fresh supply for each generation. Mine too had its own and wrongly accused: Theilhard's life was condemned from within and without the Society as his heart suffered rejection—hopefully, he sees his present acceptance from his seat above; Pedro Arrupe was faced with difficulties that will surely gain him the crown of sainthood when Pope John Paul II is no more (sorry to say, his replacement, the former Grand Inquisitor, appears to lack compassion and humanity to an even greater degree). The slain in El Salvador pray to heaven for us as we recall their blood flowing while TV cameras rolled..... Whether we would see greatness, holiness, martyrdom or a routine assignment, the same mold formed each of us.

Now, however, it was 1940, and that meant the end of Juniorate, the transition to Philosophy, and the move to West Baden, Indiana where Philosophy and Theology were housed.

Along with our material belongings and acquired books and sundries, we took the means of physical penitence. I have yet to see in any one of the myriad books on the Jesuit life, history,

54

training, or being that I have read or know any mention of our torture instruments that had been part of what was expected of us during and forever after our Milford experience. I STILL have mine today, stored in a drawer.

For the non-initiated, just like Army recruits get their duffle bags with uniforms, and so on, we were given a "cat-o'nine tails" with which to whip ourselves regularly in order to banish impure thoughts (read sex), identified faults and shortcomings.

This instrument is made of rope material, braided, with five, not nine, braided ends, the whole thing is about 30" long. We were expected to whip ourselves intermittently or regularly, I don't recall. I do recall, however, hearing my fellow recruits in other alcoves in our dormitory whipping themselves just as I am sure they were aware of my own self-flagellation. But this is not all.

Secondly, we received metal torture belts. Again, I have mine yet stored in a cigar box together with the whip. These were made of something like chicken coop wire. Now, years later, I wonder about the hygiene of such a material whose purpose was to draw blood along the entire waistline of its wearer thanks to the pointy, cut off wire protrusions on its interior which were fashioned to penetrate the skin of the wearer, inflicting sufficient pain to drive out any thoughts of physical pleasure or well being. We wore those too. The Jesuit brothers charged with the care of our earthly needs must have really worked hard to get all the blood out of our clothing when they did our laundry.

I cannot speak for my classmates, but I do know that except for a one time accidental erection while lying on my stomach on a towel sunbathing nude on the roof, I beat any sexual thought or feeling out of myself; either that or they bled out of me. Is it any wonder that at age 52, I could not attain or sustain an erection nor ejaculate? But I am getting ahead of myself.

V

Next came Philosophy for which we would move to West Baden. West Baden and French Lick were in lovely Indiana territory. A huge hotel complex, the Jesuits were able to purchase it in the early 1930's, a benefit of the Depression when it could no longer operate as the resort it had been. (It is my understanding that it currently is again a resort. The Jesuits left it long ago.)

The building, amidst a park like setting and every conceivable amenity known to man at that time, was round. A dome covered the courtyard so that we could walk along the balconies regardless of weather. Again, there was segregation: the lower floors were the Philosophers, the upper levels housed the Theologians.

Our classes were intense. We were totally immersed in philosophical thought, in its teaching, logic, dialogue and repartee. We did so in Latin. Often we continued to carry out our dialogue in English outside of the class room as we became intensely involved in the subject matter. One might say we easily became even hot headed!

There was little free time, bells continued to run our lives, and recreation periods were also busy. I think this is the time and place when I first started to play golf, I certainly had not done so prior to West Baden and recall how I enjoyed the game somewhat later during Regency.

We were also encouraged to read enormous amounts of material on different subjects. After all, the three years would serve to prepare us to go out and teach in high schools run by the Society in various cities.

We were not much older than many of the students we anticipated instructing, and we knew that our attire would be a great help in garnering the respect a Jesuit was de facto accorded.

There are three things that happened to me while I was in Philosophy-- though not necessarily in the following order:

My beloved mother passed away. I am uncertain what the cause of death was but I do know she was severely diabetic. Her diabetes was the reason I never used sugar or ate sweets outside of an occasional piece of chocolate or some ice cream because at a young age I had become convinced that diabetes was hereditary. Obviously I did not want to catch it. I do not recall the exact day or

56

month, but I do recall being told to hasten to her bedside at once with the train tickets I was given. I got to Detroit just in time to say good bye. The entire family was assembled. I am not sure if Joe had leave since the war was at its zenith. I do know that Rose's Jerry had two sisters whom I had not seen, and that Johnny, the youngest, was either born or in the oven. I think John was born in 1943.

I don't remember interacting with my family though I was with them. I do not recall if I was permitted to stay long enough to attend her funeral. I found peace knowing mother knew me safe in the bosom of the Society. Her life time hope for me, that I would be a priest, was in the process of becoming. The pleasure of seeing me ordained was denied her here on earth. And so was the pleasure I would have had to honor her with my first Mass.

Secondly, Tom Hopkins, a fellow recruit, decided to leave and return to the secular life. I do not recall exactly when Tom left, but I do know it was not long thereafter that he met Cathy who became is beloved life long companion. Our friendship continued through the years, but more on that later.

The third thing that happened would have a huge impact on me long term. I have already said that membership in the Society appealed to me because of the status that it would implicitly and explicitly afford me, the satisfaction it would give me regarding the cultural and social advantages I had seen Jesuits partake of and wanted for myself, and the life long security that the Society provided its members regardless of the world's economy.

Now I developed severe, incredibly intense and incapacitating headaches. No medical explanation was found in spite of the solicitous care my superiors availed me. Nothing helped. Serious consideration was given to my leaving the Society. Finally, I either asked for or it was suggested to me that I try to smoke. You may recall smoking was anathema in both Novitiate and Juniorate. Now it became my salvation. The headaches did not cease, but they became tolerable. I fell behind in my studies, but not to the point of not being able to catch up. I was also given a goodly amount of leniency in performance reviews.

This had a significant down side of life long consequence. It had been my firm intention to make the 4th vow, the special Jesuit vow of allegiance to the Pope. I knew that the Society had its own hierarchy, and that at least in the US, the Irish, German, and to some degree Italian members considered themselves the "double crème de la crème" within an organization priding itself in being the cream of the crop.

This little Polish guy from the other side of the tracks aspired to make that 4th vow against all visible odds…..and now saw his chances dwindling to zero. This depressed me considerably but I was not ready to throw in the towel. Instead, I gathered a second wind and prepared for what was to come next. Eventually, after considerable time, the headaches disappeared as mysteriously as they had arrived and I began the next phase of becoming astutely trained: Regency.

VI

I had been assigned to Loyola High School in Chicago. Regency consisted of yet another three year period. The 1943 fall semester found me ensconced at the Jesuit residence eager to face my first class from the other side of the room.

I would spend three years in Chicago where my assignment was to teach math and science, subjects for which I had both affinity and ability. Additionally, I coached football.

My classes went well. The kids responded favorably. I don't know if it was the inculcated awe and respect for a cassock-clad teacher, or if they genuinely liked me and my teaching style. Or, was I merely so eager as to see everything in its best light? At any rate, my reviews of classroom activities were consistently favorable. The coaching appeared to have gone well although I do not recall whom we played and whether we won or lost. For a long time, I had class photographs of each group that was entrusted to my coaching care and career. I cannot seem to locate them any more.

In no small measure, Loyola High School and my years in Chicago were to become life changing experiences for me. I was given the first taste of what it meant to be a Jesuit, how Jesuits were accorded a status that was unique and special, how Jesuits were perceived by all others, and many day to day experiences, all of them positive.

Wearing my cassock and biretta afforded me automatic and instantaneous deference in something as simple as walking across the street. Regardless of my youth, I was perceived as part of an elite group. The aura of Society membership imbued me with an importance I had never experienced before. The parents of my students looked up to me and respected my care of their sons without challenge or concern.

We were kept as busy as ever. Our prayer life and spiritual growth was as important as it had been earlier. Added to this were our work obligations whether in the class room or the athletic field. We had classes to plan and papers to correct. As part of the Society, our life was also being among our peers, or better said, those who had attained that to which we were aspiring: priesthood. Even our limited free time found itself regulated and organized.

Here also began something I had neither knowledge of or experience with until now: the social life of a Jesuit away from home, or outside of the immediate Jesuit domicile.

In my years as a student at UoD High, I lived as far from the school geographically as socially. My parents were honest, decent and hard working blue collar folk. Many Jesuit Fathers would frequent the homes of students living close to campus, and when invited to soirees of various kinds such as cocktails, dinners, or other parties.

We had had none of that at our home, nor was there ever a thought given to inviting any of my teachers, Jesuit or not. Now, however, as a Jesuit and the teacher of young Johnny, I found myself asked to dine at his parents' home. Not, however, quite so fast! I found myself invited as the result of an invitation extended to one of the Fathers who asked me to accompany him.

There were many such occasions over the period of my Regency in Chicago. I owe a special thanks to Father Finnegan for taking me along on so many varied occasions and to events that provided exposure, education, and gave much needed polish to the little Polish Scholastic. Willy Finnegan would take me under his wing during those early days of my new life. Moreover, over the years, he became my mentor, guide, and a friend on whom I could rely and to whom I could turn for the rest of his earthly life and beyond.

I owe Willy Finnegan a lot. Not only did he assist in making me a better and more astute Jesuit, his guidance and example made me a better human being. It was from him that I learned empathy and compassion, human understanding and tolerance, resilience and strength. He instilled in me the desire to become the best that I could be as a Jesuit, a man, a human being, and forever more, a Child of God basking in the Father's love.

It was Willy Finnegan's example, influence, and teaching which instilled me with self-confidence as I affirmed my own decisions and actions many years later. The ethics, values and morals which the Society promoted in us scholastics had special meaning, importance, and fortitude as interpreted and lived by the Reverend William Finnegan, S.J.

During these years in Chicago I met and made friends with whom I would continue to maintain contact through the years. One particular group with whom I spent more and more time was the Sofi family. I seem to recall that they either owned or had something to do with a golf course. I remember not only enjoying their hospitality in their lovely home, associating with the many family members, but improving both my golf game and card playing skills thanks to them. Many years later, we were still corresponding.

There were others I also befriended and whose friendship I retained over time, but my recollections begin to blur between the time I was there for my Regency, and subsequent periods of returning to Chicago in various capacities and how or where I met my then and future friends in the windy city.

My time in Chicago was not limited to being a Scholastic: some years later, I spent several summers as a chaplain at Cook

County General Hospital as well as in other functions carried out locally by Jesuits.

What I recall most about those times as Chaplain was observing a major lung operation and afterward commenting to the surgeon how grey, dirty and diseased the organ appeared. He replied: "that's not from smoking, that's how the lungs of anyone living in a major city look."

The second thing I recall about Chicago time, albeit also from Cook County General, was a sweet little old Irish woman who was approaching the time when she would meet her Maker. Speaking in the most delightful "braugh" you'd ever heard, she asked me for my name. When I told her, her gentle face contorted itself and she said, "what an awful name, what a terrible awful name. I can't even pronounce it." Without missing a beat, I retorted, "my dear lass, 'twas really O'Gutowski but we shortened it" whereupon the twinkle returned to her smiling eyes and she said: "O'Gutowski, what a lovely name, 'tis a beautiful name indeed!" I left her smiling and never saw her again. But I remember her still after all these many years.

VII

Before long, it was time to return to West Baden and the final push: Theology. We would now be on the top floors of our very own Grand Hotel, firm in our knowledge that in but a few short years we would be out in the world spreading God's truth.

For now, we were engaged in the most challenging of all our study years. We dissected scriptures, we read the works of the Doctors of the Church, we saw how Aquinas' roots reached back all the way to Augustine, and where the latter finally found his voice and strength. We learned that man does not live by faith alone, nor is Grace the only doorway to eternal life. We questioned and answered age long debates and dialogues transcending the recorded history of mankind. We learned to theologically prove God's existence and then question whether faith is or isn't ultimately a gift from God that is needed to attain salvation. We learned of the very unique and special way Jesuits had incorporated the traditions and practices of indigenous peoples into orthodox and acceptable Christian practice. The dryness of the subject matter came alive in our midst as eager minds expanded. But it wasn't all dry, and it wasn't all that lofty. We also came down to earth.

It was in the course I remember most vividly: Moral Theology. In common parlance, it was our formal sex education course, the one course which would address human anatomy, lust, desire, and morality. What was sanctioned, when it was a blessed activity, and when it was illicit. What we could or most likely would expect to encounter in the sanctity of the confessional. We, soon to become ordained life long celibates, and already avowed to chastity, now learned what those less fortunate than ourselves (for we KNEW or at least had been told that we had chosen the holier path, the moral high road), faced in their daily lives.

To accomplish this enormous task, we were presented with two anatomically correct models of both male and female. We fondly referred to them as John Upjohn and Vagina Ever-Ready. You can take it from there. Ordination came next.

VIII

June 1949. We would be ordained on the 14th of this month. We were allowed to invite our families who had not visited us thus far. Each candidate for ordination was given a specific number of invitations to both church and subsequent celebrations that began with a formal dinner.

Like everyone else, I invited my brothers and sisters and their families. Neither of my parents would have the joy of witnessing the event, and in their place I asked Willi Finnegan to join us. To my delight, he agreed to come.

Ordinations are all the same. When you're one of the candidates being ordained, the whole affair takes on its own unique meaning. To the spectators attending the ceremony, one is as good as any other. In my case, all went well and as expected in church. The celebration afterward would not be so.

An enormous brouhaha arose among my relatives. Sister Helen and sister-in-law Helen had some dispute regarding who was sitting where how close to me or anyone else. Rose and Therese got involved as well, Leo disengaged in favor of his wife. I do not recall Joe's presence although I believe he'd returned from military service by 1949. Willy Finnegan made the best of an uncomfortable situation, and thanks to him ruffled feathers were smoothed at least for the duration of dinner. The children who attended were seen but not heard. I don't recall how many nieces and nephews had come: Rose had four children by now, Leo had two, Joe had Ann's Jim.

The rift that began that day would only deepen over the years. As time went on, no one was exactly sure just what had happened when and how, but neither was anyone willing to make amends. It was never repaired in my life time and at this point in time everyone else involved has already been long dead. It was really too bad. The memories that linger could have been more joyful and I know mom and dad would have been hurt had they been alive.

I returned to Detroit for a short holiday, and said my first Mass at St. Thomas the Apostle Church near our former Helen Avenue home on June 19, 1949. It was the last time I would visit the old neighborhood for more than a drive through it. It had changed.

The euphoria of having been ordained was short lived because there was one more year of theology ahead of me. Additional course work followed. I had to take cram courses in German and French, especially the former, because it had been determined that I would continue my education in math and science, most specifically, Physics. The preparatory course work was taken at Boston College. Whatever additional theology and other work was deemed advisable was also taken care of during this time.

Finally, on August 15, 1952, the Jesuit portion of my education had finally reached conclusion with the taking of my final vows. It's completion at Bellarmine School of Theology ended with the awarding of an STL, a License in Sacred Theology. I don't know what this award was supposed to signify or of what practical use it would become other than a pre-ordained level of theological sophistication, knowledge and practice. Practice of theology in the practical sense of professional licensure like a licensed therapist or physician was highly improbable. I was now ready for the Catholic University in Washington, DC to earn my doctorate.

TO BECOME EXTRAORDINARY

It's another gorgeous May morning here on Fleeton Point. This is not where I live. I'm visiting my oldest dearest ex-wife friend. I myself live in Richmond, Virginia. These days I spend most of my energy on bridge games at the local senior center. I'm in my 89th year, still driving, aiming to reach at least 100 and my doctor sees no health issues looming on the horizon to contradict that intention: he has just had me operated for a nasty hernia!

I

As I reflect on this long length of time in which I've lived and worked, I especially think back on mid-life and the events that took place soon after I hit the half century mark. Back then, I was addressed as Dr. G., Father Ace, Ace, Father Gutowski, but never Frank. Only my family called me that, and Monika. I am still Frank, and I am still with Monika, albeit merely as an always welcome visitor and some time resident at this little point at the end of Virginia's Northern Neck that juts into the Chesapeake Bay all around. It's lovely here. I am a city kid. I'd go nuts....but I digress, oh, and everyone now calls me Frank.

Considering the mess the Catholic Church has gotten itself into with its various issues of denial or blindness concerning priestly activities that are definitely neither priestly nor morally acceptable, my story may be of interest. I did everything by the book. I did not deviate nor was I deviant. I tried to do the right thing. And at no single instance did I act without the full consent of my superiors, in obedience. At least as long as they were reasonably supportive of my choices until we conflicted over a very mundane and practical material matter: MONEY along with the use, disposition, and need of money. That was the bottom-line from which all else followed.

I was no Cardinal Law...nor like any of his minions. The Vatican conspiratorially approved of Law's criminal immorality by rewarding him with pontifical plums; the Jesuits sought vengeance for the innocent. The Pope and the Jesuits often went their own ways!

Now, when I reflect on the transitions and subsequent hardships I endured, I realize that behind all the espoused virtues, money remains the end all and be all of the Society as it does in much of society. I am reminded of the phrase, "do as I say not as I do" for the Society talks about poverty and sacrifice......as long as its own impenetrable coffers are stocked fully and securely what do they care about the hardship of others....whether they cause it or further it or allow it or promote it. I learned that what is sadly missing is true genuine goodness. Goodness for the sake of goodness alone. "As cold as Christian charity" is apt. Is what I was taught to believe nothing but a sham? The question would haunt me as time went on.

Doing the "right" thing in obedience created practical problems within the "real" world. These then subjected me to malicious indignation, surreptitious and clandestine blackmail and black-listing, propelled me into actions I would not have otherwise chosen to take, (although as Monika reminds me, I did superbly well for the duration), caused me to suffer incredible losses that have impacted life since then to this day, and exposed me first hand to the principles of social psychology regarding group behavior of which I was unaware. I thought I could be a David, but the Jesuit Goliath's force used might not right. Nevertheless, it did not win its position. It would be Constitutional principles which reigned.

My integrity is not only intact, it has triumphed over the many years after the fact. I have gained peace and contentment in my life even though I never recovered financially from vengefully imposed hardships. Moreover, my four acquired children, — and they are mine in form, and shape, and outlook, and name….give a satisfaction and joy no dollar amount can equal. The multiple frustrations, hurts, angers, and self righteous indignation in the face of such corrupt insinuations as were heaped upon me, all have washed away with the tide of life the way Fleeton Beach is washing away. What remains is that I now feel both ready and able to say, from a distant perspective and with less emotional trauma, of my experiences. Once upon a time. When I was 52.

II

In this my story, it is the church trying to thwart decency and honesty and create untenable situations which only the superiority of the human spirit, as conceived of and created by an all loving God, could sustain in spite of, not because of, Holy Mother. Or, maybe it isn't the Church "in toto", and only a special corps of its minions called Jesuits who pride themselves in not only being the Pope's army, but in all humility, think they're just one rather prominent step up above or higher than the average religious or the mere banal faithful. Jesuits are given and give themselves the status of the crème de la crème, the aristocrats of papal fealty, the rest or everyone else is but bourgeois proletariat. Once I was one of them. More importantly, in spite of them, I remain a decent, honorable man, a guileless Polish Urwisz. More power to me!

Surely the renowned sociologist and prolific writer, Father Andrew Greeley, would agree with my overall assessment and subsequent conclusions regarding the Jebs!

Forgive an old man, I am getting ahead of myself once again. It is little wonder that so traumatic a period would force memories and thoughts to insinuate themselves even yet.

At any rate, these many of my morning musings will now be immortalized on paper by my scribe. I jest not. I talk, she takes notes and writes. She talks, I listen: most of the time, she doesn't require an answer, just a sounding board; I am a great sounding board. Monika has been my friend for over forty years. For a brief period, she was my wife but of course that's getting ahead of the story once more. She has remained my friend and I hers. We're best friends. She once gave me a pillow that said, "Happiness is being married to your best friend".

Our most serious arguments were about semantics! Our bond remains as strong as any marital bond and stronger than many. These pages are taking shape upon her insistence and the encouragement of so many of our mutual friends. As long as she's willing, I'm ready. I hope I remain able. Let's go.

Thus far, I've covered over 35 years of my life from when I heard an English speaking kid call me, and introduced my family, background, education, and then some more education. Overall, I completed 19 years post high school education, and even added a 20th year while I was already teaching: I had yet to finish the calculations which would complete my doctoral dissertation at CUA when I was assigned to John Carroll for the 55-56 academic year. I would continue assigned work, leisure, recreational and spiritual activities for my lifetime-time, or so I believed. Summers were spent working as a hospital chaplain in places like Cook County in Chicago or replacing various priests at their parishes so they would have a chance to vacation.

I did not attend my graduation from Catholic U, but I had some time earlier been granted permission to fly to Washington for the oral defense of my dissertation. It was the first time that I experienced the speed of flying instead of the much slower car, bus or train rides I had taken thus far.

Years later, on a visit to Argonne Laboratories, using a computer, I redid the calculations over which I had labored manually and with a slide rule for month upon month of headache and frustration.....in a few (10!) minutes. That's what is called progress. Here's how my life progressed beyond the ordinary routine of academia. Fast forward.

III

It was around the fall of 1960. I had become adjusted to and integrated in the John Carroll University faculty as well as both the religious and local community since first arriving in 1955.

Father Lawrence Monville SJ was Chairman of the Physics Department at John Carroll University. His was a cadre of highly qualified physicists who both taught and conducted research in addition to their many external activities either as priests or family men. My work consisted mainly of teaching with little research responsibility. My free time was spent either on the golf course or engaged in frequent card games. I played bridge and poker both in house or at someone's home. As I already mentioned, I would at times substitute for a vacationing or ill priest or engage in other priestly works as needed.

Since I began my studies at Catholic U, and even more so after I arrived at John Carroll, I had fostered and maintained the friendships I had made over the years while a scholastic teaching in Chicago as well as when I served as Chaplain. The Sofis who had attended my ordination would invite me for various family affairs and celebrations over the years. I had also kept up with some of the nurses I had met, particularly one Flossie whose last name now escapes me (was it Kuscinski?). Flossie would keep in touch with me for many years and many changes in both our lives over time.

As I mentioned earlier, Thomas Hopkins had been a fellow novice but found the commitment to a celibate life more than he wanted to uphold. Tom's leaving did not end our relationship. By the time I was settled in Cleveland, I would drive to Detroit and spend most of my holidays and feasts or vacations with the Hopkins family. Tom had married Cathy and the two had first Maureen, Barbara, then little Cathy, and several more children over time ending with a son.

Holidays at Tom and Cathy's were grand. The company was great, the booze was plentiful, and the food was excellent. Cathy was enthralled by her husband's Jesuit friends and I was not the only one attending. I am not even sure if I was the only house-guest many of the times I visited there. Tom and Cathy had a refrigerator in their bedroom, and they and I and whatever other priests were around would pile unto their bed and watch TV, movies, make merry or play cards. It sounds so banal or immoral, but there was nothing untoward about our evenings other than our raucous laughter and probably a little too much liquid cheer. We had great times. I remember them most fondly. I also especially remember their daughter Barbara. She was a really great young lady who for a long time would keep in touch with me including during her time in graduate school in Atlanta where her grandmother lived, and where she intended to become a registered dietician. I also recall young Cathy spending some of her college time at Sofia, the Jesuit University in Japan.

Knowing Tom led to meeting the rest of his family. He had a married brother, Pete, in Chicago whom I met at some point while there but who sadly passed away quite young. Another brother had become a priest and was teaching in Pittsburgh, and yet another, younger brother, Joe, was in the process of becoming a Jesuit. There were also some sisters. Mary was a nurse, I believe, and Eileen married a Cleveland jurist who later sat on the bench. Of all, it was Tom's brother Bill with whom I became fast friends. Bill and Lois lived not far from John Carroll, and produced a flock of children, one after the other. The 10th one was named Robert Francis, the Francis for me.

It was also at the various Hopkins families where I was called Ace, or Father Ace. I believe that "ACE" was the nickname of a Detroit athlete, I don't remember if baseball or football, he was "Ace" Gutowski. It didn't take much to transfer that to me. And it stuck. To this day, Lois Hopkins calls me Ace, and her kids call me Father Ace. I like it. It is filled with memories of younger years amidst the multitudes of children and their great parents.

Later, much later, Bill and Lois truly became the most special people in my life. Earlier, I spent wonderful evenings and sometimes days with them. I would go to football games with a

70

group of Bill's friends when the Browns played, and on boat trips to the various wineries on the islands in Lake Erie whenever Bill arranged such a trip. I attended dinners and cocktail parties, card games and family affairs, weddings, baptisms, school plays and graduations. With 12 children, there was always something going on of which I became a part. Eventually, that included trips to West Point and the Army/Navy or Army/Notre Dame games when their oldest son was appointed to study there.

Bill Hopkins and his wife Lois never let me down. They never criticized me nor condemned me. Their all encompassing heartfelt warmth was not only reserved for me, but eventually extended to Monika and her children. Thinking back, I wonder if we would have made it had it not been for Lois. She was and continues to be an incredible force of non-stop goodness. When I think of what a Christian, a Catholic, is or should be, then it is to be like Lois Hopkins.

IV

I knew I was being groomed for the chairmanship of the department since this responsibility customarily fell to a Jesuit within the department, and our department had none other than myself at a time when Larry, born in 1897, was ready to retire. Later, we were able to acquire William Nichols, SJ, and Manuel Carreira SJ, but Bill eventually added being Superior of the Jesuit Community to his many duties, and Manny was never fully in residence, dividing his time and genius among several Jesuit universities both in the US and in his native Spain. More and more, over time, I slowly took over departmental affairs.

The world as we knew it was on the verge of turning itself upside down with cultural upheavals, political mayhem, and never before seen changes in our social fabric and America's image. Over all, this was the militarily driven quest for space, a race begun by Russia into which the US threw itself full throttle seeking not only military superiority in space, but with the expansion of NASA, peaceful endeavors as well.

When Giovanni Roncalli was elected to become Pope John XXIII, none of us knew what it would mean to allow fresh air to rush in through the windows he threw open. The laity now had masses in its native tongue devoid of unnecessary redundancy. Many things became simpler for the average person, rules inculcated for generations fell by the way side. There was a sudden realization that fish on Friday was to help the Italian fishermen and Mass on Sunday morning could not serve the many scheduled to work but who were free the night before, and so on and so forth. Less well known but of even greater significance was the impact of the new on the rules of the old as it pertained to vowed religious, whether diocesan or in community.

By the mid-sixties, the trickling of an exodus by members of religious communities and parochial priests re-examining and freshly assessing their state in life was gaining momentum. Not only the priests and nuns who left their communities and abandoned their vows were questioning. The rest of us, who had no crises of faith, would also experience attitudinal changes: the most important one of these appears to have been our new-found or reborn participation in the secular world by overtly expounding our commitments to service, partaking of external festivities and events, and as a result, the loosening of our stabilizing bonds within community.

For me personally, it meant there was less overt camaraderie at Rodman Hall, and while we upheld what had been drilled into us or abided by implicit and explicit expectations, we nevertheless were on our own. A blatant example of this was when one of our Jesuit confreres died in his room, and was not found until such time as the odor emanating from his cell overwhelmed the passers by. See how they love one another? More like out of sight out of mind, or, what you don't know won't hurt you. I myself stuck with Shakespeare's Hamlet: To Thine Own Self Be True. If nothing else, I was consistent.

The rumblings of the Vietnam situation had prompted me to become politically active for the first time in my life as I promoted Barry Goldwater's candidacy along with several of my department colleagues who, like myself, saw a quick hard hit to win preferable to a long drawn out bleeding ourselves to death. I went so far as to campaign for Mr. Goldwater from the pulpit at Gesu parish church across the street from Rodman Hall, our residence, which was administered by a group of Jesuits also. I found myself not only criticized but reprimanded for taking such a public stand at Sunday's sermon. I would never again be asked to substitute at Gesu. Time Magazine had printed one of our letters, and that too had been received amidst mixed reviews from our less hawkish associates and friends. And later, also others.

For me, this was my second confrontation between my beliefs and the reality of what is or prevailed. My first one had been barely ten years earlier in Washington, DC.

It had been a long night of working in the lab for us PhD candidates at Catholic U. Our joint research project included several young men from various walks of life and backgrounds. There was only one priest other than myself, and as was customary back then, we wore our Roman collars to and from the lab while traveling in public.

We were tired and hungry and decided, as a group, to frequent a local eatery before heading to our respective residences. As we sat down to order our meal, we were informed that one of our group had to leave. He was African American, unwelcome, unwanted, and not allowed to fraternize with us in the segregated capitol of the free world in 1953. We all got up and left amidst angry epitaphs of outrage. I decided that very evening to some day use my teaching ability to educate young blacks to help eliminate prejudice and racism, and with it the perception of inferiority, ignorance or white superiority. I had no idea how and when, if ever, I would be able to carry this decision out. For now, I thought suggesting a good start would be to support and subsidize interracial marriage.

VOWED OBEDIENCE

I

At John Carroll, things at the department were going well. Thanks to the impetus given the sciences with the launching of Russia's Sputnik a decade ago, physics had reached new and increased importance. Physicists were in great demand. Research was not only encouraged, it was promoted, fostered, funded and supported by foundations, government programs, the military, public and private enterprises as well as major industries all poised to rush headlong into the race for space.

Among our various research grants, our department had applied for and received grant monies from the different military branches who were interested in the supersonics, the ultrasonics, and the acoustics that would be so important to their technological strides in both war and peace and most of all, in the race for space. One of these grants had come to us from the Department of the Navy, most specifically, through the auspices of Assistant Secretary of the Navy, Dr. Robert Morse.

Bob Morse had been chairman of the physics department at Brown University before accepting his Presidential appointment. And, while there, was advisor and mentor to a young Iraqi student, Mohamed Salih Said, whose thesis had been completed in 1963 whereupon the university conferred the degree of Doctor of Philosophy in Physics on Said.

The research for Said's dissertation, which Morse had supervised and encouraged, had been in the field of ultrasonics to which our current project was geared. Specifically, Said's work was "The Ultrasonic Attenuation of Alkali Metals at Low Temperatures". He had grown, measured, sliced and tested sodium as well as other crystals. His work appears to have dovetailed that of Joseph Trivisonno's research in our department.

While I did not know any of the details or circumstances at the time, it was brought to the attention of our department that this young Iraqi PhD was searching for a position post haste, and that his former advisor felt his work and our research project were an ideally fortuitous marriage of talent and opportunity.

In other words, the young man was at the right place at the right time and, being actively promoted by the Assistant Secretary of the Navy whose contract we had just been awarded, virtually guaranteed him the position we needed to fill. One quick interview is all it took to assure ourselves that we had filled our slot, one quick contract offer for a post doc was all it took to retain Said's services. Said had a job and we had our man.

II

February is a dismal time in Cleveland. The skies are a never ending grey hanging higher or lower depending on the heaviness of the snows eager to descend in various tons of profusion along the snow belts' path that extends well along I-90, and blankets the New York State Throughway's path from beyond Buffalo and Rochester and on past Lake Erie's shores, into New England. Throughout, life goes on as people slip and slide and curse along ice, snow, and slush in Erie as well as Cleveland and Detroit.

That reminds me: snow and driving in it became interesting after I moved to Richmond. I'd grown up in Detroit well aware of the lake effect's furies that I then saw whipped into blizzards during my Chicago years. In Washington I had paid little attention to the weather stuck in my lab or at prayers. Now, here in Virginia, I was amazed at people's lack of ability to drive in a couple of inches of the white stuff. They appear to believe it can be outdistanced and outsmarted with an extra push on the gas pedal! Or, I find amazing the idea that schools close at the first sign of snow being released from a cloud no bigger than a powder puff. Way back dad had a car accident in winter, but it wasn't because of snow; it was because there was no stop sign where there should have been one.

O yes, I'm off on a tangent again.....forgive an old man!

It was on one of those raw days of damp, cold, windy lake weather that our newest department member, Dr. Mohamed Salih Said and family arrived in Cleveland. Early in the day, wife, mother-in-law and two babes in arms arrived and were hosted by one of the department's families, the Trivisonnos. Later in the day, the paterfamilias arrived complete with truck, furnishings, and a friend who had helped him drive. We, the department, one and all, gathered to unload the material possessions and assembled them as best we felt we knew how or could given weather, time of day, and most of all, the families' fatigue.

The job well done, we gathered to enjoy a repast prepared by Ann Trivisonno. Over wine, beer and pizza, we chatted amiably till all were ready to turn in for the night, a day well spent and much accomplished. There was only on negative note: Said's mother in law took it upon herself to launch into criticizing me and department members for a letter Time magazine had recently printed in which we suggested basically, either end the war in Vietnam quickly or get out now. As I said earlier, we were Goldwater's hawks hawking for Goldwater.....but also horrified over the reports that were given nightly on Johnson's handling of Vietnam. The evening ended quietly after Ann served coffee. In leaving, the same woman would not go till she commented how regrettable her son in law's new cohorts appeared to be. It was most ungracious for her hosts.

It was Ann's husband, Joe Trivisonno, who became the direct supervisor and co-researcher of our new staff member. All seemed to go well. We prided ourselves in a smoothly running department of congenial colleagues whose overall goal was to further our university mission in educating young men (women were allowed on campus only after 3PM in those days) in the finest manner consistent with Jesuit philosophy and belief which included catholic theology no matter your course of study.

As time went on, Joe would at times confide in me that all things did not go as he had hoped for. Young Said had a mind of his own and was wont to ignore direction or protocol. I would listen and advise patience. Although a priest, and as the only other Jesuit next to Father Monville in the department, I really had no authority or position to counsel otherwise at that point in time: I was not yet chairman even if I knew I would soon be in charge.

The university held regular parties at the start of each semester which included faculty, faculty wives or spouses, graduate assistants and staff. Our department echoed that conviviality on its own with regular gatherings at one or another faculty family's home intermittently throughout the academic year. Although I had met them during their initial move to Cleveland, it was then that I became acquainted with Said's family which initially consisted of his wife plus a toddler, Leila, and an even younger son, Robbie.

In time, I would see this family grow to include another daughter, Nadja, and a second son, Stephan, both of whom I was asked to baptize as their mother and the couple's marriage were within the teachings and laws of the Catholic Church. My contact with the family extended beyond our departmental gatherings to family gatherings, meeting their friends, and getting to know the little ones. I had similar relationships with several families both within and without the department.

Other than pleasant hours, I only recall that Said's wife was much younger than the other faculty wives in attendance, she looked more like one of our graduate students.

III

There were two distinct parts to my life: work and personal. My personal life included a lot of bridge and poker at the homes of several couples whom I had gotten to know quite intimately and well over the years since arriving in Cleveland some dozen or so years ago. Golf courses beckoned, and if the Jesuits had no memberships all of us were always welcome guests of any number of members: I liked golf, and played whenever the occasion to do so arose.

I found myself invited frequently to dinners, parties, and family events. Although I often went to Detroit for various holidays, I rarely spent them with my own family. Instead, I visited the home of my good friend Tom, former seminarian from my novitiate days, who married and had a brood of his own for me to share and enjoy along with his wife. Tom Hopkins and Cathy were my ongoing hosts. I felt as if I were family, and they certainly made me feel that way including me in every and all celebrations. Over time, I had also gotten to know Tom's brothers, one an eventual Jesuit, one lost too early in life, a priest in another religious order, and Bill. It was Bill and his wife Lois who not only became my friends early on, but whose kindness and love kept me going in days I could not yet fathom.

There were others too. I was a regular guest at the home of two couples which now, with hindsight, presented rather odd situations: in one home, the husband would leave and explicitly encourage me and his wife to spend some time necking, and cuddling…. I was so innocent and naïve, I complied without emotion or reactions to the suggestions without question.

At the time, I was still flagellating myself and girding my middle with wire prongs to stifle any carnal thoughts or desires. It made me more automaton and less a responsive human, and far from anything amorous. BUT WHAT THE HELL? I wonder now what were these men thinking of when they left their wives alone with me? That I would ……… ? I honestly still believe that we of the cloth, vowed and ordained, in the days before child molestation scandals and defrocked clergy, were looked upon more as gender neutral, or as eunuchs, asexual or sexless beings in black - not men of the flesh - and as such could be deployed to prep a spouse for further intimacy later on once we had gone home. But that's only a guess. I never asked, I stopped going to these homes, and no one ever told me. I did get to learn to kiss and neck and pet......with no reaction whatsoever on my part!

One couple whom I'd met during a rainy evening while trying to hail a cab became my friends and I was saddened when they eventually divorced. The lady would move to Florida and open a boutique in the Palm Beach area; over time I lost contact with the husband but it was my acquaintance with her which led me to visit Florida for what would become the first of many summers in which I would substitute for a parish priest during the latter's vacation, and enjoy my own change of scenery. Plus, I had a ready made dinner companion whenever I was in the Lake Worth area.

No, there was no relationship between her and me. We were mutually respectful friends who always maintained proper decorum and valued our friendship too much to even consider transgressing into something beyond or more intimate...at least I can say this for myself. Surely, it was a little bit of flirtatiousness, or do I think so with hindsight? At this point in time I am not even sure of that. She was nice, and a good friend. What I do know for sure is that I did not engage in matters either arousing or sexual. I was both vowed and firmly committed.

During one of those summers while I was the substitute priest, a woman sounding desperate called the rectory to say she was on her way to either commit suicide or to speak with the pastor. In and of itself, this is not unusual. Pastors are subject to the whims of hysterical women all too often. Some of us priests, even Jesuits, spend many hours soothing the female of the species. I braced myself for what lay ahead.

In this particular instance, this became the way in which I met someone who developed a decided crush on me which to the best of my knowledge was a first in my life. It also became an eye

80

opening, shocking event that deeply impacted my innocent quiet life at age 50.

I didn't know what to do. I had no intentions of being involved. I had no desire other than to be sweet, kind and good without hurting her feelings. She would not be put off. What a relief it would be when I was able to happily return to Cleveland, leaving her and her amorous advances on the Florida beaches. Almost.

Weeks later, she popped up in my life again: she called me at Carroll and invited me to her family in an upstate New York location----this in the fall of 1969. Stupidly, I went......I would regret going. It was very awkward, to say the least.

My acceptance of her invitation was totally misunderstood... and after a more than difficult night where I had been relegated to an extra bed in her son's room and suddenly found her under the sheets with me, I left the family home never to return there again. I think her family was as shocked by my arrival as I would be by her subsequent behavior. I was so naïve. I also learned something about myself that night: either for medical reasons or as a result of a life time of sublimation and denial, I was unable to have an erection under the most conducive of circumstances and (her) efforts. I also stopped replying to any of her subsequent efforts to contact me. I was thoroughly and severely shaken.

Memories of the summer of 1969 would not be a total loss. Because I had taught several courses at NASA's Lewis Research center, I had been invited to witness the moon launch that summer. It was an exciting, fascinating and unforgettable event. It would, however, be my last summer at Lake Worth and I would not see Florida again.

Instead, I intended to be free to teach a few weeks of summer school some of the summers while at John Carroll, when other faculty did not want to take a specific class after all. Usually they did, because it was extra income and with large families to support, summer teaching was a real benefit for many. It could mean a new refrigerator or car payment; I obviously had no such needs or wants, and therefore was not among them.

In trying to remember what I did when, I believe this is how I spent some of my time: First of all, I taught as suggested above; I do recall teaching as many as 21 hours of physics in a given semester, that each semester I taught I would teach a new (to me) course, and that the department was offering over 48 hrs. for physics majors…in time I taught each one of those courses at least once.

I spent several summers partially at Argonne Laboratories often in combination with time in Detroit where my sister Helen was battling cancer until her death in the early '60's. Helen asked that I both say her funeral Mass and give the eulogy which she herself had written. Following that, my notes indicate that starting with 1963 when I rented a car and drove to Boulder and back followed by the next summer at Estes Park…..I spent my summers in Florida until 1970 when Joe Schell SJ asked me to travel with him and try out every golf course between Cleveland and Boston, Maine and Florida, that we could find or would pass on our way back and forth. More on this in context on the following pages.

During these same years, my bridge and poker playing occasions had increased considerably. In addition to the sporadic and impromptu games at Rodman Hall with fellow Jesuits, I had become a regular bridge player at several homes in the University's vicinity. One of my fellow Jesuits frequently asked me to join one particular family: it turned out to be somewhat awkward. I learned the husband was jealous of my attention to his wife of which I was totally unaware and certainly innocently disinterested, while at the same time, his wife would accompany my Jesuit companion on various trips to places like New York City. I didn't ask, I wasn't told, and I didn't wonder… back then.

At some point in the mid sixties, Larry Monville wanted to retire and as a result, I became department chairman. It wasn't something I sought to be, it was something expected of me. With it came the administrative and personnel headaches such a position engenders.

My teaching load was reduced as was any active research participation on my part. I did, however, not lose contact with the people in my department who knew my door was always open to anything and everything of concern to them, whether personal, private, or department related. In spite of the bureaucratic matters I was now responsible for, I did not neglect outside interests. To the contrary, as chairman my relationships flourished.

IV

There were no major changes in our staff size or composition. We actively pursued and happily convinced a brilliant Spanish Jesuit physicist, Manuel Carreira SJ, to join our ranks. As competent as he was personable, we found him a most delightful addition to our ranks. A Fulbright scholar from India was less able to gain favorable response: Singal had an attitude problem that included anger and resentment toward the other department members based on nationality, religion, race and color. He separated himself, declined participation and refused inclusion yet verbally expounded his outrage against the very individuals who attempted to make him comfortable and accepted. We knew that his appointment was time limited, and hoped that this dark shadow would leave with the person who had brought it. We were wrong.

Singal made it his business to ingratiate himself with young Said. Said was no effervescent joiner or self promoting propagandist: quiet, unassuming, a loner, he did his work and our only concern had been that he found it unusually difficult to accept guidance, direction, correction and warranted criticism of his work. There were no major issues, we found no reason for any major action. Singal, however, visibly influenced Said negatively: the latter stopped attending department meetings because Singal, a Fulbright Scholar but not part of the faculty, was not included. He isolated himself at social gatherings much more than usual, or didn't attend at all, and it had been overheard that some negative accusations had been made toward department members for their prejudices and negative actions toward anyone not a snow white Christian as was the case with the Hindu Singal and Moslem Said. Moreover, this was something totally new; Said had blended right in before the arrival of Singal—no one had ever commented on Said's olive complexion or his religious beliefs.

The animosity Singal created became so extensive and far reaching, that Said's wife on occasion stopped by my office (she attended courses after 3PM, tuition free for faculty wives, to finish the degree she had begun in her pre-baby days), to tearfully discuss that a change had come over her husband, that he just wasn't the same, and that he appeared to absorb Singal's negativity. Other than to reassure her that this was a time limited matter whose effects would hopefully reverse in short order after Singal's departure, I knew not what to say.

The Singal matter occurred after the baptism of little Nadja in the fall of 1966. It was the following spring that Monika would stop at my office to voice her concern about the influence she didn't know how to stop or address. It was the summer of 1967. It was to become a major turning point.

Till this time, religion had not been an issue: I myself saw Salih joke and laugh shyly with members of the department in his quiet, reticent manner. I had seen him at university wide and departmental church (convocations) ceremonies and events. Now, even after Singal left because his grant with us ended, Said continued to consider himself the victim of racism. (The University, if not the physics department, had an international faculty even back then in the mid-sixties, and Cleveland a sizeable and active Arab community).

De facto, the attack of Israel on Egypt in June 1967 was a direct blow against the Said marriage. No one knew it at the time. It is in retrospect that we can put the pieces together and see that whatever went awry over a period of time found its primal scream at a specifically given point. For Salih and Monika it was the Arab-Israeli War. What I did not know at the time, and learned long afterwards, is that Monika's mother exacerbated the event by having her Jewish friends in Jerusalem send inflammatory mail to Salih. What hadn't ignited previously was now fanned into full flame. But that wasn't all.

Said's willful dissociation from his colleagues in the preceding semester deprived him of much needed comfort and support at a time his Arab pride was subjugated to mortal blows. His peers in the department found their outreach rejected. The local Arab community, though it banded together and I knew Monika did all kinds of things to consolidate people and opinion....reported in the Diocesan paper....was, like she herself, mainly Christian. At the same time, the Moslem community basically consisted of students too busy to take any position or divert energy to be involved, and the Moslem Palestinian community appears to have made a call to arms, violence, and retaliation. (Monika refreshed my memory on this as we write.) I know myself that this was not an easy time when Monika found herself pregnant with their fourth child. I also can recall there were continued family related issues concerning her mother that made life even worse and that need no inclusion in my story-at least not at this point on the time line. I knew about all of this less from Salih or Monika, and more from another faculty member and his wife who had had indirect contact with her mother.

It appears that Monika's mother made it her business to consort with someone well known to the department as a would be rival for my chairmanship and furthermore, to spread negative information about her son-in-law that would become fuel for future fires. When the department grapevine extended this information to me, I simply ignored such balderdash. I was dealing with concrete serious matters and had no time for gossip.

I was wrong. It was a serious matter that would explode into a deadly conflagration for the Saids with spill over effects that would ultimately change lives.

V

My concern then, as department chairman, was that Joe Trivisonno had come to me saying that Said was not coming to work, and had not been coming for some time. He had not called. There was no explanation. It was simply "no-show", day after day, week after week, and so on--far too long to not raise major concerns. Joe could not explain or find a reason to have caused this; he mentioned a brief unpleasantness in the lab a while back, but was certain that nothing in proportion to what was happening now had occurred back then. I called Said, and went to visit the family.

I learned that Said had been very upset about that lab incident, and, moreover, that he did not like working with Joe, did not like research, wanted to teach as he had done prior to his PhD studies, and was certain that people were prejudicial against him for being an Arab. A Moslem, he felt out of place at a Catholic school, believed himself to be subjected to discrimination, was overall dissatisfied with how things were going in his life, and lastly, that he physically did not feel well and had extensive stomach and abdominal pains.

I encouraged him to seek medical attention, and promised to see what I could accomplish to assure his continued place at our university, in my department, by adjusting his work and schedule to be more suitable to and in line with his interests, and lastly, to discretely inquire into Said's indicated perceptions of prejudice and discrimination.

Medically, all appeared to be well according to various test results and examinations arranged by the wife of one of Said's Iraqi friends, Dr. Mudrikah Al-Khatib who was at both University Hospitals as well as outside Cleveland, in Painesville. I learned this from Joe Trivisonno who became alarmed at his own lack of perception to help Said in this crisis and for being so insensitive in the already mentioned lab encounter. Joe went to see Said at home to iron things out, smooth things over, make peace and to demonstrate his remorse with an apology. Although both knew that their working relationship was over, they parted as friends and agreed they would continue to be amiable department colleagues.

For Said, this change meant that his association with Argonne Laboratories (Carroll had an ongoing relationship with same, many of us participated there at various times) for future

86

ventures would end, as would his ability to publish and present research as he had been doing thus far. In a "publish or perish" academic environment and discipline, this was a deliberate step into a professional dead end and I very clearly apprised Said of this fact. I could not dissuade him nor prompt him to reconsider the importance his decision would have long term.

Instead, I arranged schedules to include a teaching load for Said: he would be responsible for a section of sandbox physics which was our name for the introductory physics course for non-physics majors. He would also teach physics to declared pre-med majors. There were some additional lab related and research duties that would continue but not in Joe's lab with Joe's research project. Some switches and rearranging had to be done because of budget constraints, requirements, and funds. I stuck my neck out for this young man and the sake of his family. It was not appreciated by some in the department.

Said could not be paid from a Navy research grant if he was not performing for the Navy's benefit as had been the case till now. There was no way to camouflage his absences under contract when he had continued to draw his salary. At the same time, the current department budget was not able to hire or fill an additional full time teaching position with benefits. We had a lot of adjunct faculty: men from GE and Picker X-ray, and ABD candidates from Case Western's PhD program (we only offered a Master's), and others capable and interested in teaching a course per semester as needed. Without benefits. By the fall of 1967, I had everything lined up and ready to proceed on time, within budget, and so on. My internal manipulation was not appreciated by some of my faculty; it generated animosity among some department members who felt that Said was getting preferential treatment at my behest. Forces outside of academia had additional agendas to impact this situation, from the direction of our student body.

This was a time when the draft was culling for itself every available body to satisfy Johnson's folly, the now steadily escalating war in Vietnam and the body count that wouldn't quit.

Deferments were applied for, rested, granted or refused. Young men left for Canada, objected conscientiously, burned their draft cards and marched in protest. And so did a lot of others. One way to honorably avoid the draft quietly and in what one might call a socially acceptable manner, was to go to college. It wasn't only to go to college, it was to manage to stay in college regardless of ability, grades, talent or desire: anything to avoid the military.

In private colleges, this included having daddy donate enough to the college funds or foundations to guarantee junior would make the grade even if he didn't have the desire, or intention to demonstrate ability, talent or interest. It was a draft dodge matter of a more elite or exclusive genre and weapon. The pen on the check-book page became mightier than the sword offered by the draft boards. All too many college administrators or board members readily closed their eyes to junior's failing when dad was willing to fork over a new building, wing, lab furnishings or other sizeable contribution.

Another tactic was to align with heavily endowed as well as endowing alumni groups. Colleges expanded and grew on the backs of the soldiers risking their lives in the jungles. At the same time, the ferment of anti-war sentiment on those same campuses grew hand in hand with the civil rights movements. The late sixties had it all. And then there was Kent State. But again, I am getting a little ahead of myself.

Our department at John Carroll had by now found and hired an additional research fellow who would continue where Said had left off and also do some teaching since we had already requested, in the latest round of annual budget considerations, that the department be enlarged by one new member. Our student body was growing university wide, and with it, so were the numbers of physics majors. Physics was in its hay day, and we, as a country, expected to reach the moon momentarily.

VI

It was in this setting and under these circumstances that, near the end of the fall semester, Said's teaching ability was brought

88

into question not only to me as the department chairman at this time, but other physics faculty--most notably Harry Nash who had been at the other end of the aforementioned grapevine, and as well the Dean and the President of the college. Moreover, Said's wife called to tell me that two mothers had called their home with increasing frequency, pleading for their sons to pass pre-med because they were scheduled to be drafted otherwise, and, at the same time, threatening her with their position of influence on campus.

Not only did those calls upset and concern her, especially while pregnant, but she also shared with me the ethical and moral predicament Said faced according to his own words. Should he succumb to these pleading women with whose concerns and fears he truly empathized, or, is it not morally and ethically correct to give them - the students, their sons - the deserved failing grade rather than have them squeeze by on their path toward a medical career and maybe someday face us in the operating room with their incompetence? I saw this as a decidedly speculative long shot, but it made sense to her. I could not deny that it certainly made sense to me too. I supported Said before both Deans and University President, as well as within the department. Once more, I scored no brownie points.

I was overruled. The Fathers Conry, Britt and Birkenhauer agreed to take the matter into their own hands, placate the pleading parents, (Adjust the grades? Cash the checks? In which order?) and withdraw further employment offers to Said. By now it was half way through the spring semester, 1968. The Saids were expecting baby #4. It was March, nearly April.

Martin Luther King, Jr. was shot.

Said had no contract for the following academic year nor had he considered seeking employment elsewhere. His wife was eight months pregnant and expecting to complete her own college education in two more semesters at John Carroll where, as a faculty wife, she paid no tuition or fees. This was important to the family.

Said had said any number of times if his wife were educated and could work, their life would be easier, and so she struggled to attain her degree and had done so all throughout the prior pregnancy in 1966. She would now soon have four children five and under while she was undauntedly nearing graduation and her BA.

We at the department were aware of the family's predicament and struggle, and it was finally agreed upon that Said would get a one year final contract to enable him to locate another position elsewhere. Said signed the contract in late spring, with the understanding that he would not be given a renewal, raise, or extension but that he would be granted time necessary for any interviews. Said stopped by my office to tell me how much he appreciated what I had done for him and his family, and that I exemplified a true Christian to him. The semester ended mid-May. Said's wife expressed her appreciation to us all, and delivered Stephan on the 30th of May.

Robert F Kennedy was shot.

I was asked to baptize the new-born Said child, Stephan Othmar, right after the television funeral broadcasts for Kennedy ended. The baptism took place on a week-end afternoon at St. Louis' Parish Church on Taylor Road in Cleveland Heights where Nadja Irene had been baptized less than two years earlier, also by me.

Stephan's God-parents were Fran and Bill O'Hearn. Attending Stephan were his parents and his siblings Leila, and Robert (Nadja appears to have been napping at home), and as well Emily Evans and her fiancé, Abdul Wahab – a former class mate of Said's in Iraq, who was completing his PhD in Mathematics at Case Western. It was a good day.

At the time, Bill O'Hearn was in the process of moving from physics teaching faculty to administration. Sadly, and in retrospect, neither one of Stephan's godparents ever carried out their responsibilities toward him; not as much as a birthday card was ever received by him, nor was any interest in him ever expressed. It would seem they chose to abdicate their parts on behalf of their godchild throughout his life span to indicate their disapproval of his parents. In this case I include both Said and myself. And we know they are Christians by their love!?

Do the perceived sins of the father, even the step-father, descend unto the head of the child? I guess so; it must have been their not-unique opinion. That's why I really like these great Christian Catholics. They go to church and pray, but forget what it means to be a Christian, i.e. Christ-like. Have I now in my old age become cynical when I say, "It's their Christian spirit, see how they love one another!" No, I do not jest. It saddens me to the core of my being. There is much truth in the phrase "as cold as Christian charity."

Once again I digress. That's one of the things that happens when you're heading toward 88 or is it 89 by now, so allow me a little liberty now and then. Now, where was I in all this turmoil of civil unrest, and shootings and lootings....baby boys and frustrated families, young men becoming cannon fodder dying too soon....ah, yes.....

I don't recall whether or not Said taught or worked in the lab for the summer that year, 1968. I do remember two things, though: his wife fell into a severe post-partum depression after the birth about which I learned from some of the faculty wives, and although I was not aware of it as yet, the bottom began to fall out of physics as the Moon shot was about to be launched. With these two things added to his plate, Said set about looking to the future. It was a long hot summer that year, 1968, in Cleveland.

VII

I myself went off to Florida to once again substitute at a Parish in Lake Worth. I liked doing that. I like Florida. I like the heat. I like the golf courses I could use. I liked the welcome I would get in a community where I knew no one simply because I was the guest priest substituting for the pastor who was on vacation. I had no real overall responsibilities such as the pastor would with finances, committees, meetings, accountability and the like. My job was to show up for any and all scheduled masses and most of the miscellaneously occurring emergencies, scheduled sacraments such as confession or pertinent devotions, whereupon I had the rest of the time to use for myself, like being on my own holiday as well. It was the Life of Reilly, as they say. I had done this before, and I would do it again.

I had no real desire to do parish work although there were some Jesuit parishes including one right across the street from John Carroll, Gesu. As a matter of fact, I had a habit of helping out or substituting for holidays like Christmas, Easter, and the like in addition to performing ceremonies for relatives and friends, whenever the need or the occasion arose to demonstrate or display my priestly gifts. But being a parish priest? No, never. I was a teacher. Priestly function was just an adjunct or my means to a desirable vacation spot. The only thought I did occasionally entertain was to teach at a traditionally black college in the South: a thought that first came to my mind when we'd been refused service in a restaurant in Washington as I already related earlier. And affirmed now, with MLKJr's death.

When I returned in time to prepare for the fall semester, Said was gone. I was informed he had packed up and left for some small Pennsylvania town, had not turned in a resignation nor informed anyone at John Carroll - department or otherwise - that he was not accepting his last year's position. I heard from the O'Hearns that the move was utter chaos. The carefully planned fall schedule of classes would have to be rearranged post haste, and I felt let down and angry after the efforts I had made.

VIII

It therefore came as a huge surprise when, about two weeks into the semester, Said and his wife showed up in my office: she in tears, and he totally despondent, telling me he had jumped from the frying pan into the fire, made the mistake of his life, would do anything to come back, and what could I do for him since he had not actually resigned from Carroll?

Not only had he made a mistake, he had learned that a requirement for teaching at a Pennsylvania state operated school

92

was American citizenship....something Carroll never questioned and he deliberately had avoided pursuing. He was an Iraqi and intended to remain an Iraqi, something he was free to do with the green card in his possession. Now that freedom was time limited if he expected to have the position he had run to. It was obvious how painful this was for him, and I truly felt sorry for the man. Nevertheless, I could do nothing. Classes were in full swing, rearranged. Faculty was not interested in his return and neither was the administration. His manner of leaving had permanently shut the door of a possible return, or reconsideration, for good. I quickly recognized any efforts or attempts on my part to once again provide any support to him would not be of help to him and would create immense harm to myself personally, and professionally in as much as I held the position of department chair and as such was responsible for the morale of the department members. Very regrettable. Case closed.

Other than the usual Christmas card followed shortly by a birthday card in January 1969, I heard nothing more from the Saids. I trusted they were well, had adjusted, and life was moving along as it was wont to do.

But not quite. And, I was wrong.

DANGER: DETOUR AHEAD!

I

The New Year was not very old when I received a message from Monika to urgently call as soon as possible. Said was in the hospital. When I returned the call, I learned what had happened: Miserable, Said had attended the American Physics Association meeting in I believe Chicago after pursuing every possible job opening he had been able to hear of all fall and winter long. When he did not receive the favorable answer he had expected from Bates College, he began to grasp at straws to move himself and his family away from Clarion which they all hated equally, and where his wife was not only unable to pull herself together without any kind of even minimal support system whatsoever, but deteriorated even more into the depression that had begun with Stephan's birth. By now, all indications suggested that intensive medical or mental health care were in order and none of it was available in a remote corner of the county where they had found an affordable place to rent last minute. In his effort to move quickly, Said saw the Chicago meeting as the opportunity he sought.

As I learned on the phone, Said had returned home in the evening, driving himself from the Pittsburgh airport about 100 miles away, and literally collapsed as Monika opened the door for him. The doctor was called and came, recognized enormous blood loss, suspected internal bleeding, and Said was delivered to the nearby Oil City hospital by ambulance. Once there, five days of blood transfusions to build up his system sufficiently to sustain surgery were required before a goodly portion of his stomach and his duodenum, both inundated with ulcers, could be removed.

Unable to drive because Salih felt women only drove to search for other men, Monika had no way to travel the 30 or so miles to the hospital to visit him, or leave the children and ride with a neighbor, or anything. She had no way to a grocery store or any place else. I felt responsible, and I felt guilty.

The stomach pains Said had had two years ago were like a sounding death knell in my mind, the family in the middle of nowhere happened because we did not act soon enough to provide evident help.....and I rushed to the hospital to see Said. Afterwards, I went to the family home in Knox, Pennsylvania, with several sacks of fresh produce, meats, and other foods I thought necessary. It was to be the first of many visits yet to come.

At the time, ulcers were still treated surgically and were considered a direct result of stress and pressure unlike our current knowledge of a foreign organism or bacterial cause that is treatable till eradicated thanks to the miracle of properly prescribed medication without the former rush to surgical intervention. This was, after all, back in early 1969.

I took Monika shopping and to take care of multiple errands. I took her to the hospital, and I watched the four children in the car while she briefly saw Said. I did so not only while he was in the hospital, I continued to make weekly treks to their house for several weeks after his return home to assist in any way I could to help alleviate the family's difficulties, and until Salih was again well enough to drive.

I had some awareness that Monika had deteriorated even further from what in Cleveland had been considered post partum depression. The events in her life had not allowed time for her

96

own well being. I knew her as cheerful and outgoing, now she was tearful and listless, stressed and tired. She had not a single person as support system, not a single family member within reach. She was relieved and grateful for my hands-on help.

On such visits, Saturdays were spent doing the miscellaneous needed errands, attending to the children and their stories, and enjoying Said and Monika's hospitality. I would say Mass in the home on Sunday morning, and, after brunch, head back to Cleveland.

Looking back to this time now, how young and energetic I must have been to sustain my full work load, late night bridge and poker games, attending to my own personal affairs and yet heading off week-end after week-end to carry out my mission of mercy.

Or was it also to salve my feelings of guilt because I had been a spectator to this family's misfortune, a participant in its disintegration? Had the family not moved, had I as chairman seen more sooner, maybe, if .... they could have stayed in Cleveland..... so many if's and if only's.....but life is hard, life is earnest, and above all, life goes on.

At any rate, because I felt partially responsible for the difficulties the Saids had encountered, I also now felt needed and able to contribute. I felt good about myself substituting a little as chief cook and bottle washer to a bunch of young kids (Monika 27, the kids 5-0), and a support to someone foreign born with a great deal of difficulty acquiring a taste for the country I loved devotedly, the God I worshiped, and the daily struggles I remembered from childhood.

Furthermore, I saw myself as a benevolent spectator involved just enough to be there without really being there at all. Basically, this was a win win situation for all concerned without cost to any one person in particular. The Jebs provided car and gas, and sometimes even a few loads of groceries. Frequently, there would be a few bottles of Angelica from the Mass wine stash included, to wash it all down. Some unidentified Jebs had their own guilt feelings about this family. We all did as we could.

II

By the time spring was in full bloom, the need for my weekly sojourns had ended, and so had my further thoughts about these treks to scenic northwest PA. Salih had written me a really nice note, calling me his only real friend to whom he would forever be grateful. I was glad to have helped, but now I was once more fully embroiled in academia. New adventures beckoned.

Project Themus was on my plate, and I along with the rest of our department salivated at the thought of having a fully financed PhD program to totally conceive and develop, and to be ready to nurture its progress under our wings for full-fledged nationwide recognition for excellence. It was my newest venture and it would be the biggest feather in my cap of life achievements. Polite Jesuits would not admit to salivating. I, Polish kid from the wrong side of the tracks, cleaned up but still the me I was born to be, absolutely drooled. YES!

We prepared, we researched. We worked our tails off. We met the expectations and wishes, the hopes and the ideals. We put a proposal together that would have done MIT or Stanford proud. We were ready, and ready or not, we wanted to move. We were eager.

There are, in academic circles as in all other endeavors, processes and procedures, rules and regulations, predetermined steps and protocols as well as a pyramid of endorsements that one must scale in order to be heard, considered, or after adequate deliberation, voted on for approval.

We arrived at the appointed time. We were loaded for bear. Smooth, sleek, ready, willing and able. The meeting proceeded. It came to be our turn. We presented, we laid it all out. We felt confident and we sat back to await our green light. Someone spoke up, out of turn. (Was it I? The tension was palpable).

It was against customarily used and enforced Robert's Rules of Order. Our project sank to oblivion in front of our eyes, relegated to the almost was-es, might have beens, or could haves. THEMUS was nixed, on the spot, never to be resuscitated again.

I was furious. I knew the Dean had deliberately focused attention on the infarction of Robert's Rules intentionally wishing to squoosh my project because of my earlier support of Said. It had become something of a personal vendetta, or so it seemed to me at the time. How dare he, after our weeks and months and hours of work deny us our reward which not only was OUR triumph but would be the University's first doctoral program in a field everyone was attempting to get into.

It took years until I could accept the fact that it was not the Dean's personal vindication or vendetta toward me because of the earlier Said incident, as well that it was not because of any manner of failure or perceived short coming or lack of excellence in our presentation explaining the entire project. What appeared to have had all of these characteristics at first glance was viewed through the prism of a well informed and difficult decision making process in a world that would see a glut of physicists on the American market even before the July 1969 moon shot when PhDs in physics became a dime a dozen, some driving cabs around Boston on Route 128 where they had formerly worked, either on its periphery or not too far away at places like Raytheon, Electric Boat, and the like. Right then and there, I did not realize what was ahead. Or I didn't want to see it.

I must admit I held a grudge for quite a long time. I felt angry. I was disappointed. And I must also admit that now, with hindsight, I see a lot of dynamics which, at the time, I had neither discerned nor did anyone else take note of my unvoiced internal struggles and made me aware of them. Both getting angry and holding a grudge were feelings I'd not experienced previously. They were uncomfortable and I felt potentially sinful. My response was to immerse myself in a variety of activities while searching for another major project to satisfy my personal needs.

III

The department was running smoothly. The new man fit right in. My work was relatively effortless. I looked forward to my holiday visits to Detroit and the Hopkins family there. I rarely visited any family members. Long week-ends were spent on the golf course at our lake property near Painesville. Evenings not otherwise occupied with academically related matter were spent playing cards, seeing an occasional film, attending concerts, theater, and the frequent cocktail and dinner parties at the home of JCU supporters. Often, I was invited to even out the number of guests at a dinner party; it was not uncommon to invite one of us Jesuits to be the extra man while at the same time being viewed as Eunuch-like and "safe".

I also found myself visiting friends more often: not just for bridge games, but for the various family events such as weddings and graduations. At times, I would be asked to be the celebrant and to dispense a suggested or pertinent sacrament. I also celebrated Mass with my various hosts when I partook of a week-end visit at their homes. Alone, I read profusely. I rekindled an old interest in cross word puzzles. Poker and bridge filled my schedule. I allowed little time for thought and reflection.

IV

The summer following the Themus tragedy, I accompanied Joseph Schell SJ who had recently turned the reigns of the University over to Henry Birkenhauer SJ. Joe and I drove from Maine to Florida and hit every major golf course along the way. I was delighted that Joe had asked me to come along, and we had a great time together. It also made the time go by quickly and helped to put distance between me and the prior disappointment. Time flies when you're having fun. We did and it did. The fall and spring semester went by quickly.

I had heard nothing more from the Said's and therefore was quite surprised when Monika called me in early May just to say hello and catch me up to family news: she had come to town to see both her doctor and the Metropolitan Opera on tour at its Cleveland stop, and was staying with a cousin. When I learned that she had come to town via bus, I offered to drive her home after the matinee performance, indicating I was free to spend the night there, say Mass in the morning, and then drive back to Carroll.

On that day, I had absolutely no idea that the drumbeat of my life was about to lead me to a path I had never considered in my foggiest dreams. Thus far, my goal had been to be a Jesuit. A good Jesuit. Even, possibly, an exemplary Jesuit. One in total obedience. As formed, molded, trained, educated and vowed. No detours or deviations.

If it is true that God laughs when we plan, then He must have been laughing heartily: His plans for me would unfold in the months to come. And they were not what I had envisioned. Not at all.

As I said earlier, along with that grudge that was still echoing within me from Project Themus, I began to seek another project, one that would totally immerse me, and use all my God given abilities. I would soon find the very thing to become my next, my biggest, and my final project in life, and in which I take more pride with each passing year.

V

Project Monika. More accurately put, it was Monika's children who were of considerable concern to me, and not she herself whose need I perceived. It was not she herself, nor would it have been she without her children but only as she was part of them and they of her and, because, as their naturally omnipresent and required mother, she would be part of my next adventure. I had set no time limits and so they have become my last but infinite, ongoing, permanent, satisfying and gratifying final project. And my greatest ultimate reward in this world.

This then is where, eventually and ultimately, things took a huge turn and a life of their own, as if on a clear crisp sunny day, we became caught in the vortex of a tornado. Finely honed plans and accompanying good intentions fell by the way side as outside forces not only insinuated themselves into our lives but governed our lives

101

and actions to serve their own best interest while ignoring ours. I was catapulted from my clearly determined straight forward path into the unknown.

As an aside, and with the usual accurate hindsight, the lack of perception on my Jesuit Superior's part is quite remarkable. He was totally oblivious to at least this one of his charges. Here is the man who was to guide and preside over me and my life and work, both spiritual and temporal, and who nevertheless was totally unaware of the Themus impact, my needs and frustrations, or hurt and anger. In spite of the rigid structure within the Society, I was an individual in a great deal of human pain and need. It went unheeded.

I now think that what might have been a good course of action would have been to transfer me to another place with other demands than merely teaching. For example, teaching a light load at Loyola Chicago while serving as chaplain at Cook County. Something was definitely needed, and I was left without counsel, guidance or discernment. Maybe it just boiled down to not giving a damn about me. It certainly was not unusual considering the setting. Again, I already referred to the chill in Christian charity.

Things became interesting, and confusing. Hardship and difficulty could neither dissuade nor stop me: to the contrary, they increased my determination and firmed my commitment to follow the dictates of my conscience. I had run across something Martin Luther had said centuries earlier while facing the church: "It is neither safe nor prudent to do aught against conscience. Here I stand—I cannot do otherwise. God help me." The Jesuits were as unwilling to really hear and understand me as the attendees of the Diet of Worms had been to comprehend Luther.

I knew in my heart that the decisions and choices I was considering to carry out were good, honest, sincere and very definitely called for. At no time did I not act in total accord with the conscience that had been formed in my early training and subsequent life.

What I had not learned were psychosocial principles. Had I been acquainted with them, I would not have been as shocked as I found myself confronted by my superiors, my confreres, my friends

102

and my family. This knowledge would have indicated to me that group behavior follows certain patterns: the formation of in and out groups, behavior control induced through association, rejection, and condemnation, along with the influencing of opinion, and reinforcement for compliance or the dissuasion of dissent. I would in time face all and more including the maliciousness and viciousness that even the Society would lower itself to.

Let me hasten to add that when all was said and done, everything came out OK in the wash water of life. Today I know more than ever that my path was the high road in God's bright light. I acted in good faith, and as well, honorably as a catholic, a priest, and a man. I had no crisis of faith or doubt. Even now I have no desire to gloat if other's found their dark reward.

PRINCIPLES, FAITH AND GOODNESS

I

I was waiting at the Shaker Heights station when Monika came off the Rapid and got into the car I was driving. A brown Plymouth Fury, I had signed it out when I decided to drive Monika home. As I have said, the Society annually purchased multiple cars that were always maintained and ready for our use, first come first serve.

After grabbing a quick bite, we immediately hit the road, and soon found ourselves on the Ohio Turnpike, exiting to and staying on I-80, while following the signs to Clarion. It had been over a year since I saw Monika or the family; they'd moved to another house closer to the college during that time. While she chatted on and on, rains were pouring down until I found it both necessary and expedient to turn into a rest area so that the thunderstorm with gushing rain passed by. As she lit a cigarette, I told Monika of a recent triumph.

My own past school year on the heels of a great previous summer had been basically uneventful. But I did proudly point to my one great achievement: I had stopped smoking in the summer of 1969. It had been my first and only effort to quit, and I did it cold turkey. I was deservedly proud.

I had been more than a heavy smoker, if it burned, I inhaled it. Cigar, cigarette or pipe. Visitors would find me sitting at my desk enveloped in a bluish grey cloud. Then one fine day Bill Hopkins invited me for a boat trip to visit the various wineries on Lake Erie's islands off the Cleveland coast. We had a great time, or at least the parts that I remember were great! The rest of the time I was seven sheets to the wind. The good that came out of this drunken foray was that when I lit my first cigarette the next morning, it tasted awful and produced a lengthy coughing fit.

On the spur of the moment I decided I had enough of smoking, removed various related supplies and implements, and never touched another tobacco product. Initially, I substituted cough drops. For a while, I would instinctively reach for a lighter when popping a cough drop into my mouth. After a while, that stopped too and I am pleased to say that for the last 40 years of my life I was as smoke-free as the first 20. Well, 16 or so anyway. And I never chewed gum.

My previous experience visiting homes, particularly with two Cleveland adjunct faculty families of my acquaintance, had taught me how important it was to be affectionate and friendly. I regularly entered homes by kissing my hostess. I was surprised that my attempt to kiss Monika in a friendly manner ended abruptly with a slap across my face along with an apology, something like, "No way Father, forgive me. I thought we were really good friends. It's one thing to welcome you with a kiss when you enter our home, quite another to sit here with you in your car in the pouring rain." I was stunned and shocked: so far I had been given to understand that this was what was expected of me by men who deliberately left me alone in their homes with their wives.

Now, suddenly, I was reprimanded and yet, it made good sense. I did not need to be told twice; the occasion remained an isolated, single incident. This was, after all, in line with what I had known all along with the exception of some industrial physicists and their families' mannerisms or behaviors. I apologized. And I didn't repeat myself.

At the same time, however, the trip presented Monika with the opportunity to tell me of some of her difficulties and frustrations. She hated Clarion and everything about living there. She was aware of the job market, and as well of Salih's lost motivation or interest.

Most importantly, she mentioned that everything was not peaches and cream in the marriage and that she had been seeking some kind of intervention or marriage counseling even while still in Cleveland. She informed me that at that time she had turned to Paul Besanceney SJ, her department chairman and advisor, a sociologist who attempted to respond instantaneously to assist the young family with marriage counseling. His efforts were very short lived because they moved shortly thereafter.

She furthermore told me that my relationship with the family, including my being Salih's erstwhile boss presented a conflict of interest in her eyes, and that's why she had not turned to me even though I too was a priest. As long as I was her husband's boss, she had deliberately refrained from mentioning anything personal to me as "not being Kosher".

As I had told others before her, I would have had to turn her down even if she had asked me, as I had others before her, because I had neither training nor knowledge of what marriage counseling consisted of nor what went into it or the dynamics that would propel it. Yes, indeed, I was a priest but first and foremost I was a professor of physics. Teaching, unlike my parish counterparts whose involvement with family issues was on the daily menu, was on mine.

From what she said, it appeared that Salih was angry or disgusted because she was not a college graduate. He did not like the amount of time it took her to keep house nor what she saw as necessary to care for the children. From what she said, I could only conclude that nothing that she did was right or pleasing, and everything she said or did was subject to criticism and ridicule.

107

The fact that she found it impossible to bounce back from the last child's birth was a particular irritant resulting in Salih's telling her she was neither fit to be a mother nor a woman, based on his own mother who had nine children. The biggest shock of all was to learn how frequently Salih hit, shoved and punched her in addition to his constant verbal assaults. Day in day out she heard that she was a disgrace, good for nothing, and not a woman.

Domestic violence and assault, including verbal and physical abuse, were merely concepts that were falling into the cracks of well intentioned family health and welfare programs back in 1970. Not even the mandatory reporting of child abuse had become law as yet. While change lay ahead, women had little if any recourse back then.

II

Monika knew that change was imperative. At the same time, there appeared to be no available options. She told me of her ongoing search for some solution to improve her own condition and her family's well being. Basically, she insisted that if Salih's attention to just what his actions precipated could be gotten, that then there would be a start into the right direction. But how?

She herself knew that first of all, it was crucial that she get back on her feet physically because she was not well, and then, hopefully with the help of her doctor, a recommendation for marriage counseling? Salih's answer to her pleas for help, marriage counseling or visiting her physician with her was beating her, punching her, and verbally abusing her even more. In front of the children.

As I listened, I was absolutely shocked by the time I pulled up in front of their home on Clarion's 5th Avenue. After spending the night, saying Mass, and driving back to Cleveland following the nice lunch Monika prepared, I gave the situation a lot of thought. I drew no conclusions. I had no inspiration nor ideas on what if anything could be done, and less so, what I could do. I did plan on visiting the family again in the not too distant future.

When I next drove to Clarion, I learned that Salih had insisted on buying a house Monika did not want to live in. It was far from town and would further isolate her. She had found another place she would have really wanted if there was no way to leave Clarion because of Salih's employment; Salih had never even looked at it. He pummeled her verbally and physically into signing the papers, including embarrassing her in front of peers and their attorney. She signed under extreme stress and duress suffering from anxiety and depression.

They would soon be moving, again. It would be the third time in three years. As I got ready to leave again, Monika informed me that she had a couple of appointments in Cleveland and if she came to town, she would let me know ahead of time. The summer was drawing to a close, and my own school year was taking shape for the fall semester, and I said we'd just have to play it by ear: if I could get away, I would drive her one way.

It would be a few short weeks until I heard from Monika again. She was taking the bus to see her physician, and planned on spending the night with her cousin Vera. Did I feel like and was I free to drive to Clarion? I said yes. Except this time it was Shippenville, a few miles closer but little difference overall.

Driving back that Saturday morning, Monika told me of her efforts to find some help in the area. She had approached the parish priest, Father Zeitler, about potential marriage counseling. He referred her to Gannon College in Erie, part of the local Diocese, and its counseling program. Obviously, with her inability to drive this was impossible, not to mention that Salih was furious to learn she had spoken to someone outside the family, and that he felt no need for marriage counseling, only for her to change and become a real woman and do her job.

Additionally, Monika also told me her doctor had previously, and again this time, requested to see Salih. Dr. Glove wanted to have him come to one of Monika's appointments, because he saw presenting and potential problems both parties in the marriage needed to address together with him. For example, Dr. Glove questioned the advisability of any additional pregnancies considering Monika's past and present condition….. suggesting a tubal ligation with which Salih would have to agree in writing. Long story short, there were several visits like this each and everyone equally frustrating and leading no where because Salih refused to accompany Monika to the doctor…yet had no difficulty in showing his displeasure with her condition.

More recently a Pakistani had joined the Clarion faculty: Dr. Khan and his wife became acquainted with the Saids and Khan himself chided Salih non-stop for his attendance at Mass, for agreeing to raise his children catholic, for not insisting that Monika become a Moslem before marrying her. Salih did not take this well. He felt his pride was wounded and Khan relentlessly persisted. At least Singal voiced displeasure with the surrounding atmosphere; Khan attacked the family dynamics. And, Salih took it out on Monika.

He punched her black and blue as he felt like doing. I was not the only one to see the bruises, camouflaged in spring and summer, easily hidden in cooler weather with long sleeves and lame excuses. The situation was not good. Even Monika's mother had suggested marriage counseling and feared for the children, as had one of her gentlemen friends whom I had met.

Salih was both angry and immoveable on the matter. The subject was an anathema topic to him at all times; it became clear to me and others that it was best to no longer discuss it in his presence because it was like pouring oil into flames. I was in no position to say, do, advise, or help in any way. I did retain a modicum of friendship. I wanted to help, but I could not discern the manner or capacity of how to deploy help. I visited regularly in hopes of finding something hopeful somewhere.

I knew one thing, at least when I came and as long as I was there, there was neither fighting nor bickering or beating. I knew really very little about the real sum and substance of the Saids' marriage, nor of the root of their difficulties, the sources of their problems, or what had drawn them together to start with.

110

What I did know was that these two people fought non-stop with four young children exposed to violence, hysteria and a chaotic household, and that change absolutely had to be effected somehow someway.

III

Monika is a very intelligent, caring, outgoing and resourceful person. While I told her there was nothing I could do, she asked me if I would help her carry out what she herself hoped to accomplish.

In broad brush strokes she told me her goal was to improve, salvage and change their marriage to a productive and healthy relationship. She also told me she did not love Salih nor ever loved him but rather, that she married him to escape her mother's domineering control and manipulation by going to Iraq..... enumerating several incredibly unfortunate incidents that either altered her life or prevented her from living it. This explained why life in Iraq seemed appealing. Unfortunately, life in Iraq was cut short after a few months making a return to the US unavoidable if undesirable.

Monika also affirmed her commitment to Salih: that she had been from the day that she met him completely and totally faithful, was so now and intended to remain so.....she even reminded me that a kiss would have been an infringement on that devotion in her eyes, and hence her slap, even for a priest with no further intentions or ulterior motives, was an OK thing no matter the innocence of intent.

I believed her. The passion in her voice and speech were credible. Here was a good woman. Young, maybe a little immature or naïve, but genuine and good. She shared with me the various reasons why she had neither steadily dated nor entered earlier relationships prior to meeting Salih. It bothered her a great deal that her mother had fabricated stories of past associations and that she had informed Salih of this fiction that he took for fact. It had not been very long after leaving her previous five years of near cloistered living among nuns when she met him. Some of that time was spent exploring religious life which she learned would be impossible and so she had thrown herself into college work, and then, when it also became impossible, factory work doing both piece work on an assembly line and then, after taking a course with IBM, working for an insurance company. Basically, she'd been no where in life except with nuns, in a classroom, and with Salih by whom she was mostly pregnant. And she didn't want to change her life, only their relationship in it.

Sadly, from all appearances Salih did not deserve such dedication. No matter, I did pledge to help her in her quest for a solution, but I also told her that my friendship with Salih meant I would extend to him the same friendship or help or support were he to join her in seeking solutions, resolutions or help. And that's were we left things that fall of 1970. Until.......

IV

It was mid-morning. Usually I was in my office but for some reason, I had gone back to Rodman Hall to my room when the phone rang. It was Monika. Her voice was barely audible and I could easily sense that she was crying. She was calling from the office of a professor at the college. Earlier that morning, Salih had ordered her to sign a loan application which was clearly falsified When she refused, he grabbed a kitchen knife and held it to Leila's throat, ordering her to sign now or else. She signed. She was terrified. Could I please come? (NO-I had commitments). I tried to calm her down. I tried to placate her with soothing words and thoughts. I would come over the week-end.

When I got there, Monika had been given the keys to one of her professor's home and the latter had also arranged for a ride for her and the children on an ad hoc basis with yet another professor friend. Monika was somewhat relieved.

This good professor now also knew of what was going on and he counseled her to get out of the marriage ASAP rather than sacrifice her children to such trauma and terror. Monika agreed

112

that something had to be done, but she felt she had to first seek other options that had not been tried as yet.

For me, the week-end was tense but not unpleasant. Most importantly, I now knew one of the stressors that had increased the tension between Monika and Salih: money, and her mother's promise of funds if Salih would guarantee her a place to live in retirement. He had agreed and she had sent funds. However, the funds were insufficient to meet the current crisis without a loan and her entanglement intensified the crisis. The most obvious problem was money, or rather, the lack of it. And what of her mother possibly also living with them in retirement?

When Salih decided to buy the house, the couple lacked the necessary down payment. It sounded like Salih had been pressured into buying the house by fellow faculty. Monika did not want the house, she could not drive and it was in a rural location where she could not walk to anything, could not get a quart of milk on her own, nor knew anyone nearby. She also had seen a house in Clarion "downtown" which she loved, which was ideally located, nearly new and enhanced by everything she felt desirable....including the price. She was so sure that Salih would like it too: he refused to see it.

Now, they were stuck in an isolated location in a house that was only ¾ finished, with no funds to complete its interior (flooring, appliances, and all else) or exterior (landscaping) yard, the debt of two mortgages, no money set aside for emergencies, and her mother already calling the shots about how she wanted certain things done because she had sent Salih the funds to do so for her own future.

It would not be long when she wanted her money back because her own plans had changed (she would remarry). Salih asked me if I could help with any funds.

V

In my recent and more frequent visits, I had become aware of something new: Salih was drinking quite heavily, at least in my presence. He would get even more agitated and angry when under the influence, and seemed to ignore the medical recommendations made following his ulcer surgery. His behavior was worrisome, this was no way to handle pressures. His inebriation also increased the insults heaped on Monika. I recall asking Salih once if there wasn't anything at all that she could do that met with his approval. "She can cook" was the only thing he came up with.

Salih's complaints about Monika wanting to attend classes for several semesters were understandable because that meant additional costs for babysitters, tuition, transportation and so on. At the same time, it was Monika's only time away from 4 little kids. And, he perceived Monika's lack of a degree as a pronounced short coming.

"I came to the United States and marry a woman less educated than women back in Iraq". It was a real issue, and one Monika had worked hard to correct attending John Carroll University free of charge while in Cleveland. Now, it was obvious that Monika was not managing very well and needed help above and beyond what could be mobilized for her or on her behalf locally.

There was no misunderstanding Salih when he said "She should have finished college so she could work. I can't do this alone. We cannot separate because we can't afford it, although I wish she would go away. It's finances, we're stuck and miserable. This house is the death of us, but the children need a home. Everything has gone to hell, everything went wrong and it is her fault, she is not a woman. She needs to be punished." Monika's needed punishment became the latest mantra.

Salih had called his mother-in-law and asked her if Monika could come to spend a brief period with her to pull herself together in her mother's care. Her mother said "no —she made her bed let her lie in it; I have my own life to take care of." Salih took this as a slap in the face along with the repeated demands for the funds she had lent him just months earlier. Obviously the only existing family was worse than a dead end.

I truly prayed maybe more than ever before in my life. This family needed practical help, not faith charged platitudes. They needed concrete solutions, not pious ablutions.

Salih had had enough of Monika but didn't know how to rid himself of her. Monika remained convinced that if she found the magic potion, avenue or modus operandi, all would be well. Neither recognized the impossibility of a situation where she wanted and he wanted out. Suggesting marriage counseling had been attempted repeatedly by not only me but others but as long as Salih refused and placed blame, it wasn't a solution. What was or could be?

Early Frank

Father, John Gutowski
June 1930

Mother, Susi Glowska Gutowski
May 1933

Frank at studies (Juniorate) in
Milford, Ohio
May 1940

A customary card game at Tom and Cathy Hopkins' house in Detroit, MI
Easter 1953

Frank at Tom and Cathy Hopkins' house in Detroit, MI
Christmas 1953

Bill and Lois Hopkins on the far right with baby Ann.
Christmas 1953

Frank's Acquired Family

Passport picture
Spring 1973

Nadja, Leila, Rob and Steve
Columbia, MD
Mid 1990's

Easter Sunday AND Monika's Birthday. Last picture of all six of us
March 23, 2008

Frank and Others

Global Volunteers teaching English
in Poland
Mid 1990's

The Bridge Group at the Senior Center
Summer 2005

Frank happily surrounded
by Santa Singers
December 2008

The 3 Graces (Leila, Katie Carapico and Monika), with Frank's
birthday cake under wraps
January 25, 2008

Family Snapshots

All the girls: Monika, Leila, Nadja
and Pepper
January 2006

Stephan
January 2006

Salih and Frank on the "Elva C" touring Reedville
July 2004

Typical Frank Expressions

With Rob at Joe's Inn
in Richmond
March 2003

Humor on the "Elva C" in
Reedville
July 2004

Somewhere in a car
Spring 2005

Recovering from surgery — TGIF
April 2007

Easter Sunday
March 23, 2008

Grandfather Frank!

All four pictures were taken in short succession; it was the last time Steve's daughter Noluenn would see Frank, January 2009, shortly before his 90th birthday. We have no pictures of Frank with Robbie's Emma; and David Anthony, born February 3rd, never saw Frank at all, to everyone's regret.

The first "sticky" goes on Frank's head at Joe's Inn over lunch.

Heading back to the car after lunch with "sticky" in place.

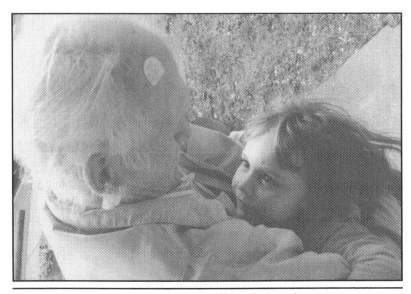

Love, adoration and second "sticky" on the ear!

One very last,
very big hug.

A TENTATIVE PLAN

I

I wracked my brain for some sort of even temporary solution. And, I thought of a plan that I believed to be workable. On my next visit, I intended to tell Salih, and indeed, I did. He was most appreciative. He was totally willing to accept my ideas, and to be free of Monika, have the children safely taken care of, and not spend any money in the process.

Only someone as naïve and other worldly as I was would come up with an idea like this. But then I was naïve, and I was not worldly wise nor worldly. This then was the idea that I presented to Salih which he instantaneously and wholeheartedly embraced with obvious relief:

I would request at least a portion of my salary. As a Jesuit, I received no salary. The salary grade attributed to me as chairman of the department was strictly a book salary for me. In other words, I was "worth" so and so much which was given to the Jesuit community who met all my needs and expenses, present and future, and who would give me whatever spending monies I requested or required.

I had access to the best food, a stable of late model cars, beer on tap and Chivas Regal by the bottle. What I did not have was instant access to what might be considered my funds: the vow of poverty did not deprive me; it fostered dependence on the generosity of the order towards its members. I had to ask to buy a suit or new underwear. Father Superior never said no, but he might have: this is to retain humility in my/our dealings. I had a little stash of private funds. This discretionary income was what I made playing poker! It included a nice little kitty to fund extra lunches, dinners, or hostess gifts when I was invited. And so, knowing the numbers and their potential, I had formulated the plan which I now presented to Salih.

I would assure that John Carroll University would determine "special circumstances" that would permit Monika to earn the semester credit hours necessary for her graduation the following spring without cost. I believed myself able to do so as chairman of a major department. We were talking about considerably fewer credit hours at Carroll vs. those required at Clarion because some of her work had by now exceeded transfer time limits.

Part of my requested salary would go for JCU related expenses such as books and fees for Monika, and some of it for her living expenses. As a result, Monika and Salih could separate for an academic year of about nine months. Monika would come back to Cleveland and with my help, complete her degree to satisfy both his wishes and her own. That would also give them both the necessary breathing room to assess their future. Monika was thrilled: she foresaw Salih's week end visits as the honeymoon they never had, kids and all. Salih appeared relieved to be rid of expenses, Monika, strife, and noisy kids. I could see the relief in his facial expression and posture. And he said so.

There was no time to lose. It was already late April 1971 and plans needed to be put into action.

II

My first suggestion was to get Monika to her doctor, and to ask Salih to please finally go with her to seek treatment for what to me looked like shattered nerves or an inability to keep things in perspective overall. She was not coping well, barely at best. Could or would she be able to cope in the scenario Salih and I had hammered out for her? He refused to go. I took her to an appointment with Dr. Glove, her OB/GYN, in Shaker Heights.

It was then that I learned directly from her physician in her presence that another pregnancy could put her over the edge of coping, that some sort of mutually agreed upon birth control was imperative and that he recommended either a vasectomy or tubal ligation. As a matter of fact, he had wanted to talk to Salih before Stephan's birth to suggest the latter at the time of delivery as being optimally performed. Dr. Glove also spoke of what he perceived as a total abdication of his (Salih's) responsibilities as a husband for the welfare of his wife.

Did Dr. Glove think being introduced as "Father" made me Monika's father and hence his candor? It was eye opening for me, it was more than what I had surmised or wanted to believe. It was worse - Salih's behavior qualified as worst case scenario. We left the gynecologist's office with a prescription for a drug called Thorazine to help Monika.

Nevertheless, and undaunted, Monika continued in her quest for some sort of answer to her problems. She fervently believed that somewhere was the answer that would solve everything; she wanted to find a way to fix things. In Clarion, she had talked to social workers and counselors found in the telephone directory, but none had private practices or knew of any local marriage counselors. The Gannon College option suggested by Father Zeitler, himself a priest but totally candid about his experience or rather the lack of in the field of marriage counseling, seemed as the only available place. There was no local mental health clinic, no local or private non profit group of any kind. The closest psychiatrist was 30 miles away.

In her efforts, the word divorce was heard more and more often, its implications appeared large, loud and clear. Monika wanted a solution, not dissolution. And she was stubborn in her pursuit of what she envisioned. Monika believed in miracles.

Finally she called an old friend whose judgment she felt would be best for both herself and Salih. He was a lawyer, a judge, a friend, an Arab, a family man, and they both knew him well. Joseph Nahra. Monika called on him, and made an appointment with him at his home. I was again engaged to provide transportation at least one way. I agreed to drive her back after the meeting which was scheduled for a Friday evening. Again, Monika planned on sleeping at her cousin's house.

III

Once again, just like to the doctor's office, I accompanied Monika to Judge Nahra's house. The advice Monika got following a lengthy and comprehensive disclosure seemed appropriate and feasible, realistic and affordable (with my promised help). This in sum and substance is what Judge Nahra said and suggested:

"Salih is an Arab, he will never want to lose his family no matter what. However, given the current circumstances, you cannot continue to live as you are living for your own sakes and especially for the sake of the children. I understand that you have both gotten into dire financial straights with the purchase of the house. I also understand the needs for a reckoning, a time for separation, for thinking and recharging yourselves and your emotional capacities.

"You need time, money, understanding and help to get along; Salih needs to become aware that he is now in an American society within which expectations differ from what he learned and knows, where wives are not beaten but instead are considered partners. Salih has to accept you as you are now, but you also must endeavor to perform as he wishes, meaning that you do finish college and are ready to contribute through gainful employment until at least such time as the current fiscal crisis ends. Taking care of your health is your responsibility; encouraging, allowing and supporting such care is his.

"I think the idea of temporarily moving to Cleveland, filing for divorce here, and thereby separating for the time being is a good one for several reasons. You can finish college in no more

132

than two part time semesters at John Carroll, and the lack of a college degree is one of Salih's criticisms of you that will be solved that way. You indicated a cousin who can help with locating rental housing, Father Frank here has offered to help you financially and to see what can be worked out with the University for free tuition and expenses. Being here alone with the children won't be easy, but it will give you time and distance to rethink your future plans, and for Salih to rethink his in light of his family.

"Filing for divorce will indicate to Salih that you are very serious about the need for some major changes in your lives and the necessity to effect them with whatever help is available to meet your needs. And, because Cleveland is so big and there are so many cases pending to be heard in family court, it will take more than a year to hear a divorce petition giving you plenty of time to meet all other goals, and expectations. Take good care of yourself and let me know how and if I can be of further assistance."

Following this extensive and practical advice, I drove Monika back home where she proceeded to take Thorazine as prescribed by her doctor.

The stress and difficulty of her situation further debilitated Monika who found herself with a severe case of mononucleosis, it would be for a second time, which left her both exhausted and lethargic, as well as incapable of dealing with her responsibilities.

When Salih called a few weeks later to ask me if I could stay with Monika and the children because he wanted to go on a Canadian fishing trip with some of his co-workers, I informed him that I would need my Superior's permission first before being able to say so, but that I had no other pressing matters at the moment because the spring semester had just ended. He informed me that Monika was zonked out on the couch most of the time and no longer gave a damn about anything so I would really be of great help. I reluctantly agreed to request permission.

By that time, my Superior was aware of my concerns about the Said family because I had already suggested that I would need my salary by fall in order to assist them. My Superior, Paul

Besanceney SJ, knew Monika because he chaired her department while she was a sociology major at John Carroll and was also aware of the family situation from earlier contacts. He now thought this would be a good thing for me: I would see first hand how foolish my ideas of helping this family were when faced directly with a single parent household, however brief a time. He expected me to be cured of my far fetched idealism after spending a week with Monika, kids and caboodle, while Salih fished. I went.

IV

I did not realize that while Salih had wanted me there, he did not want others to know that Monika was not well enough to have been left alone, and that he had entrusted me with her care while he went away without even telling her how to reach him in any potential emergency because he knew she was safe with me in residence. Now, suddenly, he put on an act of the "embarrassed" husband, returning home to find his wife in the company of someone else. Salih was furious that I walked out of the house and greeted his friends and companions when he returned, accusing me of deliberately embarrassing him in front of his fellow faculty. I was stunned.

That night, Salih once again got terribly intoxicated. Hours later, a sobbing Monika arrived next to my bed in the guest room. Salih had tried to force himself on her against her wishes and in spite of her poor health, telling her this was her punishment and what she deserved. I could neither sooth nor calm her, so I got dressed and ready to head back home after making a renewed effort to console Monika.

Several hours later, Salih himself also came to what had been my bedside apparently fully expecting to find a compromising situation. Instead, he found me dressed, up and reading at the side of the bed, with Monika in the bed that had been assigned to me in the guest room, calmly asleep.

Salih was unsteady on his feet as he glared at me: I still remember the look in his eyes. Fortunately and thank God, he quickly saw for himself that he had nothing to worry about. I did not feel I owed him any explanation since none was warranted, and he didn't either. I did say I was waiting for daylight to hit the road back to Cleveland and that the week of his absence had gone well. He muttered an apology, and thanked me for my help in being there. And, he added that he hoped that I would please come soon to further discuss my ideas of providing him and Monika with the promised and much needed help. I said I would try to do so.

In the course of the night's events, while trying to calm Monika, I also learned that Salih had not slept with her since his ulcer surgery, and yet she had found condoms in his suit just recently as she readied it to be picked up by the dry cleaner. He'd never used one with her. Birth control was one of the matters Dr. Glove had wanted to discuss, especially in light of Monika's Catholicism and papal dicta.

Dutifully, Monika had also written to her father in law in Mosul, Iraq. She knew an Egyptian couple on the Clarion faculty who translated both her letter and his reply: How saddened he was at the possibility of divorce; how much he missed all of the family, how he hoped that his son would heed the advice of those older, wiser and more experienced than himself and make the effort to restore harmony in his home for the sake of the whole unit because that was his obligation before Allah. Monika really loved and respected her father in law; Salih paid no attention. Another rampage followed: she had involved the Egyptians in his affairs and injured his pride once again. Amidst tears, Monika told me on the phone how kind her father in law had been and how disappointed he sounded, just like herself.

I am not sure if I noticed it then, or later, or whether my recollections are embroidering my hindsight: something in Monika's attitude, perception and manner changed dramatically after the above condom discovery. Something was very very different.

V

It was now late May/early June 1971. I had no definite summer plans other than the demands of the Said situation. Monika started to pack her things, and I carted several car loads of boxes to Monika's cousin's house in South Euclid, a suburb of Cleveland, not far from John Carroll University and my Rodman Hall home.

This same cousin found a house available for rent via her friends. It was not far from the University, convenient to shopping, transportation, and all other things Monika would need with her children, no car, and living alone. I promised to help in any way I would be able to, including my idea of bringing prepared food from our dining room on the days Monika had classes that interfered with meal preparation. I offered to babysit as my time allowed. Now I know how foolishly naïve and idealistic I was; back then I thought I was practicality personified and reality incarnate.

At the same time, I was talking to family, friends and colleagues about my plans to help Monika. Some thought I was crazy. Most shook their heads incredulously. Some gave me advice. The advice came from fellow priests and consisted of: "if you get involved with this family, be really involved and marry the woman." From a parish priest named for a good scotch I heard, "Why marry, get yourself a little whore like I have." By Walt Farrell, a fellow Jesuit and friend, I was told, "this is a young woman, you are not giving her a chance to meet people her own age and maybe find someone to fall in love with." It was obvious that none of the so called celibates understood either my intentions or my goals. They appeared to see things through a sexual filter. This was not the nature of the relationship and my goal was to provide temporary crisis intervention and help. I myself foresaw this intense involvement lasting for no longer than the year it would take for Monika to graduate. Maybe I would add a few months beyond to help her settle elsewhere into a new job. No more, but no less.

One old Jesuit saw it differently. Father Zurlinden SJ was half as old as God when he took me aside and said, "Don't do anything half assed. If you truly care and want to help this family, you must marry the mother, not treat her like some harlot in your debt after you're done."

No one appeared to understand or accept the fact that romance, sex, attraction or human desire had nothing to do with my course of action. I knew it. Monika knew it.

In June of 1971, our physical contact consisted of celebrating the Eucharist and receiving communion: it was Christ's body that became one flesh with us individually while jointly facing the altar. Every trip to Cleveland till this time included my saying Mass in one of the Rodman Hall chapels with Monika as sole congregant in prayerful participation.

I was totally imbued with the fresh air John XXIII had let in the windows of the Catholic Church, and the teachings of Vatican II which were stirring controversies and newness within our faith. My understanding and the current thought of the time convinced me that the Eucharist, bread that had become Christ's body being ingested at Mass, His blood that was drunk in the form of wine, were no different than a man's penetration of a woman and the deposit of semen left within her. Communion became a fulfilling sexual act without physical sex. Monika did not disagree. Our bodies were joined in Him, with Him, and through Him, in the unity of the Holy Spirit. I believed myself right; Monika believed me. She suggested that what Teresa of Avila had experienced was an orgasm, later called her ecstasy. We would be no less.

My family was notified of my intentions and the reaction was mixed: some had little to say, a few objected loudly. I recall my niece Rita, who had recently left the convent after 20 or so years as a nun and who now was a psychiatric social worker, tell me she thought that Monika saw me as both Father and father figure. I don't remember Rita meeting Monika that early, but maybe she did.....or she was able to discern things because of her professional wisdom and experience, things that I did not see.

In an effort to have a support system for Monika, I took her to visit friends whom she did not know from her past association with the university. We went to the Graffys, a well to do couple in Beechwood at whose house I played frequent bridge along with Frank Smith SJ. Phyllis Graffy was floating in her pool mid-morning enjoying what must have been one in a series of early morning drinks. She did not bother coming out of the pool to greet us. Later, she made the remark that I should watch out for the shameless fat tart I had a lot of nerve to bring and whom she need not get to know. I shook my head in disbelief, and then laughed. Maybe her husband Bob was right when he thought his wife had a crush on me???

Next, I took Monika to visit the Owens. Fred and Marge were a dear couple with three children. Fred had been at Carroll, he worked for Picker X-ray in town, their two young sons were typical teenagers and their daughter was about to marry. I had been asked to perform the ceremony. As it turned out, it would be one of the two last weddings I performed that month, the other one was my nephew Bob to his bride Sally who had been a nun together with his sister Rita.

We had a great visit, a delicious meal, and I left with Marge's blessing and promise of helping Monika while she toughed out her year nearby. It was nice. Sometime later, we would visit their daughter Marty Sorce and her new husband in the Youngstown-Akron area as they hosted a post honeymoon party. Like her parents, Marty was a delight.

By now, we were close to and yet still far from moving ahead toward the ultimate goal of implementing my project: perfectly open and above board, even if some had intimated their concerns at the impossibilities of the endeavor! No one had nixed my project. It was now mid to late June. I believed I had a green light, or I assumed that I did.

And then several bomb shells torpedoed all good intentions out of the water.

DERAILMENT

I

Paul Besanceney SJ, Monika's one time advisor and chair of her department, the one Jesuit to whom Monika had turned for help and marriage counseling several years earlier while still living in Cleveland and a faculty wife, had earlier become Superior of the JC Jesuit Community. As such, he was my superior. And, as such, he assumed authority that was not his to take. He called Monika and requested that she come to Cleveland to meet him in his office.

Monika, the good catholic boarding school graduate trained totally in obedience and subject to ecclesiastical authority made immediate arrangements to do so. After all, he was a priest, and as such was to be instantly obeyed. He had also been a trusted faculty advisor, trusted enough to entrust him with personal issues.

When she arrived in one of Rodman Hall's public rooms, she was informed by Father Besanceney that she was NOT to consider moving to Cleveland because as a former faculty wife she would be an embarrassment to the university and its faculty and staff especially considering the nature of her husband's departure, and that although she was a student in good standing, she must not continue her studies at John Carroll and had no business to assume that her presence would be either welcome or acceptable, and lastly, to make sure she understood, that her place was anywhere except there, in the Cleveland area. Moreover, he informed her that he was forbidding her to consider the move.

Did he have the authority to tell Monika what to do? Of course he did not. Did she assert herself and tell him to fry ice or sit on a tack? Of course not. Instead, although totally shattered, she obeyed him. He was a priest. He was authority. That is how she had been taught. If a Jesuit-or any priest- said "jump" she would only say, "Father, how high do you want me to try to jump?"

II

I lugged the boxes stored at Vera's house back to Clarion. That's also when I learned that Monika had now consulted Ray Pope, Esq. to initiate filing for divorce in Clarion now that she could not come to Cleveland. She was naïve enough to believe that the time frames mentioned by Judge Nahra were equally applicable in this small northwestern PA town and county. Again, in spite of good intentions, she was wrong.

It was shortly after this time that I was informed by my Superior, the self same Besanceney, that if I wanted my salary, I would have to leave Rodman Hall, the Jesuits' residence, and find another place to live. I received this news with very mixed emotions, and without seriously considering just what that would mean for me myself. I anticipated the opportunity to discuss this rationally before any action would be taken.

Monika and I still had no romantic or physical relationship up to this point. After all, her consistent goal was to solve her marital problems, and mine was to retain my celibate life. She believed and was committed, and so was I. I was also aided by the very real and tangible instruments I had had since my novitiate days: they had served me well.

III

Major shifts were in the air. Monika was committed to accept any and all difficulties while seeking solutions and improvements as long as she believed that Salih was equally committed to her regardless of how he displayed said commitment. The condoms in the suit pocket in the earlier spring were the catalyst. Finding them shocked Monika to reality and out of the escape into a thorazine haze. Monika needed her wits fully. She rallied with a new found sense of purpose. Now, it would soon be summer.

What had changed? Now with apparent evidence that the necessary commitment between two people was a figment of her own imagination, in spite of four children, and as well a clear explanation why Salih was so eager to have her off the proximal and immediate scene, divorce was no longer just an option. In other words, there was no marriage to solve or save. She felt that her viewpoint was endorsed by a recent book on marital relations written by an ordained professor at Yale's theology department. I forgot his name, but I do recall that in sum and substance his position was that only a genuine total marital commitment between and by both parties constituted a marriage which would then be emotionally insoluble: Monika now felt she was a party of one.

Although Besanceney had thrown multiple monkey wrenches or flies into our well-intentioned ointment-balm, I cannot credit him alone for the shift that took Monika and me from friends to lovers somewhere in late June or early July. I was a new and clumsy lover, Monika, a scared needy partner. Vera was the generous and understanding enabler who provided her home for the liaison that had now begun, although it could not be physically consummated. Two babes-in-woods clinging to each other. Monika considered her marriage to Salih as a mere paper formality in wait of its coup de grace. She had stopped believing in its existence. It had ended with a left over condom lost in tweed.

Salih's anger and frustration reached new and higher levels as the money promises crashed and burned along with his anticipated hope for freedom. As usual, he dissipated his rage by assaulting Monika's body. Some local people became aware of what was happening. Betty Farnham three houses away, and Mary Haws, wife of the local veterinarian, actively took a stand in support of Monika. Mary spent time cheering Monika while bringing to her kitchen bountiful baskets filled with self-made edibles of all kinds as well as a dozen water glasses and other dishes: Salih had smashed every single drinking glass and several dishes during his uncontrolled outbursts.

Both women had, in no uncertain terms, suggested to Salih that he would be better off spending some time elsewhere because they felt his presence was causing more harm than good, in spite of logistical difficulties. It was summer, and no classes were being held. Angry and insulted, Salih packed up and went to Pittsburgh where his Uncle Yunis was completing a PhD in library science at Pitt.

As Nietzsche would have us believe, as long as Monika had a why – faith in her marriage – Monika was seeking a how. That myth now having been dispelled, divorce was not only logical, it would only affirm what already was anyway, while ending hypocrisy and dispelling illusion. Monika appeared to gather a new or second wind. When the chips are down....or when the going gets tough, the tough get going.

IV

Salih in the meantime continued his threats from afar. While not present to punch and hit her, he ranted about how he would come and kill Monika; she just had to wait and see how he would punish her. The repeated threats terrified Monika who first called her attorney and then the local police. The former promised to not ignore her plight with a prompt filing, the latter that there was a squad car somewhere in the county at all times, and if and only when Salih physically forced entry into the home, a call would dispatch someone. Great. By then she might be dead. In 1971 there were no domestic violence programs, laws, or other protection.

142

This was especially true of rural north western Pennsylvania's Clarion County.

Enter Betty Farnham, newly recovered from yet another miscarriage. Betty called her friend, Grace Urrico, the other half of their well loved piano duo. Grace was away for the rest of the summer attending to parents in Rhode Island. Her townhouse was empty. Could Monika and the children use it temporarily? Yes of course.

Night after night, at dusk, Betty would come with or without her husband, pick up Monika and the children and take them to Grace's house to spend the night. The thought was that Salih would be more likely to await darkness to carry out any of his threats. Daylight was friendlier and safer. In the morning, she once again came and took the family back home in time for breakfast. Betty was absolutely incredible. This continued for several weeks.

In early August, Monika received the official documents scheduling the divorce hearing for later that month. She was informed that Salih had likewise been officially served to appear in the offices of Judge Robert Filson who had been designated as the "master" in front of whom depositions would be taken and decrees determined, in line with then effective Pennsylvania laws. They may still be thus even now, I don't know.

Monika and I spoke almost daily on the phone. I tried to reassure her and encourage her. I hoped to infuse her with self confidence and the strength to "stick to her guns." By the start of August, I was too busy to drive to Clarion more than a couple of times on the spur of the moment, because the matter of my salary, residence, and status had not been resolved and the fall semester wasn't far off.

At the same time, Monika could not come to Cleveland at this time; once or twice at best and then only in conjunction with a ride from me. As a single parent without any security, separated and facing the possibility of divorce, her mobility was curtailed. Vera and Joe welcomed her as ever. They were a God

143

sent during these circumstances. Vera had never been surprised that the couple would divorce based on what she had seen even while they lived in Cleveland. Joe had never visited their home, but knew enough from his wife and children, plus Monika's visits, to support the situation.

Left without a dime, nor the ability to get anywhere from her isolated location, Monika was fortunate in the friends who helped her by providing food and all else she needed for the children and herself. In addition to Mary and Betty, next door neighbor Leah Nanz provided ample hugs and patient listening day in and day out...along with a big bottle of vodka on August 24th, the day the divorce was final. Marilyn Carter, the children's Kindergarten teacher, and her daughter Karin offered support. And so did the Garcias.

V

The days were difficult. Salih did not respond to any of the legal notices associated with the divorce petition. He did not object, contest, seek custody, or indicate any position whatsoever. Even though he had been officially notified of the impending hearing, he ignored it. He did not respond in any manner, nor did he appear as requested. Property could not be settled but child support was determined at the minimum Monika had intimated as appropriate given his financial situation. Full custody was awarded to Monika. Pennsylvania provided no alimony. Monika didn't know that. The divorce was final on August 24th. Monika was penniless. She realized their joint checking account had been cleaned out, and so had the meager savings along with a considerable number of US Savings Series E-bonds.

When it finally took place, the divorce had become anticlimactic and even uneventful. Practically, Salih provided neither for his children nor for Monika. I sent the $500.00 from my poker winnings, it's all I had. It paid the lawyer and some milk and bread. There was a support order on file, but Salih simply ignored it as he did anything else at will. Again or still, Monika's

144

friends supported her and the children. Salih did nothing but he did stay away. Monika's mother was not heard from at all nor did she respond in any way. She was otherwise engaged at the time! Shortly after the divorce was final, Ernie Spittler SJ and I drove out to see Monika. We only stayed for the afternoon but we did bring a storehouse of supplies from Rodman Hall's coffers. I handed Monika whatever bills I had in my pocket, and so did Ernie.

After Labor Day, Monika's mother also came to introduce her new husband and to let him meet Monika and her children. It was a difficult visit for Monika, so Bob Cihlar SJ and I drove out to visit and bring a little lightness and relaxation to everyone. We had a pleasant visit but we too returned to Carroll that same evening. Our brief almost-liaison after Monika's divorce petition was filed became a memory. Although I no longer considered myself to be the virgin I had been for more than 52 years after spilling my seeds. I was unsure of my feelings or actions; she even more so. Monika sought comfort, affection and kindness. She had perceived a sense of incest without its remotest possibility.

The semester was about to begin. I had no idea how to accomplish what I had hoped to do, and whether I could indeed effect anything at all. The financial situation for Monika was untenable, yet there was no silver lining to be seen anywhere. Monika's inability to drive presented a big handicap, but the lack of a vehicle was equally problematic even if she could. She lived in the affluent Ghetto outside Clarion, Marianne Estates, postal zone Shippenville. It was isolated, remote, impractical and desirable only when one had appropriate income, a car and the ability to drive.

CHANGE OF VENUE

I

My request for my salary had never been reviewed or been acted on so I re-approached the subject with both the University's President and my Superior. Without hesitation, they informed me that I could be receiving my salary in short order, but that they expected me to take a sabbatical for the present academic year even though the semester had already begun, and, that I was expected to vacate my room at Rodman Hall within two weeks as well as my office in the science building. I was stunned. I had fully expected to remain at Carroll in my position as department chair without any sabbatical or other leave of absence. Everything that I had thought would work to the advantage of all concerned had gone to hell in a hand-basket.

Monika had been granted the divorce within weeks when it had been expected to take months well beyond a year's duration. But that would have been in densely populated Cuyahoga County, not Clarion which had more deer than people. Now, I had no place to go. Monika was not able to complete her work at John Carroll, and attending Clarion State would mean at least a couple of extra semesters worth of work because some of her credits were either too old or otherwise unfit for transfer. All the careful planning, assessing, gathering of information and potential logistics had become useless.

When I walked back over to my office after the meeting with Birkenhauer and Besanceney, my heart heavy and hopelessness in my soul, I realized that Harry Nash had already removed my name from my office door and fastened his own on it as the new chairman. Obviously the decisions had been made a while before I was notified.

Even so, it was another shock: Harry'd been angling for the chairmanship from the first day I was so designated. He had disliked Said, he was…no comment. My thoughts suffice. It was now nearly mid September, and I had to make some quick decisions. I knew my salary would be forthcoming month to month until I returned to campus and taught, all nine months of it. How would that then work with Harry in my place? I needed a temporary place to live immediately. The rest would get sorted out soon enough.

At 52, I had never lived anywhere but with my parents or in the bosom of the society since I was 17. I had no idea what to do or think. I owned nothing; I didn't even have a social security number. I felt the best solution was to move in with Monika in Clarion. I would have time to help her since I was not working elsewhere, my income would support us both for the immediate duration, I would help her with course work and direction to get her degree as quickly as possible, and the children would be better off with me there. After all, it was the children as much as their mother's health and well being that had been and continued to be my motivation. I would not have thought of doing what I now embarked on had Monika been childless, I had no interest in her as a woman but only as a mother who needed to be well enough to meet the demands of her state in life. It was a given and always understood that the children ultimately were my primary motivation. By me.

II

I packed my things, including my books and other items in my office. Bob, who had been to Monika's with me only a couple of weeks earlier, helped me load one of the larger cars, and we headed to Clarion. We unloaded the car while Monika prepared dinner. When we were done, Bob observed that Monika was adding as much wine to the dinner as to her gullet: it prompted a phrase we often remembered with fond thoughts of this kind man. "Are we having cooked stew or stewed cook?" Bob drove back alone the next morning. We kept in touch, we even visited his mother and he brought her to see us. Sadly he passed away much too soon and too young not too much later.

It wasn't until the morning after Bob had left to return to Cleveland that I realized I had no car. I called Carroll, and requested that this be corrected at once. I was told that a Plymouth Valiant was available to me at Blue Book value to be deducted from my salary.

At this point, Paul Besanceney had been elevated to Provincial and left John Carroll for Detroit. He was replaced as Superior by Bill Nichols SJ of the physics department. I was relieved. Bill came at once to get me and take me back to John Carroll to pick up the car we would affectionately call Susibell, and which would serve us well.

Bill had also brought along several bottles of Mass wine for my use. In spite of my earlier indiscretion, I had most sincerely confessed my sin and was upholding my vows. I saw no problems with saying Mass privately for us and neighbors and therefore did not request faculties (permission) from the local bishop. Bill, as my immediate superior, agreed.

All the while, the current situation here and now was preposterous. It was strange, it was awkward. The boys' bedroom had been the guest room whenever I had been there previously. Now it would be my room again, on a little more permanent basis. I also shared the children's bathroom. Monika was at the other end of the house with her own room and bath. And there were no transgressions planned or carried out.

III

For me, every day became a new adventure, the change was horrific for me. Now, in retrospect, I can readily admit that I was in a state of cultural, professional and personal shock with little adjustment assistance or ability. I took one day at a time, sometimes an hour at a time. There were countless moments when I wanted to scream in pain or head for the hills as fast as I could run. Or drive. I did not allow myself to think because the result of thought went against every fiber in my body. I had descended into a hell.

The children were terrific. Leila, a little shy, was articulate and vocal in her open welcome of me. Her sentiments were echoed by her brother Rob. Both had had their share of hardship in their short lives; Leila had served as her siblings' steady anchor without support, and provided any support of her own for herself. She was wise beyond her years. She told me of their collective fears when hearing their parents' fight, the little ones seeking comfort with her when the noise of papa hitting mommy and mommy wailing got too much.

Rob was very dear but also very evidently missed his father. It had been less than 6 months since I myself had seen the bruises on Rob's back because his father in a fit of rage had sent a shovel slamming across and into this little boy's back. Now, he asked me what he could do if anything to let his father know he'd forgiven him.

It saddened me more than once to have had a hand in trying to arrange an outing for the two for which Rob would wait for hours at the dining room window for a father who never came, time and time again. Nevertheless, Rob appeared resentful of his mother, a characteristic he appears to have carried into adulthood. In plain English, he obviously hates her guts as is clearly seen in how he treats her. Like shit. It was something I was never able to change.

150

Nadja was starting Kindergarten and did not know what to make of all the changes nor of the present, new, situation and I really did not know how or what to communicate to her. Her long hours at the Exton's home just two doors away gave her the space and escape in a safe and caring environment that she sought. I had baptized her years earlier. Now, rather than being with the rest of us, she would spend her time with the Felds, Ostrows, or Palmers as well.

At school, there were some episodes suggesting anxiety, as when she thought a little piece of clingy toilet paper surely was a tape worm which was exiting her body. I picked her up at once and brought her home. I also took her on quite a few midnight excursions to the Oil City ER because of the abrupt random onset of severe ear aches. Eventually she would have her tonsils removed, ending this difficulty in her young life. And later, we went back to the ENT doctor who ended her severe nose bleeds through cauterization.

It was Rob who would comment on my nightly drives to the emergency room with his little sister when he recalled how Steve had to suffer with a piece of metal in his foot which Papa chose to ignore. Rob was clearly torn between emotion and reason.

Stevie was an absolute delight. He clung to me like a baby Koala. Curious and inquisitive, one of the first days when he followed me into the bathroom was to cry out in shock, "You have a broken penis!" Unlike him, his brother and his father, I had not been circumcised. Stevie had also been baptized by me a few years earlier. He was just 3.

Stevie was like a sponge soaking up everything around him. I got an enormous kick out of this little tyke who attached himself to me as if glued on. What a long way this was from an incident Leila had told me about: her father kicking Steve roughly and forcefully off the bed when he was just having a little gleeful fun that quickly became trauma and tears.

I do recall driving through a toll gate with Stevie once when the attendant made the comment: "Your grandson sure uses big words." Steve's ability to use adverbs with facility was quite extraordinary for one so young; his language development advanced even then.

IV

After a couple of weeks, and Bob's second trip with the remainder of my things, I began to settle in more comfortably, and as well understand the routine that had been established with school buses and various activities. I began to feel somewhat at home. I knew it was a time limited commitment, and I felt that I could manage for less than a year. I gave no thought of what would lie beyond that year. I assumed it would be life at Rodman Hall once more.

My quarters continued to be in the guest room, and neither Monika nor I had any desire to change that or to pretend that we were anything other than what we were: friends. I attributed the June episode to the stress and pressure we were under.

It was early October when we first heard rumors that something was underfoot to have Monika declared an unfit mother because a catholic priest lived in her house, and furthermore, that the children would be taken away from her as a result of this depraved circumstance. We heard this from neighbors; there was no indication of any kind that Salih had any connection to these rumors although he probably was aware of them as well.

Not given to believing in rumors, we ignored the tattle tales until Monika's friend Mary cautioned us, and shortly thereafter, so did Betty. We never learned who had begun the malicious gossip, what if any of it was true, and whether we should be concerned with what was indicated. Both of us were incredibly naïve when it came to worldly things.

We did encounter two confrontations at a local Clarion store where a couple of families ran into us while shopping. While one made a scene, the other very obviously snubbed us visibly with much to do. It wasn't too long afterwards that we learned both marriages were facing difficulties, both separated, and one of the

152

wives sadly contrived to become pregnant in hopes of holding a husband who had already walked out the door.

We became aware of something very interesting: the people who condemned my actions the loudest, who called me crazy (Ed Carome of the Carroll physics faculty) or other things, who insulted me and Monika to our faces or behind our backs, were people who themselves had unresolved marital issues awaiting resolution such as in Ed's case, leaving Jean plus six or eight kids for a woman in the art department. But no one made him take a sabbatical! I will refer to this again later.

Once Mary apprised us of the seriousness of the allegations, we drove to Jamestown, NY, and applied for a marriage license. A week later, on a Wednesday because he had no office hours, Dr. G. Alan Haws and his wife, Mary, drove with us to Jamestown to bear witness to the civil marriage ceremony between Frank Gutowski and Monika Smith Said. It was a beautiful ride on a gorgeous fall day with the results of God's generous paint brush in evidence throughout the drive. I love fall because of how God shows off that time of year.

Following the legalities, Alan and Mary took us to a lovely restaurant for dinner, and then we all went back home. Mrs. Gladys Walter who hailed from either nearby Knox or Kossuth had spent the day with the children. We were exhausted and relieved. And we again each went to our separate rooms.

Although we were now legally united, neither of us was sure of how to deal with this new development which, like so much in the last few months, had not been in our plans or hopes or dreams or the wishes for our futures or our lives. Marriage was only a piece of paper to ascertain the children's safety and security. Otherwise, it would not exist. We had gone to Jamestown because it was far enough away and did not have the then current requirements of Pennsylvania law for obtaining marriage licenses.

Once again, we had responded to what came toward us from the outside and not what our hearts and minds directed us to do. Instead of the pro-active plans I'd formulated with Salih's

153

agreement, we were reacting to fears induced by environmental stimuli beyond our control. It was October 13th, 1971. I had work to do to get this family on its feet, and this was my time to do so before returning to Carroll once more.

V

The following week-end, I think it was Saturday, Salih came unannounced to take the children. A few hours later we received a telephone call from the police to at once drive to the Oil City ER to pick the children up. Salih had been stung by several hornets and is highly allergic. It was most upsetting to see him barely conscious with tubes everywhere, and most unsettling for the kids whose outing turned to trauma. We took them home as requested and stopped for some sandwiches at the A-frame Italian restaurant on the way out of town.

As we arrived at home, police awaited us. It appears that Salih tore the tubes loose and, barely able to navigate, left the hospital before being well enough to be discharged. An APB had been put out for him because he was considered a danger to himself as well as anyone else on the road he might encounter. Was he here? No. We had no idea where he was and it would be weeks before we heard from him again.

The next time we did see him would be memorable and again traumatic. Salih came crashing through the kitchen door, possibly inebriated…cursing and shouting that I had upset his plan. By helping Monika, I prevented him from punishing her as she deserved. He shouted that he did nothing for her financially in order to bring her to her knees. He wanted her to come begging, back to him, because of her incompetence and inability in managing on her own. He wanted to punish her with humiliation and devastation. She deserved to be punished. My presence had screwed up his plan, he had intended to allow her to flounder in Cleveland to show her how both dependent and incapable she was, that she was forced to rely on him and his benevolence because alone she was worthless and nothing. On and on, relentlessly repeating himself.

154

Luckily some neighbors who knew him arrived and ended the scene. As he left, he added that I would learn that he had to be avenged.

We would next see Salih in court. I am unsure at present, but I think it was early November, for the purpose of enforcing the child support order and in order to settle property matters. The former was settled, there were no agreements regarding the latter. Soothing the kids and Monika after those events was no simple task. I do remember that shortly following the above scene, I moved into Monika's bedroom. It was shortly before Thanksgiving. I would remain there until I believed my project complete. Neither one of us was sure of what we were doing but it felt right, it was legal, it felt good, and Monika relaxed considerably. Practice made perfect!

VI

Thanksgiving brought a surprise: a few days before the actual holiday, my brother Leo and his wife Helen came from Detroit with a fully prepared Thanksgiving dinner in the trunk of their car. We celebrated and feasted with fabulous Polish foods and American foods prepared a la Polonaise. There was a secondary motive to the gathering.

Helen believed I needed to be rescued and had convinced Leo to make the journey. She came fully prepared to physically remove me and take me back to John Carroll, where I, the pride of the family, belonged and ought to be. Somehow somewhere their daughter, my niece, Rita had told them of my activities, and now they took it upon themselves to make sure I, the kid, got back in line as told by my older brother.

It didn't take long, however, for them to see how integrated we had become, how well we all got along and how basically OK and normal everything was. They left a few days later, their mission abandoned, their ideals crushed, and their faith shaken. Sadly, I never saw Leo again; it took Helen many years to ask for me, but by then I had no desire to see her and so I didn't.

VII

I sometimes would lie awake at night, wondering how to negotiate current developments with my state in life. After all, I was both an ordained priest and a vowed Jesuit. And I really was not interested in forsaking either. I had absolutely no crisis of faith, but I was committed to a young family who had no recourse.

Finally, before Christmas, I drove to John Carroll and met with Father Superior who as already mentioned earlier was now Bill Nichols, for the purpose of applying for laicization. Bill was stunned. But then so was I. Neither he nor I had the faintest idea whether this could even be attained, and even if, what the length of the process would be. And if, then what would happen? I told Bill that we had had a civil ceremony because of our fears regarding the children, I also told him that just a couple of weeks ago I had made my move into Monika's bedroom, that till then we did indeed lead celibate lives, and I also confessed to the June-July episodes.

Surprisingly, it was Bill who astutely put his finger on matters and lifted any guilt. Whereas I might have been more willing and ready than able, Monika's libido would not budge as long as she held the slightest hope of salvaging a marriage. Finding the condoms indicated infidelity, the one thing she would not tolerate or get passed, and the straw that broke the camel's back of trying, of principle, in spite of the other enormous problems and difficulties.

Apparently it is one of those commonly held beliefs that men may stray randomly at will, but that women, at least 50 years ago, were not inclined to do so as long as they believed in the sanctity of their marriages. For women, an affair was a flag announcing, "it's over, it ended, I am free."

Although I had heard of this before (didn't I actually already include the concept somewhere along the line on these pages crediting someone else?), it would be much much later during one of our discussions that Monika did tell me that indeed, she could have never kissed me let alone anything else, because she was committed to her state in life, maybe even more to it than to Salih himself. Principles and honor superseded matters of instinct, desire, want or need. The appearance of condoms had ended any of that.

When I left Bill's office, I fully expected to return to John Carroll for the fall semester, but in a slightly altered state. Instead of a priest wearing a cassock, I would be a lay man with a family, just like most of the rest of my faculty peers.

VIII

It was around the 1971 Christmas holidays that Monika began to complain of ever increasing pains in her abdomen. At times she doubled over with pain. We made an appointment with her gynecologist in Cleveland a few days later and as well with the kids pediatrician, in order to take care of both on the same day in the same location. It was January 1972.

Dr. Glove's examination and test results indicated a potentially dangerous tumor on one of Monika's ovaries and immediate surgery for its removal was indicated.

The tests indicated an additional diagnosis: although not with 100% certainty, there were early indications that Monika was, in all likelihood, also pregnant. There was no assurance at this early stage, pending further testing for accuracy a little later. This created complications as the surgery could possibly be contraindicated or jeopardize Monika.

In 1972 even an unintentional abortion was illegal, and only under the most special circumstances could an exception be made; waiting to be positive was too risky because of the nature of the tumor. Monika's pain and my concerns overruled any other considerations. We did not, for a single second, consider potential implications of possible life, religious perspectives or other issues of morals or ethics in line with catholic teachings. Our sole overriding concern was Monika's pain and prognosis as well as the four children who needed their mother. We followed Dr. Glove's direction without question.

Dr. Glove, the head of OB/GYN at St. Luke's Hospital, made all arrangements such as consultations with other doctors including a psychiatrist. Just like Dr. Glove had said for some time, it was the latter's opinion any further pregnancies were detrimental to Monika's mental health given post partum depressive episodes that appeared to have increased in severity during the two pregnancies Dr. Glove supervised.

This gave the green light to perform the operation. At the same time, Monika would have the tubal ligation that Dr. Glove had already recommended since her last delivery but could not perform without her husband's consent. I concurred. I was also now in a position to sign the necessary documents. I never gave a single moment's thought to how that would relate to catholic teaching. Actually, it never occurred to me till now as I write of these past events that those thoughts had not entered my mind at that time. Back then, the immediacy of suffering and circumstance precluded any reflection whatsoever.

Unsure of whether Monika was covered by anyone's health insurance, Dr. Glove was incredible: we never got a bill from him, nor from any other attending doctor, nor from the hospital.

Miraculously and totally unexpected, Monika's mother and her husband Lew had agreed to come to take care of the children. Monika was shocked and surprised that her mother actually came through when needed. Apparently it was a first. She was sure that the new husband, Lew Hopps, deserved a lot of the credit and he said so himself. He would hear of nothing else other than being there for a child and grandchildren when any kind of emergency such as this arose.

It was obvious when we returned home that Monika's mother was overwhelmed by the household activities surrounding four children, but she had done what she could and the children were safe and taken care of. We were grateful. There was a positive spill over effect: Monika's mother had been keenly critical of her housekeeping and related activities, referring to not only her own competence and excellence in home management which she had actually formally studied, but she had never factored 4 children into the whole! Now she gained a new appreciation for both Monika's and my new-found competence. It was a milestone!

Monika's recovery was uncomplicated and she soon was back on her feet. The biopsy reports came back negative and explained the tumor consisted of hair, nails, and other derma related materials. The lab reports affirmed an early stage pregnancy that had been terminated, but there was no evidence of cancer.

I was relieved all around: for Monika, for the children, and for the progress of my project without additional impediments in an already difficult situation. I would not have wanted a child at my age and with my new found responsibilities. For Monika, it was a matter of physical and mental health.

Roe v. Wade would come into being a year later but for us right then and there, there was no moral or ethical debate on the subject at the time nor would there be later on. The procedures performed were a D&C, a tubal ligation, and the removal of a benign ovarian tumor. At the time, Monika's nerves had settled down considerably, but I still harbored some concerns. I also wondered how many D&C's that were so frequently performed at that time included similar circumstances. I still wonder about that.

Next on my agenda was to find a good psychiatrist near our home into whose care I hoped to commend Monika. I did so, though I don't remember who recommended him. Mary? Betty? Leah? Does it matter? I made an appointment, and took Monika to see Dr. James Markham in Oil City at his office right near the hospital to which I'd been before.

IX

This is as good a time as any to talk a little about Monika, the woman whose unfortunate situation prompted a good part of my story. A brief overview of her life is not out of line at this point, because her visits to Dr. Markham unfolded much that had gotten her to where she now found herself, and me as well. Her mother's role in our lives would also become quite significant.

Initially, I took Monika quite often to see Dr. Markham but after a few weeks, her appointments were scheduled only once weekly and not too long after that, reduced to bi-weekly.

His assessment and opinions were formed quite quickly. He saw no need for any medications, indicated no evidence of any major mental illness or related diagnoses of grave concern. He saw no indications of character disorders, nor what I understood to be psychotic behaviors. He furthermore decried the earlier Thorazine episode as the all too frequent and unfortunate inappropriately prescribed medications by someone outside of one's medical specialty. He did provide Monika with some sleeping pills if needed to help her rest because Monika complained of frequent repetitive nightmares that interfered with restful sleep. Monika felt no need to take them, but stored them away.

At various times I would participate at Monika's appointments because Dr. Markham felt it would benefit me as well. I liked Dr. Markham. He and I developed a great deal of personal and professional respect for each other, in the interest of his client and my charge. I could not utter wife, it was foreign and anathema to me, regardless of my true dedication. Monika was and remained a term limited project which I intended to carry out in full.

She as well as I had lost control of our lives, plans and selves. Monika had put so much energy and effort into what she believed to be a marriage, its demise was incomprehensible to her. She truly mourned and grieved. Sometimes she appeared inconsolable. She had at an earlier point once visited Salih in an attempt to communicate calmly on the many unsettled issues. To no avail, the visit was a disappointment and emotionally devastating. She would not make a second attempt. When thereafter the divorce was indeed final, legal, and the end of that would-be union that had in actuality ended long before then, she lacked the capacity to accept it, even though she had initiated it. She bore some responsibility, yet would or could not see her part in this. Reality was very sad and bitter, accepting it very difficult. How deeply wounded Monika had been would become evident over the lengthy time of the healing process.

It was those times that made me question my decision. It made me feel inadequate, and it made me feel helpless. I can only say that thanks to the insight and support of Dr. Markham, those times became fewer and further in between as Monika learned to accept her own mistakes, take responsibility for her own actions, and to forgive herself for initial faulty judgment: she should have never married Salih because she was as unfair to him as to herself; her lack of marriage preparation, maturity, or knowledge of what marriage or family entailed and then blaming herself for whatever faults, accidents or mistakes was pointless because none were made intentionally or willfully.

Ultimately I managed to make the point that if God forgave her, could she herself do less? That worked. We were much happier and at peace.

In other words, there was nothing wrong with Monika herself. She lacked experience and exposure to the normal, the norm, the mundane, average, customary and ordinary. At issue was to bring her up to speed, to teach patiently, to mentor, guide, help, praise, support, instruct and encourage. Monika was living in the world but she'd never acquired the skills to be of the world or as part of the environment in which she was physically located. Some of the causes for her difficulties also originated in her being moved from Austria to the US, too long to go into here, and as well, the exposure to wartime. The prescription was lots of TLC, together with educating and mentoring.

This was meat and potatoes for me. It was just what a great Jesuit teacher does best! My role of savior and rescuer now took on more direct and practical importance by adding another dimension. My attention would include taking care of Monika to a greater degree than I had anticipated but somewhat differently. I would be guiding and teaching her in word and deed, along with the children. I realized this was more involved than I had intended to become. And, although this was a lot more than I had bargained

161

for, this was the heart of the matter. Good old Zurlinden had been right, after all, exhorting me to marry. This now was what marriage was all about.

Monika's only presenting complaints had been how she hated Clarion; she refused to discuss anything pertaining to her mother or their relationship. Dr. Markham felt an exploration into Monika's feelings regarding her mother was warranted, because she so vehemently had insisted that the subject was off limits. I did not participate in those discussions. All I knew is that Monika did not want her mother around, really tried to get along, but was constantly put on the defensive, a defensive she handled poorly and turned into verbal slug fests on paper.

I also learned early on, and would do so in giant increments as time went on, that Monika's mother could not be stopped when she decided on whatever she decided on, regardless of anyone else's feelings, opinions, wishes or wants. After all, I had had my first taste of her at the Trivisonno's years earlier, and it was nasty. Somehow she had become totally convinced of her own consistent entitlement regardless of issue at hand.

In the course of her therapy, Monika developed self efficacy and self assurance. She shed a lot of the negatives she'd both absorbed and integrated during the years of verbal and emotional abuse which had begun early in her life, and that had been a lot more permanently damaging than the bruises which had eventually healed over time. The invisible scars lingered and festered. Eventually, Dr. Markham suggested to Monika what he considered some positive steps to transcend the past, and correct the present while opening herself to really great future possibility. He didn't just suggest. He put his money where his mouth was and made it happen.

X

One of the complaints Salih had had was Monika's lack of a college degree. At the same time, her diligent efforts to rectify this situation were thwarted by his impromptu move to Clarion without thought or consideration beyond his own feelings of pride. The financial situation made it clear that after attempting a couple of courses at Clarion state for one semester that the expenses were too great, the costs too high when she would have to take an additional full time year's worth of courses to have enough credit to graduate. In addition, she would have to change majors because Clarion had no sociology department (at least then) which added even more course work. Completing college would open up new possibilities for Monika, something that I myself had already considered earlier. But it would do an additional thing I had also hoped to effect: get her out of Clarion.

Dr. Markham saw a lot of Monika's difficulties as Clarion related. Monika was a fish out of water, a canoe without a paddle up s—t creek, totally out of place in Clarion. She had good friends, but the overall life style was something that exceeded her adjustment capacity.

Moving there had been a grievous mistake, considering, and one she had attempted to avoid by voicing her objections before it took place. Unfortunately, it was the dynamics between the two plus Salih's own background that had him ignore her pleas. This mistake had been avoidable, and would have been under other circumstances. Her adjustment difficulties were extensive enough even in a more, to her, amenable setting without adding the isolation or desolation of a county that had more deer than people, no public transportation, and was at a distance too great for a single day's change of scenery. On top of that, some of the friends she so easily made came and would again leave the area just as fast. They too felt similarly, were able to gain jobs elsewhere, leaving her to feel even more isolated and abandoned. Yes, college would be a way out.

Both Monika and I explained the presenting financial constraints in time and dollars to Dr. Markham. Within weeks, he had obtained necessary forms, information, details and the ins and outs of submitting Monika's application to the Pennsylvania Department of Rehabilitation citing that her health and well being were, due to present circumstances, in jeopardy of further deterioration unless she were able to adequately prepare herself for gainful employment. Or something to that effect.

Long story short, starting in early 1973, PA-Rehab agreed to pay all college and related expenses such as books and fees plus a living and transportation allowance. For the two plus years that Monika attended Clarion State College, Monika's benefits were the equivalent of entry level work in a profession. In addition, her student and our financial status qualified her for low interest loans with PHEAA, the Pennsylvania Higher Education Assistance Act, for each of the two years she studied for the completion of her BA.

Monika finished her course work and had one grade of "I" to complete in Economics 102 in the fall of 1975. Nadja's tonsillectomy had taken her from the classroom and besides, she didn't like economics and procrastinated. John Bodoh, both Dean and family friend, turned it into an F, telling Monika that she had enough on her plate and he would adjust an elective to serve in its place. Monika was as relieved as she was angry because of her GPA. Nevertheless, she had matriculated at last after 16 years of effort.

When he wrote about us a year later, Jeremy Main referred to Monika as growing up in New England, the poorly adjusted child of an upper middle class family. He would also refer to her initial foray into the graduate world jungle: She wanted to continue to an MSW, applied to Smith and was turned down, not for academic reasons but because of logistics: she couldn't drive, needed a placement, and had to be available to attend periodic conferences. These were all impossibilities from her location. It would be Nadja who eventually realized Monika's dream of a Smith degree some 14 years later.

I am, however, getting way ahead of myself. Monika may have been busy studying, but it was my life that would experience a killer upheaval and devastation in the next spring.

THE UNEXPECTED: FEAR AND CHANGE

I

We Jesuits became captives of the Society in adolescence, and would be enfolded by its system till we expired. Our lives were based on tradition and principle which were as firm as Gibraltar and equally immoveable. We were imbued with a certain series of convictions. These included the adherence to a set of externals giving way to the formation of our esprit de corps as well as steady growth in spirituality.

Vatican II rattled the entire system. Instead of a fresh breath of air, it rumbled like an earthquake through institutions and organizations within the church and outside it. Among these, the Society of Jesus.

Our lives were as if governed by the beats of an evenly ticking metronome, the cadence and rhythm of the beat that had sustained Jesuit life for generations. Suddenly the winds of change blew through our stable structure as if it were flimsy scaffolding. We in the US swayed as if we were bamboo in Bangkok, especially the older priests who knew nothing else and believed that nothing else could or would exist in life - AMDG.

Change is a difficult thing to accept; it can be impossible to adapt to it. The more deeply ingrained…read the older we are…the harder it becomes. The Jesuits faced sudden and abrupt change as a community and an order themselves. Pedro Arrupe died in the midst of the alterations. Catholicism underwent a catharsis, and no place more so than in the US where much of it was welcomed with open arms by a public ready for it. Not so within the walls of Jesuit life.

It wasn't just language with the cessation of the Latin vulgate's use. Or food and drink, or new rules about fasting or abstinence. We lost our bells, those incantatory systolic beats of our training in formation. Once the bells were gone, what was left? Who really cared that much about whether we read at table because most of us were gone half the time anyway and the other half of us had our thoughts engaged elsewhere. Who really cared about whether we wore cassocks or black suits or sweaters, sport shirts and shorts? Whether we arose praising God or retired giving Him thanks? We could and would and did henceforth and so on, if we chose to, totally on our own.

But the bells! Nothing could replace them even if we didn't need reminders. Were only they symbolic of really what being a Jesuit was all about? What about spirituality? Godliness? Christ-like living? Caritas?

If I wasn't then I am at least now uncertain just what that really meant. What was the esprit de corps of a group of men who had allowed one of their company to die alone and not be found till he smelled? And a growing spirituality? Just what does that really mean? We didn't aspire to become holy, we aspired to be the best that we could be within the parameters of our lives and the expectations placed on us. Holiness and sainthood were accidental by-products of a life well lived or in modern times, lost in the pursuit of excellence for Christ's sake: martyrdom.

As the years have passed, my perspective on religion has changed considerably. Oddly, I have no qualms nor issues with the teachings of the Roman Catholic Church as it relates to the Life of Christ, His Mystical Body or the Communion of Saints. I believe

166

in the Old Testament's fulfillment with the New and its Trinity. But I have a lot of issues like so many Catholics and other Christians of several denominations about the place of the church, a man made organization, in the world. The need for a clergy or the place it now attempts to occupy. My faith today in my eighties is as strong as it has ever been. My faith in God, the Trinity, the redemptive aspects, and the life in a hereafter are firm. Is it important to fast on Ash Wednesday, not eat meat on Fridays during Lent, attend weekly Mass regularly, and tithe? HELL NO.

God in all His magnificence couldn't care less about us little worms and our activities day to day as long as we abide by the guidelines He gave to Moses. God did NOT dictate the commandments of the church! Those came from a group of men obsessed with controlling and manipulating for their own gain. How else did the Vatican get so rich!

God is much too busy running the universe. And yes, I do believe He runs every nuance and detail, including those of our lives, in as well as with His Benevolence. I just don't have to slide around on my knees to give Him credence and worship! Or say any suggested set or litany of proscribed prayers. Nor do I believe in funding any one group proclaiming it knows better than the next group in what form or structure He expects adoration. Religion by definition proclaims itself for the good; men running it may or may not follow.

And what about tolerance? Because my church teaches the evils of abortion, does that mean I have the right to curtail your ability to obtain a medically safe, sanctioned and insurance covered procedure when YOUR faith believes life begins at birth or quickening as opposed to mine which believes conception is the prime moment. I abhor the lack of tolerlance among catholics, and the meddling of Catholic Bishops in American politics when it comes to matters of health, welfare, and other social matters that serve their own intentions more than their flocks'. A good example is the take-over of Catholic hospitals that will not allow any number of procedures to be performed for religious reasons, depriving their patients of access. And Benedict, the Nazi Torquemada of the twenty first century, represents a loving God? P-lease!

I think He doesn't give a damn about buildings and formats, but how well I live my life thanks to the grace which He gives me. God expects me to be tolerant and loving, and to be the best that I can be. I've become a strong advocate for the corporal works of mercy, a lot more than the purposes of the Church's commandments. Increase taxes to meet the deficit, don't cut entitlement programs for those less fortunate while the rich get richer. Just when and where are we our brother's keepers?

If Proverbs speaks of the Virtuous Woman, then I am the Just Man. Once again, my thoughts are wandering, reign me in and let's get back to March 1972.

II

Bill Nichols called me in mid-March to request I come to Cleveland and meet with him. As usual and to be efficient, Monika called and ascertained appointment times both for her own overdue post-surgery check up with Dr. Glove, and for the kids' routine doctor visits with Dr. Friedman.

As luck would have it, the schedule of appointments spanned two days, plus I did not know when or how much time I would need to meet with Bill which meant no transportation for Monika and kids. What to do? I called Lois Hopkins.

It had been some time since I had spoken with Lois or seen her and Bill. Not only had they not thought that my ideas were good, nor viable, but I had really behaved badly at their home and continued to have all kinds of guilt feelings for crashing drunk through the buffet table at their daughter Mary's wedding. What a mess I had made in my alcohol induced merriment. (Now, not having had a drop for a few years, I regret it even more.)

When I asked Lois if Monika, the kids and I could come to their house, I got an immediate positive response. "Come, stay, call us so we know when, we're looking forward to it. Of course you're having dinner with us, and we'll arrange for sleeping space."

When we later got there, it was like old home week or homecoming for me. Monika and the kids found themselves in the bosom of a huge loving family like they had never experienced before. They fit right in with the Hopkins' twelve children, most in residence, and Leila and Rob were the same ages as Jazzer (Jim) and Ginny (Virginia), Nadja and Steve were the children that just hadn't be added by Lois and Bill. And Schatzi the dog was a loveable mutt not unlike our own Schatzi the Dachshund.

Our visit to the Hopkins would be the first of countless such visits, each one gave us an infusion of love, of what family life was all about, advice on child rearing both what to do and what not to do, and so much more I can't even list it all. Lois was absolutely super, Bill the steadfastness that I wanted to mirror, and the kids....fantastic. That included ours among them!

III

My meeting with Bill Nichols was less joyful. Since I had been his "boss" in the physics department, and was his senior both in the Society and in age, Bill found it very awkward to have been given the job of hatchet man. He apologized. He told me it was not his doing nor his choice. He hemmed and hawed before getting to the point.

But first, and without much ado he asked me how things were going, how life among the family was turning out for me as well as for them, and how I felt about this new role in my life. Bill knew I was married, but because it had been told to him in confession, the knowledge was a confidential matter. In the role as Father Superior he had no such knowledge, and as a representative of the Provincial and the Order, he asked me if I intended to return to religious life in community at Carroll. He informed me that my leave of absence from the Order, as well as my sabbatical from the University, would soon end, and that my return would automatically reinstate me fully. Understandably, the University wanted to know who its projected faculty would be for the fall semester.

In retrospect, the fact that Harry Nash had usurped my place so surreptitiously and instantaneously, moving into an office that was still officially mine, never came up. I wonder what the plan for me actually was. Was I to boot Harry back out of the position he had coveted far too long? No matter, it never came up.

Furthermore, Bill assured me that any legalities would easily be "rectified", alluding to the fact that I was married without actually saying so and retaining the confidential nature of this information. The Society had ways and means to adjust that which it considered important, expedient, and necessary.

I obviously was taken aback. I had not expected this. Actually, I had not expected anything except next year's contract as the reason for Bill's earlier call.

Now I learned that next year's contract had not come because there would be none unless I complied as indicated. Bill could not look me in the eye. I am certain that he was as much at a loss as I was shocked. I couldn't think fast enough to say anything at all.

The pregnant silence was broken by Bill with the next bomb shell: it had been decided and approved that whatever it would take to pay Monika off and get her both out of my life and far away from the Jesuit Community's field of vision had been approved. I just had to name the dollar figure. The rest was just logistics that would be taken care of.

I don't think I knew what shock was until that moment. I wasn't just shot full force fatally in the chest. I was about to be inundated by the Tsunami-like force of a clever, astute, highly educated, articulate, and incredibly cruel machine that lacked feeling, compassion, caring or the capacity to comprehend what Christ was all about.

Inhuman describes it well. Nietzsche and "Deus ex machina" took on new meaning! Was God really dead, and the Jesuits were the first to know? Had they killed Him? Or, at least as far as they were concerned, did their discernment supersede the essence of His teaching? The dialectic might be used to rationalize anything.

They had replaced the God of Abraham and Jesus with the golden calf of dollar signs, thinking not only that money could buy anything but reducing Monika to a whore, a thing, an object to be bandied about at will or with enough loot. Dear dear Father Zurlinden! Wasn't one of the reasons she had suffered so with Salih that she had been treated like chattel? And now, here, more of the same. A bunch of old misogynists dismissing the honorable course of honorable people seen with their myopic vision through a looking glass, most darkly.

I would not tell Monika of the insult heaped on her, she'd had enough in her life without such as this. It would be months before she knew.

"Pfui Teufel!", Monika would say eventually when she heard this. But not without commenting, "we should have taken the money, it would have turned into a win win situation for all of us long term with minimal impact on anyone and our relationship would not have been affected." I can't say I agree, I don't know. At that very moment, then, I was so outraged and disgusted with my fellow Jesuits for even suggesting such a course of action, that I ended the meeting and left.

There was more to come.

JOB REWRITTEN

I

It would take a while for me to recover from the shock. My salary would still come for another five or so months as I had extended the 9 months into 12 payments. Beyond that, I had no ideas at all. I did tell our friends what had transpired, and Jose Garcia immediately suggested legal advice, as did Peter Konitzky – two Clarion State faculty members. I had never dealt with a lawyer in Cleveland or anywhere else for that matter except across a bridge table. Monika suggested I call Judge Joseph Nahra. I did and he recommended a law firm, and from its staff, Lucille Huston.

The most difficult, heart wrenching, hopeless, helpless and non-productive period of my life was about to begin. Lucille and one of her associates and I would meet countless hours on countless days in pursuit of an avenue that would either retain my academic status on the faculty of John Carroll University, or reinstate me, or compensate me for any losses.

My goal was simply to continue as lay faculty the way most of the faculty lived. I could see no difference in walking over to Rodman Hall or driving a few miles from my home. I didn't necessarily have to be chairman, but I did intend to teach.

Teaching was my first love, the only thing I knew and had ever done in life, and physics was the subject that I had been educated to teach.

There was much agreement in several other academic communities which had become aware of John Carroll's actions, it seemed to them that this was a non-issue. I had heard via the grapevine that John Carroll had contacted Salih in order to formulate a case against me. I could not imagine what or how, but their behavior increased my disgust while it affirmed the decisions I had made.

II

Finally, John Carroll presented its case in response to my request to honor my tenured position. I stood accused of insinuating myself into a marriage in the guise of priest and upon Salih's request, as a marriage counselor, causing its demise, and considered to constitute both grave misconduct and moral turpitude. These two constitute the only two causes for which a tenured faculty member could be dismissed.

The number and magnitude of shocks was starting to leave me numb. As I reflect on those days and their events, I realize I could write or dictate or scribble notes for Monika's transcription which would take longer than I might expect to live. Tons.

Now, nearly 30 years later, I look back on the small minds, insignificant intellects and above all, uncharitable souls so devoid of what they proclaimed themselves to be. Even if Monika, who has just completed another graduate degree at Loyola, Maryland, has assured me things have changed, and that I had been at the wrong place at the wrong time, too near Vatican II and what had been expected to be reactionary behavior among religious conservatives such as Jesuits. I am too old now to bother. Then, I was badly wounded and when I was down, they chose to kick me even harder. That to me is neither Christ-like nor at the level of the Humanism the Society expounds.

Now, in my 80's, this period was a lot of water over the dam of my life that simply got backed up. I pity all those who were willing to malign me, falsely accuse me, and who tapped into Salih's hatred, anger and vengefulness by exhorting him to perjure himself under oath. This, to me, is an unconscionable act before God, the Constitution and our Judicial System. The number of insinuations and lies perpetrated by the Society and/or the University were mostly just that, lies. And they held about an equal amount of water: zero.

I had had no prior exposure to the double standards with which the Society conducted itself. Indeed, I found it shocking to see the lengths to which they would go to proclaim themselves self-righteously, under the most incriminating circumstances.

For example, I knew perfectly well that one of my Jesuit confreres would cavort annually in New York City with the affluent wife of a bridge partner — as did others--, but everyone closed their eyes. The self same Jesuit now testified that Monika would call him at 3AM even citing a specific date, to indicate her instability. It just so happened that Monika did not know him or for that matter, his phone number even less so. On the designated date we were asleep together, it was long after our marriage. Who needed this kind of crap? "No one is such a liar as the indignant man" (Nietzsche). In this case, men=Jesuits.

Finally, let it all be on their conscience, and let a just God decide. I am reminded of the late Bishop then still Msgr. Gaughan who made a silk screen for Monika during this time which reads: "It is a terrible thing to fall into the hands of a just God." Indeed, we did- both short term and long term. And so will all others. Emphasis on "Just".

While attorneys harangued, I was also busy. Lucille had reviewed everything we said and did and listed for her. She had even received letters from Monika's mother exhorting her to help us, referring to and reflecting on the horrible circumstances from which I had liberated her daughter, and including nothing more than a few negatives about Salih. I still have a copy of at least one of her letters. I like to remember her from that.

Although Lucille was not a Catholic, she learned a lot from me about Catholicism, and felt we had to be squeaky clean in compliance with not only our faith, but our Church. In simple terms, that meant we had not married in church and as all good Catholics know, that meant we were living in sin. We really should marry in church. Well, that wasn't the easiest of assignments since Monika was divorced. On the other hand, I know enough about theology, church teachings, and procedures and agreed to at least give it a shot. In the event we could succeed, great. And if nothing else, we would gain some important time and show good faith by trying.

III

One simple procedural thing I knew was the importance of jurisdiction. One cannot simply walk into a parish and request whatever. Monika had gotten married in the Diocese of Providence, Rhode Island. She had already told me of the complications surrounding the case which would mean they had extensive documentation. We wrote to them at once.

Providence replied and informed us that they had transferred jurisdiction of the matter to Greensburg, PA and not Erie in whose Diocese we resided. No reason for this determination was given. We contacted the Greensburg Diocese, and requested that we be put in touch with the marriage tribunal. We learned that they had already received all pertinent files. I do not recall what the date of our initial trip to Greensburg was, but my guess is that it must have been late spring early summer 1972, and not much later than that.

Directed to the Diocesan Chancery Office, we were introduced to Monsignor (later Bishop of Gary, Ind.) Norbert Gaughan who would supervise the handling of Monika's petition when she completed the application process. It was a very lengthy process in which every nuance and detail was considered to play a major part. There would be many meetings with Msgr. Gaughan, many forms to fill out and extensive statements to prepare.

Monika's was a difficult case, as I was about to learn. We are presently now working on this section together for obvious reasons.

Initially, it appears that Monika and Salih considered themselves married as of the beginning of April, 1962. Both

176

were too naïve or unfamiliar with what the legal marriage process entailed. They had met the preceding Christmas Eve at a party. They began to date afterwards. During the last week of March, having reached the age of majority on March 23rd, Monika joined Salih in his efficiency apartment appreciating that at last she was 21 and if not ready for self determination, then at least legally able. It was Monika's first and only real relationship with anyone. Salih knew Iraqi habits, not the legalities of the US.

About a week later, it was during the birthday party for friend and fellow graduate student that Abdul Rahim Al-Khital delighted in seeing Salih so happy with Monika. After a brief repartee, he officiously declared them married according to Islam and its customs as he knew them. April 5th. Monika remembers details of Rahim's birthday and the many guests joining in the change of venue on behalf of the young couple.

While that was fine for them at the time, it wasn't long before Monika and Salih learned that Rahim's sweet incantations were officially meaningless according to law, and if they wanted to get married, they had to do so after blood tests, applications, and so on as mandated by Rhode Island. By the time all the requirements had been met, it was the end of the month. The license was finally issued in the first days of May.

No wedding date had been set at this point. When Monika approached her local parish the same week, St. John's on Atwells Avenue in Providence, in order to learn what would have to be done to arrange for a marriage ceremony, the pastor was away and his absence was expected to be of considerable length.

In his place was a Dominican priest from Providence College whose function was primarily to pinch hit while retaining his teaching position at the college. A very kind man, he gave Salih and Monika some general guidelines and informed them that the completion of a fairly lengthy course of instruction about marriage would have to be completed before other applications would be given consideration and a final scheduling of the ceremony made.

177

The instructions were to begin within the week, Father wanted to assure that everything would be completed and in order before the return of the pastor later on. And so, Salih and Monika went to St. John's for as many sessions as were required as conducted by a college professor who just happened to also be a substitute priest (how well I know all about those!) for the duration. I gather from what Monika says with a lot of subsequently gained wisdom and experience, the sessions consisted of the blind leading the blind blindly in regards to marriage related material. The evenings were most pleasantly turned into interesting discussions about Middle East politics, and other then current topics.

The required number of sessions were completed and documented. Salih had no qualms about signing the most important required document presented to him after extensive explanation and discussion: his solemn promise to assure that any children born of the marriage would be baptized and raised within the Catholic faith. After the successful completion of all mandated matters, they bade farewell to the kindly Dominican.

When the pastor returned, things were scheduled to continue. It was now June. Instead, things took a detour. While he approved of the pre-Cana instruction and noted that Monika's certificates attesting to her receipt of prior sacraments were adequate, he also informed Monika and Salih that a marriage between a Catholic and an Infidel could not take place unless certain dispensations were given. Requesting those would be a lengthy and difficult process that would have to be carried out by a Diocesan Office, not a local parish – and with that, he referred them to the Diocese.

Because of her Austrian heritage, Monika had already become acquainted with a German speaking Hungarian priest, Msgr. Varsanyi. The latter had since become Chancellor of the Diocese, and was anything but enthralled with Salih and Monika's plans. He also informed them that an American Diocese also had no jurisdiction when it came to approving a marriage between an Infidel and a Catholic. If they really wanted to pursue the matter, it would have to be decided by the Apostolic Nuncio in Washington. He alone could make the appropriate decisions. The matter was sent to Washington. It would take several weeks before a decision was handed down to the Diocesan Chancery. REQUEST DENIED.

It is my contention that at that point Monika wasn't just furious and desperate, but rather, that she became like a barn stormer assaulting ecclesiastical offices, representatives and most particularly, Msgr. Varsanyi who was only the messenger.

Monika's period was due and didn't come. Earlier she had lit candles in the Franciscan Chapel down town praying for pregnancy ASAP because she feared abandonment as Soraya had recently experienced. God or biology responded.

She had also, since the time that the matter had gone to Washington, visited a good friend, the father of a fellow boarding school student from Portugal, who was a physician. Dr. Seabra affirmed that she was pregnant and happily congratulated Salih and her on the good news, promising to do all he could to guide her to delivery when the time came, at Roger Williams Hospital. (Which he indeed would then do.)

For one so young, inexperienced and naïve, Monika actually gave a good argument for her position. She had been told that if Salih had not been obligated and as well also desired to return to Iraq when his studies were complete, a dispensation might have been more seriously considered. With a probable move to Iraq, it was felt that her own faith could become jeopardized and that therefore the Sacrament of Matrimony would be denied her.

Monika eloquently wrote in rebuttal that God's gifts and graces bestowed when receiving a Sacrament and its inherent blessings were God's way for strengthening her against the eventualities they so quickly suggested. That in Iraq, the importance of the Sacrament could make the difference between a faithful life lived fully and a life without the comfort of faith. Moreover, Salih had signed all suggested and required documents assuring that any children born of their union would be both baptized and raised according to Catholic teachings and what kind of example did

179

such a prejudicial decision demonstrate to him, already insulted with the word Infidel, when he was a devout believer in the mercies of Allah who, after all, was God.

Astounded by her eloquence, Msgr. Varsanyi told Monika that he would forward her case directly to the Vatican, and also add the news of the impending birth of Salih and Monika's first child. It was now sometime early or mid September.

I myself find Monika's sense of conviction and faith pretty awesome for someone only 21. The fact that she refused to use the marriage license sitting on some shelf waiting to expire in order to fully adhere to church teachings in spite of the advancing pregnancy back in 1962 also spoke in her favor-from a church perspective. Salih was both more conservative, practical and concerned. He wanted to be sure the child would be legally born within wedlock and the clock was ticking.

By the end of September, Monika became Msgr. Varsanyi's daily phone call. Any news yet? O great(yuk)! Vatican II delayed everything in Rome, requests regarding such mundane matter as a dispensation for marriage had little if any priority regardless of extenuating circumstances. On the morning of October 3rd once again, there was no news. The license would expire at the end of the day. It would mean new blood tests, document scrutiny, official translations, and applications, none of which were cheap or easily had.

At noon, Salih came down town and met Monika's elevator as she came out to lunch from the Turks Head Building. He carried a lovely bouquet of flowers in his hand, took Monika's elbow and walked with her to the Rhode Island Superior Court where he produced the nearly expired marriage license for the justice of the peace who married them both in a few minutes, attended by some court staff, whom Salih tipped generously. Then he and Monika walked back across the canal, up Westminster Street to the entrance of the Turks Head Building and he watched as the elevator door closed behind her for the work-afternoon.

It would be another three months before Rome responded. This time, it was in the affirmative. Monika and Salih had moved into Blessed Sacrament Parish by then and she called the rectory at once. That same evening, January 3rd 1963, in the sacristy because the sanctuary was denied them in their religiously mixed marriage, Monika and Salih formally exchanged their vows and promises before God, their witnesses, Marlene and Nicky Cesino, and her mother. Six weeks later, the same priest, Father Maynard, would baptize Leila Marie attended by a broadly beaming father and triumphant mother.

This then, in totality, is what constituted the entire case presented for consideration. Msgr. Gaughan sighed audibly. He would call us.

IV

In the meantime, the academic wheels were whirring. John Carroll insisted on a formal hearing within its confines. One might call it a kangaroo court. Lucille was not in favor of it, she wanted to take the matter public. She was also running for political office and was looking for a constitutional legal feather in her cap that she hoped I would put there to advance her political standing.

John Carroll's entire case hinged on proving my moral turpitude and grave misconduct. To futher its position, it had engaged Salih with what I was later told was more than adequate and very desirable compensation to testify. They were counting on making their case based on his testimony that I had de facto wormed my way into his home and destroyed it in the process. It started out well, but their momentum got lost very quickly.

Carroll's lawyers presented all kinds of evidence which would have been laughable had it not been so maliciously intended to destroy me and my credibility. They had me wining and dining Monika all over the East Side of Cleveland, practically promenading to draw attention to ourselves, giving times and places, situations and occasions.

Fortunately, Lucille had been prepared for such tactics and with my schedule, and the support of friends and documented

181

alibis nothing whatsoever could be made of it because none of it happened nor was any of it either true or accurate. I already talked about any and all contacts and their occasions earlier. I now gladly recited them here, once more, under oath.

Salih's testimony was called upon. He first talked about how he participated in Cana conferences to learn how to be a good husband in a Catholic marriage. He named when and where he had begged me to be the marriage counselor he so desperately needed with the problems his wife gave him. He was the wronged and jilted husband trying to support a wife and many children, all of whom born according to the Catholic church's ban on birth control, and with his full support of their catholic upbringing after he himself assured their baptisms. He put it on so thick that the hardest heart would melt in response to his pain and suffering. Meek and mellow. I never blamed him although I found his willingness pathetic; he had, after all, fallen into the Jesuits' hands.

Until he was confronted with facts, such as: Monika's health and what his role was in helping her become well; how he helped her overcome her serious post partum depression in 1968 and its lingering effects; what of or about his visits with her physician as a result of the latter's request, (there were none) and more of the same. His verbal and physical abuse was also questioned. Yes, of course, she didn't meet his standards and expectations. He listed a variety of complaints that really were immaterial to the issues at hand. When asked if he ever hit or punched her/his wife, he looked around the room and answered in a strong voice: "Of course, doesn't everybody?"

The assembled gentry shuddered. Nevertheless, although not overtly considered guilty as charged, we were informed that the University would not reinstate me to my position. We went to civil court. On assignment, we learned that the case would be heard in Federal Court. The ACLU, AAUP and OEO all provided briefs of support for my reinstatement.

182

V

Federal court threw all of the earlier hearing who-shot-John testimony suggested by John Carroll's charges out, whatever the proper legal term for this is. Instead, it took a different approach based on the charges Carroll had brought against me. In the matters of insinuation or counseling, there were no findings or conclusions to support the charges, this became immaterial or moot. I was no longer subject to accusations regarding grave misconduct or moral turpitude reaffirming my personal and professional integrity. Federal Court saw this as a ridiculous attempt by the University to substantiate its desire to be rid of me by lowering itself without dignity to grasp at straws.

The Court was clearly cognizant of Carroll's real motive: I might possibly offend its board and fund raising efforts; the bottom line was money. The conservative Catholics who constituted students, their parents, alumni and any VIP's on the Board of Directors or who were in any way related to the University might frown on donating to an institution that would condone a priest who became a lay man and married a divorced woman with four children. It could, might, or most definitely would create scandal which meant less money.

Bastards all. To me, it was depriving a 54 year old man of the job he needed to support his family, giving no assistance to help him relocate, and depriving him even of references for a job well done for many years in a highly visible and respected position is what is scandalalous. But I didn't know all of this then. I am once again getting ahead of myself. They were bastards, SJ or not. They probably still are! The case continued.

When Federal Court finally did rule, its ruling was of infinitely greater significance not only for me, but for others who followed me. Mine would become a precedent setting case in which the principle of separation of church and state was invoked and affirmed.

In other words, a Catholic University has the right to terminate a member of its religious community who is also on its faculty according to its religiously determined standards whereas a lay person teaching on the same faculty at the same university is held accountable to different standards and protected by civil rights.

What that meant was that by taking the vows of my religious community, in this case the Jesuits, I had forfeited my civil rights, rights that every other American proudly possessed and defended with his life.

At the same time, another physicist in my (former) department left his wife and six kids while taking off with a fellow faculty member! That was acceptable and fine. He was a layman, his actions didn't endanger Jesuit coffers! O tempore, o mores!

While I lost the principle, I did win a year's salary to forestall an appeal to a higher court, something I was in no financial position to pursue anyway. I hope some others have since then, or maybe will in the future. I believe this is a sorry state of affairs if endorsed by our Constitution which promises protection under the law to its citizens. Maybe that means I wasn't a citizen any more either!? I felt hurt and bitter.

I wish I could have appealed as high as the Supreme Court because in my heart I believe this ruling is an injustice to countless people who have dedicated their lives to do good and thereby placed themselves unaware at risk for potential future harm. Maybe someone has done so by now; I have not kept up with the matter.

We would spend many hours reviewing this case because it was such a bitter pill to swallow. Everyone suggested that I appeal, but I had had it. We couldn't afford to deplete the few resources available to us. We needed money to survive, and, I was really down.

During all this time, Monika's petition for annulment was in the works and it was not going well. Salih had sent his responses repeating what he had said at John Carroll. He pretty much was a Catholic without actually having been baptized in the way he demonstrated dedication to church related matters on behalf of his family. His children were baptized, he took his family to Mass on Sundays, and he sought marriage counseling from a Jesuit. His wife was impossible and unstable. She had to be crazy and did not know what her or a woman's responsibilities were, and he deserved to be pitied.

After comparisons of depositions between Salih's statements and others who had been questioned, there were huge discrepancies but no way to really refute or determine cause. The church does not annul a marriage, it declares it never was and therefore is null.

As we sat in Bishop Gaughan's office reviewing the entire matter, I mentioned in passing that in light of Salih's pronouncements, maybe Dr. Markham should be consulted. After all, he was a respected professional in a pertinent field whose opinion would carry some weight, whatever he would say.

Msgr. Gaughan did not know that a psychiatrist had become involved in Monika's life, and agreed at once that this was pertinent and significant information, either way.

The meeting was cut off suddenly: a priest stormed into the room to announce Roe v Wade had just been passed by the Supreme Court. It was January 1973. We left.

VI

Shortly after our meeting, Msgr. Gaughan called once again. He had heard from Dr. Markham who positively asserted that Monika was both mentally healthy and competent. At the current time, he was unable to add anything that would prove of benefit to our case before the Tribunal. He would prefer to desist from submitting an ultimate, binding opinion at present, but would appreciate the opportunity to possibly do so at a later date should new or additional information suggest it in the not too distant future.

While Monika had been hesitant to discuss any matters pertaining to family or her mother at any length and, because it was an extremely difficult subject for her that in her own opinion had little to do with her presenting problems, Dr. Markham had thus far not probed into the past beyond the most immediate. He had, however, surmised that there were issues to explore to various degrees even if he did not know their substance.

It would be only a few days till Monika received a phone call requesting her presence in Dr. Markham's office, out of sequence and unscheduled, but at her discretion and convenience. It was important but neither urgent nor hurried. I drove Monika to Oil City for the appointed time set by my work schedule.

When we got there, Monika learned the reason for Dr. Markham's call and concerns. It appears that Monika's mother had somehow learned that she was in Dr. Markham's care. She had searched for his location and called Dr. Markham, demanding to discuss Monika with him. According to already then prevailing confidentiality laws, Dr. Markham refused to speak with her without a signed release from Monika, and let her know this through his secretary. Undaunted, this woman began to pester and harass Dr. Markham, calling over and over again with her demands. She would not accept the legal restrictions or implications. She informed Markham's office that as the patient's mother her authority was enough to access information. Monika was 31 at the time. Dr. Markham was amazed by the chutzpah, and did not hesitate to say so to me with an explanation of such indications of entitlement, and their further implications.

Dr. Markham told Monika what had happened, he did not ask her whether she would sign any releases. Her look was enough to drop the subject. It gave ample occasion to broach that erstwhile hesitancy on Monika's part to include anything pertaining to her younger life or her mother. The white elephant lying in the middle of the therapy session space would now be not only raised, it would be examined. There was a great deal to be examined. Much, but not all, would become of interest to the Greensburg Marriage Tribunal which would decide to further stretch its investigative arms. I too became a listener as things unfolded before me.

VII

Monika explained to Dr. Markham (and me – but in this portion of our writing her memory is sufficient and I will review) that:

She married Salih to escape her mother, because she had been unable to do so in any other way known to her up to that point in time. Her mother had had no direct role or presence in her life since she was about 8 or 9 years old and her involvement with Monika's life earlier past infancy was peripheral at best.

While the war did play a role in some events, other children of Monika's acquaintance had mothers who stayed with them whereas her own mother was always absent and rarely present. As a result, Monika had spent a lot of time with neighbors' families in the remote little town to which they had fled, untouched by bombs. The circumstances of losing these families would become life time trauma her mother demanded be denied.

Later, Monika was farmed out to neighbors, cousins, and last of all, for two years while still in Austria, to a family whom Monika had learned to love as her own, and who would hold this position for life. She now had a real mother! That love and friendship continues and is now spanning generations!

Torn unwillingly from this family, as well as her home land because her mother had various issues of what Monika had both seen and been told by family and friends as being arrogance, pride and greed when compared to others she knew and loved, Monika found much of the same in the new country.

Here, however, she spoke neither language nor knew habits or traditions. Once again, she found herself left with strangers in their homes where she was not even able to communicate her needs, wants, or feelings. Once again, her mother was off. It appears that two very kind teachers took some steps on Monika's behalf and for her well being, Mrs. Margaret Burke, 7th grade at Horace Greeley High School in Chappaqua, was one of them. She decried the instability and insecurity from which her student obviously suffered and suggested the more structured environment of a boarding school. Monika's mother would follow this directive.

Monika would spend the next five years in catholic boarding school run by a semi-cloistered French religious order. She was happy there. Her life was regulated, safe, secure and certain. She had no home to go to on week-ends or for vacations like the other students, and got to know the nuns well. Her eventual desire to join them was thwarted because her parents had not been married in church, making her a bastard in the eyes of the Catholic Church, and therefore unacceptable to religious life.

An excellent student, Monika never considered not continuing her education, and applied for admission to various all girl colleges. She received several partial scholarships that were included with her acceptance letters. One college offered her tuition, room, board, books and fees and a sort of work study program. It was from Notre Dame in Baltimore. Monika was ecstatic. It was not to be.

Her mother did not allow her to accept the once in a life time opportunity because it was too far from Rhode Island. Monika was devastated. Instead, she went to Rhode Island College, and was forced to live alone in an apartment her mother provided. That, however, was against college rules for Freshman girls back in 1959. The Dean requested to see her mother. Angrily, her mother accused the Dean of interfering and refused to abide by regulations; Monika was forced to leave her studies. (The alternative offered by the Dean was to have Monika live with a faculty family in exchange for babysitting, as was done by several other students-Monika's mother said NO. In late 1959, the planned dorms had not been built).

It appears that the 19 year old applied for and got jobs in factories, continued course work both for business and college, and also continued to live alone. Attractive and vivacious, Monika had no trouble getting dates: no sooner would her mother hear of them from the two women she had hired to report back to her, then she interfered: she did things like have a young man's week

188

end pass revoked at the Coast Guard Academy (he was the son of Wisconsin Senator Gaylord Nelson!!) before the two ever even went out together; she stopped other dates through priests and authorities left and right, calling one the N word and another also an N word with a different meaning. Monika was welcomed and introduced to young men and their families by her pastor, but her mother exploded and forbade such contacts.

Monika could not turn around without constraints: when she finally wrote her uncle in Austria about returning there and working in his factory or office, her mother informed the entire family that Monika's life as an uncontrollable whore and harlot was so despicable and of such great pain to herself as mother, that she did not wish a plague like Monika on anyone, least of all her relatives. This was corroborated by the Tribunal's investigation.

Monika had met Salih and three months later moved into his efficiency apartment at 21, married him three times in succession.....and believed herself to have escaped at last.

Dr. Markham informed the Marriage Tribunal with a summary of what he had learned, and recommended that the Tribunal further investigate this young woman's earlier goal to escape manipulation and control over and above anything within normal limits.

For the Tribunal, this would be enough to launch an in depth inquiry.

The Tribunal requested that Monika submit a list of individuals in Austria who knew both her and her parents; past teachers and others in the US who had knowledge of Monika and her mother. The church interviewed countless people here and abroad. Their conclusions dovetailed Dr. Markham's. Basically, her mother's narcissistic control pre-empted Monika's natural maturation process and forced her into immature actions and decisions, based on a non-developed, defective reasoning process that indicated premature marriage as the only way to escape. Her mother was not interviewed, she would be contacted only to verify relationship and whereabouts.

It would be mid-May when Monika called Greensburg to learn if there was anything new regarding her case. Things were in process, there was nothing else to tell her as yet. She would be informed of anything pertinent as it developed.

Monika and the four children left for Europe shortly before Memorial Day, and were gone for half the summer. I, on the other hand, stayed behind to try to figure out what in God's name I would do, should or could do, and how the hell I would go about doing it.

Some time after Monika returned, she called the Marriage Tribunal to find out if there was any news. Yes there was.

The Marriage Tribunal of the Diocese of Greensburg decreed that for reasons of Defective Consent, no marriage had ever existed between Salih and Monika.

In other words, a decree of nullity had been granted, meaning that "Monika was free to marry Frank whose was already duly laicized and freed from his vows, of which celibacy was specifically cited, "by re-script from the Congregation of Faith and the Society of Jesus"".

People frequently believe that individuals with enough money or clout or connections are able to obtain an annulment. That is not true. The church does not annul existing marriages but it may, under certain circumstances and extensive investigation, determine that there never was a valid marriage between the parties based on a series of criteria weighed against presenting evidence.

In Monika's case, in spite of Salih's protestations, it was learned that he had no role in the matter of declaring the marriage null and void nor was he able to detain such a determination. It had been Dr. Markham who had put the church on the path of discovering cause. (The opposite can also be true as seen in the Kennedy case and its subsequent reversal).

Once a Decree of Nullity, asserting that there never was a marriage to begin with, was handed down, Monika was free to marry me in church. Msgr. Gaughan agreed to witness the exchange of our vows.

On August 28th, chosen in honor of her father whose birthday it was, and in the presence of the children, Bill and Lois Hopkins from Cleveland and Salih's uncle, Yunis Mohamed Aziz, Monika and I were married. This had not been part of my originally conceived project, but it was both good and appropriate under the circumstances.

Monika forgot the camera in the last pew at St. Emma's Chapel in Greensburg....we didn't get a single picture, but we did have a wonderful dinner to which Bill and Lois treated everyone, plus a gigantic wedding cake. The latter, unfortunately because of the blistering heat of the day, slid apart into its individual layers in Susibell's trunk. It still tasted good.

THE REAL WORLD

I

Over time, we had been to court several times with Salih. He would not pay child support, and he did nothing to see his children. When he was supposed to come, they would wait for hours, and he did not show up. He claimed he didn't have to pay since he didn't see them.

The court had awarded Monika the house in full because all other assets had been moved. Then we found out the bank was about to foreclose because the mortgage had not been paid for longer than any bank anywhere had ever allowed a home-owner to remain in the property. The second mortgage had also not been paid. It was privately held by the prior owners, very kind people whose name was Baldacchino who had built the house but left Clarion when he got a better job in a preferred location. A few additional loans were outstanding as well. In total, there was no equity in the house at that point, only debt against the deed.

A great guy by the name of Russ Christie whom the kids affectionately called Rice Krispies, was manager of the local bank branch and knew us. He lived near us and knew what had happened and where we stood. He also encouraged whosoever to help us end up with the house. It would allow him to act, too. What a great human being!

The deed in Monika's hand, we renegotiated the outstanding indebtedness and for now, somewhat precariously, we were safe. We also knew we could not afford the house with so much outstanding debt, and would have to move. But at least for the time being, we had diverted some stress.

II

Not so on the employment scene. I was 54. I had been a tenured university professor who had become department chair. My degree was in physics, about the worst discipline to have a degree in after the moon had been conquered. I had never looked for a job in my entire life. I had four children to support, and their mother to get back on her feet both health wise and emotionally. I was totally overwhelmed with what might lie ahead.

Although I had gotten a social security number at the time I moved out of Rodman Hall, I did not have a single credit card. I learned how important that was when trying to purchase something at Sears for which I did not have enough cash on me at the moment.

Later that same evening, Sears called. A very nice young lady asked me all kinds of questions, and probed into my credit worthiness with ever increasing incredulity. I fit no prior applicant profile; the digits on my social indicated it was fairly recent, yet I was ending middle age. I was born in the US so where had I been all these years? I explained patiently who I was, and why I was where I was given recent events.

Blessings on this kind woman whose name I never knew but whose nationality she shared with me: she was Polish, calling from Philadelphia. She would see to it that I got a Sears credit card at once. And she did just that. It was my first credit card ever! To this day I think of her and thank her, and I can only hope that she reads this and remembers because she had a significant impact on my and my families' future.

In the nearby college library, I spent hours looking into materials dealing with career changes. I researched books to learn how to find a job. Although I was familiar with resumes, it was in my capacity to review the ones sent by applicants either for jobs or graduate assistantships. I myself had never written one. Now I would have to.

The library also had The Chronicle of Higher Education on file, as well as Physics Today. I responded to every single ad that even remotely resembled anything I knew I could do or had done at any level from post doc to department chair. I had not been a great researcher and had been long gone from any lab. My forte was teaching. That de facto meant academia in some manner or form. Therefore, I did not apply to industry except for several positions which former students pointed out to me. They too helped.

NOTHING.

Not a response, not a no, nothing. I was sending inquiries into a big black hole in the sky or ground, at any rate to somewhere where no one gave a damn to at least have the courtesy to reply to my expressed interest in a given position.

Forget interviews! Since not even my initial contacts were acknowledged, they did not see any further probes. So, I wrote more letter....at a time when I had no word processor and typed on my very old Royal.

III

Monika did not help much, if at all. She'd been through the job seeking process with Salih when he returned from Iraq and earlier, before they had actually even left for Iraq. She also saw how disenchanted he had become during their last spring in Cleveland, and even more so afterward when he would have done anything or taken nearly any job to get out of Clarion. Job searches filled Monika with enormous anxiety; the prospects appeared to be non-existent; possibilities of what next were dim. I needed support I didn't get.

Luckily, Monika's stipends from the Department of Rehabilitation went a long way especially in her expert handling of household finances. And, she was qualified to apply for student loans, as well as additional grant funds. She did, she got them, and we squeaked along with more money than she could have made at some local job full time. We were, however, also depleting the kitty I had gotten at my Carroll exit.

I am unsure at this moment how often we went to court because of Salih's non-child support payments. In those days, the laws had no real teeth so a man could ignore his obligations, which is more unlikely today. We did not go to court all that often, I think it was a total of three times before we moved away in 1976. Maybe four?

The sum and substance of the court order that was entered, as amended from prior and other court orders, was that Salih was to pay $170.00 toward the care of his four children. He was considered responsible for extra or unusual things, including braces on their teeth and similar needs. The children would remain on Salih's health insurance, and they were his income tax deductions. He would be responsible for financing the college education of all four in full. He was to have the children two weeks in the summer, and alternate week-ends but details were supposed to be worked out on an on-going basis between the parents such as, he was supposed to call in advance to indicate when he would come, want to have them in the summer, or to communicate if he had to change day or time unexpectedly. And, the support order amount was subject to review and cost of living increases.

After some incredible scenes where he arrived with the police who took him away ranting and raving totally out of control, the court order was changed to supervised visitations only at the local office of social services near the court house in Clarion.

The last visitation order was signed by a different judge. Bob Filson had excused himself from the case. First of all, he saw me almost daily because by then I worked in the court house, and secondly, he had a farm off the beaten path somewhere in the

196

southern part of the county on which piles of trash and garbage had been thrown illegally. On examination, said trash and garbage contained a considerable amount of mail and other things bearing the address of one Mohamed S Said as recorded on court orders he'd signed previously. This had gone over like a lead balloon with the judge! He laughed as much as he was furious. And so he excused himself from the case.

I realize I am skipping around a little bit, please bear with me, a lot of things were going on at the same time in the early to mid seventies until we moved away from Clarion and had other things go on in our lives that might be equally confusing when we get there!

For example, there was an overlap of John Carroll's case against me with the annulments process; of Monika's attending Clarion State with my employment issues; the housing situation; child support and visitation matters regarding the children. All of the above were part of my life, for better or for worse. I was on a roller coaster.

IV

My rising frustration with employment was unending. I was now applying for anything and everything including in the local papers. A response came expressing an interest in my experience in education. I was told that interviews would take place at a given time and place; if I was interested, come. You bet I was, and I went.

The young man who met me in some local motel lobby was canvassing the country side for potential salesmen for an outfit called something like Commercial Trade Institute, which was out of Chicago, and whose products were a series of correspondence courses mainly geared toward recent veterans whose benefits would pay the costs of the course material and bestow a certificate of completion to the complying individual. And, when he was done, GIJoe could possibly take another course or another or another.... till the VA money ran out. Remember the time frames: this was early seventies. VIETNAM made VETERANS.

197

This was also the one and only time in my life to the best of my recollection, that I cried till tears streamed down my face, I sobbed but not only for myself. It was August 9th, 1974 and Nixon resigned. To me, this signified so much shame, so much disgrace, and so much humiliation for the land that I loved. I really dissolved out of pain for my country.

Around that time, I got the call that I had the job. I learned the required spiel, after correcting language misuses. I had my little kit, and I would hit the road every morning, return every evening, extended my hours because some people would be available only at night, traveled through Clarion, Franklin, Venango, Mercer, Jefferson and Armstrong Counties. I left earlier, I came home later. I hated every moment of every day or mile. I barely broke even. Susibell was getting a beating she didn't deserve, and neither did I. I began to search for something else.

And I found it. It was an ad for the US Chamber of Commerce, seeking a membership coordinator and promoter. Again, an interview, again a job offer, again, a spiel to memorize and repeat over and over and over exactly as it was written, the expectations that everyone would seek to join was high, the reality low. People who had a two bit machine shop did not need to be part of the US Chamber, and neither did the local Veterinarian or vegetable stand. There were some people who did have an interest, but most of them were members already in both local and national Chambers worth a mere renewal. Basically, I was selling a magazine called Nation's Business and the business of the nation held very little interest for me.

Our friend Katie has often joked saying, "fake it till you make it" but I just couldn't. I am too straight forward and honest to want to divest anyone of their hard earned money for a magazine they wouldn't even glance at, or deprive them of benefits better used in another manner more conducive of their life style and intentions rather than a correspondence course they were unlikely to complete. I am an honest man, not a con-artist.

With these jobs, I felt like a fraud, like a shyster. It did not help nor make it easier that Monika echoed my sentiments. While I didn't let her see me shudder as I left the house each morning, I knew that she saw Willy Loman in me when I got home at night. It was awful, and what's worse, it generated no income. My heart was not in what I was doing, this was going no where. They say nothing happens until someone sells something. Good. Let them. I wish them all the luck in the world, but this is not for me.

One never knows what God has in mind. My next stop came from someone I met because I had met someone who knew someone who mentioned that a job was coming down the pike. A family by the name of Mortland whom I had met somewhere along the line and befriended, would become instrumental in catapulting me out of my awful dire straights. Alec Mortland became a life line.

V

CETA, the government's Comprehensive Education and Training Act was seeking a coordinator for Clarion County. The Mortlands informed me of it, had a contact who had an inside track, and told me how, where and when to apply. I did. After a while, I learned that I had the job.

Now I had an office once again, and I had a secretary. Cleone McGregor was terrific. I could not have asked for anyone nicer or better to guide me through the maze of the local political scene of elected officials, government agencies, programs and services.

Bob Filson's office was down the hall. As we got to know each other, I learned why he had removed himself from the Said case that I mentioned earlier. He was a really nice person to get to know and occasionally have lunch with.

The whole concept of being back within a quasi professional atmosphere, however bureaucratic, was uplifting for me. Work became pleasant again. I liked what I did, and who I worked with. I also liked my client population who were, to a large extent, people who had been hit hard by economic fluctuations in a county that did not offer much opportunity in those days. These were people I instinctively knew from childhood: the hard working men and women I had seen at our house as I was growing up. Loving, tough, unpretentious and rough, but genuine, real, authentic, with a good sense of humor and loving hearts.

The family was doing OK. Monika was handling things infinitely better and nearing the end of her studies. The kids were all good students, had friends, and were like ordinary kids everywhere. Salih had not kept the bi-weekly dates for supervised visitations as the designated supervisor would always call to tell us ahead of time, nor had he requested them any time in the summer. He had not contacted us at all.

My brother Joe came to see us for a few days, without telling anyone back home in Detroit where he was going. I was touched that he took the long trip alone while in failing health. It was good to spend time with him. Shortly after his visit, we learned he had succumbed to the cancer that had been eating him alive.

Several friends from Cleveland came at various times, including Monika's cousin Vera and her family. We continued frequent treks to the Hopkins because we really enjoyed it there and one summer Lois allowed two of her kids to come and stay with us.

With four kids, there's never a dull moment.

VI

Something else was happening at that time. Monika had some concerns regarding Leila's friendship with one of her teachers who had come to the house as a guest a couple of times and made Monika feel ill at ease. I didn't share her reaction and told her so. I was very wrong not to trust her instincts; I regret this to this day. Later contact with the young man didn't change her mind. It would be many many years later that I learned how accurate Monika's radar had been. The no good bastard teaching at the parochial school was molesting several little girls, including Leila who had the tremendous fortitude and guts to return to Clarion as an adult and report him to the police in spite of the local pastor who maligned her because of me. These holier than thou Catholics are disgusting a lot of the time. Those guys surely were. The teacher disappeared next day.

Rob had a bad accident: going through a pair of doors that open with a bar across the middle, he caught his middle finger and severed its tip. Thanks to the presence of mind of Sister Rita OSB, his teacher, who I believe was right behind him, the finger was put into salt water and we rushed Rob to the Oil City Hospital 30+ miles away where it was reattached so that although he has lost a little length, he retained the finger nail to protect the damaged tip. Salih did come to see him then; he even brought him a Polaroid camera.

Nadja was repeating second grade, but had changed schools in the process. She was the youngest by far in her class, and although she learned well, we felt—along with some professionals, that her life would be a lot less stressful with a little more maturity. She had multiple ear infections and later would have her tonsils out. Severe nosebleeds ended once she was cauterized, it would be while wearing her white First Communion dress.

She was then, and continues to this day, to be a very special person who's exceedingly bright. It would be but a few years later before we would lock horns regularly, and mostly at the dinner table. It would take even more years for me to muster the gumption to apologize to her for not understanding her well enough to be the supportive parent she sought and deserved. Instead, I had abruptly or compulsively chastised her, embarrassed her and above all, hurt her deeply at a precious and vulnerable age, no matter that those were not my intentions. I should have known better. It remains one of the few regrets in my life that I can't redo.

And then there was Steve. Urwicz! That's Polish for what Spitzbub is in German as Monika told me, or Rapscallion or hellion. He really was. His energy and curiosity were boundless. He was in the ER more than the other three combined; his nose broke at least twice, and the accidents got worse in proportion to how he got older throughout the years! He was and is charming, smart as a whip, never stopping and unstoppable, and always on the go, loving and loved! The worst of his accidents happened on the soccer field in high school and would negatively effect his future athletic participation.

All the kids were terrific, but this one proclaimed himself to be mine from his first day in first grade when he argued with his teacher that he was not a Said, he was a Gutowski.....so vehemently, that we were called into school to address the situation in person to affirm his birth name.

I think having the kids kept me as young and as energetic as I was in spite of my age and work load. Once again, because I really love the kids who after all were the real reason for my life change, I am letting my thoughts wander hither and yon remembering.

VIII

While I worked for CETA, we finally had a buyer for the albatross of a house in which we were still living. I had done extensive work in completing the interior. When he had visited, my brother Leo showed and taught and discussed with me what needed or could be done. He left me to do the work for which my next door neighbor, Chuck Nanz, lent a frequent capable hand.

Outside, I had planted some shrubbery, made paths and established a large rock garden for which I moved really large rocks or boulders and transplanted all kinds of plants I had either found, been given, or was invited to dig up for transplanting into our yard. My efforts produced the equity that had been lacking when we had been given the debt ridden property. But not much.

We found a house we really liked in town that would not increase our debt load and from which Monika and the kids could walk everywhere, and we got ready for our move.

Another adventure! In the last minute, something happened that prevented the movers from coming at the appointed time. In their place, a group of young men whom we'd met and fed came to our rescue. They were the Mormon missionaries assigned

202

to this area, strong young men of God, ready willing and able to pack, carry, load and unload our belongings. Except for having the large king-size mattress fly off the truck near the Clarion River bridge. (We retrieved it without damage or further incident). The day ended with great success. We would see the young men often afterwards. Although we made it clear we were contently Catholic, we nevertheless appreciated their family evenings at our home, teaching us as well. We also were now finally relieved of a huge financial burden.

My sister Therese came again, this time with an old friend, after we settled into the house. We also hoped that Sister Maria Matteo, my old nun friend from I don't remember where, would come again. She had last been to see us right after her return from Rome where she had witnessed the canonization of Elisabeth Seton, the foundress of her religious community. Unfortunately, she was not be able to make it. Matt would not see us again.

We all enjoyed the house, including Schatzi the Dachshund and Agamemnon the Maine Coon cat. All the kids had begun music lessons earlier and were continuing now that they could walk to the college for their lessons. We could go swimming at the college pool.

Monika found a part time job in a doctor's office that allowed her to run the household without problems. Her income was minimal, but she hoped it would tide her over between graduation and the real job for which she had applied at the local social services office. She was very disappointed when she didn't get it; it went to someone she knew. Shortly thereafter, a friend working for social services got killed in a head on collision. It was very upsetting to Monika who felt the accident could have been avoided had the newly hired person not needed a few weeks before beginning--a job that Monika could have started at once.

As it is wont to do, time passed quickly and 1976 began. Monika now had an incomplete and no more college monies were forthcoming. In a couple of months she would leave her part time job because she broke some bones in her foot at work. Workman's

Comp would be short lived. Her opportunities were limited, grad school was impossible in time and place. For me, CETA funds were running low and therefore the funding of my position's continuation debatable. The feelings of fear and desperation reared their heads and we had few ideas of what would come next.

My work with CETA had gone well and given me a modicum of satisfaction. One of my proudest achievements was to participate in the inception of a nursing program for qualified and eligible candidates who would not otherwise have been able to obtain such training. Alec Mortland's wife Joyce had been an inspiration to make it happen and one of its first graduates subsequently.

I had more self confidence about locating a better and different position, but I still lacked a lot of the skills for a successful job search. And, my age was not in my favor.

FAITH AND HOPE

I

We bought the New York Times every Sunday and looked through the various ads for professional occupations usually listed following its "Week in Review". One of the listings there, week after week, was for an outfit called Bernard Haldane that listed multiple locations and indicated its ability to assist in locating and negotiating upper level positions with commensurate salaries.

With Monika's encouragement, I made an appointment at Haldane's Cleveland office. When I went there, I was impressed by what I learned about job search techniques, job preparation, networking, negotiating and more. Additionally, there were some incentives for those willing and able to sign up on the spot. I did, and forked over what the price tag called for with a heavy but hopeful heart.

I really did learn a lot at Haldane. I also had some of my sense of self restored, but best of all, the weeks of sessions gave us frequent week ends with the Hopkins family where we soaked up a hell of a lot of good family vibes otherwise missing in our livers. Bill and Lois, as ever, were great to be with and so were all their kids with ours.

In time, I was ready to put my new found knowledge to work. In spite of my recharged self confidence and arsenal of skills, I was a 57 year old man with no past. I did everything I had learned, over and over and over. My network expanded geometrically. I expended my energy and other remaining resources. Nothing happened.

We had consistently been subscribers of Time Magazine over the years, so when Time began its marketing campaign for a new publication under its umbrella that was to be called "MONEY", we signed up as charter subscribers. Neither Monika nor I knew anything about money and maybe we would learn something. The subscription would change our lives.

II

Sometime in early spring, Monika read an article in the above magazine which described the magazine's role in helping an individual sharpen his financial acuity. The author of the article was Jeremy Main of Money's board of editorial writers. Monika decided to send him some favorable comments on the article, and to let him know how much I could benefit from the same kind of counsel and support given the article's subject. 1976 was in its infancy.

Not long afterwards, Jeremy Main called me. He wished to come to see me and further discuss whether I would be a suitable subject for a future article. Anything that might help me was welcome, even such a long shot as a potential article. I said yes.

Starting with Jeremy's first visit, we all found ourselves caught up in a whirlwind of activities which none of us had ever experienced. Jeremy himself came a few times to interview me and as well to get to know the whole family. One of Time-Life's best photographers, Martha Holmes, also came to Clarion and would spend two long week-ends with us. She followed us in our daily activities, planned some activities for us, and treated us to picnic fare and restaurant meals.

Lastly, we were invited to spend several days in New York City at the offices of Time-Life, in conference with a panel of experts gathered together to provide guidance, stimulation, motivation, and instill courage in both Monika and me regarding potential future paths, possibilities and opportunities suggesting exploration. It was an enormously beneficial time spent both in session and for the remaining time in which we were treated to concert and ballet performances as well as restaurant fare we'd only ever read about before. While Monika and I were housed at the Hotel Dorset next to MOMA, the children were at their grandmother's house in nearby Connecticut for one of their rare extended visits.

Back in Clarion, we eagerly awaited the July copy that would tell all about us all but especially me and the predicaments a highly educated former priest faced. Jeremy Main had done his homework. While he researched my life story for verification, he informed me of something I did not know but which would explain the difficulties of my path.

It appeared that John Carroll University would not only NOT give me any references for any of the academic positions for which I had applied again and again, but they also denied my ever being on their faculty or knowing me. Had I known that, I might have appealed the court decision, or filed another suit against them. Now, it was just the final straw or the bitterest pill of all to learn just how low my former confreres would stoop in the name of Christ Jesus. Earlier I had been hurt, now I wasted no more time on the likes of those I once esteemed.

The July copy hit the news stands and our phone rang with well wishes and curses from around the community. I also received calls from various individuals who had further ideas for my future or job leads to explore in the present. Some former students also called from as far away as Texas and California, offering to support me for any position I would apply for. It was very gratifying and restored my former positive outlook. There was also some gratification in knowing that John Carroll's despicable and covert actions were now public domain. The calls I received reflected this; and it felt good.

I was also contacted by several potential employers and while I was not guaranteed any position, I was asked to submit my credentials to several places seeking to hire someone with the kind of diversified solid background and experience I appeared to offer. I did so at once, and in short order several packets with my complete credentials were in the mail.

III

A few weeks went by, and I was asked to present myself in metropolitan Boston, in New York City, near Stamford, and south of the Mason Dixon Line in both Baltimore and Richmond.

We called Monika's mother and asked if the children could visit her again while Monika would accompany me in my travels from place to place. We set out from Clarion with children, dog and cat, certain we would only return to pack our things once we knew where we would end up. I was filled with hope and optimism, Monika dreamed of Boston.

My first meetings were scheduled to be in NYC. While interesting, I was offered a lot of pie in the sky depending if and when and so on. In other words, there was nothing of substance concretely available for my immediate future there. I could not afford this.

Stamford was very promising and desirable. The first round of interviews went well, and I was waiting for the second round schedule. Jeremy Main himself had referred me, and we would be in the vicinity of all the family Monika had in the US.

While Monika had some familiarity with the area as a whole, I did not. At best, I had driven through there and I wasn't even certain of that. Nevertheless, I joined Monika in gathering local information from the local Chamber of Commerce along with looking into housing and schools that were affordable and which could accommodate all four children.

We saw a realtor and met the principal-priest of a local parochial school. We were concerned that things would go smoothly since the school year was about to begin. Overall, I felt a great degree of confidence and comfort envisioning myself to be making a career move into the kind of setting to which I had become accustomed over a life time.

Bad experiences and frequent disappointments had been tough teachers, so even though I expected to be in Connecticut, I nevertheless decided to use the interim waiting period most efficiently and make a quick trip to Baltimore and Richmond while waiting, and to see what the opportunities there would avail themselves to me.

Baltimore appeared to be a great opportunity, but like an earlier trip I had taken to this city also on behalf of a position, I felt uncomfortable in the milieu in which I would find myself there professionally.

Richmond, on the other hand, was a position on an academic campus and the opening would be in conjunction with several departments coordinating their activities with some government funded partnership programs not unrelated to my recent CETA experience. I was ideally suited for the position, I was offered it, but it was funded to coincide with the Federal budget and therefore would not begin until October 1st. I asked to think about it for a few days because that date was nearly a month away, the children had to get settled in order to begin their school year, and the Stamford possibility was alive and well even if I also had no contract in hand.

We headed back to the Hopps' home in Rowayton where the children were eagerly awaiting us. The last couple of weeks had been difficult and uncertain as summer drew to a close, and they were eager to know our, and especially their own, future. Our arrival was – I am not sure what I would call it. It was anything but welcome. I call it incredible.

Monika's mother appeared unable to talk in a normal voice but rather screamed hysterically about our incredible nerve to move into their home, that we better get out immediately, neither she nor her husband had any intentions of supporting or hosting us, and too much more to fully recall this much later except

209

that it was a terrible scene for everyone concerned, was totally unnecessary and uncalled for, and I could not fathom what might have prompted it.

There was a message to call the Stamford offices to set up a meeting for contract negotiations. I never called back and never went there. I packed the children, cat and dog and we drove straight through to Richmond where we had already called Pat Mears, the oldest and married daughter of my dear friends, Lois and Bill Hopkins. By the time we got to Pat's, she and Mike had readied rooms and beds and we collapsed.

We stayed there a while until we first of all got the school situation under control. All four children would be attending a parochial school north of Richmond, Our Lady of Lourdes, the only school that could accommodate all four children. It would determine what part of town we would chose for our home.

We then moved to an inexpensive motel room, while we searched for local housing and awaited the anticipated government contract and the start of my new job, on or about October 1st. It arrived on September 30th, and Nadja announced that it was she who had prayed that her birthday would be dad's good luck day. And so it was!

We would also learn what had happened with Monika's mother: it appears that the parochial school we had visited to potentially enroll the children had contacted her for whatever they needed to know, and set off her hysterical fear we were planning to settle on her turf. One can't reason with an unreasonable person so the matter was never mentioned again later on for any kind of clarification.

IV

In Richmond, it wasn't long until we found an affordable house half way between the children's school and my work. Fortunately, the Clarion home had sold easily. That meant we could afford the new house, and would move our things directly from one home to the next.

Rob went with me to pick up everything from Clarion and proved a great help and good companion for the trip. Even when we lost the brakes heading down one of Pennsylvania's many hills, he kept his good humor and faith in my driving ability. Not so when we finally arrived: The large heavy door from the truck rolled down and it looked like his foot had gotten crushed beneath its weight. Pat Mears took Rob to the ER while the rest of us unloaded things. Luckily, Rob was OK. Soon we were settled in, unpacked, and life moved forward.

Monika did a few volunteer things to acquaint herself with the local community. She initially felt ill at ease in Richmond, but after a few months she applied to join VISTA and that gave her all the opportunity she sought in order to integrate herself into the various activities she preferred. Eventually, VISTA also became her stepping stone into the Virginia Commonwealth University School of Social Work.

While my job went well, I was not satisfied. I differed with some of my superiors in how to best carry out the various projects with which we were all involved. Both our perspectives and our vantage points were very different: I came from a science background, they came from education and public administration areas. I sought concrete, measurable results based on the evaluation of facts gathered from structured endeavors. Their perspectives included flexibility and fluctuation to accommodate at the risk of losing precision.

I remembered Admiral Rickover's statements to the effect that education courses are one course taught in different ways rather than the knowledge of content. It didn't help to recall that! It made things difficult for me and I did not regret the end of the grant-funded position. I don't think that the others involved with this grant felt any different than I did.

The house we had bought and in which we lived did not meet our needs. Once Leila had graduated from 8th grade and started at St. Gertrude's, and Rob had his heart set on attending Benedictine where he wanted to participate in junior ROTC, the school needs also changed. Nadja and Steve switched to St. Paul's, we joined the parish there, and moved closer to it, from Bellevue to Westwood Avenues. Everyone liked the new house, or at least they said they did.

Because my first love and greatest interest was teaching, I was delighted when someone offered me a semester's worth of physics classes while he went on sabbatical. It would be the first time in 8 years that I stood before a class even though I was not on the faculty or even considered a full-fledged adjunct. However short term I was standing on a campus. Leila was very proud of my teaching assignment and came to visit me at class.

Now, I had no qualms about openly stating what I thought of John Carroll's behavior when they denied my existence or refused to give me the references which I had earned. My substituting became a spring board to teach evening physics courses, adjunct, at J. Sargeant Reynolds Community College for many years even beyond what was considered customary retirement age.

While I taught some of the time, I still needed a primary day job to feed my family. I tried several things short term for a while: my physics background impressed a group of men vested in energy and green conservation and development projects. They decided to hire me. It was interesting. Unfortunately, however, their cash flow was stretched to its limits. My salary was more liability than benefit at this early stage of their venture, and their concepts would become timely and desirable many years after we parted our ways. Right then and there, they were ahead of their time. They had also hired me too early in their fledgling company's history because they had become aware of my availability and were impressed by my credentials much more than they needed me at that point in time.

My brief foray back into the classroom, now at a community college, had put me in touch with both local and state educational programs for science teachers throughout the Commonwealth. While it was an honor to serve on various committees, I needed something more concrete. When I learned that Charles City

212

County needed someone to teach physics at its High School, I applied and was hired.

V

There were several Charles City County High School teachers living in close proximity to our home, and we commuted together, taking turns driving. The camaraderie we formed during our daily trips was warm and friendly, but it did not extend beyond our job related associations. We never socialized. Unlike them, I was not of color.

Teaching in this rural Virginia setting, so close to both Richmond and Williamsburg with their affluence and multiple institutions of learning was eye opening. Overall, I had never experienced poverty as I did there. It was a different kind of poverty than I was familiar with. And it was not just that the school budget itself did not include lab equipment and supplies, the likes of which I assembled at home in my own basement to facilitate the learning process with some visual and hands on experiments.

I had experienced poverty in my life. I had come from what I knew to be poor circumstances, but ours had been a different kind of poverty. Dad worked daily, even throughout the depression, when he kept his job, literally, by brewing beer for his boss. We had little, but what we had was maintained with pride.

My parents and my siblings, and from them I myself, acquired tastes and life styles based on what we saw and read and were exposed to. That's how Joe became familiar with classical music and shared it with me, read magazines, and purchased books all of us kids read over time. Dad read the Polish newspaper, and although I don't remember mother reading much, she would always also leaf through the paper and comment on an occasional gossipy tidbit. The emphasis in our home was to reach higher and become better; if dad's sweat poured before machines forming the injected metals into Chrysler body parts, then it was expected that we would become educated and thereby attain easier means to earn our livelihood.

Here, now, I was faced with students who came from dire poverty not only as a result of lack of material goods. Theirs was an impoverishment of the soul, of not being familiarized with main stream values, of not learning how to evaluate priorities, without inspiration to aspire or the skills to learn to transcend beyond the status quo. There was a bitterness and melancholy I felt, and in spite of loud music, happy voices, and frequent laughter, I discerned a heavy weight of hopelessness regarding expectations. I want to believe that over my years at the school, I threw out enough positive vibes that some good ultimately came of our daily contact. Later, I would learn I indeed had done so.

Things at home were going smoothly. It helped me a great deal when Monika got a Virginia driver's license as a surprise for me after taking lessons with an instructor from AAA. She bought me a bottle of Chivas Regal on her way home from passing the road test to celebrate. She had, in the meantime, also completed her MSW and was working; her salary at the time equaled mine and we were pleased to meet our financial obligations with relative ease for the first time, together. We worked hard, the kids studied well, and life became what might be considered as being normal or average.

We were not receiving nor had we received any child support. One attempt to pursue this ended with a partial past due payment made via the court system, but that was short lived. We were audited by the Internal Revenue Service and learned that we had overpaid and received a refund. Another time, we were again audited because Salih claimed the children on his return: luckily we had all the documentation so we could demonstrate that we had provided 100% of the children's support.

Another time, after a renewed interstate court demand for support, Salih sent plane tickets to have the children come for a visit. Unfortunately he did not call ahead to ask us to agree on a given time. When they came, it was too late because we were already on our way somewhere; without his willingness to verbally communicate, we were unable to make alternate arrangements. This happened one time only.

214

Monika liked her work, she was also very busy with several volunteer commitments which she thoroughly enjoyed. Her love of music opened doors for committee and board work, and with it, we once again both felt we had at long last returned to the kind of social setting in which we felt contently familiar. Even though I worked long hours, I found an occasional bridge game that gave me pleasure, and as well a pleasant round of golf.

We had frequent dinner parties and other gatherings, and Monika was again reveling in being a good hostess. One of our frequent guests was a woman by the name of Nina Abady whom Monika had met as a result of some fund raising efforts for the renovation of a down town theater.

I did not know then, but would soon learn, that Nina had taught at Virginia Union University, one of the historically black colleges, located near our home in Richmond. Her position on the faculty had been very prominent not only because of her teaching, but because of the various other functions she held on campus. When Nina learned of my daily treks to Charles City County, my background and credentials, she took it upon herself to recommend me to Virginia Union and before long, I was the one man physics department carrying out what had been a dream of mine for more years than I could remember: to teach at a black southern school in order to promote the sciences in an underserved population. Thanks to Nina, I had achieved one of my major life time goals.

There would be several rewarding features in this: I saw one of my students receive a scholarship to Johns Hopkins, I saw several others doing well, and the son of the University's President would choose graduate work in physics after being my student. All this was immensely gratifying to me, especially since I had missed academics for so long.

VI

Having four teenagers at one time proved to be overwhelming for me. It was now around 1980, I was over 60, and I was not feeling well. My doctor, Peter Goodman, suggested

215

that I sounded depressed, and referred me to a psychiatrist. I don't remember the name, but I do know the office was on Lake Avenue, not far from Monika's best friend, Katie Carapico, who had then recently lost her husband.

The psychiatrist prescribed Milltown tablets. I took them as prescribed, regularly. I also began to drink more heavily.

Drinking had been a problem for me most of my adult life post ordination. It had started gradually even during Regency when I wet my feet in social circles I had heretofore only aspired to join. I also developed a taste for the finer spirits; I acquired a liking for scotch, and among scotches, the names of Haig and Haig, Chivas Regal or Johnny Walker Black were my preferences. While at John Carroll, these were readily available, and beer had been on tap. Back then, I had enjoyed beer with every meal and snack or made it a snack in and of itself. There had been episodes I would prefer to forget: crashing through Mary Hopkins wedding buffet table; the drunken winery trips on Lake Erie; the Browns-Steelers games where I consumed thermos bottles filled with Martinis… and countless Martinis or Scotches consumed over card games.

After leaving the Society, I could not afford this indulgence. I maintained my driver's license with its "REV" for as many years as it was valid. Having that "REV" on my license had prevented me from being cited with innumerable DUI's by Cleveland's finest more often than I want to recount. Now, driving under the influence was a memory I was glad to forget. I had only gotten really seriously drunk twice while we lived in Pennsylvania: both times at the home of near neighbors within walking distance of home.

Because of our budget limitations, liquor was out, but we learned to make wine. I don't remember who gave us the first wine making kit complete with all necessary paraphernalia. I think it was Bill Hopkins, my friend who owned and operated a liquor store in Cleveland Heights. Over time, we made an adequate blackberry wine strong enough to pass as a sort of port.

Back in Clarion where we lived out in the country near fields and hedges of blackberry bushes, the children would help us pick blackberries near our home: the amounts we would eventually prepare were actually quite staggering! A couple of large plastic garbage pails full of berries gathered amidst thorns and spiders each of several years would produce several dozen bottles which we would seal with paraffin in the hopes of aging them to perfection. Unfortunately they would be drunk before that happened! In addition to blackberries, we also tried other fruits: elderberry which I liked but Monika thought awful, pears which didn't work at all, apples that made a sort of rose, and peaches which became better fermented fruit served over ice cream than any type of liquid refreshment.

Our wine making ended when we left the Clarion area and moved to Virginia. For a while, we rarely drank anything except as we had guests after we had settled there. I think the kids may differ on that recollection; seems to me that Nadja remembers me drinking when their mother had to go out of town for work now and then - I do not recall this.

Once we moved to Westwood Avenue, my drinking resumed in earnest, especially after Monika befriended a family of alcoholic women. One in particular, who lived near us and had commuted to evening classes with Monika while herself aspiring to the Episcopal priesthood, would spend countless afternoons sloshing sherry and engaging in theological discussions with me in our kitchen while Monika would make tuna salad with crackers for our stomachs in order to absorb some of the booze. In time, our drinking would continue at her home as well at the various social events to which she invited us. And my own drinking increased beyond what I want to admit.

I was buying cheap Vodka and whatever beer I found on sale. I was also experiencing increasing pain in both my hips which I attributed to old high school foot ball injuries revisited. I accompanied the boys on most mornings and every Sunday on their paper routes in spite of a great deal of discomfort. Sometimes I would finish the rounds with a few hefty shots from my stash hidden under the basement steps.

217

There was one episode when Rob and Steve both found me near collapse after treating my cold with excessive numbers of OTC cold tablets washed down with liquor. I nearly passed out and was disoriented: actually, both boys would tell me afterwards about the incident that scared them a great deal, and which I did not recall whatsoever. The only thing I remembered was that now –thanks to this incident--I knew how I could commit suicide if I wanted to: take the whole bottle of those same damn pills with a whole bottle of booze. Life would end. Obviously, with such thoughts, my entire frame of reference was not well. I no longer liked myself, I no longer liked my life.

VII

I taught at Virginia Union every day, I taught two nights at the community college, and most semesters, two nights at VCU as well. I was tired and asking myself, is that all that was left for me in this life? In spite of seeing the psychiatrist, I was increasingly depressed. I was also increasingly dissatisfied with both me and my life. Now that things were overall less stressed or chaotic, I felt a let down that dragged me down with it.

The kids were all fairly well on their way: my primary intentions had been to see them safe. Monika had finished the education I had committed myself to help her attain. By finishing a Master's, she'd done more than intended.

In therapy, I reflected on how I came to be where I was, and what my precipitating intentions had been before I undertook what would become enormous life changes with adherent problems and difficulties I had not chosen nor agreed to. I could honestly say that with hind sight I would have had the same goals, but would have pursued them differently.

MY WAY

I

Here I was: the project I had taken on was nearing the end of its anticipated duration. I was over sixty years of age and had not for a single day lived life outside of some sort of constraints. Initially it was my own family while I was young. I had joined the Society at seventeen, long before I was mature or old enough to make such a permanent commitment.

Mother had said I would be a priest and I did as I had been told. And from the society, I took on a ready made family that would make more demands on me than I could possibly have anticipated regardless of the cautionary words given me by well meaning friends facing what I was about to undertake. I saw myself going to my deathbed without ever having really lived, and I was terrified of living since the lack of financial security frightened me. No one had adverted to the fact that not only was I late beginning social security payments, but my life time pension contributions up to that point also remained in the Jesuits' coffers as well. Obviously, my depression came from both within and without me. How much longer would this project take to be completed? I asked myself time and again.

II

Monika hated the word project. She hated being referred to as my project. We got along splendidly even though we had both arguments and differences of opinion. After all, how many couples did we know who could spend half the night discussing how many angels danced on the head of a pin? Or similar topics. We were "in sinc", hand in glove, two peas in a pod...for most things but not everything. We were the best of friends and most caring lovers.

Although she was more ebullient and outgoing than I, Monika and I had much in common regarding how we looked at life and circumstances. We shared values and outlooks, perspectives and priorities – or at least most all of them. We also both lived in our heads more than we dealt with our emotions, or better said, while Monika was emotional, I was more controlled. Neither of us knew how to handle feelings well, whether our own or each other's.

From the very start, we agreed that I would never take Monika dancing while she would never play bridge. She learned to forget about dancing. I did not forget about wanting to play bridge. I maintained I could not love because I had no idea what love was or what it meant to love someone, anyone. Monika assured me of her love; at the same time she would say that while she loved me with all her heart, she was not in love with me nor had she ever been in love with me at any point in time.

It is no wonder that the parents of one of Rob's friends apparently told Rob we were weird. When Rob told me this, I just laughed. We were different, no doubt about it. But, we had done exceptionally well under extremely difficult circumstances in raising the four children, seeing to their education, providing a home that provided diversity, cultural experiences, intellectual stimulation and both an exceptionally eclectic atmosphere as well as broad exposure.

It was my sister Theresa's last visit to Richmond that helped me come to terms with what I saw as my future and what I needed to do so it would come about as I intended. Theresa and I drank

220

ourselves into oblivion for several days, but when she left, I felt better than I had had in a while. I also did not know that I would next see her on her death bed in Detroit, barely able to recognize me. For now, I had a newly found and renewed sense of purpose. It did not include old projects. It was I.

One Saturday in early 1981 I took Monika to dinner at a restaurant we both liked, The Flying Cloud. After a couple of Martinis, I suggested to Monika that the time had come to conclude this project, and that I was hoping to move on as soon as I was assured that she had found someone else to be with and take care of her.

III

I had no idea what kind of someone I was thinking of, all I thought of was of my own exit. I was sure that Monika, an attractive and intelligent woman, well educated and financially on her feet, would find a man who would gladly take care of her now that the children were almost grown and gone.

I did not advert to the fact that Monika had never really dated anyone and that she had no intention of doing so now: she was my wife for life. And she said so.

I wanted to live on my own. I wanted to drink when I wanted and go to bed when I felt like it, to sleep in the morning until noon and watch football without interruption or emergency. My golf clubs hadn't been used except for a few rare exceptions for the past ten years. (Eventually, Rob took them to Tech and I never saw them again).

I was tired of being at anyone's beck and call whether child or spouse or employer. I wanted for once in my life to experience what it was like to not be responsible to anyone or for anyone; to be by myself, to be myself. I had never been there, never done that, and the clock was ticking so it was now or never would be. I wanted to play bridge. I wanted out.

What I did not consider was how Monika would react, or indeed that she would react. However much she disliked being called my project, my leaving was anathema to her. She was shocked; she didn't believe me. She cried and carried on. At the same time, she was concerned about my drinking which was totally out of control and blamed it for my desires.

I reeked of liquor even after taking a morning shower. My car had countless empty beer bottles or cans behind the passenger seat. I didn't see any more point in seeing the psychiatrist, but I did get in the car with every intention to kill myself by driving full speed into the stone supports from the railroad trestle at the bottom of Lombardy near VUU.

In the last minute, I instinctively turned the wheels and hit the brakes, without actually changing my mind; I did not repeat this a second time. I had enough. I missed my solitary life, I needed to be alone. Ending my life was not the answer, living it was.

My hips had also gotten worse. I no longer walked up the stairs and decided to sleep in the family room. Now, looking back, I did make it down the basement to my hooch stash. I wanted to be by myself and that therefore meant that I would leave Monika.

I was very concerned about finances. The old fears birthed during the depression returned. Back then I witnessed the loss of my father's real estate investments. Now I needed a double hip replacement and feared the medical costs. Would our hard won home be lost to cover my expenses? The mere thought generated nightmares. I called an attorney we knew from church. He drew up a new deed by which I gave Monika the house in its entirety. Monika was not pleased.

IV

Monika's upset would have consequences, some of which I would only understand years later. Her own experiences seeing Dr. Markham had made her very aware of her own reactions and feelings, and to recognize when she could or could not handle herself adequately. As a result, she now went to see her gynecologist who viewed her situation as being related to both pre-menstrual syndrome as well as early menopausal symptoms.

To help her feel better, Monika was given a prescription for Ativan, to be taken as needed on certain days a month. Unbeknown to Monika herself, to me, or to anyone else at the time was the fact that Monika cannot take or tolerate or may be allergic to the whole spectrum of medications into which Ativan falls. Would it have made a difference to me then? No. I wanted out. I wanted to be on my own a lot more than I wished to be with anyone else no matter how pleasant or compatible.

Now, I saw Monika as intermittently belligerent and cantankerous. Out of the blue and without provocation her moods would swing erratically. While we would have heated discussions and arguments in the past, I now found us bickering and squabbling non stop all too often. Monika did some off the wall things including once when we had a guest; she had several accidents and was being totally out of character, and frequently unlike herself. I felt I was the cause. Blaming myself was a very unpleasant sensation I wanted to eliminate.

I really pushed to have her find my replacement. Finally, she appeared to have met someone. Was this at last my ticket to go? Little did I know how this would ultimately unfold.

Monika did indeed meet someone. Although she became temporarily infatuated, her lack of desire, interest or experience turned everything upside down. The situation became disastrous. But more on that a little later.

I was about to make the biggest mistake of my life, one I would regret deeply at various times even though I learned to live with it in my own way. Eventually, it all came out in the wash. I would, however, never completely recapture what I lost back then. Looking back, I should have simply suggested a temporary separation to get my own needs and wants taken care of because experiencing life on my own, just once, is what I myself was after. A cruise might have done it, who knows, now it's 20/20 hindsight.

Instead, while Monika and our youngest, Stevie, accompanied a girl friend with her children to Key West for spring break, I packed my things and moved out. When Monika returned, I was gone and with me, the station wagon which Steve had been using to drive to school. I had traded it in for a new car of my choice even though Monika's mother had just bought 4 new tires for Stevie's safety on the old wagon.

Monika did not share my plans or intentions. She had never wanted to be a project; now she didn't want anyone in my place. She'd never even given this a thought. I was fully aware that Monika, having met someone to please me, began to feel so guilty and torn that she stopped attending weekly Mass and monthly confession which she had done all her life until now.

On the one hand, pleasing me continued to be important to her, even if I wanted to leave. Obeying me was also an issue, for even if it had been an ignored topic in recent years, my niece Rita had been correct when she declared that Monika looked at me like the father she had missed in her life. At least she had always deferred to me as such. The nature of our ongoing relationship both then and since certainly only lends further credence to this assertion, as does the nature of our affection, and the devotion we continue to have for each other.

Right then and there, and in response to my requests to find someone else, Monika had met someone who turned out to be anything but honorable, was most likely a sex addict, was someone whose community reputation with women preceded him, and someone whose questionable behavior could or would ultimately be explained by the removal of a brain tumor long before he would eventually die much later on.

Not only was there to be no relationship such as I had envisioned it in Monika's future, she would, to the contrary, learn how tragically bad things could get. Eventually, when the man in question began to harass, stalk, and threaten Monika with his gun, I moved back into our house to make sure Monika was safe and protected. That ended that.

V

Being back together gave us some much needed time to calmly discuss where we ourselves were heading. Monika did not want a divorce. I did not want to be married. Once again in our lives, the deciding factor came from outside ourselves.

I learned that signing the deed over to Monika was of no relevance if I incurred extensive medical or other bills for as long as we were legally married, Monika would be responsible for my expenses. This scared me more than anything else. I was getting older, she was still young. Her earning power was at her lifetime high, mine was dwindling. In my mind, I created nightmarish scenarios of dire fiscal straights caused both for her and myself. Indeed, I was a child of the depression and like a victim, I relived its stress.

We needed to have a formal, legal divorce. I again spoke with our attorney friend who detailed the necessary sequences to obtain one. First on the list was no cohabitation for a minimum of six months because we had no minor children between us. Since I knew that the matter would be simple and uncontested, I paid the lawyer's fee and asked Monika to take care of filing the paper work. Obediently, she did so. Her mother would testify.

ON MY OWN

I

I looked for and found a furnished room that was reasonably priced. I was also now old enough to receive Medicare and whatever supplemental insurance to cover the majority portion of anticipated expenses came from my employment at Virginia Union. I moved.

Shortly thereafter, it was now summer, my hips were scheduled to be replaced one at a time but within the same hospital stay. Stevie came to see me every day in the hospital as long as I was there. Once I was discharged, Medicare provided a specified amount of time for rehabilitation. I agreed to spend the approved time in a rehabilitation facility. Once that had been completed, our good friends Evelyn and Howard Maxwell drove me to Monika's mother's house where I received excellent if awkward care for several weeks, until I was able to again be well on my own.

If I say that it was awkward, then that's reflection on the reason why Monika's mother suggested my going to her house: she was very much in favor of a divorce, and did not want me to return back to Monika's care because the completed portion of the six months separation requirement would be invalidated. It would be only a few months later that she would also be the person volunteering to testify at the divorce hearing; she was the only one who really wanted our divorce.

Whatever problems she had with me began long before the children had stayed at their Connecticut home years earlier. Things certainly did not improve when I asked her to please respect us enough to not interfere in our lives, and now, the prospect of our impending divorce made her a quite evidently pleased and happy facilitator.

II

I realize I am skipping around: there was a lot going on at the same time, overlapping or dovetailing. While a lot of things were going on in my life, in our lives, at home and at work, the children were maturing and each one became a unique and special individual in his or her own right.

My pride in all of them remains the greatest pride I have in my life, my participation in raising them, and above all, allowing their mother to be a mother, is what I became increasingly proud of as time went on. Even now in my advanced years I look back with pride. I will, therefore, briefly write about them at this point, and then return to the telling of my own endeavors. Life goes on!

Leila had skipped her senior year and began college a year early at Virginia Commonwealth University; she had met all requirements for high school graduation by the end of her junior year, except two classes which she immediately took at VCU. When she was given her high school diploma, she had a year of college credit to her name. Up until now, she had spent her summers working at the Jewish Community Center day camp; she also held several other jobs from newspaper delivery starting in 8th grade, to sales clerk and other jobs. She studied abroad for one year, developed interests in international affairs and programs, and was an incredibly productive young woman for many years to come. At some point, she returned to a graduate program at UVA to obtain a BSN.

Soon after Leila's decision to start college early, Rob began to explore college options and decided to enlist in the Army. His experience with Junior ROTC at Benedictine had been a good one; he progressed through the ranks, and benefitted overall from the structure and discipline offered. It was a horrible evening when Monika had to sign his documents with the Army recruiter because he was not yet of age to do so himself. After his 1982 graduation from Benedictine, he left home for basic training and subsequently went straight to Virginia Tech's Cadet Corps. Although Rob would come for many of his vacations, he had, de facto, left home. After he finished college, the Army sent him to Germany and at the end of his tour of duty, his life would continue in Berlin with a career playing the trombone he first started to study in second grade in Clarion.

Nadja's educational accomplishments took her from positions of responsibility as student council president and as well her interests in business via Junior Achievement along with her various jobs in department stores and for newspapers from private school to public school where she took college courses as her regular curriculum. She would attend Smith for four years, gain experience in various public relations positions and ultimately return to graduate school: at the Duke Divinity School she received a Master's degree with honors; as a PhD candidate at William and Mary she's ABD till her dissertation is completed and defended.

Steve continues as he evolves and I see him as both being and becoming. He struggled through college not because of academics but because of his multiple interests and commitments in other areas. Actually, he had left high school early, obtained a GED and attended college after having been invited to the Governor School for the Arts after his junior year in high school. His audition tapes were self produced! When he finally got a Master's degree, it was while also producing several CD's, recognition for published articles, forming a corporation and adoring his young daughter. Everything is a never ending adventure for Steve. Stay tuned!

As I already said earlier, Monika's experience brought me back home following our divorce. We sorted out a lot of things that needed to be resolved. I did not want to accept Monika's tremendous hurt upon my leaving. I know from the children that she totally lost her resolve to move forward one day when everyone was at home and she pulled a framed photograph of me off the wall, destroyed the frame, broke the glass and tore the picture into pieces. Rob told me he tried to reassemble it like a puzzle and to reglue it, without luck. Monika herself would later regret the outburst, and attempt to get the negative from Manny Carreira who had taken the picture years earlier. No such luck. He never responded. Maybe part of the JCU gang?

She turned her attention to work. She would also sell the house, and plan a move which promised to further her career. Our relationship would soon settle into a new and comfortable groove. It would continue and thrive over the coming years of our lives.

III

Now divorced, I slowly got my bearings as a single man. Initially, my small abode was a pleasant place to come home to. After I was attacked by some hoodlums who stole my wallet and pushed me down some stairs…thank God my hips survived in tact….I sought to move elsewhere. I found a small apartment, gathered some furnishings from the house Monika was emptying for sale and relocation, bought myself whatever else I wanted or needed, and set up housekeeping.

I also learned ordinary practical things I had never learned at any other time in my life. I learned how to cook and I studied nutrition. I made quarts of a chicken vegetable stew that was not really the so called Brunswick stew but that's where I had gotten my inspiration. I froze portions. I began to enjoy nightly bowls of ice cream that became dinner and which I would do for the rest of my life. I was not a big fresh fruit eater, but did have a daily banana. I made stacks of pancakes and would freeze several meals worth, the same was true of the omelets I made now and then.

Most of the time, I ate cereal for breakfast with the powdered milk I mixed daily.

Mixing milk powder was one of my efforts to be thrifty and cost effective. Saving money and living frugally became both a challenge and a game. I saved regularly. I kept the hot water heater off most of the time except for a few hours to shower and do the stacks of dishes I allowed to accumulate. I never turned the heat on in my apartment: with units all around me except the outside wall with the window, I simply wore a few layers and felt no cold. I also did not turn the air conditioning on because I love heat. When it got too unbearably hot and humid, I would remove clothing and turn on a fan. It pleased me to save, and the children benefitted from my savings over the years, most of all Steve.

For a while back then, in my first larger apartment while I was still working part time, Stevie would stay with me: it was traumatic for both of us. While Monika thought he was well off with me, both he and I knew things were disastrous. I was drinking non stop. I had become a falling down drunk, blacking out now and then, totally out of control. For Steve, my actions, behavior and demeanor became a nightmare. He loved me like no one else, and he was appalled by me, also like no one else had ever been. I became a disappointment of which I myself was keenly aware. I hovered between feelings of failure and sensing a new beginning. I didn't know what the hell I was doing, or would do. And I no longer knew why I had been so eager to leave Monika when I did.

How much I had affected Steve already earlier because of my drinking became all too evident in his last year at St. Christopher's when he portrayed the father in Thomas Wolfe's play, "Look Homeward Angel". His ability to mimic a functioning alcoholic descending into drunken oblivion was what he had seen from me.

His performance was stellar; my example an abominable inspiration. We've never really talked enough about this, and I believe we need to do so. I owe Steve the heartfelt apologies I myself feel and which he so very much deserves. Time rushes on, this is time I must make soon when he visits me because I don't know how many more opportunities will present themselves over the time that is left me.

IV

Currently, back then, I had expected to teach another year or so at VUU. But, as the fall semester began, I found myself physically locked out of my office on campus and in receipt of a letter informing me that my services would no longer be required. They had smelled me. Literally. I was a drunk and as such had no place on a Baptist –or any other- campus. My reaction at the time was outrage. Older, wiser and more mellow, I still do not agree with how VUU handled this, but I do see the prudence in what they had to do. It would be much later that I would be able to admit my own responsibility for its happening, regardless of how things were carried out at the time. It would also be years before I would stop drinking completely.

For now, I increased my hours as a tutor with a service that engaged competent people to help high school students with their work, SAT preparation, and the like. I also tutored college students, and prepared individuals for the GMATs or LSATs and similar entry examinations for advanced professional study. I concentrated on Math and Physics, but also found myself tutoring Latin and English. I continued to teach at VCU and JSarge adjunct and in the evening. There were several community activities which drew my attention, such as the Richmond Senior Center, the Shepherd Center, several educational programs as well as various university sponsored research studies in which I qualified for participation. I had a pretty full schedule and my income was adequate for both my needs and some enjoyable additions.

And, I began to date! For the first time, at age 68, I dated! And not just one woman. By joining several social groups, women swarmed all over me when they learned of my availability. This was something totally new to me. Whether a casual bridge game at the Senior Center or a ferociously competitive game for Masters' Points at the Bridge Club, there would always be at least one lady eager to catch my eye or more. I suddenly had the opportunity to make up for what I missed in my youth. And I did.

Although surrounded by a plethora of willing women, one particular lady caught my eye and would eventually spend a considerable amount of time with me and as well on my behalf. Our relationship would eventually end only because she desired marriage, whereas I did not. She would marry soon after we parted. Before then, however, I learned an awful lot from her about how to care for myself in my present circumstances and for the future.

It was she who familiarized me with many opportunities and services available to senior citizens. It was she who taught me about wills and power of attorney, medical directives and leaving my remains to medical science. And she also showed me how I would be able initiate the application process to qualify for more affordable housing both better and less expensive than I was occupying at the time. If she reads these pages, she will recognize herself at once, and hopefully see that I continue to think of her, gratefully.

As I said, my lady friend assisted me in my quest for better housing. Although I ended up across the street from where she had hoped to see me, I would move into what has since then become my last and final residence, God willing.

My apartment is relatively small. It's an efficiency apartment consisting of a bathroom, kitchen, living room and an alcove to sleep in. I could have had a larger unit in the same building, one that would specifically separate living and sleeping quarters more distinctly. What I have suits me well. It's not much different in size than my room at Rodman Hall had been, and larger if I add the areas for cooking and bathing.

I am content here. I have room for everything I own, and plan to own. Since being here, I have acquired little except books and CD's. Everything else in my quarters is new only if it had to be replaced, like the microwave and the television. I am truly content.

By the fall of 1989, my schedule became reduced to tutoring and related activities. I was now 70, receiving my full social security that was larger because I had waited, together with my full if small TIAA-CREF pensions: although I had asked Monika if I should put her down for survivor benefits, she had declined the privilege because she felt I deserved every cent due me in the present.

<h1 style="text-align:center">V</h1>

Foot loose and fancy free, I embarked on expanding my horizons with travel. I joined Elder Hostel. With them, I would visit places I had only read about and had never expected to really see first hand. I went to Alaska and Hawaii, I traveled to Central America and Europe. I walked through the Louvre and amid Greek and Roman ruins. I participated in a Global volunteer group teaching English abroad, and spent time in Poland, the country from which I claim my heritage. Rob came from Berlin to join me in Poland.

The Elder Hostel catalog became my smorgasbord of what to do or see or go to. There were workshops and spiritual events; I went to monasteries and learned about the activities carried out by monks so different from the Jesuit life style I knew. I learned about bee keeping and fruit preservation, jam preservation and fruit cake baking. For the first time, I actually studied the music I enjoyed life-long. And the women!

Most Elder Hostel events had a lot more female participants. That meant that we men had our pick of companionship. In time, I met several women with whom I would share hotel rooms; they were thrilled to have a man escort them around, I was thrilled to only pay half the cost of various rooms or ship board cabins. While these were platonic relationships, it would be only one woman who started our arrangement by insisting up front that there would be no "sheet music" in any of our accommodations. And, there never was. Not with this one individual and not with any of the other similarly symbiotic relationships that would happen over time.

I enjoyed women. I enjoyed people. I liked the trips, the adventure, the newness of it all. I was less eager or interested in sex. Monika and I had had a very satisfying sex life. I wasn't looking for anything new or different. It was hard enough to get things going with Monika when I was 20 years younger. AIDS was scary. I found more satisfaction in not embarrassing myself with any potential shortcomings in that department. I was OK without even a hint of sheet music. As a matter of fact, it would be my last Elder Hostel trip when my companion decided sex would be included on the agenda, that I packed up and left, never to attend another one of the scheduled events. By then, I had also been traveling for over a dozen years and was not too far from 80 and quite honestly, a bit tired.

In addition to my extensive travels and the many hours of tutoring that afforded them, I also became active in other areas. I regularly read newspapers for the blind; I also volunteered to teach adult GED candidates.

One of Richmond's social services agencies called me and asked if I would participate in a program that taught families and individuals about budgeting and household management. I did this for several years, and continued with my clients until the last of them passed away. Afterwards, I did not continue in service to others.

I became a life time member at the Senior Center, and enjoyed several days weekly there, mostly playing bridge but also other card games. Eventually, I was asked to teach bridge and did so for several course-sessions. Other things at the Senior Center interested me as well: it had a full schedule of programs ready to be explored. I tried them nearly all at least once.

There were several study programs that interested me. I signed up for memory retention and brain function, for overall health and hearing, for stroke prevention and heart health. These have been of various duration, both long and short term, and, as some ended new ones began. I continue to partake of a few even as late as now, 2007. One of these is a University of Alabama stroke study. As a scientist, I believe in furthering science which will serve the benefit of all long term.

At present, I am also appalled by the decreased emphasis on the sciences overall both for students and corporations, in pure and applied research, because that will ultimately mean that the position of the United States in the global economy of today will decrease in importance. We need scientists, we need research, and we need funding for both. Right now, our universities are turning out incredibly competent and well educated PhD's, and the larger percentage return to their native China, India, and other countries. There needs to be a warning bell in the financial community that this cannot go on long term, because where science withdraws in importance, money will follow down the tube.

Education has been my lifetime interest and commitment. I am therefore very interested in science education and the advancement of science. At some point, we had a special program at John Carroll for science teachers. I don't know that it is still going on. I have had no contact with Carroll all these years, no one kept in touch with me except Bill Nichols.

Bill would come to visit us in Clarion, in Richmond, and the last time, in Columbia Maryland where he called Monika and announced himself. I think he was genuinely concerned about the welfare of my soul, a kind and gentle man put into difficult and awkward positions. Last I knew, his memory was failing and he was relieved of his teaching assignments. Someone so brilliant as he had been, it saddens me even now.

Sorry, I am off on another tangent, this one especially close to my heart, but I'm back!

EQUANIMITY

I

Although life continued to be busy for me, it had also become calm. Gone were the stressors of an earlier period when I had no idea what the hell I was going to do. Now, there was a well defined rhythm to my day to day life. Overall, much in my existence reminded me of the years in the Society; it was comforting in its familiarity. No chaos, no stress. Nothing unpleasant, no demands, no expectations from others, nor their disappointments which I could not avoid to elicit.

In the meantime, Monika was focused on her career. In her efforts to further herself, she made several mistakes and ran headlong into more than one dead end with the best of intentions. I tried to comfort her; I knew only too well how trying to do everything right can turn into a wrong. In Monika's case, there was an additional handicap, because she thought that she could replicate what I had done for her. She felt she could automatically and indiscriminately do much good for another person as I had done for her and her family, and willy-nilly poured all her extensive cash resources —many of them thanks to me---into her effort. She totally neglected to assess probability of success based on historical evidence or a consideration of the beneficiary's ability to perform.

It was with the utmost gentleness that I told her that what worked for us was not only what I gave but what she had brought along. It was her share of the input that had made our efforts successful. "Look what I had to work with: YOU. Everyone else is no Monika." Sadder but wiser, she realized how right I was and how foolish, hurtful and even harmful her efforts would become in the long run in spite of good intentions.

Although it becomes quite easy to regurgitate thoughts, events, or memories that are not directly part of this recollection effort, this is my story and I shall quickly assert that whatever Monika did, any joy or pain, success or failure, did not impact my life any longer. Our friendship was solid, but we promised each other we would be concerned about our own lives within the framework of our relationship, and not what pertained to any issues or relationships regarding others, whether associates or bosses or lovers or friends. After all, we were now free agents to blunder or triumph in our activities. And, we both did some of both.

When I became aware of some difficulties Monika had encountered, I point blank told her she could not count on me to bail her out again. Eventually, I would pay extensive attorney fees for her because of an uncouth group associated with one of her employers. It was the only actual hands on help I would give her over many years.

If Monika had been upset with my leaving, we had weathered that storm and resumed the friendship we had had all along, which had grown to be even better over time, and which we now enjoyed in full bloom. I would tell anyone who asked why we were not together, that our marriage had nearly destroyed a most perfect friendship. Even so, I was convinced that only the fewest understood me fully when I said so. I dare say that now, after so much time and water over the dam, I have learned to love Monika in ways I was unable to do earlier. It includes large doses of respect, affection, and appreciation.

II

There were times when I truly regretted having left Monika, even regretted the mere idea of having wanted to leave. No one I had known before, and no one I have met since understood me as well, allowed me to be as I chose to be (most of the time!), gave me the freedom and the space to be who I was or am, trusted me so completely that there simply were no issues or concerns regarding trust, and met me on my own intellectual wave length when and if and where or what my mind construed or pursued. I think I had to leave Monika to learn to appreciate what I had had in her. It was meeting other women that showed me this. In her own way, Monika is as unusual as I am; she is as principled and as both moral and ethical, our values are the same. Maybe that's because ultimately, I also raised her to mature adulthood!

In time, as the years passed by, I began to fully understand that the cause of our frequent, destructive and negative squabbling was as much my drinking as it was largely attributable to Ativan. Monika's reaction to what apparently is a commonly used anti-anxiety drug was unusual and rare, her response became an exaggerated, and highly agitated opposite of the reaction to what is commonly anticipated. A pharmacologist would call it "bizarre" but not unheard of as regarding such a drug reaction.

A lot of the blame I had heaped on Monika's bickering and our joint squabbling needed to be placed at the feet of this medication and the doctor who did not have the specialty required to prescribe it. The rest of the blame lay in the empty beer and vodka bottles I was hiding with little success.

I've often wondered whether this combination had not generated a fight or flight response within me, and with it, prompted my desire to rush away when I decided I had had enough and wanted to leave. It was, after all, I who wanted to go for quite a while before I actually went, contrary to many others who were of the opinion that it was Monika who dumped me. She didn't. It was I who had wanted out.

III

For a period of time, Monika and I saw little of each other. She was too hurt to see or talk to me. I was too busy enjoying new found freedoms. Eventually, the pull of gravity exerted by and on each of us brought us back together. We became one heart and one soul once more if indeed we had ever ceased to be.

Monika and I would never again share a bed even though we spent week ends and weeks together, either at her place or traveling elsewhere. At the same time, nothing could or would come between us. We were truly one: in mind, spirit, thought, and action. We were also chaste, and in fact, celibate. If Monika had considered herself committed elsewhere, she upheld an equally sexless relationship that defied termination and felt honor bound. My invitations or desires went unheeded. It was my own fault. We simply did not discuss the physical intimacy we once had that I myself believed we could regain. It had become a moot point, never brought up; not mine, nor hers, through the years.

It was really the only subject not brought up during our continued relationship. Beyond her affirmed celibacy, I know nothing about Monika's sex life. I too continued a celibate life but I cannot declare chastity. Once the sex genie was out of the bottle so late in my life, I saw no point in re-confining him to such limitations. Instead, my prurient interests found satisfaction in the library of books, videos and DVD's I accumulated to assist me as I developed a strong right arm. Like the bumper sticker I saw now and then, I became a dirty old man, in solitude. I would never use my torture instruments again and that's enough on this subject.

At some point, when I anticipated that Monika would wish to remarry, I had entered a request to have Monika's and my marriage declared null and void. The Diocese of Richmond Marriage Tribunal was assigned jurisdiction. Although it went through the proscribed and customary details to ascertain the validity of such a claim, after a lengthy period of time and necessary investigation, it did indeed issue a formal decree of nullity.

The cause would again be Defective Consent but not on Monika part but because I myself had entered a sacramental marriage not as a life time commitment, but with what had ultimately been an intention of leaving, once the project was completed. And, I had done exactly that. I did so even if it was probably a couple of years sooner than would have been wise for Steve's sake. Considering my drinking, nothing was wise at the time.

Monika would be free to marry. She had a Decree of Nullity in hand allowing her to enter a sacramental marriage were she to choose to do so, but her partner at the time would have none of it. Threatened with the refusal of absolution in confession, they went their separate ways to live in different states. By the time he thought better of it, she knew better than to agree to yet another hopelessly impossible situation.

As a matter of fact, unlike me when I got a taste of the abundant selection of available woman following our divorce, Monika withdrew and never dated anyone after the Decree of Nullity was issued. And, while I myself have stopped doing so now, she still hasn't agreed to go on a single date. Not even with me! Warm friendships-yes. A little flirting to keep spirits alive? Why not. But beyond that, nothing more. We continue as soul mates. I doubt that this would ever again change as long as we both shall live.

We would meet for lunches, I would take her to dinner now and then. We also traveled a fair amount together for short periods. Our travels were limited, mostly because of Monika's dog who had to be cared for. We spent a few days at the beach, a few days in the mountains.

IV

At some point, in the late '90's, in autumn, we drove to Clarion to visit Salih. I had no idea how he would receive me considering the past. I had not seen him since separating from Monika a dozen or so years earlier. Prior to that, he had come to Richmond several times both alone and with his friend Fifi El-

Sadat, the Egyptian widow whose husband we had known too. Such visits were cordial or uneventful. They would all head to the beach together.

I recall only two things: one was seeing Salih walk between his sons down our alley way and how similarly he and Rob walked as opposed to Steve's up and down bounces. The second was Rob returning from having walked him back to his hotel room not far from our house, and being quite upset because Salih had begun to rant and rave about some political matter with an intensity that nearly got him killed crossing a busy street. Luckily, Rob held or pulled him back in time.

There had been little point in making an issue about child support. He owed his children thousands of dollars of back support monies, health insurance and their college tuitions, and other things such as the very tragically awful experience Nadja would encounter regarding her braces that he was to have paid in full.

Years earlier, Salih had been fired from his teaching position at Clarion State. We were told at the time that he had refused to submit to the periodic evaluation by which merit pay increases, and places on the tenure track were determined along with peer and student satisfaction, as well as other pre-determined criteria.

When we heard that he had simply walked out, I was not surprised. I had seen that same kind of arrogant pride at John Carroll when Triv had attempted to suggest some corrections many years earlier. I also knew that with his record, his age, and the market for physics, he was washed up professionally for good at age 50. And indeed, he has not worked since then. What an example that is for his children, no matter their age. Additionally, he affixed blame for his situation, again, totally on others. No comment.

I was surprised that Salih welcomed me with such warmth when we visited him at his Strattanville place. I had replayed my life often in my mind, and had often wondered how he felt about the events of years past as time went on. I frequently swayed in my reflections of that time long ago. If only...... was a recurrent theme for me but without regret. I had moments of fleeting sadness

242

to know the man did not have the pleasure of his family, especially since I was a participant in making that happen. And yet, I also knew that it was his own fault to be as he was, just the same.

I took the car and drove up to Cook Forest, followed the roads along the Clarion River where we had all gone so often when we lived in the area, to the ice cream stand in Sigel or Sligo or whatever the name of the place was. It seemed like another life time.

Eventually, as I drove on the familiar roads, I reconciled my own thoughts with the reality of facts. I may have raised Salih's children, but it was not something I had planned. Neither could I attribute all the blame or guilt for the past on my fellow Jesuits. They may have altered our plans and taken matters into their own hands, but they did not initiate the course of events. That had been generated by Salih himself when he failed to perform adequately at the jobs he had held at John Carroll, his leaving there without any concern of how that impacted the rest of his young family, and the arrogance and anger he displayed when people were genuinely trying to help him for his own benefit. It was a good trip, a good ride through the beautiful fall foliage, and reinforced my own peace of mind.

V

On the same trip, we also saw Mary and Alan Haws in Clarion, and spent a delightful evening with them. We drove back to Columbia by going through Western Maryland and enjoying even more of the colorful leaves, of what I always called "God showing off."

We took several trips to New York to attend opera performances at either the New York or Metropolitan Opera, both at Lincoln Center. While I felt that the Mariinsky was a disappointment, running into old Richmond friend Helen Scott Reed was a delight. Steve would meet us there if he was free.

While Monika lived in Columbia, MD., we also attended symphony and opera performances in both Baltimore and

Washington so that I sometimes would drive twice monthly to spend a week end with her, and attend such a performance.

The last longer trip we took starting out in Columbia was to Cleveland where we visited Lois Hopkins and saw a few of her children who happen to be living in the area, all adults with families of their own. They still called me Father Ace and welcomed me as if I had been there most recently.

It was now nearly summer 2000. I had turned 81 early in the year, and when Monika called to discuss which series for concerts and opera we should renew, I declined. Driving up from Richmond on I-95, circumventing Washington on the Beltway, and driving back before the crack of dawn on Monday mornings to avoid the morning rush and to also be sure I was back at the Richmond Senior Center for my noon bridge game became too strenuous for me.

I didn't want to risk a car crash. I had already had a couple of fender benders in recent months which caused the cancellation of my insurance policy. Now I was driving a state condoned uninsured vehicle for which I had to pay a fee. Another accident was too risky at this point. I needed to be able to drive locally, and give up my long hauls at the newer excessively high speeds. I am a fast driver, but cars zipped past me when I was doing over 70. Twice a month of this was just too much. I had had enough.

Monika can be very persuasive: we compromised on attending all opera performances but only those concerts I really especially wanted to hear. Harolyn Blackwell was to sing at one of them, and I had developed a great fondness for her voice. Any additional tickets would be Monika's to use or give away. It turned out we simply cancelled one of the series in favor of the other, problem solved. Somewhat.

VI

While in Columbia, Monika had completed two related programs at Loyola. She was happily back in a Jesuit educational setting, acquiring the training and skills to become a pastoral

244

counselor, and followed this with yet another post graduate certificate.

Work had had its ups and downs for reasons unrelated to me and therefore not included here. She had enjoyed being an intern at Howard Community College where she met and made a new friend for life in Julie Knox-Brown, whom I too found to be utterly delightful. Another friend and neighbor, Pam Pennix-Green, had introduced Monika to ad hoc work for the federal government which would become a most pleasurable activity.

Speaking of Julie reminds me of Monika's friend Gundl from Austria who came for a lengthy visit in 1997. Gundl and I hit it off as if we had known each other all our lives. Gundl's only negative comment was her dismay that we were not married any longer. She thought us perfect for each other. Of course at this point we ourselves thought so too but not enough to change the status quo because everything has its reasons.

What makes Gundl's visit significant is not that Gundl herself drank a little too much too often, but that we went to a restaurant where everyone ordered some kind of drink except I. I had stopped drinking completely, cold turkey, a year ago in the preceding spring and did not intend to ever take another drink as long as I lived. I had not joined AA or anything else, I had simply one day decided I had polluted myself enough over time, that it was costing money I could use better elsewhere, and that I could not answer the question: WHY. So I quit and that was that.

Before I had made that decision, I had become aware that the various hostesses at our bridge games would move liquor bottles located within my vicinity to somewhere else in order to be out of immediate reach from my seat. I also had begun to notice that no one else but I drank anything at all, and that I would often leave someone's home feeling a little too happy or conducting myself somewhat too boisterously. Drinking always tasted good to me, I liked booze of all kinds. But if my drinking was noticed in a negative light by more than a few others, then it was time to stop. From the day that I quit, until today, I did not have another drop of any alcoholic beverage-- except for one occasion.

Monika had asked me to stay with the dog while she had to attend a work related week in Washington. I arrived to care for the dog, and she left. It did not take me long to discover the well stocked liquor cabinet. I wanted to just sample this and that flavor. Then I wanted a few more tastes of other bottles. Long story short, Monika came back two days sooner than expected. She arrived on Thursday instead of Saturday morning.

As she entered the house, I was walking down the stairs swinging a nearly empty bottle of vodka and slurring "Hallo, you're back so soon, I didn't expect you for another couple of days." The front door was open, the air conditioning going full blast, the dog looked pathetic and unhappy and Monika's expression showed disgust.

Leila had come back with Monika because she had flown into a DC area airport from where she was returning. Although she had anticipated spending the week end with her mother before getting a ride back to Richmond, Leila now packed my things along with me into my car and drove me home at once. I know she too was disgusted with me, and I felt at least equally disgusted with myself. It was, however, the one and only time that I relapsed in all the years since I quit drinking in the spring of 1996. Nevertheless, it was both very embarrassing and inexcusable. Mea culpa.

This last incident took place in Reedville to which Monika had moved permanently. Monika's work commitments had changed and she found life in Reedville less costly and less demanding. The only thing she missed about Columbia in addition to a few very good friends with whom she would maintain contact, were the afternoons at the Meyerhoff, Baltimore's excellent symphony hall down town. With my no longer wanting to accompany her there, her own interest shifted. It didn't wane, it just didn't hold the importance it had held when we both would attend together.

I myself found Reedville infinitely easier to get to. It was a shorter distance on more leisurely roads than the intense interstate race track called I-95. When our bridge games on Mondays changed to alternate weeks, I found myself heading to Reedville quite often. It was during those times that Monika and I would talk about getting back to writing the memoir we had begun already quite some time back. Still, nothing happened and I was approaching my 85th birthday.

VII

When I learned that I needed eye surgery and subsequent care, it was without question that I called Monika to let her know the dates and times, the length of time she would have me at her home recovering, and when I was expected to be able to return to my home. Of course she agreed to do so without question.

The following year was Rob's 40th birthday. Monika prepared a great deal of feasting for Rob's and family friends. It would be the last time I saw Salih who also attended. As before, we got along great. He did make a few remarks about Monika, but I didn't pay attention to comments that had no significance after so many years. I myself had given a lot of thought to things by then, and I was at peace knowing I had been right to do as I did.

GOLDEN TWILIGHT

I

For some time, already prior to my eye surgery, I had begun to feel a strange sense of foreboding that my short term memory was deteriorating. I became aware of it especially when I spent long periods driving, such as I had going to Columbia. I would play mental word games with myself while driving, I distinctly remember that now and then I perceived a distinct sense of loss of a thought or concept or name or something I knew I should know. This bothered me a great deal and also worried me. At that time, no one but I myself was aware of it. Now, however, Rob made some comments to me that indicated he had noticed too that I wasn't the sharp tack with whom he was accustomed to converse.

I redoubled my efforts to do cross word puzzles, but noticed how much more difficult they were becoming for me. I did the ones early in the week, but as the week went on the difficulty of puzzles increased until Sunday; and I no longer did them every day. I didn't even attempt the Sunday New York Times puzzles any more, nor did I want the frustration of the Washington Post's which Monika saved for me weekly.

I did not like the feelings I had or the future I might face, it frightened me. My sister Rose had suffered from dementia so severely, that she did not remember her own children by the time she died. And she had not been drinking earlier in her life like I had been. I did not fear death but I did fear pickled brain, dependence, being a burden, vegetating.

II

As I spent more and more time in my apartment, I found myself increasingly reflecting on my past life. I felt totally at peace with myself and my God. I had no fear of dying, and I had few concerns about an after life. Monika and I spent hours discussing whether there indeed was a place called hell, or if hell was any place from which God was absent. I was no longer concerned one way or the other because I knew my life would end with my Maker, in whichever form.

I believe that I have fought the good fight, kept the faith even if it morphed into something other than my studies had indicated. I believed in God more firmly than ever, and yet found much of religion superfluous and redundant. I liked the Einstein phrase when he said that" "my sense of God is my sense of wonderment about the universe." I recently have copied that to hang on my refrigerator and I believe it fully. I am in awe of God's creation, and only an omnipotent loving God could have created it.

The course of my life became an infinitely more intricate one than I would have ever imagined. I did some really daring things following my own convictions. I still believe I did the right thing at the right time, and I would do it again and again if the occasions presented themselves although I now marvel at my own energy levels which I no longer possess. Now, I became consistently aware of how quickly time passed and how little I accomplished within it, day to day, week to week. I seem to be racing through life going no where. And, I feel very aware of how I am slowing down.

It became evident in my weekly activities. I was or am very definitely slowing down. I drove less and spent less time in Fleeton with Monika. I enjoyed her visits and would treat her to lunch when she came to town. I played bridge only once a week now, on Thursdays.

Nadja continued to stop by with some home made goodies with what seemed some regularity. Leila came by now and then too. The girls were getting somewhat concerned about my housekeeping and eating habits. And I forgot things that I should have remembered, like a routine check up with the dentist and with Dr. Peter Goodman.

When I finally realized that I was to have gone to see him, I had also noticed something strange happening with my stomach. Peter would have me admitted to the hospital at once when I finally got to his office on a Tuesday in late April 2007 for an immediate emergency hernia operation. In some ways, it would spell unforeseen problems and the hopes of continuing this writing effort.

Here's why: I didn't tell anyone I was going into the hospital. When she couldn't reach me by phone, because my friend Bootsie had also not heard from me about the week's bridge game and called her, Nadja panicked. She called the police and fire department, and it caused quite a stir in my apartment building including with the management.

Monika, on the other hand, had spoken to me earlier in the week when I had mentioned receiving a package from Rita. So, she first called my niece Rita in case I had decided on an unexpected trip there as I had spontaneously done in the past, and, when that turned out to be a dead end, she secondly, later in the morning when his office opened, called Peter Goodman who of course knew exactly where I was and how.

A few days later, Monika came to pick me up. She took me home to her house in Fleeton, and I spent the next two weeks recovering, and then an additional 10 days after I saw the doctor who checked my incision. While there, Monika wasn't sure if my very obvious memory loss was anesthesia induced or age related. One morning I sat across the breakfast table from her and said, "I know I have known you for a long time, but where do I know you from?" Monika's face showed her shock. Anesthesia or not, this was a bit much.

III

It would be a turning point. Even though I remembered our mutual past a day later, Monika gained a new awareness of my struggles to remember and the girls' concern for me. Leila made a good case for me to move to Mommie's place: she knew Monika loved me and I loved her. And Leila would tell each of us of the other's love, repeatedly! It did not move me to move!

Just like she had had a hard time earlier admitting I was a drunk at various times, so Monika now found herself wishing to but no longer able to deny my increasing dementia. She knew, just like I had been saying for some time, that either we do the memoir or we won't finish the whole thing together any more or we would be living together and thereby expediting the process.

We spent the next three weeks together reviewing our old notes to get my memoir done. Because of the most recent events, I decided that my life as written down would end with this lengthy visit that not only had me recover physically, but which made me realize that if not now then never. How much time would I have left to finish what we had begun?

IV

The next blow came at my scheduled visit with Peter: he indicated I was not to continue driving any longer. That meant, I would not longer go to Reedville and Monika's house in Fleeton under my own power.

I was, de facto, losing my independence faster than my mind and when Monika drove me home a few days later to an apartment rearranged and spotlessly clean thanks to the girls, I was not sure of what the remainder of my life would hold in store for me.

It was then and there that I decided to tell Monika to use what she had and not count on any additions except as she herself knew my life to continue. I promised to add thoughts over time as they would possibly occur to me and mail them at various intervals. I would add a little of my ongoing discernment to the introduction I had begun some time back. I thought of adding to it as we neared the completion of our effort, if indeed we ever would reach that point. And that's how we left things. It's a good place to end my formal effort to create my memoir at age 88.

Even so, Monika gave me a stack of envelopes, addressed to herself and stamped for easy mailing. As time went on, I mailed them with regularity as thoughts and memories that occurred to me irregularly night or day, sometimes more and sometimes less.

There will be no more lengthy periods for thought and reflection while I drive along to Fleeton. There will be just my own occasional observations and glimpses into a past while sitting in my Lazyboy. But there will also still be memories re-birthed with the help of another: my best friend, my alter ego, my soul mate and my scribe. The woman I love. Monika.

Well, I won't be made a liar of long term nor will I turn maudlin in my dotage: Surely over the months ahead there will be additional ideas, thoughts, reflections or memories I myself will want to add; I shall jot them down and Monika will get them, in person or by mail. I may do that for a long time to come! After all, I continue to think, and therefore I am and continue to be. And the rest?

AMDG

Summer 2007

ADDENDUM

Frank would come to Fleeton only three more times. Once with me, for a couple of weeks, when no bridge was scheduled. Then again, when Steve came to help hang a picture — an Arabic Calligraphy I had had especially commissioned which said "PEACE"— along with his sisters and me. And the last visit with all four of the kids, on Easter Sunday 2008. It just so happened that in 2008 Easter Sunday was also my birthday.

We had and would continue to celebrate Thanksgiving and Christmas at both Leila and Nadja's homes respectively. Frank's birthday was celebrated in various ways such as a little luncheon gathering at a local Chinese restaurant earlier in 2008 for his birthday #89.

Leila and Nadja were truly taking good care of his various humanly needs. They provided transportation to doctor and dental appointments, researched resources for geriatric medicine and administered regular pedicures and hair cuts. Nadja baked and Leila bought groceries, or reverse, they both did an awful lot including laundry and housekeeping chores. If it was a burden for them they carried it out with a great deal of warmth and love and any complaints were solely about their concern for Frank's well being.

They also saw to it that Meals-on-Wheels and other services were plugged in as was feasible or as Frank would allow such services to be delivered to him. It wasn't always easy because he feared any infringement on his independence, and the possibility of running out of money when someone came to clean or bring food; he also didn't want anyone making a fuss over him or critique his housekeeping and cooking.

In addition to visiting him at his place and then driving him to do whatever errands he wanted to do before we'd go to have lunch, I stopped by whenever I went to Richmond to join him for his routine walks which had shortened quite a bit, and I went to Richmond often to take those little walks. Our last such walk was Valentine's Day 2009.

Frank had a lengthy schedule of medical appointments when I spent four days with him in a Richmond Motel in the summer of 2008. It was around this time that he was diagnosed with an abdominal aneurysm.

Frank knew, as did all of us, that this was exactly what my friend Gundl called it: a death sentence. [Ironically, it would be Gundl herself who died within weeks, a month short of her 69th birthday and a year before the celebration I had planned with her for her 70th. She and I had been friends for all of my then 67 years. Gundl knew and loved Frank!]

When confronted with the inherent risks of a major operation at his venerable age, Frank decided against it. The aneurysm was too advanced for the less invasive procedure, which also meant it was at greater risk to rupture. Even now, Frank was enjoying his bridge games, he was not taking any medication because he had no other ailments. He was ambulatory and able to care for himself. He was in his apartment and had no desire or intention to leave it. We deferred to his wisdom.

No matter how his various doctors encouraged him to come to live with me, as I did myself, he declined such offers and suggestions. He began to deteriorate even more rapidly than before. In January 2009, a psychiatric evaluation indicated that while he was on the border of having to go into some sort of assisted living situation unless he came to live with me, that was stretching the facts as far as was conscientiously, realistically possible.

256

Leila invited his bridge buddies and friends to celebrate his 90th birthday on January 25th. Leila made a really lovely party with all the trimmings and goodies that go with such an event. It was a lovely afternoon, and it was evident that Frank's mind was with us only half the time.

My own fear, which I did not dare voice at the time, was about safety. Frank, of course, knew all about electricity and had taught E&M countless times. Now, his occasional attempts to change cords and rewire appliances caused me to shudder in fear of fire.

I knew for certain that he could not continue on his own. Both girls were adamant that he had to get more care because they themselves could no longer provide adequately given the time and distance involved, and with Nadja's baby due momentarily.

In the week between the appointment with the psychiatrist and the birthday party, I had given notice to the apartment management group that Frank's move would be within 60 days, or no later than the end of March. Bishop Walter Sullivan indicated he would see to it that Frank could be accommodated by the Little Sisters of the Poor.

When Stevie and I went on a vacation to Argentina and Uruguay on January 26th, it was with the knowledge that shortly upon our return, Stevie would help move Frank out to my house unless he preferred to go to the home: the third choice — to do nothing — that Frank had always pointed out as an additional alternate was no longer viable or available.

It never came to that.

Frank passed away on February 24th, 2009. The death certificate was signed on the following day by his then physician, in absentia.

He never saw David Anthony Cipriani II.

AMDG
At last, with Love